DEEP ROOTS

Edward R. Rosick

To RGD

For being there from the beginning

PART I

He who fights with monsters should look to it that he himself does not become a monster, for when you gaze long into an abyss, the abyss also gazes into you.

—Friedrich Nietzsche

CHAPTER 1

KEVIN CIANO GOT OUT of the shower in the cramped confines of his bathroom when the rat crawled on his left foot. Misshapen front claws raked across his toes and he instinctively jerked away before looking down to see the creature—thin, gray fur, with eyes leaking blood—slowly moving forward. Without thinking, Kevin grabbed the creature by its long-scaled tail and smashed it onto the wet linoleum floor.

Once.

Twice.

By the third blow the rat lay dead, its head a dripping lump of broken bone and brains. Kevin dropped the bloody mess into the wastepaper basket and made a mental note to take out the trash before he left for work.

That'll teach me to buy bargain-bin rat poison. He washed his hands before drying off the rest of his six-foot tall sinewy body, moving into his bedroom to get dressed. *Next time it's nothing but the best for the little bastards.*

Thin blades of early-morning sunlight worked their way through uneven metal venetian blinds that covered the window of his one-bedroom house on the east side of Detroit. Fatigued, Kevin looked at the clock on the nightstand next to his bed. 6:32 A.M.

He shut off the alarm which was due to go off in eight minutes. Beside the clock sat a 5 by 7-inch faded color picture in a cheap plastic frame. As Kevin started putting on a pair of worn but clean jeans, he glanced at the picture for a moment, at the smiling faces of the three people—an older woman dressed in a tie-dyed t-shirt and jeans in-between a lanky young man with long light-brown hair tied in a pony tail, which hung lazily over his bare left shoulder, and a petite, attractive, dark-haired young woman wearing a loose-fitting simple white dress that stopped midway down her tanned thighs. The young man had a tight smile as if holding something in, while the young woman beamed a joyous grin that could not be faked. Kevin stared at the photo for a few seconds more, then walked back into the bathroom to finish drying his hair.

As he started to vigorously rub his head with a towel, a sudden pinprick of pain in his right shoulder caused Kevin to flinch.

"What the hell?" He turned his head and expected to see an inflamed zit or insect bite. After all, the man had seen more spiders in the house the last four weeks than he had in his entire thirty years of life. However, it was neither a zit nor spider bite, but rather a raised area of skin the size of a dime on the front of his right shoulder. He cleaned the steam off the bathroom mirror and looked closer.

The lesion was a perfect circle, like a tiny bicycle tire implanted underneath his pale, freckled skin. There seemed to be no redness or discharge. Cautiously, Kevin ran his left index finger over the raised flesh. It was hard and devoid of any sensation.

No pain, no tingling. A small circle of nothing.

Another piece of artwork to go with the rest. He briefly

looked at his forearms, enveloped with a menagerie of prison tattoos and scarifications—concentric circles, jagged pentagrams, crisscrossing triangles, and other geometric designs—then looked away. They were forever a reminder of his time at Fairview State Penitentiary, of his dealings with Charles Readona, times that he wished with all his heart he could forget.

Kevin touched the lesion one more time. *Probably an ingrown hair. Guess it beats growing out of my ears.*

By the time he had finished drying his hair, the thought of the lesion had completely left his mind.

After finishing getting dressed in a white shirt and a simple, red-striped tie, Kevin sucked down a cup of cold coffee and made his way outside. The late September morning was unusually cold, and he considered going back inside to get a jacket, then dismissed the thought for fear of missing his morning bus.

Kevin looked up and down the block of Miranda Street for any two-legged predators. Except for three large raccoons working diligently to get into a garbage bag on the overgrown lawn of a boarded-up abandoned house across the street, there were no other living creatures in sight. He walked toward Lincoln Street where, four more blocks north, he would pick up a Detroit Metro bus for the six-mile ride to Woodward and Greenlawn and his ten-dollar-an-hour (*cash only*) job. He was almost at the corner when he came upon a fresh splatter of blood on the cracked sidewalk.

Someone must have gotten popped during a fight.

Kevin bent closer to the crimson puddle and flashed back to his prison time, sitting across from a fat, balding psychiatrist with bulging eyes and an enormous Adam's apple, who would flash card after card of Rorschach inkblots.

"And what of this one?" the shrink would say in his condescending voice, staring over his too-small glasses at Kevin.

"I don't know," Kevin replied, knowing that he should

give some bullshit answer but was too tired, too damn defeated to muster up an ounce of energy to lie.

"And what of this one?" the shrink said again, mercifully holding up the last of the cards.

The inkblot was different from all the rest; while the others were pale blue in swirling patterns of unrecognizable shapes, this one was dark crimson with sharp edges jutting out from the center of a small shape that appeared vaguely feminine.

"Why is that one a different color?" Kevin had asked, staring intently at the Rorschach, like looking into the face of a long-lost friend while trying desperately to remember their name.

"What do you see?" the shrink asked, his voice rising in excitement.

"I want to know why it's a different color," Kevin said with more force. "What kind of mind-game are you pulling here?"

"Now, Kevin," the shrink had said, his voice back to its usual arrogance. "I thought we were learning to control that anger. You know it's your anger that got you into this unfortunate situation, and it's your anger that—"

Kevin slapped the card out of the shrink's hand so fast it was like a magic trick. "You want to know what anger's really about?" Kevin's face found itself mere inches from the shrink's. "Try spending twenty-four hours out on the block and you'll learn more about anger then you could in school!"

The outburst cost Kevin a month in solitary.

A loud crack of a slamming door erupted in the air and Kevin was brought back to Miranda Street. He blinked hard and looked around.

Dark shapes moved behind the thick plate glass windows of a run-down one-story house to his left. Knee-high grass covered the lawn and dozens of empty beer and liquor bottles were scattered across the tiny wooden front porch that was tilted precariously on buckling supports.

Just another illegal business transaction gone bad. He looked down at the blood, then back at the house.

Kevin had learned in the joint to avoid the crack addicts and meth-heads. Both were unpredictable, psychotic, and willing to do anything to get their fix. Everyone avoided them—the Aryan Brotherhood, the Black Warriors, the Hispanic Shorn.

Everyone except Readona.

The shapes moved again, and Kevin imagined the group in the house, cachectic men and women in various stages of dress, leering at him like hungry vampires, mouths agape in eager anticipation of their next meal, eyes watery and gums grey and decayed.

Kevin carefully stepped around the blood splatter and quickly made his way to the bus stop.

He had used the same bus for over a month and there was a different driver each time. Kevin imagined an entire warehouse full of bored men and women dressed in navy blue DETROIT METRO BUS DRIVER uniforms waiting each day to see if they were going to be chosen to drive the great unwashed masses back and forth along the deserted streets of Motown.

The bus pulled to a stop a moment later and Kevin got on and dropped three quarters into the till. He scanned the seats—all empty except for an old white woman sitting in the second row, wearing a filthy pale green sweatshirt and jeans two sizes too big. She appeared to be having an animated conversation with a stuffed teddy bear she was holding close to her face.

"You need to sit."

Kevin looked to his right: it was the first time a bus driver had ever spoken to him.

The driver, a large black man with hands the size of small hams, motioned with his head. "You need to sit," he said again. "New policy. Some mutherfucker brought a lawsuit against the city last week for falling down and bruising his ass when he wouldn't sit down when the bus started rollin'. Now none of us can drive without everyone sitting."

"No problem."

Kevin turned to walk to the back and saw that the old woman had stood up and was holding out the teddy bear like a sword in her right hand. Kevin took a step forward and the woman snarled.

"Man, will you sit? She ain't gonna hurt you," the driver said. He calmly turned around. "Tisha, sit your skinny ass down and behave or I'll throw you off my bus."

The woman snarled once more at Kevin, then did as she was told.

Kevin walked by her but the woman totally ignored him, immersed again in deep conversation with her bear. He picked a seat in the back row and sat down.

As the bus started moving, Kevin finally remembered the dead rat in the trash.

CHAPTER 2

D ON'T YOU HAVE THE latest Rotting Flesh disc yet?"
Kevin looked up from the counter of Honsey's
Movie and Music store. A teenaged boy, fourteen or fifteen,
stared back at him. The kid's long black hair was greasy and
unkempt. Dark brown eyes looked out from sunken sockets
and his cheeks were scarred with acne. Two girls the same age
as the boy—dressed in the similar dirty dark-blue jeans and
black t-shirts—stood on either side of him.

"Don't think so," Kevin answered. "I can check to see if
it's going to—"

"That's fuckin' bullshit!" the kid loudly interrupted him.
In two quick steps he was at the counter and slammed his
bony fist down on the hard plastic. "I was fuckin' here last
week and some other fuckin' counter-clown told me it was
gonna be in today."

"It's not in today." Redolent odors of pot and the punk's
stale breath washed over Kevin; a rush of adrenaline sped up
his heart. "You're welcome to check back tomorrow."

The kid glanced at his companions and shook his head.
"You hear that?"

The two girls gave high-pitched giggles.

"You're welcome to check back tomorrow," the kid echoed. "Man, you are one stupid asshole."

Kevin felt the familiar anger boiling up and he let a small stream of it escape. "I've heard enough of your mouth, boy," he said in an even, low voice. "Now why don't you and your little friends get the hell out of here."

The boy stepped away from the counter and began scratching an angry looking zit on his face with his middle finger. "You don't own this fuckin' store. And who the fuck are you to tell me to get the hell out of here? You're just a fuckin' old man who's too fuckin' stupid to do anything but be a fuckin' counter-clown at a second-rate sound shop."

Kevin let his fingers glide over the handle of the baseball bat under the counter.

It would be easy. One swing and the punk's head would explode like a ripe Halloween pumpkin.

Kevin took a deep breath and cleared his throat. "Listen—none of us want trouble here, but if you keep copping an attitude, then—"

"I love trouble!" the punk interrupted again. He pulled up the front of his over-sized t-shirt, revealing his pale belly and a stainless steel semi-automatic pistol tucked haphazardly inside his jeans. He patted the butt of the gun and smiled at Kevin. "Maybe I should just teach you about coppin' an attitude with me."

Kevin let go of the bat and took a step away from the counter. His heart was beating so hard he was sure it was visible under his shirt.

"C'mon, Caleb, you're freakin' the old man," the girl to his right said to the boy. "Dusting him would just ruin all the fun we were gonna have today." She reached over and ran her hand up and down his crotch and smiled seductively at Kevin.

The boy kept tapping the butt of the gun with his finger.

Finally, after what felt like an eternity to Kevin, Caleb pulled down his shirt.

"Maybe you're right," he said, running one hand up and down the girl's skinny ass. "Guess you're just a lucky guy today to find my bitch needin' some dick."

"I guess so," Kevin muttered, his heart still pounding wildly.

"I'll be back," Caleb said over his shoulder in an exaggerated Austrian accent as he and his girlfriends walked toward the door. On their way out, he casually pushed over a rack of used R & B CDs and cassettes, sending a hundred square plastic containers spilling out onto the floor, then stomped on a pile of them like they were cockroaches.

Kevin waited for five minutes until he moved out from behind the counter. He looked up at the clock over the door: 5:50.

Near enough to closing time. He placed the SORRY-WE'RE CLOSED sign on the door, dropped the shades, latched the two deadbolts, and walked to the back to get a broom and dustpan.

Next, he put back up the music rack and was just starting to sweep up the broken CDs and cassettes when a loud banging on the front door almost caused him to knock the rack down again.

For a grim moment, Kevin imagined Caleb standing outside, holding his shiny pistol with both hands out like a cop on a TV show. He would wait to hear to click of the deadbolts being unlatched and then start shooting, pulling the trigger with his skeletal finger until the clip was empty and Kevin lay dead.

There were more knocks and a muffled voice outside the door. Kevin took a step back, holding onto the broom handle so tight his fingers turned ghostly white. The voice outside the door called out again and Kevin strained to make it out. It didn't sound like that kid.

Maybe it's Honsey coming by the check up and here I am, closed early with who knows how much merchandise ruined.

After a third round of impatient knocks, Kevin took a deep breath and unlocked the door with trembling hands.

It wasn't a punk kid with greasy hair, nor was it Adam Honsey, a late middle-aged man built like a retired heavy-weight boxer (which he was). Instead, the man standing before Kevin was short and thin with a thick head full of black curly hair, and eyes with irises the color of dark chocolate. His name was Caesar Rameriez, Kevin's best friend for the past twenty-one years.

"What's with the closed sign?" Caesar asked, walking past Kevin into the store. "If Honsey comes strolling by and sees that you've closed up early he'll throw a—" He stopped speaking at mid-sentence and gazed at the floor. "Somebody have a little accident?"

Kevin ran one hand through his thin-cropped light brown hair that was already starting to go gray at the edges. "Something like that." He picked up the dustbin and handed it to Caesar. "Help me out and I'll tell you a story."

"So, you going to call the cops?" Caesar asked after he and Kevin had finished sweeping.

Kevin shook his head. "Don't need the hassle."

"That you don't." Caesar looked around at the cramped confines of the store, its shelves neatly stocked with used CDs, DVDs, cassettes and videotapes. "Was the rest of the day any better?"

"It was good up to that point," Kevin answered. "Think I made about two hundred in sales, and except for an old man who I had to kick out for jerking off in the porn palace—" He pointed to a curtained-off room in the back of the store— "I didn't have problems with anyone."

Caesar frowned. "How did you know he was beating his meat?"

"Honsey's got a video-cam back there with a monitor under the register. Any time someone goes back there I try to remember to check up on them."

"Lucky you." Caesar looked around and chuckled. "You ever realize that it's like a time machine in here? Videos, cassettes, secret back rooms for porn—it's like stepping back into the early 2000's."

"I'd give my left nut to find a time machine and go back to then," Kevin said quietly. He looked up at the clock, then handed the broom he was still holding to Caesar. "Put this in the back for me. I've got to stash the money in the safe and get out of here—my bus is due in fifteen minutes."

Caesar waved him off. "Don't worry about the bus. I'll drive you home."

Kevin shook his head. "I don't think that's a good idea."

"Why not? My stylin' 2009 Impala not a good enough ride for you?"

Kevin looked up from behind the counter, where he was trying to remember the combination of the small safe Honsey had embedded in the floor underneath a worn piece of carpet. "If you drive me home, we'll end up picking up a six and Maria will be pissed at you for being late."

Caesar waved him off. "She'll be fine." He pulled out his cell phone l and began to type on it. "I'll text her and let her know what's up."

Kevin slowly turned the dial of the safe. "I think she hates me."

"She doesn't hate you. If I ever caught that vibe from her, I'd set her straight in a second."

"How you going to set her straight?"

"I'll tell her it's my way or the highway."

Kevin laughed. "She's the best thing that ever happened to you. Even if she is young enough to be your daughter."

Caesar looked down at Kevin from above the counter. "Fuck you. She's only ten years younger than me."

Kevin laughed again. "Caesar, she just graduated from high school a couple years ago."

"So what? Last spring you were still locked up." Caesar stepped back and put up his hands. "Look, K, I've been hearing about our age difference from her old lady ever since we got together. Just lay off, okay?"

"Sure." Kevin tried to concentrate on opening the safe and still his trembling hands.

"I didn't mean anything by that cut," Caesar quickly said in an apologetic tone. "I had a rough day. They laid off four more workers at the shop today and there's talk that some Chinese firm is going buy us out, and we all know if that happens our jobs will be shipped out."

Kevin finally got the combination right and opened the safe. "It's okay. And I meant what I said—Maria's a good woman. I don't want to see you two go bad."

Caesar's phone rang, the ring tone that of a braying donkey, and he looked at the text.

"Maria. Says she's going to her Mom's to plan their trip up to Traverse City so it's no problem if I give you a ride." He held out the phone toward Kevin. "See? She doesn't say anything about hating you."

Kevin stood up and good-naturedly pushed the phone away. "Fine. I believe you."

"As you should." Caesar put the phone in his pocket. "You get one yet?"

"What?"

"A cell phone."

"No."

"Shit, K, you're the only person in Michigan without one."

Kevin shrugged. "You know me—always the rebel." He closed the safe and carefully replaced the carpeting. "Ready to go?"

"You know it."

Kevin went to move from behind the counter when he eyes fell upon the baseball bat. *It would have been easy. It would have been so easy and so terrible and—*

"Kev? You coming?"

Kevin looked up. "Yeah. I've had enough fun here for today."

CHAPTER 3

CAESAR PULLED THE IMPALA onto the cracked driveway of Kevin's house. "You really need to find a new crib," he said, reaching into the back seat to get the six-pack of beer that they had picked up at a party store.

"I've got my eye on a new riverfront condo. I'm just waiting for the market to cool down until I drop a down-payment on one."

"I'm serious, K. This place is nasty." He looked up and down the street. "Is there anyone else living on this block?"

"You counting the crack-house residents?"

"No."

"I think there's a young couple living a few doors down, least there was last month, and an old man at the end of the block who sits on his porch and yells at the feral cats running across his lawn."

"Like I said—you need to get a new crib."

"If the state of Michigan wants to pay the rent for released cons for one year, they can put me anywhere they want," Kevin said as he and Caesar walked into the house.

Kevin turned on the light, illuminating the tiny living

room and adjoining kitchen. Caesar took two beers from the six-pack and put the rest in the refrigerator.

"To your first month of freedom," he said, tapping Kevin's bottle with his.

"I'll drink to that." Kevin drained his half his bottle and loudly belched. "This was one of the things I missed the most in prison—just sitting back and having an ice-cold beer."

"Don't you mean to say having an ice-cold beer with your best friend?"

Kevin smiled. "Of course that's what I meant."

"Thought so." Caesar put his beer down on the floor, then cocked his head back slightly and sniffed. "Don't take this personally, but it smells kind of funky in here."

Kevin sat up. "Damn, I forgot." He walked to his bathroom and came out a moment later with a wrapped plastic garbage bag.

"What the hell do you have in there?" Caesar asked.

Kevin walked over to Caesar and thrust the bag at him. "A rat."

Caesar flinched and plastered himself against the couch. "Don't fuck with me. What's in there?"

"I told you," Kevin said, a wicked grin spreading across his face, "a rat."

"Why the hell do you have a rat in there? And you better tell me it's dead!"

"It's dead. It crawled on my foot after I got out of the shower. I smashed its head in." Kevin opened the front door and gave the bag a heave out onto the front lawn. "I'll put it by the curb tomorrow morning."

"That wasn't funny," Caesar said, starring coldly at Kevin.

"C'mon—it was kinda funny." He laughed and drank more of his beer. "Remember when we finished ninth grade and went down to the Rouge River with a pint of sloe gin and Jenny Leadbeter?"

Caesar took a deep breath and a smile formed on his face.

"I remember you had the hots for her."

Kevin nodded. "You had finished off the pint, me and Jenny were getting all cozy and then some rat the size of a beagle came lumbering up the side of the riverbank toward us and—"

"I freaked out and puked all over Jenny." Caesar laughed and took another drink of his beer.

"I was so pissed at you," Kevin groaned.

"Not as pissed as Jenny!"

"You got that right." Kevin finished his beer. "What ever happened to her?"

"Last I heard she was a Missionary in Uganda or someplace like that."

"It's funny where life takes us sometimes, isn't it?"

Caesar nodded. "That it is." He looked around the living room. "You call the landlord about the rat problem?"

"Not yet. I doubt if some rich-ass slumlord living in Bloomfield Hills is going to be all over that pronto. Anyway, I'm the only person alive without a phone, remember?"

"I'm buying you a phone tomorrow," Caesar said.

"I'm not a charity case. I'll buy a phone when I can afford it." Kevin got up from the couch and grabbed his empty bottle. "You need another one?"

"Sure." Caesar finished his beer and handed the it to Kevin. "Might as well bring the rest of 'em in here. No reason to be getting up every few minutes to get more."

Kevin returned from the kitchen and placed the six-pack on the floor. Caesar grabbed anther bottle and opened it up. "You sleeping any better?"

Kevin shrugged. "Not really."

"Maria has been listening to this podcast about stress. It's not my thing, but I can't help but hear them in the morning when I'm getting ready for work. Anyway, this guy, I think a Doctor named Rossi, was talking about how unresolved stress can make all sorts of crazy things happen—headaches, rashes, shit like that—and he also talked about how it can lead to clinical depression."

"You saying that I can't sleep because I'm depressed?"

"Give yourself a break; you were in a rotten place for six years. That alone would make anyone depressed."

"But I'm not there anymore." Kevin opened up two beers and handed one to Caesar. "And there's no way I'm ever going back again." He took a long drink and sat back into the couch. "So, if anything, I should be happy about my future, not depressed."

Caesar sighed. "You know what I mean." He stood up, walked to the small front window of the house, and looked outside. "Can't believe it's already getting dark this early. I'm not ready for winter."

"Me neither." The deep-throated beat of a bass rift grew in the air. Kevin joined Caesar by the window. "New customers at the crack-house?"

"Uh huh." A tricked-out black Nissan 380Z sat idling in the street as one figure dressed in dark clothes stood on the porch of the house. Kevin watched as dark clothes exchanged something with a portly man dressed in a two-sizes-too small wife-beater t-shirt and some baggy shorts.

"Cops ever pay those folks a visit?" Caesar asked.

Kevin shook his head. "I don't think the cops know this block exists."

He sat back down on the couch. Caesar remained standing and looking out the window.

"Chill out, Caesar—they're not going to bother your car," Kevin said.

"Sure. They probably only jack expensive imports." He joined Kevin and they sat in silence, quietly drinking their beer.

Caesar placed his second empty bottle next to the six-pack, then looked at his watch and sighed. "I should get going. Four A.M. seems to be coming earlier and earlier these days. I really need to see about getting on the afternoon shift."

"There's some nights I don't fall asleep until four."

Caesar looked at Kevin before grabbing another bottle of beer. "Is it something from . . . you know, being at Fairview?"

Kevin shook his head and said nothing.

"Look, I'm not bugging you," Caesar continued, "but if something about that place has got into your head and is fucking with your sleep, then—"

"Nine months ago," Kevin said, staring out into space. "Nine months ago, to the day, I slit a guy's throat."

CHAPTER 4

CAESAR'S EYES OPENED WIDE. "Fuck!"

"You can't tell anyone, Caesar. Not Maria. Not *any-one*."

"Kevin, we've been best friends since fifth-grade when you saved my life. You can tell me anything and know that I'll keep it to myself."

Kevin shook his head. "I didn't save your life. All I did was stop a couple of eighth-grade assholes from beating on you."

"No," Caesar interrupted with conviction. "You saved my life, K. You didn't even know me, and you saved my fucking life."

"Fine. I saved your life." Kevin got up and paced on the tiled living room floor. "But this . . . it can't ever get out. I shouldn't even be telling you."

"It won't get out. You got my word. And you know that's as good as gold."

"I know." Kevin took another long drink of beer, placed the bottle down in the far corner of the living room, and crossed his arms.

"It was after last Halloween. Up until that time things were going good . . . at least as good as things could go in that hellhole."

"I remember," Caesar said. "You were pretty up—on your final stretch as you called it."

"Yeah. My final stretch." Kevin shook his head. "It's funny how you can adapt to damn near anything. After my first week there I was sure that I wasn't going to make a month, and by the time last year rolled around it was usually just a numbing routine."

He motioned to Caesar with one hand. "You got any smokes on you?"

"No. Maria made me quit a couple months ago."

"No problem. One more bad habit I don't need back." He picked up his beer and sat back down on the couch. "So, there I was—working at the shop DynaCore had set up in the prison yard, making bullet-proof vests for two dollars an hour, taking an occasional college credit course, and keeping to myself. I thought I was so fucking smooth."

"What happened?" Caesar asked in a quiet voice.

"I got careless and cocky. Two of the worst mistakes in prison." Kevin sighed and wrapped his fingers behind his head. "It was a typical fall day up there—colder than shit outside, snowing like mad. Hardly anyone was in the yard. I was going nuts staying in my square—my cell—so I went down to the rec room."

Kevin finished off his beer. "I almost never went down there when it was crowded—too much of a chance of bad shit happening. But I was so damn bored and figured if something started going down, I would just leave.

"A few other guys and I were shooting basketball, nothing serious, when a half-dozen members of the Black Brotherhood showed up and wanted to play a game. I should've walked away but I didn't. I was bored and sick of being afraid—no, not afraid, but always being on my guard. I forgot that's what had kept me alive and mostly trouble free for all my time up to that point."

"What happened?"

"We played the game and ended up kicking their ass. Leon Means—I still remember the fuck's name—all two hundred and fifty muscled pounds of him, got into my face and started spouting all this black racist shit, about how we cheated and how white guys could never beat black guys in hoops one-on-one. I just started laughing at him and went to walk away when he took a swing." Kevin gave a bitter laugh. "I blocked it without even thinking and dropped him cold."

"You killed him with just one punch?"

Kevin's brow furrowed. "No. He wasn't the one that I killed, but I made him look bad to his homies, and by doing that I put a death sentence on myself."

"But they didn't kill you. Not unless you're a ghost." Caesar gave a nervous laugh.

Kevin stayed silent for a moment, staring again off into the distance.

"They started toying with me," he finally continued. "Would gang up and beat my ass in the shower, shoved and tripped me in the chow-hall, whispering that when I least expected it, they were going to kill me."

He unbuttoned his white shirt, pulled off his t-shirt, and pointed with his left index finger to his back.

"They shanked me in the shower. A half-inch to the center and he would have sliced my aorta and killed me on the spot . . ."

Caesar inspected the two-inch jagged scar just below Kevin's right shoulder blade. "Was this what put you in the hospital for a week? When you told me you had pneumonia?"

Kevin nodded. "Didn't need you to freak out on me. I had that covered for both of us."

Caesar pointed at Kevin's shoulder. "What's that?"

"What?"

"This," he bent closer to Kevin, ". . . this circle shaped thing on your shoulder."

"I think it's an ingrown hair."

"Doesn't look like any ingrown hair. It looks like one of your prison tats . . ."

"It's nothing." Kevin put his t-shirt back on and stood up. "Anyway, when I got back to my cell, the Brotherhood got word to me that they were going to finish the job. I knew they would."

"What'd you do? Go to the guards?"

"Fuck no! Those guys were overworked, underpaid, and were not going to give me 24-hour protection."

"What'd you do?"

"You remember Billie Knottmier?"

"The big smelly kid in our ninth-grade class?"

"Uh huh. You remember how he used to tie up cats, hang them on trees and beat them with a baseball bat?"

Caesar grimaced. "Billie was one sick fuck."

"There was this guy—is *still* this guy—in Fairview named Charles Readona. He had this motley band of a dozen or so followers—rapist, pedophiles, murderers—that made Billie look like a saint. And none of them were even close to being as sadistic as Readona."

Kevin paced back and forth. "Readona looks like a no-body, just a run-of-the-mill white-trash lowlife. Maybe five-eight, gaunt, with thin receding black hair, big ears and small sharp nose . . . but he had these dark brown eyes that even in the light of the afternoon sun could turn as black as coal."

He stopped, reached for his beer, realized that it was empty, and continued his pacing.

"I had spent five years keeping to myself, staying out of trouble, not joining any of the gangs, and then, when I need-ed help, there was no one. Not until one of Readona's mon-sters came up to me in the chow-hall and told me Charles—

that's what they called him, *Charles*—wanted to talk to me about saving my life."

"Why you?"

"Don't know. And at the time, I didn't care." Kevin finally stopped pacing and crossed his arms tight against his chest.

"Two of his men took me to Readona's cell. He was sitting there on the bottom bunk, dressed in a prison-green T-shirt and ratty looking jeans, just another con. He looked up at me with those freaky brown-black eyes of his and said 'Kevin'—like I was some long-lost relative—'Kevin, we all know that you're in a bad spot and I've decided that we're going to help you.'"

"He offered to help you out of the goodness of his heart?"

"No!" Kevin's voice was loud and high and he stepped away from Caesar. "Sorry . . . It's just that I was so damn afraid . . ."

His voice trailed off and he shook his head.

"You've never been afraid of much of anything in your life."

"I was then. It was hell, always wondering when the Brotherhood would finally kill me. Day after day, week after week . . ." His lips were pursed tight. "They were going to kill me. Less than a year until I was out of that shithole and they were going to fucking kill me and there wasn't a damn thing I could do about it.

"I asked Readona what he wanted in exchange for help. He told me all I had to do was kill one of the Black Brotherhood. Slit the guy's throat and then Readona and his men would make sure that I was never caught for the murder and that the Brotherhood, or anyone else, would never fuck with me again."

"And you believed him?"

Kevin stared at Caesar. "I know it sounds insane, but I was at the end of my rope. I was sleeping an hour or two a night, I stopped going to the mess hall to eat. . . . I just wanted it to end." Kevin ran his hands through his short hair. "I did exactly what Readona said. Waited in the shower, grabbed the guy from behind, slit his throat and went back to my cell."

"Fuck." Caesar took a deep breath. "You had to do it though, right?" He said, sounding as if it was as much as a question as it was a statement to convince himself. "If you hadn't, they would have killed you, so instead, you killed one of them."

"Yeah. That's about it. From that day, to the day you picked me up last month outside the walls, no one from the Brotherhood—hell, no one period—ever messed with me again." He tapped his head several times against the couch. "I don't know why I told you . . ."

"Because you needed to get it out," Caesar reassured him. "You keep shit like that inside, it'll eat you up. Damn, K, no wonder you haven't been sleeping."

Kevin weakly smiled. "You're a good friend, Caesar."

"Damn straight I am." Caesar got up and patted his taller friend on the arm. "You know you can always tell me anything."

"A regular Dr. Phil now, are you?"

Caesar laughed. "I wish I was getting his paycheck." He looked down at his watch. "I gotta roll."

Kevin nodded and walked Caesar to the door. "Thanks for the beer."

Caesar turned around. "I know I've never served time, but I know it was hell in there for you and you did what you had to do to survive. And maybe I'll go to hell for saying this, but between me and you, I'm glad you did." He pulled his car keys out then turned again to Kevin. "You doing anything a week from Saturday night?"

"Let me check my calendar." Kevin reached up in mid-air and pantomimed opening a notebook. "Nope, looks like I'm free."

"Great. I might be able to score a couple tickets for one

of the last Tigers games."

"That's cool, but doesn't Maria want to go?"

Caesar shook his head. "She's going to Traverse City to see her Grandma."

"Then I guess it's a date." Kevin opened the door and watched as Caesar made his way to his car. "Thanks again for the beer and listening."

"What else do you expect? You're my boy, K!"

Kevin watched Caesar drive away before he closed and locked the door.

My boy. He stood in the silence of the living room and stared into the gloomy darkness of the night. *Would you still think I'm your boy if you knew that after I slit the throat of a 17-year-old kid that I cut out his still-beating heart?*

CHAPTER 5

For Kevin, the rest of the week passed by in totally unremarkable fashion—no rats crawling on him, no
street punks causing a hassle in the store. Honsey, while initially pissed at the loss of merchandise, was grateful that the
incident with the punk kid hadn't escalated into bloodshed.
At the end of the week, Caesar stopped by the shop and
dropped off a cell phone for Kevin.

"I told you I'm not a charity case," Kevin had protested.

Caesar had waved him off. "Pay me when you get the
spare cash. Besides, the phone only has five hours of call time
on it—after that you buy your own damn timecards."

Kevin sat on his couch that Saturday evening, absently
flipping the cover of the phone open and closed and allowed
himself a moment of relaxation. Life was getting better.
Slowly, but still, better. He wasn't in prison anymore; he was
earning money and he had handled himself well with that
asshole kid.

"And you're going to see the Detroit Tigers tonight," he
said out loud.

When was the last time he had been to a ballgame?

Must have been twenty years ago. I was just a kid, dad was still alive, and all the world seemed so much simpler.

The phone suddenly started buzzing and Kevin almost dropped it. Opening the cover, he pushed the small handset icon. The tiny screen lit with the following text from Caesar:

Hope U didn't 4get bout 2nite. Ill b over in a few. Ur guna luv it!

Kevin smiled and closed the cell phone shut. He got up from the couch to grab a jacket when a sharp bee-sting pain bit into his right thigh. He quickly unbuckled his jeans and dropped them to his ankles, expecting to see a spider chewing into his leg.

He found instead another raised area of skin like the one he had discovered on his shoulder.

Kevin sat down on the couch and carefully examined his leg. Unlike the circle-shaped lesion on his shoulder, this one appeared as an elongated oval, one inch long and one-quarter inch wide. The raised skin was slightly darkened, like a thick piece of black thread embedded underneath pale flesh.

What the hell is going on? Kevin stepped out of his jeans, walked into the bathroom, and took off his shirt.

The raised circle on his shoulder was still there. Was it bigger? Kevin peered in the mirror. It definitely looked larger. Grown from dime-sized to penny-sized.

And thicker.

Riper.

He sat down on the closed toilet seat and took a deep breath. *Maybe I picked up some type of parasite in prison, but if it was that, it probably would have popped up earlier.*

He touched the spot on his thigh and ran his index finger along the raised skin. Similar to when he initially found the lesion on his shoulder, there was no more pain, just a slight numbness. Under his finger, the growth on his thigh was glassy smooth, bringing up a vivid memory of being nine years old at his maternal grandmother's funeral. His mother had made him go up to the casket by himself to see his dead grandma, then kneel and pray for her soul to go to Heaven.

Except Kevin didn't kneel and pray. He stood there, dressed in a suit and tie like a little gentleman, and stared at his grandmother's hands. They were so yellow, appearing so unearthly he was convinced that somehow, the funeral director had cut off her real hands and replaced them with fake plastic or wood ones.

He peered around to make sure no one was looking at him, then reached into the casket and touched her hands. They weren't plastic or wood. They were made of cold flesh that had lost its life.

That's what the lesions on his thigh felt like.

Like death.

There was a loud knock on the door. He put his shirt and pants back on, then ran into the living room and answered the door.

"Didn't you get my message?" Caesar asked after walking inside. "You look like you just got up."

"I'm almost ready."Kevin, buttoned his shirt and grabbed a pair of shoes.

"Good, because I'm ready for a night out with the wild man of Detroit!" Caesar flopped down on the couch. "We sure used to tear up the city in our younger days, didn't we?"

"The key word in that sentence is 'younger,'" Kevin reminded him. "I'm just looking forward to going to Comerica, having some hot dogs and cold beer, and watching the Tigers win their way into the playoffs."

And having something to take my mind off of my shoulder and leg.

"Sorry, K. We're not going to see the Tigers."

"We're not?"

Caesar shook his head. "The guy who was going to give

me his tickets decided he wanted to go. But that's okay. I got us covered."

"Yeah? Where are we going?"

Caesar gave him a wicked smile. "To see fire."

Kevin looked out the window of the Impala and hoped a stray bullet wouldn't hit them as he and Caesar drove down Van Dyke Road. On every other corner, street dealers standing under busted lights hawked their wares while hookers stood waiting on the periphery for an easy mark.

"C'mon, Caesar, tell me where we're going," Kevin whined.

Caesar pulled out two tickets from his shirt and gave them to Kevin. "I told you: we're going to see fire."

Kevin read one of the tickets, a cigarette-pack sized parchment paper:

COME ONE, COME ALL
TO SEE THE HOTTEST SHOW THIS FALL
COME CELEBRATE LIFE AND DEATH WITH YOUR FRIENDS
AND NEVER EVER BE THE SAME AGAIN!

He handed the tickets back to Caesar. "What the hell is this about?"

"It's like a celebration of the Autumn Equinox."

"That's not for another couple days."

"So, they're a little bit early, okay?" He stopped at a red light and looked anxiously around the streets. "Is your door locked?"

"Yeah."

Caesar pushed hard on the accelerator when the light turned green, and the Impala jumped forward. Caught off-guard at the sudden movement, Kevin was pushed backwards and his loose seatbelt slid below his waist, almost touching his thigh.

"If you're so worried about getting carjacked, what the hell are we doing around here?" Kevin asked anxiously. "This area of town makes my neighborhood look serene."

"You'll see," Caesar slowed at the next light and turned left onto Harper Avenue. "We're almost there."

"There's nothing down here except burned-out buildings occupied by burned-out addicts."

"In that, my friend, you're mistaken." Caesar slowed the car and pointed out the window. "We're here."

On his right, the large Spanish Baroque-styled three-story tall building occupied half a city block. The red and brown granite exterior had been liberally painted with multi-colored graffiti, while the quarter end of the building was a menagerie of rotting timbers and fallen stone.

"Nice place," Kevin said with a hint of weary sarcasm. "We going to take the deluxe or standard tour?"

"Let me park and I'll fill you in." Caesar pulled his car into a large lot filled with at least a hundred cars.

In less than a minute a very tall, very thin black man wearing a full-length, red leather jacket knocked on the driver side window.

"Tickets?" the man spoke up in a baritone voice.

Caesar handed them over and the man motioned with one hand adorned in rings of sliver and jade on each long finger.

"Park seven rows down," the man instructed. "Wait for escorts before you get out of your car."

"You've brought me to a Halloween show and we forgot our costumes," Kevin said as they cruised the rows of cars looking for a parking spot.

"No, it's a fire show, in celebration of the Celtic New Year. Halloween is what developed out of Samhain."

"Since when did you become an expert in Celtic mythology?"

Caesar frowned as he pulled into an open spot. "Just because I work in a machine tool shop doesn't mean I don't pick up a book to read." He looked out the window for the escorts then turned back to Kevin. "Peter, a guy that used to work in the shop with me, started this performance artist group, MCFM—Motor City Fire Masters—a couple years ago. They go around to different trashed buildings like the Grand Ballroom, Michigan Central Station, now Eastown Theatre here, and put on these crazy-ass shows."

Two men dressed in black leather jackets, one average sized and the other almost as tall as the ticket-taker—with shoulders as wide as a Detroit Lions offensive lineman—walked up to the Impala.

"Looks like our escorts are here," Kevin guessed aloud.

He got out of the car and noticed the faint odor of cannabis wafting from one of the men.

"Is this on the up and up?" Kevin asked Caesar as they followed the two men toward the building. A gunshot and the wail of an ambulance could be vaguely heard in the distance.

Caesar nodded. "Sure. One of Peter's cousins is a big shot in the Detroit Building Inspection Department. He makes sure they don't get hassled. Plus, the local cops love it when MCFM has a show! It drives out all the dealers that normally do business in these abandoned buildings."

"That's good. Sure would hate to go back to the joint because I was involved in a staged pagan ritual."

"C'mon, , you know I'm not gonna take you to a place where that would happen."

They stopped in front of the large double-oak doors of the building. Their escorts each took hold of large brass circles attached to each door and silently pulled them open.

"Wow . . ." Kevin stepped into the cavernous foyer of the Eastown Theatre. The walls and high ceiling were a mix of classical style architecture, complete with a fifteen-foot-wide marble staircase that stood in the middle of the room. Though the latter's snow-white texture seemed to have faded with the passage of time.

"Look at that woodwork!" Caesar pointed to the intricately carved wooden framing around the faded red tiling of the walls and ceiling. "Pretty damn impressive."

"That it is." They walked by a dozen or so young people standing in the foyer—some dressed in sweatshirts and jeans, others in leather and stilettos—and walked up the dirty marble staircase.

"Can't believe someone hasn't stolen these steps," Caesar commented.

"Probably the fact that each one weighs a thousand pounds or more has deterred your common Detroit thief."

"Fair point,."

They opened another smaller set of doors to the auditorium and a cacophony of Celtic music and human voices filled Kevin's ears. On the auditorium floor in front of a massive stage were three-hundred or so people milling between widely spaced aluminum folding chairs. A hazy blue cloud of cigarette and pot smoke hung high up in the domed ceiling; the auditorium lights filtering through it cast a surrealist glow on the crowd below.

"C'mon, , let's go in back. I'll introduce you to Peter and the gang." Caesar pushed Kevin through the animated crowd of men and women, a juxtaposition of dreadlocks and bald, all leather to full body paint, innocent-looking girls with flowers in their hair to thickly muscled men wearing animal skins with faces covered in war paint.

"I feel old in here," Kevin said as they made their way back.

Their trek was blocked by three male and three female dancers dressed only in dark green loincloths, who were pantomiming monkeys, cows, stags, and other animals.

"Can't see this at a Tigers game!" Caesar cackled.

One of the women—tall, with ebony skin, cropped hair, long fingernails sharpened to points, and leopard spots painted on her upper nude body—slinked toward Kevin. The woman seductively moved around him, lightly running her nails up and down his back and chest, her fingertips lightly stroking his neck and face.

Primeval scents of musk, perfume, and sweat filled his world and Kevin felt his pulse quicken. Her light green eyes never left his. She smiled and crouched down in front of him, sliding her fingers down his chest to his abdomen and hard over his crotch before moving down his thighs.

Directly onto the new lesion.

A sharp sensation of a bee sting in his leg startled Kevin. He instinctively slapped her hand away and stumbled backward.

"Kev—you okay?" He heard someone say as if in an echo chamber.

Kevin blinked and looked around. The dancer had stood up and was frowning and saying something unintelligible to her cohorts.

"Kevin, what's going on?" Caesar said.

"Nothing!" Kevin quickly mouthed, "I'm sorry," to the dancer, who shook her head then turned to join the other dancers in with the crowd.

"Why'd you freak out on that girl?" Caesar asked.

"I don't know," Kevin lied. "Just thought it was getting a little too weird. You know I'm not into public displays of affection."

Caesar laughed uneasily. "Next you'll be telling me you're joining the priesthood!"

Kevin pointed to the stage. "I thought you were going to introduce me to your friends."

"Follow me!"

Pushing the stinging pain to the back of his mind, Kevin followed Caesar to the front, where they made their way around various technicians and workers as they continued setting up lighting fixtures and numerously large scaffoldings. The acrid smell of kerosene and propane hung heavy in the air. Kevin initially noticed that there were multiple fire extinguishers placed both under the scaffolding and off to the sides of the stage.

"I hope your friends know what they're doing," Kevin spoke. "A fire in this old building could make a good night turn really bad really fast."

Caesar waved him off, and then smiled.

"Hey, Peter!" he yelled to a well-tanned Native-American twenty-something man. He was lean, but muscular at around six-feet tall, dressed up in a dark T-shirt with faded jeans, joined near the back of the stage with another man and two women.

"Good to see you," Peter said as Caesar and Kevin approached him.

The other man was African-American, mid-twenties like Peter, a bit taller but even more muscular. Of the two women, one was pale, almost as tall as Peter with large breasts, spiked blond hair, a pair of two-gauge barbells through the corner of both eyebrows and nasal septum, and a sharp face that would have made her at home in the centerfolds of girlie magazines Kevin would steal as a kid from his dad's closet. The other woman was shorter, five-five, with dark brown hair that fell straight down framing her face that held full lips, high cheekbones and strong yet feminine chin. She was slim and tanned, although not as dark as Peter, with no visible piercings but elaborate multi-colored tattoos on both arms; on her left, Kevin could make out a Celtic cross covered in ivy inside an elaborate triquetra; on the right was a maze of Celtic knot-work with interspersed lettering too small for Kevin to read. All four of the performers wore the same dark t-shirts with a rainbow-colored Mobius knot on the front, especially prominent on the blonde's noticeable bosom, with the words NOW AND FOREVER MCFM! printed in smaller white letters below.

"Didn't think you were going to make it," Peter told Caesar.

Kevin noticed that Peter's ears were thin and pointed like a dog or coyote's and his front teeth were all tapered to a point.

Caesar guffawed, "For as much as I paid for these tickets you think I would miss it?"

"It costs a lot of money to put on a show like this," Peter said, glancing over at Kevin. "Who's your friend?"

"I'm Kevin Ciano. He extended his hand to the taller man

The man met Kevin's hand with a firm grip of his own. "Nice to meet you, Kevin. I'm Peter."

"Sorry. I'm terrible at introductions," Caesar sheepishly scratched the back of his head. "Kevin, this is Delmond—"He pointed to the black guy, then to the tall white girl, "—the beautiful Roxanne, and last but not least, Sherri."

Kevin nodded to all three. His eyes lingered a moment longer on Sherri, and she held his gaze.

"Did Caesar tell you much about the show tonight?" Peter asked him.

"No. I think he wanted it to be a surprise."

"Surprises can be fun," Sherri said, then laughed, a light, easy sound that immediately put Kevin at ease.

"Where do you want this?" asked a middle-aged Hispanic man dressed in loose jeans, a flannel shirt, and work boats.

He pointed at a fifteen-foot-high three-tiered scaffold being moved by a forklift. What interested Kevin was not the scaffolding itself but its attachments: hanging from each level top to bottom, were ten, eight, and six slaughterhouse meat hooks suspended with thick nylon rope.

"You can leave it right there for now," Peter replied. "We'll have you move it later in the show."

"Fine by me," the man said. "I'm being paid by the hour."

"C'mon over and see my creation." Peter motioned Kevin and Caesar to look up at the meat hook-adorned scaffolding. "You like it?"

"Looks like you're getting ready to go fishing for whales," Kevin said.

Peter laughed again, put his hands up over his head and grabbed the lowest set of hooks hanging seven feet above the stage. He smoothly pulled himself up until his arms were at ninety-degree angles, looking like an Olympic gymnast.

"So then," he said, grinning down at Caesar and Kevin, "are you ready to see a show?"

CHAPTER 6

KEVIN GASPED ALONG WITH the crowd as the dancer on stage, a stunning Asian woman in her early twenties dressed in a sheer white silk dress with nothing underneath, ducked under a flaming sword swung at her head by a stocky black man covered by a ragged coat made of brown animal furs.

"That chick has got some balls!" Caesar shouted, his gleeful voice muffled by the loud pounding of drums that fueled the rhythm of the dancers.

Kevin nodded. Five rows back from the stage, he could feel the heat that emanated from the various swords and sticks and torches that were part of the show. The oily stench of kerosene and propane that he had only faintly noticed backstage were now front and center. Mixed with the odors of cannabis and sweat, it gave the theatre a thick, redolent atmosphere. Kevin didn't mind. The sound, the smells—they all fit perfectly into the primitive performance before his eyes.

Caesar tapped Kevin on his arm. "How much longer you think the show's gonna go?"

"Don't know. Just sit back and enjoy."

He guessed the show had been going for at least an hour. It had started with a group of twenty dancers bounding up the center aisle, expertly wielding flaming torches that they twirled like batons. Onstage, Peter and Sherri—both dressed simply in earth-tone full-length smocks—were theatrically born in a huge explosion of fire rising out of a Volkswagen beetle-sized faux boulder. Through action and pantomime, they appeared to have a lover's quarrel: Roxanne, nude except for a swatch of animal fur around her groin, appeared as the temptress coming between Peter and Sherri. Delmond, wearing a full-length black-wolf costume with only his face uncovered, looked to Kevin to be acting as the trickster, going from one character to another and urging them on.

There was a scene break, with another group of scantily clad male and female dancers back onto stage, again twirling torches and flaming spears.

"Man, if I wasn't with Maria I'd be hitting' on Roxanne!" Caesar said loudly in Kevin's ear.

Kevin snickered. "You think she's doing the deed with Peter?"

"No way. Peter's with Delmond." He tapped Kevin on the shoulder again. "You should ask Roxanne out."

"I don't know. I'm six years out of practice."

"That's no excuse," Caesar insisted. "After the show I'll—"

He stopped in mid-sentence as the lights dimmed and the music increased in volume. Sherri came back on stage, now in a torn sheepskin pullover. It was cut in a revealing V, exposing most of her breasts and extending down to her upper thighs. She appeared frightened and lost, dancing aimlessly among ten-foot-high Christmas trees with exaggerated phallic tops cut into their spiky leaves.

A dozen large men, each at least six feet tall with oiled-up bulging muscles and dressed as cavemen, emerged from both sides of the stage. They crept closer and closer to Sherri until, an arm's length away, there was a huge explosion center stage, bathing Kevin and the entire audience in a flash of brilliant heat and light.

The music quieted to a soft moan and Kevin's eyes slowly adjusted back to the dim lighting. On the middle of the stage were Sherri and Delmond, the latter now costumed as a goat, complete with long, bony legs and cloven feet. The cavemen stood on the either side of the couple, holding their flaming clubs high and chanting in a rhythmic beat.

The goat-man Delmond moved close to Sherri and pawed at her sheepskin, and each time she rebuffed him with a hard slap to his hands and arms. After a few tries, Delmond stood back, bellowed in lustful rage and tore off the costumed goatskin around his waist and groin.

"Holy shit!" Caesar gasped.

Delmond's thick, long cock stood straight out pointing at Sherri. She gazed upon it, eyes wide. Delmond took two steps back, snarled like a lion before a kill, then grabbed his member with one hand and began to wave it back and forth.

Without warning all the lights in the arena went out except for one dim spotlight on Delmond and Sherri. He thrust out his hips and a three-foot long jet of flame shot out from his dick. Sherri threw up her arms for protection, there was a thunderous pounding of drums, and then all the lights in the theatre went out.

"That was the wildest shit I've ever seen!" Caesar exclaimed after the lights came on. The dancers with flaming torches and spears came back onstage, signaling another set change. "How the hell do you think they did that?"

"Shooting fire out of your dick? I thought every guy knew how to do that."

Caesar punched Kevin on the arm, just missing the lesion on his shoulder. "Fuck you!" he laughed and shook his head. "I wonder how they're going to top that?"

"Looks like we're going to find out," Kevin said as the

lights dimmed, the dancers left, and an eight-foot-tall funeral pyre occupied the middle of the stage.

The spotlight focused on a person rolled up in a fetal position in the center of the collection of logs on top of the Pyre. Slowly, with grace, the person stood up. It was Sherri. Totally nude. Kevin could now see that besides the tats on her arms she had two more—a large, multi-limbed tree on her back and a phoenix rising out of a ball of fire on her chest. He watched, mesmerized by her slow, sensual dance to the Celtic music booming in the auditorium. Kevin grew hard in his jeans and squirmed to relieve the pressure on his growing erection. Below, the dancers gathered around, holding clubs with flaming phallic heads.

The spotlight shifted to the back and right. There stood the fifteen-foot-high scaffold, now covered with thick, black plastic tarps, giving it the appearance of a smooth mountain wall. And on that wall, suspended by multiple hooks and ropes, hung top to bottom, were Peter, Delmond, and Roxanne.

"You could not pay me enough to do that!" Caesar exclaimed. The suspended trio were motionless, like puppets held in stasis by an unseen, sadistic master.

The music quickened in rhythm and both Sherri and the dancers below moved with it. The spotlight jumped back and forth between her and the hanging trio until there was a sudden lull in the music.

Peter, Delmond and Roxanne pushed off with their feet on the covered scaffolding, swaying back and forth in perfect unison to the beat of the music. Peter gestured to the dancers, and they began to thrusting their flaming phallic torches near the bottom of the pyre with menace.

Kevin's heart pounded erection straining in his jeans, both aroused and fearful as the music quickened and the torches grew closer to the wood. Peter looked at the dancers below with a regal gaze, then sneered at Sherri and pointed at her. In perfect unison the music reached a crescendo, the dancers thrust their torches to the wood and the pyre exploded in a geyser of flame.

The entire crowd in the theatre sprang to their feet. The heat from the fireball was so intense, Kevin turned away, shielding his eyes. When he looked back, all he could see were empty scaffolding and a deserted pyre with thick clouds of smoke rising from the top.

Thunderous applause filled the auditorium as the lights came on and dancers again filled the isles.

Caesar, a huge smile on his face, turned to his best friend. "That was incredible! What'd you think?"

Kevin continued to stare at the smoking pyre and hoped with all his heart that Sherri wasn't hurt. "I think your friends are either the bravest or craziest people I've ever met."

After most of the crowd had left, Caesar and Kevin made their way to the back of the stage. The oily smell of burnt kerosene and propane still hung heavy in the air and stung Kevin's eyes.

Caesar called out to Peter, who was talking to Roxanne and Delmond, both now garbed in nondescript brown bathrobes, next to the remains of the pyre. Sherri was nowhere to be seen.

"Man, when you left the shop and said you wanted to do something more exciting with your life you really meant it," Caesar said when he reached Peter.

"I take it you two liked it?" he asked them.

"It was fantastic!" Caesar gushed. "How 'bout you, Kev?"

"Same here." He cocked his head and tried to look past the scaffolding, which had been stripped of its black covering. "That last scene with the pyre and explosions was incredible. I'd be interested to know how Sherri manages not to get burned to a crisp."

"That was a sacrificial pyre," Roxanne said matter-of-factly. "Who says she didn't get killed?"

Kevin frowned and she broke out in laughter.

"Just fucking with you! There's a trap door that she drops through just before the explosion." She pointed behind him, "Here comes the bride of fire now."

Kevin looked over his shoulder. Sherri was walking toward them dressed in the same sheepskin pullover she had worn in the penultimate act.

"Has anyone seen my robe?" She saw Kevin looking at her and tugged at the shoulders of the garment, slightly closing the opening of the V cut.

"Why? You look adorable in that," Roxanne teased.

"I'm serious—where's my robe?"

"You're so cute," Roxanne continued teasing her. "Caesar and Kevin have already seen you naked—why the sudden modesty?"

"That's different. It's part of the show," Sherri groaned. Kevin thought he could detect a hint of blushing on her face.

"Check over by the spare propane tanks," Delmond said. "I think I saw it in a box there."

"You guys want a beer?" Peter asked both Kevin and Caesar. "We're going to chill out for a few minutes before breaking the rest of the set down."

"Sure." Kevin and Caesar gathered up six chairs from the auditorium floor and brought them back to the stage.

"I'm glad you could make it to the show," Peter said to them after Sherri had returned, finally wearing her robe.

"When did you have the ears done?" Caesar asked Peter, curiously staring at each of them on the sides of his head. "They look great."

"Thanks." Peter grinned. "Three months ago."

"You mind me asking what it signifies?" Kevin asked.

"Not at all," Peter said. "I'm half-Mocarian—we're a small tribe in Michigan—and my totem animal is the dog. As part of my life journey, I'm doing everything that I can to bring myself closer to that totem. I know that may sound strange, but it helps give me strength to do the three-person suspension." He pointed at the scaffolding/meat hook conglomeration in the back. "Without my totem there's no way I could hold five hundred and twenty-five pounds."

Kevin's eyes widened. "You're telling me that you're suspending not just yourself, but Delmond and Roxanne?"

"That's right," Peter answered with pride. "There's only two other groups in the world as far as I know that have attempted that."

"Now I'm even more impressed," Kevinsaid. . "What's it like being suspended?"

"For me it's two things," Peter responded, "The first is to see how far I can go in making the suspension an integral part of the show while pushing the limits of static rigging. On a more personal level, it's about pushing away the fear of body pain and attaining a new level of spiritual consciousness."

"I do it because it makes me cum," Roxanne interjected, giving Kevin an exaggerated wink.

Peter looked at her, shook his head, then turned back to Kevin. "Caesar said you were an old friend. Said you'd just come back into town."

"That's right. Been away for a few years."

"Where you been?"

"Lay off, Roxy," Sherri interjected. "You're going to make the guy feel like he's in an interrogation room."

Kevin shrugged. "It's alright. I've been living up in Northern Michigan."

"I love it up there," Roxanne said. "Where at? Traverse City? Harbor Springs?"

"Near Fairview," Kevin said off-handedly.

Roxanne took a long drag off a cigarette and blew out the blue smoke in tight small circles. She looked at Sherri. "Isn't that where the prison is?"

Sherri sighed and reached for a beer. "Yeah, Roxy. There's

a prison there."

"There's a lot of places to work up there, not just the prison, right Kev?" Caesar asked him.

Kevin nodded. "Lot of places." He turned to Sherri. "It's got to be a trip, being up on that pyre when the flames go off."

"That's why she has hardwood floors instead of shag carpeting," Roxanne said, pointing offhandedly at Sherri's crotch. "Don't want to burn any pubes!"

Sherri flipped her off. "It's not too bad," she said to Kevin. "The worst part is when the trap door opens. No matter how many times I do it, it still feels like I'm on a roller-coaster."

"So, I have to ask," Caesar said, turning to Delmond, "how in the hell—"

"Do I blow fire out of my cock?" Delmond finished the sentence for him and laughed. "Believe it or not, you're not the first person to ask me that."

He stood up, opened his robe, grabbed his dick and pulled it up. "See here?" Kevin and Caesar leaned forward. Delmond was pointing to a small pencil-eraser sized hole just below his scrotum.

"That's an opening to a fake urethral hole. Runs all the way from there to the end of my glans." Delmond grabbed the head of his cock and used both thumbs to push away his foreskin and open the urethra. Kevin could see that underneath it was another small round hole.

"During the show I have a small can of butane hidden in my costume. Connected to it is medical catheter tubing that goes into the fake urethral hole and up and out thru my dick. I turn the gas on, hit a lighter-flint I have palmed, and voila! One flaming dick!"

"That's wild," Caesar thought aloud. "How the hell did you get that hole, that tubing, all that shit done?"

Delmond glanced at Peter, who gave an almost imperceptible nod.

"There's this doctor named Irwin Rothstein," Delmond

casually said. "He has a place over in Creektown where he lives and does utterly fantastic shit."

"Dr. Rothstein is the most talented body morphing artist we've ever met," Peter added. "He did our piercings, he did Delmond's urethral implant, he did my teeth and ears. The man can do things that most people would think are impossible."

"He can't talk to the dead like Nehemiah the witch-doctor," Roxanne said, looking at Sherri.

"You are being such a bitch tonight! Just because someone doesn't have M.D. or D.O. after their name doesn't mean they're not a healer. And I never said he could talk to the dead."

Kevin looked at Peter, who shrugged. "It's a long story, one not worth getting in the middle of a disagreement between these two ladies."

Roxanne took a drag off her cigarette and blew the smoke directly at Peter. "It's just that I can't believe someone as intelligent as my dear Sherri believes that people can be cured of incurable diseases by faith healers."

Sherri sighed. "And I told you that I saw Reggie walking around, looking as healthy as any of us, a month after he was told at the cancer clinic that he had only a couple more weeks to live."

Roxanne dropped her cigarette into her beer bottle and looked at Kevin. "You believe people can be cured by faith healers?"

Kevin put up his hands, palms out. "I'm just an innocent bystander."

"You ready to tear this shit down?" It was the scaffolding guy, standing with three bored-looking young men dressed in the same work garb as the older man.

Peter turned back to Kevin and Caesar. "Looks like it's time to finish up. Thanks again for coming to the show."

"Glad I came," Kevin said. "It takes a lot of guts to do

what you guys do."

"Hope to see you again," Sherri said, shaking Kevin's hand. "Have a good night."

They walked off the stage and were halfway to the auditorium doors when Kevin stopped. "You think Sherri would go out with me?"

"Sherri? I thought Roxy would be more your type." Before Kevin could retort, Caesar waved him off. "I'm just giving you shit. Yes, I think Sherri would go out with you. Go ask her before they leave."

Kevin took a step toward the stage, then hesitated. "I don't know . . . I mean, I just met her."

Caesar frowned. "Who are you and what have you done with my best friend? The first to talk to a table full of girls at the bar when we were young studs?"

"That was a long time ago. We were both younger and braver." Kevin crossed his arms and sighed. "And I wasn't an ex-con."

"Fuck that," Caesar waved him off. "Grow your balls back and go ask her!"

Kevin steadily took a deep breath. "You're right—I was the man back in the day, wasn't I?"

Caesar slapped him on the back. "That you were, and still are. I'll wait here. Don't come back without a yes!"

His heart pounding, Kevin walked back to the stage. *I wish I had pounded back a few more beers.*

He forced himself up on stage where Sherri and Roxanne were having a discussion next to the scaffolding. He went to turn away when Sherri noticed him first.

"Hey, Kevin," she greeted, a smile on her face. "You forget something?"

"No."

That was brilliant.

She said one more thing to Roxanne, then moved closer to him. "Oh. What's up?"

He cleared his throat. "Listen—I know we just met, but I was wondering if you'd like to get together sometime."

She beamed. "That would be nice."

"G-Great." Kevin nodded, then felt a knot form in his stomach. "Problem is, I don't have a car. Unless you want me to pick you up in a bus—"

She smiled again and touched his hand. "Don't worry about it. Give me your phone number and address and I'll come over and get you."

After they exchanged numbers and said their goodbyes, Kevin turned, walked down the stage steps, and turned to look at Sherri. She was still watching him, and he waved before slamming his thigh—and the lesion—into a chair on the floor.

A sharp, hot, jolt of pain erupted in his thigh and up into his groin and balls. Kevin grabbed the chair with both hands to keep from falling.

"Kevin!" he heard Sherri yell from the stage. He turned to look at her.

Sherri's face was tight with concern. "What's wrong? Did you hurt yourself?"

Kevin forced himself to smile. *What the fuck is going on with me?*

"I'm fine," he said through gritted teeth. "Just hit my knee kind of hard on this chair."

Sherri stood on the top of the stage steps. "Are you sure?"

He waved her off. "I'm sure. See you this weekend."

Caesar met him half-way down the auditorium. "You okay?"

"Yeah. Just hit myself in the wrong spot." The pain was still there but quickly subsiding.

"You know, you've seemed just a bit off tonight," Caesar said as they walked back through the foyer. "You sure you're okay?"

"I haven't been out on the town for six years," Kevin said.

"Just taking me a while to get my sea-legs back." He carefully made his way through the entrance doors, being careful not to let anything touch his leg. Or more specifically, the lesion on his leg.

"So, what did Sherri say?" Caesar asked.

"Said she'd go out with me," Kevin said as they walked out into the cool night air.

"Of course, she did. Never had any doubt in my mind."

Kevin chuckled. "Always the optimist," he said, the pain in his leg still throbbing like a muted, far-away voice.

CHAPTER 7

KEVIN TOOK ANOTHER SHOT of Mohawk vodka and coughed. The cheap booze burned his throat and made his stomach feel like it was washed in acid.

He placed the shot glass down on his folding table in the kitchen, then squinted at the tiny clock on the electric stove in the corner. The black hands behind the yellowed plastic read 7:32.

A half –hour before Sherry said she'd be here. Guess I should get this over with.

Kevin had been thinking about how to deal with the lesions on his shoulder and thigh the past few days, ever since he had gotten home that night from the fire-show. He could picture Sherri's tattooed, technicolor body straddling his hips, riding him before he turned her over while still inside her and fucked her both hard and slow. Then he thought about the lesions, what happened when they were touched too hard and her possible reaction to them . . .

Kevin stood in front of the cabinet mirror and starred at his right shoulder in the dim bathroom light. *It's gotten bigger. No matter how much I tell myself otherwise, it's bigger.*

Tearing open a package of four-by-four gauze pads, Kevin took a deep breath and placed two pads over the lesion.

There was just a slight sensation of pressure and heat. He held his breath and pressed down harder, his pulse quickening in anticipation of a hot needle of pain. Except there was just more pressure.

"It's getting better," Kevin said, taping down the pads. He undid his belt-buckle, dropped his pants and looked at the oblong-shaped lesion on his thigh. To his chagrin this one also seemed larger. *But that's what the other one did—got bigger first, then no more pain. I'll take that deal.*

He pushed down the pads on the thigh lesion and immediately, there was a deep, dull ache traveling from his thigh into his balls, like a tooth with a rotting cavity. Kevin pulled the pads off and took two deep breaths. It hurt, but he had learned in Fairview how to tolerate simple pain.

Slowly and more carefully, Kevin taped down three pads on his leg. The three shots of vodka helped dull the ache and he had just finished getting re-dressed when there was a soft knock on the door.

He checked his hair in the mirror and then walked to the front door. Sherri stood on the porch, holding a bag in her hand.

"Hi, Sherri," Kevin greeted before stepping aside and waving her in. "You have any trouble finding the place?"

"No." She walked past him, and a hint of patchouli wafted past, lighting up the room. She put down the bag on the kitchen table, then turned and took off her leather jacket. "You got a place to hang this up?"

Kevin shook his head. "Whoever built this house had an aversion to closets." He took the jacket and let his eyes linger on her for a few seconds.

Sherri had on a simple V-necked knee-length blue dress, black high heels, and her shoulder length light brown hair hung loosely over her shoulders. She wore a simple hemp necklace with a perfectly circular quarter-sized Petoskey stone hanging just above her cleavage.

"You look very nice," Kevin commented

Sherri smiled. "Thanks. You too."

"Yeah—I got out my best jeans and cashmere sweater," he patted his chest with his one free hand on the black thin cotton sweater he was wearing, ",for the occasion."

She laughed. An easy melodic sound.

"I'll put your jacket in my room," Kevin said, just to say something.

When he came back to the living room she was sitting on the couch. Kevin sat in the vinyl-covered chair across from her.

"So where would you like to go?" he asked.

"It really doesn't matter . . ." She pointed to the bag on the kitchen table. "I brought over some spiced rum if you want to just stay here."

"If that's what you want to do . . ." Kevin's voice trailed off and a moment of uneasy silence filled the air.

Sherri finally spoke. "I'm fine with staying here, but if you want to go out, that's okay too."

"Let's stay here." Kevin grabbed two glasses from the kitchen and came back into the living room with the rum bottle. He filled each glass half-full of the dark liquid and handed one to Sherri.

"That's pretty smooth stuff," Kevin said after drinking a mouthful.

"Unless you're used to it, I'd be careful." Sherri took a small drink and smiled again. "It'll creep up on you real fast."

Especially mixed with three shots of vodka.

"Thanks for the advice. I'm sure you wouldn't be impressed if I passed out on the floor."

Sherri giggled and sat back on the couch. "I wouldn't." She took another sip of the rum. "I was wondering . . . you going out with anyone right now?"

"No. How 'bout you?"

She leaned forward on the couch. "Not really."

Kevin echoed her, then said, "That can mean a lot of different things."

Sherri put down her glass on the floor. "I was seeing Roxy for a while." She nervously laughed and played with her hair. "Last winter I broke up with my boyfriend of two years. It was a really tough time, Roxy was there for me, and things just happened."

Kevin shook his head. "I've been accused (*and convicted*) of many things, but never of being a prude." He took another drink. "So, are you still seeing her? I mean, are you still—"

Sherri waved him off. "We're not sleeping together anymore. Roxanne is a very intense person, and it just got too hard to be with her in certain ways. I still deeply care about her, and we're still able to work together, but as for anything else," she shrugged, "that's in the past."

"Thanks for telling me." Kevin took another drink of the rum, already feeling the languid humming in his head from the alcohol-induced buzz.

"Sure." She ran a hand through her hair. "It's just something I wanted you to know. So, you said that you were living up near Fairview?"

Damn. Here it comes. He had decided at the beginning of the week that he was going to be honest with her regarding his past, then spent the next five days trying to figure out how to tell her of his recent past without sounding trite or pitiful.

"Um-hum."

Her eyes kept locked on him. "Not much to do up there except work at the prison."

Kevin took a deep breath and didn't try to hide the sigh. "Look—I want to be clean with you here, so . . . I was incarcerated at Fairview for six years for assault and battery. I got out a little over a month ago."

Sherri tightened up and an invisible cloud of tension

came alive in the room.

"I'm not a nutcase or a serial killer," Kevin said quickly. "It was—damn, I know this sounds like a cliché—just a bad situation that should have been a misdemeanor at most, but it turned into a felony and I essentially got fucked."

She fidgeted on the couch. "You mind if I smoke?"

"Feel free."

She'll be out the door before she's done with that cigarette.

"Thanks." She pulled a pack out of her purse, then dropped it. Cigarettes scattered on the floor and she fumbled trying to pick them up.

Kevin reached down. "Let me help you."

"I can get it." She forced an uneasy laugh. "Sometimes I can be clumsy as Hell, which, considering I play with fire on a regular basis, is not a good trait to have."

"Look—it's okay if you want to leave."

Sherri shook her head. "I don't want to leave." She lit a cigarette and sat back on the couch.

Kevin tried to smile and failed. "I probably should have told you I was an ex-con before I asked you out."

She took a long drag off her cigarette and blew out a thin line of blue smoke. "That's okay. I'm the one who said the other night that surprises could be fun, right?"

This time Kevin did manage to smile. "You did." He stood up and headed for the kitchen. "Let me get you something for those ashes."

He came back with an empty beer bottle. "Best I have." He placed it in front of her then sat down on the chair.

"Thanks." They remained quiet for a moment before she finally spoke. "I have two older brothers in the Army. Right now, they're both stationed in Afghanistan. My fraternal twin, Sam, was in Fairview for five years for cooking meth."

She took another long draw off her cigarette.

"I went up to that shit hole at least once a month to see him. My mom would never go—said she couldn't stand to see her baby boy in a cage."

"It must have been hard to see him there," Kevin commented.

Sherri nodded. "He was a small guy, no bigger than me. He told me he was raped the second night he was there."

She took another drag off the cigarette then dropped it in the beer bottle. "There was this one guard there named Thomas—"

"White guy, about five-ten, one eighty, with short gray hair?"

"Yeah. You know him?"

"He was there the first two years I was there, then retired. No-nonsense dude. If you fucked with him, he'd fuck with you. But if you didn't, he was as good as they came."

"I got to know him. He watched over Sam, made sure the predators didn't use him." She looked at Kevin and he could see her eyes were moist. "But Thomas wasn't there twenty-four seven." She took a long drink. "Tell me right now, Kevin. Tell me if you were one of those predators."

Kevin cleared his throat. "First week I was there three guys tried to rape me in the shower. I ended up in the prison hospital with a nasty concussion and a broken right hand. The guys that tried to rape me also ended up in the hospital—two with broken jaws, one with busted nuts."

Sherri frowned in confusion.

Kevin awkwardly smiled while recollecting the fight in his mind. "I kicked him in the balls so hard that they pretty much exploded."

Sherri lit another cigarette. "What happened after that?"

"After that no one fucked with me (*except for the Brotherhood and Readona, but we'll leave that part out right now*)." He took a long drink. "I hated the bastards who preyed on the weak. I did things in jail that I'm not proud of, but I never was one of them. *Never*."

She starred at him for a long moment and Kevin swore

he could hear the clock ticking on the wall.

"I believe you," she finally said. "Peter's told me what a stand-up guy Caesar is. I've found that most stand-up guys don't hang around assholes."

Kevin shrugged. "I never said I wasn't an asshole."

Sherri laughed and Kevin felt the tension in the room disappear as fast as it had formed. "How 'bout a smart-ass?"

"I've definitely been accused of that." He held up the bottle of rum. "Ready for some more?"

She shook her head. "I'm already getting buzzed. I could use a glass of water, though."

"Sure thing." Kevin quickly stood up and felt the full rush of alcohol slam into his brain. He took a deep breath as he walked to the kitchen, making sure he didn't stumble or fall.

"Here you go." Kevin handed her the glass of water and sat down on couch. He reached down for the bottle of rum, thought better of it, then poured himself some more anyway.

"Where's Sam at now?" he asked.

Sherri's eyes glistened with tears. "Probably at the bottom of the Detroit River."

"Damn." Kevin reached over and laid his hand over hers. "I'm sorry."

"He was clean for three months, then got back into dealing. A month after that he disappeared."

"Maybe he decided to disappear. Being in the joint—" Kevin shook his head, "—does things to you. It makes you want to crawl into a corner and never come out. Maybe he decided that he wanted to find another corner and get away from all the bad shit around him."

"The bad shit was *in* Sam. That's what he never could see. You can never get away from what's inside you. You either deal with it or you don't." She wiped her eyes with the back of her hand then drained half her glass of water. "How 'bout some more rum?"

Kevin poured another glassful of the dark liquid and re-topped his own glass.

"On the anniversary of his disappearance I got this envelope with this in it." Sherri tapped the Petoskey stone with one slim finger. "We went up with my family to Sleeping Bear Dunes when we were thirteen. Sam had just had his first girlfriend break up with him and was depressed as hell. When we were walking along the beach, I found this stone, polished it, and gave it to him. He wore it every day." She sighed. "He's not coming back."

Kevin nodded and said nothing.

Sherri lit up another cigarette, then motioned toward Kevin. "How'd you like the show last weekend?"

"It was great. The whole creation story, the love and death thing, the finale—it takes a lot of brains and guts to do what you did."

Sherri smiled, then laced her fingers behind her head and stretched out her back. Kevin tried not to stare at her chest, her nipples visible under the thin material of her dress.

"So, you don't think we're a bunch of freaks with tats and piercings?" she asked in a half serious, half sarcastic tone.

"No," Kevin said with more intensity than he had planned. "You're all artists and performers . . . Hell, you have more guts than I'd ever have to do something like that . . ."

"You have any tats or piercing?" Sherri asked.

Kevin took another drink of rum moved closer to her and pulled up the sleeves of his sweater.

Sherri's eye's widened. She reached down to his arms, then stopped and looked at Kevin. "Can I?"

He nodded.

She ran her fingers delicately over his scars and tats, like a blind woman reading Braille. "I've seen a lot of tats and scarifications in my life, but nothing like these. There's an order to them, a chaotic but paradoxical theme." She traced two in particular, the scarification being a bisecting amalgam of straight and curved lines holding solid circles, the tat being two simple designs of a cross just touching a pair of curved bisecting lines.

"I've seen these before," Sherri finally murmured.

"You've seen these scars and tats on someone else?"

"No." She kept her hand on Kevin's arm and lightly traced the two scars and tats. "In a book I read at a friend's house. I think it had to do with Germanic magical runes—symbols and letters used for connecting to the spirit world." She looked up at him. "Where did you get these?"

"At Fairview." He put his hand over hers. "Although the guy who did them didn't strike me much as one who was into magic and spirits."

She stopped tracing the shapes with her fingers. "Maybe I'm way off base. I was pretty high that night."

Kevin laughed nervously. "That certainly can skew one's perspective."

"That it can." She turned her hand over so that their fingers were now intertwined. "These scars and tats—do they hold hope or pain for you?"

He looked into her eyes, light, vibrant green like morning grass in springtime, and swallowed hard. "Both. The guy who did it was—*is*—a very fucked-up man." He took a deep breath. "When I look at them, I can't help but think of him."

"But they also hold hope?"

"They remind me that even the worst things can be endured. That when it seems all light is gone, that somewhere, there still is light, and if you keep fighting long enough, you'll find it."

He moved in and kissed her, tentative at first, then deeply and passionately as she kissed him back, her hands never leaving his arms.

They talked and kissed their way through the late hours of the night and early hours of the morning. Kevin tried twice to get her into bed, but each time Sherri rebuffed him. A small part of him was frustrated, but he pushed that part down with surprising calmness and ease.

The sun crept slowly up the eastern horizon as they lay quietly on the couch, their bodies entwined, Sherri's head resting on Kevin's chest. He brushed away a lock of hair from her forehead and kissed her warm skin.

"Sun's coming up," he whispered, afraid to break the spell of happiness which had bloomed with ferocious intensity.

"It seems to do that every morning."

Kevin chuckled lightly. "One night with me and you're already turning into a smart-ass."

"Nah." Sherri disengaged herself from him and slowly got off the couch. "I've always been a smart-ass." She smoothed out her dress and walked to the bathroom.

Kevin sat up, rubbed his eyes with the palms of his hands, and looked at the closed bathroom door. He couldn't remember when, if ever, he had felt as comfortable with a woman as he felt with Sherri. In the span of a night and morning, he had given her a complete rundown on his life: how his life had changed at fifteen when his dad died of esophageal cancer courtesy of half a dozen cigars a day combined with 25 years of breathing in the toxic fumes at the Bower's Steel factory. Barely passing high school and then excelling at Henry Ford Community College in political science and creative writing courses, leading him to consider applying to law school.

Except all that changed when his girlfriend Lisa came up pregnant just before he was going to transfer to the University of Michigan. Instead of moving out of Detroit, Kevin became engaged and took a job at Bowers.

He hated the work—the heavy-metal smell, the roar of the refineries, the foreman always screaming down his back. Every night after work was a time to drown his self-pity in booze and pot, and it probably would have continued until he died the same death as his father or he ended up hanging from a noose in his basement. But then had come that night in Monroe, when it became crystal-clear to Kevin how shitty life could truly become.

"Kevin? Are you sleeping?" Sherri's voice sounded distant and quiet.

He forced his eyes open and stretched his arms over his head. "No. Just getting my second wind."

She walked over to him and grabbed his hands. "I'm tired. Walk me to the door so I can go home and sleep."

When they reached the door, Kevin put his hand around her waist and pulled her close. "You can crash here if you want."

"If I go lay down in your bed, you're not going to join me?"

He softly kissed her, then smiled. "I never said that."

"Uh huh." She tapped him on the nose. "We're not sleeping together on our first date."

Kevin sighed. "I was hoping you wouldn't say that.""

She gently laughed and pulled away. "It's not that I don't want to, it's just that . . ." her voice trailed off and she ran her finger down over his cheek. "I really like you."

He reached up, held her hand, and kissed it gently. "I really like you too."

"You're a good man, Kevin Ciano," she said, staring into his eyes. "I can see that in spite of the bad decisions you've made, at your core you're a good man."

A grainy memory suddenly flashed in his mind of holding down a skinny, black seventeen-year-old kid in the prison shower and slashing his throat with a long, sharp knife. He watched with morbid fascination the blood flow in rhythmic spurts from the boy's severed carotid arteries and pondered how amazing it was for such a small person to have so much blood.

"What are you thinking about?"

Kevin blinked once, twice. "How glad I am that you

came over." He was amazed how smooth the lie came out.

"Even though you're not going to get laid?"

Kevin forced the bloody memory out of his consciousness and kissed her on the forehead. "Even though I'm not going to get laid."

She kissed him deeply, then pulled away "You know what they say," she said, digging through her purse for her car keys, "good things come to those who wait."

CHAPTER 8

KEVIN CLOSED THE COVER of his cell phone and sat down on the couch. He looked at the new wall clock he had hung the other day and noticed that it was ten minutes fast.

He grinned. *Better fast than slow.* That was one of Sherri's sayings, mostly pertaining to sex.

They had consummated their relationship the third time she had come over, and for Kevin it was like a recurring, wonderful dream suddenly made real. After six years of isolating himself from others, he was able to again share in the energy of someone alive and joyful, giving Kevin that one thing he had almost lost in prison: hope.

He looked at the clock again. It had a large, red LED readout for the numbers, and the day and date above. 5:15 P.M. Saturday—the first Saturday night in three weeks that he wouldn't be spending the evening, and sometimes the morning, with her.

Kevin absently pushed the dust on the linoleum floor around with his bare foot. Things had changed so fast since Sherri had come over to his place that night. Almost as fast as things changed six years previously during that night in Monroe, a tiny, nagging voice in his head said.

But that's not ever going to happen again. The bad shit is finally over.

And it was getting better. The universe, at least his insignificant speck of the cosmos, seemed to be slowly righting itself. A steady job at Honsey's, Sherri . . . the positives were outweighing the negatives, and he intended with every ounce of his strength to make sure it stayed that way.

The roar of a racing car snagged Kevin's attention. He looked out the front window, saw nothing, and stepped out onto the sagging wooden porch. The crisp autumn air was thick with rich odors of decay and death. He looked up in the sky, a thick layer of overcast blocking out the thin rays of the early evening sun giving the world a gray, monochrome hue.

Kevin gazed over at the crack house. A tricked-out brown classic Ford Gran Torino—he guessed 1973—sat in the street, its big-block V-8 engine idling nosily, like a dinosaur digesting a large meal. The driver of the car, his face streaked in shadows, starred at Kevin, who had the sudden urge to flip the guy off. Out of the corner of his eye, Kevin saw Caesar's Impala turn onto the street and he immediately let go of the crazy thought.

"Hola, amigo," Caesar said a moment later as he walked in, carrying a six-pack of beer. He wore light brown chinos and a white shirt with a flashy tie of red and orange.

"You didn't have to get all dressed up just to see me," Kevin said.

Caesar put the six-pack in the refrigerator and brought two cans into the living room. "Had a meeting at a new plant in Lansing today. They want me to be the liaison between our plant and theirs, so I had to look the part." He opened both beers and gave one to Kevin. "Maria's not really happy about it—me being away more—but it's a raise, so . . ." he shrugged and took a swig of beer.

"You slumming today?" Caesar continued, pointing at Kevin's torn sweats and coffee-stained sweatshirt with a Detroit Lions logo on the front. "I thought you said you were working Saturdays this month."

"Honsey and I were working until one this morning on a new website. He's setting up an online store that we think is really going to help his business take off."

Caesar raised his eyebrows. "Since when did you become a computer geek?"

"I took half a dozen computer courses at Fairview." Kevin took a long drink of beer and loudly burped. "Your hard-earned tax dollars at work."

"I got no problem with my tax dollars going to help guys learn a trade when they're in the joint." Caesar leaned forward on the couch. "You think this online thing will take off?"

"I do. And Honsey said he'd do profit-sharing with me."

"Damn! That's great!"

"No complaints from me."

"Where's Sherri tonight?"

"At her mom's. I told you that fifteen minutes ago when you called. You starting to get senile on me?"

"Cut me some slack. Between Maria being sick these past couple weeksand extra hours at work, my brain ain't working the way it should." He took another drink of beer. "Still having mind-blowing sex with Sherri?"

Kevin frowned. "C'mon, man—do I ask you about your sex life with Maria?"

"You don't because you'd be jealous if I told you how awesome it was."

Kevin smiled coyly. "In your dreams."

"K, my dreams are now my reality. And I am happy for you, man. After all the shit you've been though you deserve a run of good luck."

Kevin finished his beer and held out his empty bottle to Caesar. "You ready for another?"

Caesar shook his head. "I'd love to, but I need to get home. I told Maria I'd take her out tonight since she's feeling better."

"That's okay," Kevin said, a dejected look on his unshaven face. "Just let your best friend sit here all by himself on a Saturday night."

"C'mon, Kev, don't be saying' shit like that. You know I—"

"I'm just busting your ass," Kevin said, smiling. "Glad you could stop by."

"Next weekend I want you and Sherri to come over. Maria is a great cook and she's been asking to meet this girl that has stolen my boy's heart."

"That sounds great. I'll talk to Sherri about it when she gets back into town tomorrow."

"You make it happen," Caesar emphatically said, pointing at Kevin. "Don't be getting pussy whipped on me, you hear?"

Kevin threw back his head and laughed. "You've been pussy-whipped since your first girlfriend in seventh grade!"

Caesar grinned and opened the door. "Do as I say, not as I do." He slapped Kevin hard on the back and laughed. "It's going to be just like old times!"

Kevin stood on the porch, his face in a tight grin, and watched Caesar leave. When the Impala was out of sight, he let out a huge breath and backed inside, his back still tingling from Caesar's slap.

It could have been worse—he could have hit me on the shoulder.

The lesions were still present, the original one on his shoulder and the other on his thigh. He had tried putting various home remedies on them—vinegar and baking soda, honey and lemon—along with some over-the-counter antibacterial ointments in the hope of making them go away.

Nothing helped.

As much as he tried to deny it, they were getting bigger, slowly growing from dime-sized to now the circumference of a quarter or even a half-dollar. He kept them covered, telling Sherri they were Nazi-related tats that he had been forced to get in prison and would be getting them lasered off as soon as he had the money. She had gone with the explanation. At least for the time being.

As soon as I build up some cash I'll head to a doctor, he told himself, as much as he hated the thought. I'm sure they're just strange zits. *Something that someone can take out in a few seconds and won't I feel stupid then for not having it done sooner!*

There was a loud knock on the door and Kevin jumped up. What did Caesar forget? He opened up the door without a second thought.

But it wasn't Caesar.

It was a monster.

CHAPTER 9

"WHAT THE MATTER, CIANO—YOU look like you've seen a ghost."

The middle-aged man named Johnny Bismarck who stood on the porch was two inches taller than Kevin. Beneath a head-full of dyed black hair, Bismarck had a handsomely chiseled face with pale green eyes that could look golden yellow in certain lighting, and fine, porcelain white teeth. In contrast to Kevin's lean frame, the man was visibly muscular under a tight-fitting navy- blue cardigan sweater and freshly pressed black dress slacks. In any other setting he could pass for a banker or lawyer or doctor.

In the coal-black world of Fairview, Bismarck was a monster.

He was one of the remorseless predators that had preyed on inmates like Sherri's brother, a child-raping pedophile that incessantly bragged about the number of girls and boys he had tortured and abused. Bismarck was also one of Readona's closest associates, and had a 35-to-life sentence, one that Kevin assumed would keep Bismarck in Fairview until he was dead.

"What are you doing here?" Kevin kept his voice low and controlled. "How the hell do you know where I live?"

"You're a con," Bismarck said in a condescending tone, like a grown-up talking to a petulant child. "It's all public record." He took a step forward. "Aren't you glad to see me?"

"That's far enough. I'll ask you again: what are you doing here?"

Bismarck smiled, showing off his Hollywood smile. "I need a favor from you."

Kevin stared hard at the larger man and let a small steam of anger in his gut form. He moved forward and Bismarck stepped back, almost falling off the rickety porch. He awkwardly grabbed hold of the railing then immediately pulled his hand back. A jagged piece of wood, two inches long and thick as a school pencil, stuck out at an awkward angle from his palm. Bismarck swore under his breath and pulled it out. Blood immediately pooled around the wound and began to drip down on the rotting wood. He looked up, his eyes dilated in anger.

"You made me bleed."

Kevin formed his hands into tight fists. "That's not bleeding. Stay on my porch five more seconds and I promise you'll learn all about it."

"You always acted the tough guy," Bismarck spat, pressing down on the wound with his thumb. "But you and me never went for a go."

"You wanna go, then let's go. The only guys I ever saw you give shit to in the joint were those that were too small or too scared to stand up for themselves. But now it's just you and me. No Readona or any of his other freaks to get in our way."

Bismarck let out a high-pitched, nervous laugh. "You're wrong—Charles is always around."

Kevin felt a shift in his world, a small, almost imperceptible movement that gave the illusion he suddenly had entered a house of mirrors at a two-bit circus. He unclenched his fists and took a step back.

"You're as fucking crazy as you were in the joint," he said, desperately searching for the anger that had given him strength just a moment before. "I'm not saying it again: get the hell off my porch and out of my life before I—"

"Before you what?" Bismarck sneered before bringing his wounded hand to his face. A sucking sound escaped from his lips before he pulled his mouth away and spit out a wad of crimson colored sputum. "You're not going to do a damn thing, Ciano. At least nothing that could get you sent back to Fairview."

"Say what you have to say, then get the Hell out of here." Kevin needed time to process the living nightmare that was unfolding, and if that meant he had to listen to Bismarck, then that was a price he was willing to pay.

Bismarck licked his wound again with a serpentine tongue. "That's more neighborly." He moved closer. Kevin could smell the faint odor of flowery expensive cologne.

"Aren't you curious how I got out?" Bismarck asked, head slightly cocked to one side.

"The question has crossed my mind."

"The last little prick who said I raped him recanted. I went before my parole board a day later, and voila!" —Bismarck spread his muscular arms open wide— "Here I am!"

"What a lucky man . . ." Kevin made no attempt to hide the sarcasm in his voice. "I don't suppose the parole board gave any thought to the others you got your disgusting hands on?"

Bismarck pursed his lips. "You only go to prison for what they find out. The other shit," he gave a shrug, "is just bonus."

A sudden thought flashed in Kevin's mind. "You ever know a guy in Fairview by the name of Sam Musgrave?"

Bismarck shook his head. "Name's not familiar. Why?"

"I met the guy's brother down at Ricky-O's bar last week,"

Kevin lied. "We got to talking and he told me Sam was tight with Charles for a while before he pulled his head out of his ass and realized what a sick fuck your master is."

"You have no idea who Charles is, do you?" Bismarck crossed his arms, bulging biceps stretching the fabric of the sweater. "You could have been one of his favorites if you would have just—"

Anger came boiling back into Kevin. "If I would have what? Pretend he was something more than a sadistic fuck who sat on his bed and jerked off while you and five others held me down and scarred me up?"

Kevin wanted Bismarck to snap, to come forward so that he could hurt him. Instead, Bismarck licked his lips and uncrossed his arms.

"You were our best work," he said, motioning toward Kevin's arms. "I bet they healed up real nice. Why don't you take off your shirt and let me have a look?"

Kevin moved forward. This time Bismarck stood his ground so that they were now almost nose-to-nose.

"Why are you here? What do you want from me?" Kevin asked.

"I need you to rob that shitty little music and video store you work for."

"Honsey's?"

"Yes."

What the hell? How does Honsey figure into any of this?

"Since when are you into petty theft?"

"It's an expensive world," Bismarck said casually. "I like nice clothes and fine food."

"You're fucking crazy. I'm not ripping off Honsey. He's a good man. He's helped me out, he's—"

"Look," Bismarck interrupted, putting up his hands, "it's just money. I'll do most of the work. All you have to do is—"

"Fuck you. I'm *not* ripping off Honsey!" Kevin balled his hand into a fist and struck it out as fast as a rattlesnake hitting a petrified rabbit. The blow hit Bismarck just below the sternum. He let out a guttural whoosh! and stumbled back.

"That's your first and last warning," Kevin grit his teeth and flared his nostrils. "Leave now, never come back, or I'm going to beat you to death right here, right now."

"And I told you that I know you're not going to do a thing that will send you back to Fairview."

Kevin smiled, a humorless movement at the corner of his lips. "Are you willing to bet your life on that?"

Bismarck smoothed out the front of his sweater and backed down two steps. He gave a crisp *tsk tsk tsk*. "All that beautiful anger. What a waste in such a conflicted little boy like yourself." When Kevin began to advance upon him, Bismarck put up his hands, palms out.

"Pull it together, Ciano. Even if no one in this shithole of a street cares what you do, I guarantee that if anything happens to me, your little throat-slashing escapade will see the full light of day."

Kevin immediately stopped. "I had a deal with Readona." Out of the corner of his eye he saw a couple people emerge from the crack house to see what the ruckus was on their little corner of hell.

"The deal's changed."

It had always been Kevin's greatest fear. The thought that Readona was just playing him, spinning a great and awful lie that would one day come back to eat him alive.

And now the day was here.

"No one's going to believe you or him." Kevin tried to keep the fear out of his voice.

Bismarck smiled, a huge, hungry smile, and heartily laughed. "Of course, they'll believe us. You did it, Kevin. You killed that kid. Not me. Not Charles. *You.*"

"The area was cleaned." Kevin's voice was high, fast, almost stuttering. "The body, blood, prints, the knife—"he stopped in mid-sentence. The knife, an eight-inch-long razor-sharp carving knife from the prison's kitchen.

What had happened to the fucking knife? Hadn't Readona told him to open up a shower drain and drop it in there? He had done it, hadn't he? But Kevin couldn't remember. All he could see in his mind's eye was the kid on the floor in a spreading pool of blood . . .

"Starting to see the picture now?" Bismarck taunted. "We have the murder weapon, we have your prints—I got some so perfect it gives me a hard-on—and that means we have you."

"You're bluffing," Kevin scoffed in a desperate attempt to find some way out. "You don't have anything. I dropped the knife in the drain, just like Charles told me to do."

"What did you just say to me a couple minutes ago?" Bismarck frowned as if deep concentration, then broke out in a large grin, Oh yeah, it was 'are you willing to bet your life on that?'"

He turned his back on Kevin and walked down the rest of the steps.

"Wait." The words escaped Kevin's lips before he consciously realized he had spoken.

Bismarck stopped, turned halfway around, and stared at the group of four people that had gathered on the porch of the crack house. He raised his still-bleeding hand to his mouth then blew a delicate kiss toward them. Kevin saw one of the women on the porch flip him off before they shuffled back inside.

Bismarck finally turned to face Kevin. "You'll be back with us, Ciano. Back with Charles . . ." he let his voice trail off and the image of his words burned into Kevin's mind.

"Or," Bismarck continued, his voice suddenly light and conversational, "you can help me with this small favor."

Kevin closed his eyes, took a deep breath, and forced himself to say the words. "I'll need to think about it."

Bismarck nodded slowly, as if contemplating a great rev-

elation. "Think fast. Like I said, I need some new clothes."
He winked at Kevin. "Give me a call. Soon."

"I don't have your number." Buried deep in his gut Kevin
felt a laugh form, a mad sound starting to grow, and he was
sure if he started laughing, he wouldn't stop until he died.
Here he was with a murderous psychopath, asking for his
phone number like a shy fifteen-year-old boy asking a girl out
on a date.

Bismarck bent down and squeezed his hand. Blood
dripped onto the sidewalk and he slowly, carefully, formed
seven numbers on the gray sidewalk in the dull orange glow
of a fading October evening.

CHAPTER 10

⸢T⸣HE SHARP CRACK OF gunfire entered Kevin's dreaming mind like a psychotic thief kicking down a door. There was a second blast, then a third and fourth. Kevin bolted upright in bed, his body drenched in sweat, looking wildly around his bedroom. There were two final sounds—gunshots, he was sure of it now—and then silence.

Crazy fucking crackheads. Catching a stray slug would be a helluva way to start the day.

After a moment, Kevin sat up in bed and felt something warm and wet on his left side. He looked over, and in the dim light coming through the drapes, he saw blood.

Son-of-a-bitch—I'm shot! He scrambled to turn on the nightlight in his room. The 40-watt bulb gave feeble illumination to the crimson streaks on his sheets and pillowcase, along with caked blood on his arm and shoulder. Kevin's sleep-blurred vision came into focus, and what he saw made him nauseated—bits of flesh mixed in with the blood, one piece at least an inch long and half again wide, like fresh shedding from a human snake.

He frantically pulled the sheets off his bed and used them

to clean his arm and shoulder, looking for a bullet wound, but there wasn't any. No hole, no evidence of a bullet entry.

Just a hair.

At least he thought it was a hair. An inch and a half long black protrusion from his right shoulder, it curled in a tight circle like a pube, but it was thicker than any hair–the width of a pencil lead—and tapered to a sharp point at the end. The skin around it was pink and moist, like a freshly healed wound.

The hair grew out of the lesion. The revelation blossomed in his mind and crowded out everything else—the blood, the gunshots, Bismarck. He stood up and looked over the rest of his naked body. The lesion on his leg was red, like a large blood-filled blister. And his arms felt strange, like when you lay on a limb too long and it felt foreign and dead. In the hazy brightness of the room, Kevin could only see the swirling patterns of scars and black and white tattoos he had lived with for an entire year. He walked on unsteady legs to the bathroom and turned on the light.

The hair on his shoulder looked even more surreal, like something from a Hollywood special effects studio. Kevin reached across his chest to touch it, then reconsidered, remembering all too well the pain from the lesions themselves. And if it grew out of *this* lesion . . .

He looked down his body at the lesion on his thigh. Was it ready to pop into another crazy hair-like thing? Kevin turned ninety degrees and looked at his back. On his right shoulder blade, he thought he could make out two small, raised circles of skin—perfectly round, like someone had implanted peas underneath his flesh.

He spent another five minutes frantically searching every millimeter of his skin for any other lesions, but found nothing.

At least not yet.

Kevin moved closer to the mirror and looked at the hair

on his shoulder, even though deep down in the subconscious recesses of his mind, he didn't believe it was a hair at all.

"What the fuck are you?" Kevin spoke out loud. The hair, fortunately, said nothing in return.

Did Readona infect him with something? The thought seemed far-fetched, but...

"If it's an infection, why don't the scars and tats have hairs growing out of them?" Kevin asked, as much to steady himself as to try and reason things out. He looked at his arms again. The intricately designed scarifications interwoven between the black and white tattoos appeared the same as ever.

He peered again via the mirror at the hair on his shoulder, then looked through the medicine cabinet. On the top shelf he found what he was looking for: a pair of rusty tweezers that had been left there by the previous tenets.

He looked at the tweezers more closely. In the serrated teeth he saw two small brown pubic hairs. Kevin grimaced, turned on the hot water, grabbed a bar of soap and built up a good lather before vigorously scrubbing the tweezers between his hands. When he felt it was as clean as he could get, he grabbed the hair at its base and pulled.

Kevin dropped the tweezers. Hot, sharp fingers of pain erupted in his shoulder and shot down into his biceps. The hair was still there, pinpoint droplets of blood dotting the bulbous skin at its base.

It's just a hair. It hurts when you try to pull a hair out, right? I remember my dad complaining when I was a kid that he was getting hairier as he got older and imagined himself as a gray sasquatch in his twilight years. Maybe that'll be me—Kevin the abominable snowman of Michigan!

But what if it's not just a hair? What if it's some crazy infection you picked up in the joint? Or worse, something that Readona put into you?

Kevin walked back into his bedroom, put on his pants, grabbed a flannel shirt but then thought better of it. He grabbed his phone, hit the contacts icon and scrolled down to Sherri's number and stared at it, his finger hovering over the send button.

No. I can't lay this on her. Not yet. He highlighted Caesar's number and called.

"Didn't think you were going to pick up," Kevin said after Caesar answered on the fifth ring. "You sleeping in late?"

"Nah. Me and Maria were just getting out of church."

"Since when have you started going back to church?"

"Since Maria asked me." Kevin could almost see the grin on Caesar's face. "You should get a kick out of this. We go to St. Peters."

"The same St. Pete's we were altar boys at for two months before we got kicked out?"

Caesar laughed tiredly. "One and the same. Fortunately for me, Father Joseph has moved on to a diocese in Chicago. I'm sure if he would have seen me, there would have been big issues."

"Yeah. I'm sure . . ." Kevin paused and looked at his shoulder. The small drops of blood had congealed into a ring of dull red around the base of the hair. "Listen, Caesar. I was wondering if you could come over?"

"I guess . . ." He paused. "Kevin, you okay?"

Kevin looked at his shoulder. "I don't know. Things have . . . changed."

CHAPTER 11

"YOU REMEMBER THAT STRANGE-LOOKING lesion I had on my shoulder?"

Caesar had gotten over to Kevin's house in fifteen minutes and was sitting on the couch, still dressed in his church clothes of freshly pressed brown Dockers and a pale blue dress shirt. Kevin was in his jeans and had carefully put on the largest shirt he owned, a long-sleeved denim that he had bought at the Fairview prison store.

"Yeah, I think so." Caesar sat forward on the couch. "What about it?"

"It's easier to show you."

Caesar's eyes opened wide after Kevin took off his shirt. "What the hell's sticking out of your shoulder?"

"It's a hair, or something like a hair, that came out of the bump. I tried to pull it out with a pair of tweezers this morning and . . ."

"And what?"

Kevin took a deep breath. "It was like someone had stuck a sewing needle into my shoulder."

"I've never had that happen to me when I pulled out a

hair." Caesar moved closer to Kevin and peered at his shoulder. "It sorta looks like a hair, but," he shook his head, "it's hard to see in this light. You got a flashlight?"

"Yeah. In the bottom drawer of my nightstand."

Caesar came back a moment later holding a large black Mag Lite and peered intently at the hair. "Man, this thing is weird."

"Make sure you don't touch it."

"Don't worry." Caesar carefully brought the flashlight even closer, and Kevin swore he could feel the infinitesimal pressure of the light's photons hitting the hair.

"It's so damn black," Caesar said. "It's like it's sucking in the light without giving back any reflection."

"I thought it was just a fucking hair." The chilly air rose goosebumps on Kevin's exposed flesh and he gingerly put his shirt back on. "But it's not just a hair, is it?"

"It's weird looking, I'll give you that, but what else could it be besides a hair?"

Kevin shrugged but said nothing.

"Any idea what caused it to come out of the bump? You do anything different last night?"

Kevin thought of Bismarck, of their confrontation on the porch, the insanity of watching Readona's henchman write his phone number in blood on the sidewalk . . .

"Earth to Kevin—you still here?"

Kevin blinked. "Yeah. I'm just tired."

"So last night . . ."

"No."

No reason to burden Caesar with any more shit from Fairview.

"Just another night in paradise."

"Did you tell Sherri about this?"

Kevin shook his head. "She hasn't seen the lesions yet."

Caesar frowned. "How's that? You stay dressed when you guys have sex?"

"I've kept them covered up. Told her that they were some Aryan-nation shit and I'm ashamed of them."

"What are you gonna tell her now?"

"I don't know." Kevin sighed and absently rubbed the stubble on his chin.

"You need to go see a doctor," Caesar told him with conviction. "We need to figure out what this thing is."

"I'm not going to any damn doctor." Kevin got up from the couch. "I can't afford it. The state still hasn't gotten my Medicaid card to me and it's not like I have dead Kennedys falling out of my ass."

Caesar thought it over for a moment. "Here's an idea—I found this cool doctor named Rossi who works in a pay-what-you-can clinic off Grand River. He's been taking really good care of Maria. We can call over there right now to see if he's working."

Kevin shook his head. "I'm not going to any fucking doctor." He walked over to the window and looked outside. A brisk north wind was blowing piles of dead yellow and red leaves in a tight circle on his brown lawn.

"I want to find out for myself what this is," Kevin finally said more calmly. "If I go to the doctor, they could tell me anything and I'd wouldn't have any background to know whether or not their opinion is worthwhile or worthless."

Caesar cleared his throat. "There's still a lot of good people out there, K. The world's not out to get you."

Kevin stared at him. "It sure felt like that six years ago."

"The past is dead," Caesar, said with such force that it surprised Kevin. "I know shit has happened to you, but that's over. I don't want to let whatever's happening to you now put you in another bad place."

Kevin's face softened somewhat. "Always the one to see the glass half-full." He walked over to Caesar and sat down next to him. "Look, if I can't get a handle on this, whatever this is, I promise I'll go see this Rossi guy. But right now, I'd really appreciate it if you could take me to a library."

"Fine," Caesar said. "Let's go see if anyone in this town still reads."

Kevin took another sip on the glass of whiskey while sitting cross-legged on his living room floor, surrounded by print-outs from the library. Caesar had dropped him off an hour earlier. Since then, he had been methodically reading the fifty or so pages of information he had culled out of the hundreds of thousands of hits he had gotten back with search items including infections, hairs, growths, and cancer.

"Menkes disease," Kevin read aloud from a sheet he hap-hazardly picked up, "commonly known as kinky hair disease (*maybe common to doctors but certainly not to ex-cons just out of the joint*), is a neurodegenerative genetic disease character-ized by a copper deficiency and generally manifested early in life ... Kinky hair, yes. Everything else, no."

Kevin crumpled up the paper and tossed it into a grow-ing pile of papers at the far end of his couch.

Maybe I'm just over-thinking this. Wouldn't be the first time. He finished the glass of whiskey in one long gulp and sighed. *Maybe it's like what my grandmother used to say about me, that I thought too much about the wrong things and too little about the right things.*

He took off his shirt and looked at his shoulder. The hair lay curled on his skin, as if it were peacefully asleep.

It's probably just something totally normal, something ev-erybody gets when they get older.

Just a hair.

CHAPTER 12

Adam Honsey squeezed between two ceiling-high shelves packed with used CDs and motioned to Kevin with one heavily scarred hand with knuckles that were knotted and misshapen. "Hand me the drill."

"I still think I should have done this," Kevin said, watching Honsey squirm his stout frame to put in two final screws to hold the shelves tight against the walls. "It would have been a helluva lot easier for me to get back there."

Honsey grunted and carefully threaded the screws through the wood and into the wall.

"Probably would have," he finally admitted, handing the drill back to Kevin. "But I'd rather blame myself than you if any of these CDs came crashing down."

Kevin smiled as Honsey inched his way out of the tight confines. "Can't argue with you there."

His boss returned the smile, showing two lower front teeth missing. Kevin noticed that the larger man was flushed, his forehead damp with drops of sweat.

"You feeling okay?" Kevin asked.

Honsey put his hands on his hips and took a deep breath.

"Yeah. Why?"

"You look a little winded."

"I'm not winded. Just haven't had enough coffee yet this morning."

"I know what you mean.'" Kevin's head pounded and his stomach rumbled from all the whiskey he drank the night before. He had almost convinced himself to pull out the hair, pain be damned, but had finished off the bottle of booze instead and ended up passing out on the couch.

Honsey yawned loudly and looked at his watch. "Quarter to nine," he said to Kevin. "Probably should get things ready to open."

"Will do. You gonna stay back here and work some more?"

He shook his clean-shaven head. "I'm gonna go back in the office and have that cup of coffee before I tackle more cleaning. By the way, a guy I know is putting on an MMA event in a couple weeks," Honsey said as they walked toward the office. "Winner of each weight division takes home five hundred dollars and he's short on middle-weights and light heavyweights. You interested?"

"No way." Kevin stood next to the office door as Honsey filled a large coffee mug emblazoned with a Detroit Red Wings emblem. "My fighting days are long gone. Besides, I was a boxer, remember? Those MMA boys are into all that fancy stuff like kick boxing and Jujitsu . . ."

Hosney waved him off. "That don't mean shit. I'd put money on someone who can use their fists like you any day of the week."

"Thanks, but like I said, my fighting days are done." Kevin playfully punched Honsey on the shoulder, who rolled his eyes in amusement. "How 'bout you? It'd be a kick to see Adam 'Lionheart' Honsey back in the ring."

"Last time I was in the ring—twenty years ago, I got a broken jaw and a concussion in the first two minutes . . ."

Honsey shook his head and laughed. "Nobody wants to pay to see a fat old man get his ass kicked."

"I don't know," Kevin mused aloud, "never underestimate the blood lust of the American public."

Honsey pointed a meaty finger toward the office entrance. "Get out of here, tough guy, and open my store."

An extra five-hundred bucks would be nice, Kevin thought as he went through the steps of opening the store: unlocking the cash register, making sure the CDs, videos, and vinyl were sitting neatly on their shelves, flipping the closed sign to open.

But not at the cost of getting back in the ring.

Kevin had done a half-dozen amateur boxing matches when he was seventeen and eighteen, winning them all by knockouts. However, he had never enjoyed it like other boxers and quit once he started community college.

When he got to Fairview, he started back up. Boxing was one of the few sanctified means in prison to take out your aggression, and Kevin took full advantage of it, viciously beating the first three men to step in the ring with him. He quickly learned that his boxing prowess only made him a mark outside the ring for guys who were looking to up their prison-creds. After getting goaded into two fights in the prison yard—each landing him a month in solitary—Kevin hung up his gloves for good.

I never much liked getting hit in the face anyway. And now I sure as hell wouldn't like getting slammed on my shoulder, back, or thigh.

After Caesar had left his house the night before, Kevin had examined his leg. The lesion on his thigh was still intact. Kevin imagined a hair curled up underneath the skin pulsating softly like a hungry leech, ready to eat its way out and stretch its coal-black body into the world.

He had covered the lesion with three thick pads of gauze in the morning before heading into work and hoped he wouldn't find them soaked with blood by the evening.

An elderly black man with close-cropped graying hair and wearing a thigh-length dirty yellow winter jacket covered with strips of duct tape was the first customer of the day. Elder Jackson—or so he called himself—had started coming in two weeks earlier and would spend hours in the porn section, happily humming to himself while he intently read every back cover of all the videos. Kevin had asked Honsey what to do about the man.

"Is he jerking off back there? Is he bothering any of the other customers?" Kevin had answered no to both. Honsey finally declared, "Then leave him be. He's probably just killing time moving from shelter to shelter."

"How you doing, Elder Jackson?" Kevin said to the old man as he ambled to the counter.

"I'm doing jus' fine!" He smiled, showing off a row of yellowing teeth. "I got some money today to buy me somethin'!"

"You're the first in the store. Take your time looking things over."

Elder Jackson gave him a slight but heartfelt bow. "Thank you, Kevin." He went to make his way to the back when he turned around. "Is that nice young lady coming in today to see you?"

Kevin smiled. "No, she's working all day today."

"That's too bad." The old man's smile faded for an instant, then reformed. "I mean, I'm glad she has a job, but I was looking' forward to maybe seein' her again. She's so very nice."

"I'm sure she'll be in sometime this week," Kevin said. "I'll tell her you're looking forward to seeing her again."

"I'd 'preciate that," Elder Jackson replied. "You make sure you treat her right, you hear? Ain't very often a man gets something special in his life."

Kevin watched the elderly man trudge back to the porn

section. *He may be old and crazy, but he's right on about Sherri.*

Kevin was still lost in thoughts about her when the buzzer to the front door went off again. A greeting smile instinctively formed on his face even before he fully looked up and faded instantly.

It was Bismarck.

He was wearing a dark brown suede jacket and matching slacks with a multicolored sweater underneath. His black hair was slicked back, and his face was tanned and flushed as if he had just come from the tanning booth.

"Good morning, young man," he said to Kevin, gazing around the store. "Do you have a minute to talk to me about your fine store?"

Kevin's lips were pursed tight. *He's come here to rob the store. He knows that I'm not going to help him, so he's decided to do it himself.*

As the monster walked slowly to the counter, Kevin let his hands drop to the baseball bat underneath. He decided that if Bismarck pulled a gun, he would try to smash his head in or die trying.

"Chill out, Kev," Bismarck said within inches of his face. The sickly-sweet smell of breath mints filled the space between the two men as Kevin's sweaty hands gripped the bat even tighter.

"What do you want?" Kevin demanded.

"To see how you're doing." Bismarck took a step back and looked from side to side. "Get a lay of the land."

Kevin heard someone clear their throat and looked to the side to see Honsey walking to the front.

"Can I help you?" he asked Bismarck.

"I hope so!" Bismarck beamed like a little boy getting a new bike. "I've been chatting here with this wonderful young man about trying to find the second album by a favorite group of mine called the Dead Kennedy's."

"You mean Plastic Surgery Disasters, released in '82?"

"That's the one!"

"I might have a copy in back," Honsey said. .

"I'll go look," Kevin quickly offered, but Honsey waved him off.

"No. You stay up here."

Beads of sweat dripped down Kevin's sides underneath his shirt. Bismarck watched Honsey disappear into the back, then turned toward Kevin.

"Where are the security cams?"

Kevin's hands began to ache from holding the baseball bat so tight. *If I bring it up fast enough, I could catch him in the chin. He'd be out before—*

"Kevin?" Bismarck snapped his fingers in front of his face. "You still with me, boy?"

Kevin took a deep breath. "Aren't you going to ask me for the money?"

Bismarck frowned and then broke into a loud laugh. He immediately covered his mouth, still chuckling underneath his breath. He again moved close to Kevin and winked.

"You think I'm here to rob the store?" he spoke in an unnaturally quiet voice. "C'mon, Kev, this rip-off is going to be a bonding thing—something special between you and me. I wouldn't think of doing it on my own."

Kevin forced himself to loosen the grip on the bat. "Then get the fuck out of here."

"Sure. In one minute. After you tell me why you haven't called."

Kevin tried to swallow, his mouth suddenly dry. "I'm still thinking," he finally responded.

Bismarck nodded slowly, as if contemplating a great mystery of the universe. "Think about this. Either decide yes right now or I'm telling your boss everything."

There was a solid, rhythmic thumping noise coming from the back. Both Kevin and Bismarck turned to see Honsey walking toward them, carrying an album jacket.

"That's my only copy," Honsey handed it to the customer. "It's in near-perfect condition. It listed at fifty dollars, but I'll sell it for thirty."

Bismarck turned the album jacket over in his hands, examining it like a jeweler inspecting a fine watch.

"I guess it's a deal I just can't pass up. Oh, by the way," Bismarck continued, looking at Kevin, "how about that thing I asked you about? You going to be able to help me out with it?"

Kevin stared at Bismarck and stepped over the precipice. "Sure. I think we can help you."

"So that's a yes?" Bismarck grinned.

Kevin nodded. He saw Honsey looking at him with a quizzical frown.

"That's so wonderful!" Bismarck chuckled. He turned to face Honsey. "I can't believe you also have this album in cassette. Do you know how long I've looked for it?"

Honsey stared at Kevin. "You told him we had a cassette of this?"

"I thought I saw one this morning on the middle of the third shelf," Kevin replied..

Honsey starred at Kevin for five seconds before sighing. "Fine. I'll go look for it."

"That was quick thinking," Bismarck said when Honsey was out of earshot. "I'm impressed."

"What the fuck are you pulling here?" Kevin said, doing nothing to keep the anger out of his voice.

"Just having a little fun."

"You've had your fun. Now leave."

"Okay. Give me your phone number so we can chat about our rendezvous."

"It's two three seven—"

"No," Bismarck interrupted, "let me see your phone."

Kevin handed over his cell and watched with impotent

rage as Bismarck put the numbers in his own phone.

"There," Bismarck said, "that wasn't so hard, was it?" As he handed Kevin's phone back to him Honsey emerged from the back.

"What's going on here?" Honsey asked.

Bismarck brightly smiled. "Kevin was just giving me his phone number in case I had any more questions. I'm just so happy to see that personal customer service isn't dead in this great city of ours." He looked at Honsey's empty hands. "You couldn't find that cassette?"

Honsey looked at Bismarck and snatched the Dead Kennedy LP from the counter. "No. I didn't find it. In fact, I think I've changed my mind about the sale."

Bismarck's face registered surprise. "What?"

"I'm gonna keep this," Honsey kept his voice firm and steady. "It's my only copy, and since there's been no transaction, it's still mine." He pointed one meaty finger at the door. "Now get the hell out of my store."

Kevin stepped out from behind the counter, bewildered at the sudden turn of events. "Listen, Mr. Honsey, there's no—"

"You know what," Bismarck sneered, ignoring Kevin while taking a step toward the older man, "I don't think I like your attitude."

"That's a shame," Honsey said. While his voice was still calm and controlled his face was red and the veins in his neck bulged out like fat worms. "Maybe you'd like to try and do something about it."

"Hey hey hey!" a voice triumphantly cried out. Kevin looked over his right shoulder to see Elder Jackson carrying a DVD high up over his head like a hunter bringing home a trophy kill. "I found me The Wiz! It used to be my granddaughter's favorite movie. Just wait 'till she sees I got her very own copy!"

"That's great," Kevin forced a friendly smile, still watching Honsey and Bismarck out of the corner of his eye. "Let me ring it up for you."

Honsey looked at Bismarck, then at Elder Jackson.

"We have other customers to deal with," Honsey said to him, "so unless there's something else we can do for you . . ."

Bismarck stepped back and shook his head. "I'm all set." He turned and walked out, not saying another word.

"That gentlemen couldn't find what he wanted?" Elder Jackson asked.

"Seems that way," Honsey said, gazing at the door.

"That'll be $12.95," Kevin said to Elder Jackson.

"Oh." Elder Jackson jammed his hands into his pockets and came up with some crumpled one-dollar bills and some change. "This is what I got," he said, dumping the money on the counter. "If you'll hold it for me, I can go collect some bottles for deposit money and—"

"This is enough," Honsey stepped around the counter and sweeped the money into his hands. "You go and enjoy that movie with your granddaughter."

"Thank you very much!" Elder Jackson said, snatching up the movie. As soon as the door closed behind him Honsey turned to Kevin and tapped him hard in the chest.

"What the hell was going on with you and that big asshole?"

"What are you talking about?"

"I'm talking about giving him your phone number. What, you think I'm stupid?"

He knows we're planning to rip him off!

"You're doing a drug deal with him, aren't you?" Honsey continued, again tapping Kevin in the chest before tightly crossing his arms. "You're setting up deals here in my store!"

"No! I swear it's nothing like that," Kevin said, his mind racing. "I told you when I started that I was never into that shit and I never will be."

"And I believed you," Honsey said, his eyes dilated and

the veins in his neck still distended. "So, if it wasn't a drug deal, what was it?"

"He asked me out."

"What? Like out on a date?"

Kevin gave a small shrug. "Yeah." He tried to give the best sheepish grin he could muster. "Look, I know you've seen Sherri in here with me, and I really like her, but when I was in prison, I realized that I like guys too, so . . ." he gave another shrug. "Anyway, I apologize for that whole scene. I should have just told the guy to meet me after work."

Honsey waved him off. "It's fine. None of my business how you want to get your nut off." He took a deep breath and gave a small chuckle. "Guess I'm just getting too old to understand your generation.'"

Kevin watched Honsey walk to the back with the Dead Kennedy's album. *And I'm getting too good at lying to both my friends and myself.*

A buzzing from his pocket brought him out of his thoughts. He pulled out his cell and looked at his message screen. There were three dark blue words against the yellow background:

See U Soon!

It was from Bismarck.

CHAPTER 13

KEVIN STOOD ON HIS porch and looked at the huge maple tree on the abandoned lot next door in the light of the setting sun. Leaves of red and yellow hung on knurled limbs that coursed out over the street and sidewalk, a canopy of color in a sea of concrete and asphalt.

There was a sudden unearthly high-pitched yowl to his left. Kevin glanced over to see a pair of cats mating furiously, the male's rear pounding like a piston into the scrawny backside of the female. Ten seconds later it was over, the animals disengaging and nonchalantly going their separate ways.

Kevin took one last breath of the air thick with odors of natural gas, courtesy of Detroit's last oil refinery six blocks west, before going inside. While fluffing the pillows on the couch he glanced up at the clock. The red numbers read 6:37 P.M.

She should be over any time now. Sherri had to work a 10-hour shift at the hair salon but promised that as soon as she was done, she would come over. He had used that knowledge to get him through the day after Bismarck had left. Kevin had been on edge and snapped at two customers before Honsey took him aside and chewed his ass. He spent the rest of the time looking up at the clock and counting the minutes as if they were pennies of gold.

Kevin had tried rehearsing what he was going to tell Sherri about the lesions—*about the hair*—all the way home on the bus, failing miserably. It wasn't that she didn't deserve to know, or even that he was afraid if it would scare her or freak her out.

He was afraid that she would see what was happening to him and leave.

The knock on the door was three fast taps. Sherri's knock. Kevin's hand was on the deadbolt when he stopped. It had to be her, but yet . . .

He carefully pulled aside the window shade and looked out. A red, rusted '99 Subaru Outback sat in his driveway. Sherri's car.

"Thought you weren't home," she said, entering the house as soon as Kevin had opened the door.

Kevin laughed. "Had to make sure you weren't the bogeyman."

Sherri shook her head then pulled his head down to hers for a kiss.

"I missed you," he said after they moved apart.

"I missed you too." Sherri hung up her jacket in the small closet next to the door and looked into the living room. "See you haven't got that 56-inch plasma TV yet."

Kevin put his hands on his hips. "I've decided that's too small. Think I'll just go for the 78-inch home theatre set after I win the lottery."

Sherri giggled. "You're probably the only man in Detroit without a TV."

"It rots your brain," Kevin replied in mock seriousness, "and I need all the gray matter I have."

"I think you have plenty of gray matter," Sherri took his hand and led him over to the couch.

"Why's that?" Kevin asked, sitting next to her and making sure his leg with the lesion was on the opposite side.

"Because you picked me as your girlfriend."

He kissed her again, this time long and deep.

Sherri giggled again as her hand ran up his thigh and rested on the bulge in his crotch. "You weren't kidding when you said you missed me."

You have to tell her. You have to tell her right fucking now.

Kevin gently but firmly pushed her hand away and stood up.

"I have to tell you something," he confessed. "The things I have covered on my shoulder and thigh—they're not nasty tats and scars."

Sherri sighed and crossed her arms.

"Look, before you get all pissed off," Kevin hurriedly continued, "I was hoping they were just some type of ingrown hair, or weird zit, something that would just go away on their own."

Don't fucking leave. Yell at me, hit me, just don't fucking leave.

Sherri cleared her throat. "So, you lied to me."

"I did. And I'm very sorry."

Sherri slowly uncrossed her arms. "Don't do it again," she said, her voice holding a hard edge. "If you can't tell me the truth, then we shouldn't—*won't*—be together."

Kevin nodded. "Fair enough." He took a step back, pulled off his sweatshirt, and removed the pads over the hair on his shoulder. "This thing came out of a raised lesion I discovered on my shoulder a few weeks ago. I have another large lesion—no hair thing yet—on my thigh, and two smaller lesions on my back."

Sherri frowned. "You lied about a hair?"

"I know, right? It seems stupid but . . ." He felt both relief and shame. "It's not like any hair I've ever had or seen."

Sherri moved closer and peered at his shoulder. "Kev, to

me it just looks like a really thick hair."

Kevin put his hands in his lap and felt sweat running down his sides. "Just don't touch it, okay?" he pleaded. He swore he could feel Sherri's warm breath wash over the hair as she looked at it from different angles.

"You know, you might be right," she commented after a moment. "It's not like any hair I've ever seen. And I've seen a lot."

"What do you think it is?"

"I don't know, but I can help you look online to see if we can find out if anyone has anything like this."

"Caesar and I went to a library yesterday and I printed out some stuff," Kevin said, grabbing a handful of sheets from underneath a magazine with his free hand.

"You've told Caesar about it and not me?"

"I've known Caesar forever. He's like a brother to me." He squeezed her hand. "I'm sorry I didn't tell you earlier."

Sherri kicked at a dust ball on the floor and nodded. "It's okay . . ." She pulled her hand out of his pointed and at the papers. "What did you guys find?"

"We printed out some info on rare diseases having to do with hairs." Kevin picked up a small pile sitting on its own. "To me, the closest anything comes to is a condition called Morgellons."

Sherri read the first couple pages and then sat them down on her lap. "It sounds like what you might have."

"You need to read it all. Morgellons disease was named in 2001," he recalled the information from memory, having read the papers over and over the night before. "It always starts with the sufferers complaining of intense itching, strange lesions, and then even stranger, hair-like protrusions from their skin that can't be identified as any known subject. There's even a Morgellons Research Group examining the number of theories about it, like are they infections, parasites, nanotechnology gone crazy?"

Kevin shook his head and tapped the papers with his finger. "Of course, most doctors tend to say that it's a psychiatric condition called delusions of parasitosis—people just imagining that they have hair or fiber-causing parasites under their skin."

Sherri pointed at his shoulder. "That's one helluva imaginary hair."

"That it is." They sat quiet for a moment before Kevin carefully put back on the pads over the hair.

"I get the feeling you're not convinced what you have is this Morgellons condition."

"People with Morgellons have no trouble picking these hair-fiber things out of their skin," Kevin said. "They also universally complain of intense, almost unbearable itching." He looked at his shoulder, then at his thigh. "My . . . things are a little itchy every now and then, but nothing at all like Morgellons. And forget the part of having no trouble pulling the thing on my shoulder out." He sighed again and shook his head. "I don't know. Caesar says I should go see a doctor."

"I agree." Sherri took his hand and held it tight. "I can call in tomorrow. You can call Honsey and tell him you're sick. We can go down to the Health Department on Seven Mile and we'll get this checked out."

Kevin pulled his hand away and stood up. "All people working at the Health Department clinics in Detroit are overworked and underpaid."

Sherri looked up at him but said nothing.

"And what if I do go?" Kevin continued. "You know they're going to just tell me that thing on my shoulder is just a hair." He pointed at the pile of papers. "Go on—read about how people with Morgellons are told they're crazy. Believe me, I've had enough of psychobabble from shrinks to last me a lifetime."

"When were you seeing a psychiatrist?" Sherri asked in a quiet voice.

Kevin's shoulder's slumped. *Great job there bringing that old shit up.*

"When I was at Fairview," he explained. "It was some new type of program for first time—" He made quotation marks in the air, "violent offenders."

"What did they do to you?"

"Do? You mean like shock therapy and shit like that?"

"Yeah."

"No shock therapy, but some weird shit like having me undress, lay in this empty room while all these flashing lights went off around me for hours on end. That went out for a few weeks every other day."

"What was it supposed to do?"

"I have no idea. When I asked, they just said it was 'part of the treatment.'

"What else did they do?"

"A ton of talking, looking at inkblots where I guess I was supposed to see my dad sexually abusing me or some crazy bullshit like that . . ." Kevin sat back on the couch and in his mind, he was back in the small, white-walled room with one table, two chairs and three video-cams staring down at him with all-seeing glass eyes. "The shrink was this creepy little dude named Dr. Robert Eugene Denison. 'Call me Bobby,' he would always say in this sing-song voice." Kevin chuckled. "Just to piss him off, I'd call him Dr. Bob.

"He and I would sit in this room for hours and hours and he'd ask me a thousand questions about crazy shit, like 'what do you think of necrophilia, Kevin?' or 'have you had any dreams about eviscerating animals with your teeth, Kevin?'"

"That's seriously fucked up," Sherri guffawed. "How long did you have to see him?"

Kevin rubbed his eyes. "Seemed like forever. But I think it was probably my thirdand fourth year there . . ."

"No wonder you don't like doctors." Sherri moved close to Kevin. "So, what are we going to do?"

Kevin smiled and put his arm around her. "I like the sound of that. The 'we.'"

"I know." Sherri sat up. "We could see if Dr. Rothstein will look at you."

"Rothstein? Who's that?"

"He's the doctor that did all of our MCFM body-work. There's nobody better at avant-garde body modifications. He's a little eccentric, but he seems nice, so—"

Sherri's words were cut off by the sound of Kevin's cell phone ringing.

"Shit," he said. . "I thought I set that on vibrate."

He pulled the phone from his pocket and starred at the screen. It was Bismarck.

"You gonna answer that?" Sherri asked.

Kevin continued to stare at the number as the phone continued its incessant ringing.

"Kevin?"

He finally looked up at her. "No," he said, putting the phone down on the table like it was a piece of radioactive waste. "I'm not going to answer it."

After two more rings the phone went silent. Sherri reached up and stroked his cheek. "If I don't ask you who that was, you won't have to lie to me."

Kevin looked at the phone, looked at Sherri, then took her hand and kissed it. "I'm falling in love with you," he said.

"And I love you."

Kevin pulled her close and kissed her long and deep. When they finally pulled apart, he told her everything about his six years at Fairview. About Readona, about Bismarck, about getting the tats and scars. All the bad shit from Fairview that he had kept bottled up for the past six years.

Everything.

Except killing the seventeen-year-old boy.

CHAPTER 14

S HERRY SAT FORWARD ON the couch and dropped the stub of her cigarette into an empty beer bottle. She had stayed mostly quiet except for a few questions here and there for the past two hours as Kevin told her the tortured story of his six years in Fairview up to his recent encounter with Bismarck.

"That's a hell of a story," she said when Kevin was finally out of words.

"Yeah. Emphasis on Hell."

She stroked the top of his hand. "Is there anymore you need to tell me?"

"No." Kevin had a snapshot memory of the black kid he murdered laying in a pool of his own blood. "That just about does it . . ."

Sherri nodded, then picked up the beer bottle shook the mass of cigarette butts to and fro. "I really need to quit smoking."

Kevin took the bottle from her and dropped his half-smoked cigarette in. "We'll quit together." He pulled Sherri closer. "I'm sure we can think of something else to give our mouths to do."

"I'm sure we can." She sighed and looked into his eyes. "I think you should tell Bismarck to go fuck himself. You're not in Fairview anymore. This prick can't hurt you."

Kevin frowned and sat back from her. "I told you I did some bad shit for them in the can. If they take that to the law—"

"So what? You beat up some people, you ran some drugs—like that's not in the norm in the day of a life of a con." She moved closer and took his hands. "I've never did time, but I heard all the stories from Sam, some worse than yours, and I know there's no way you're going back to jail for what you did there."

I don't think slitting a kids' throat is just a story.

Kevin shook his head. "I can't chance it. I know you think I'm being paranoid, but . . ." his voice trailed off and he was suddenly aware how tired he was.

"I don't think you're being paranoid, Kevin" She kissed him then sat back. "But I do think that if you rip off Honsey, Bismarck will never let you go."

"I'm not going to rip off Honsey," he said emphatically. "And you're right: doing that would just get me in that much deeper with Bismarck." *And Readona, Don't forget the man who's pulling the puppet strings.* "That's one thing I don't want." He sighed and wrapped his fingers behind his head. "I've got to figure out a way to get him to fuck up, so he gets sent back to the can and not me."

Sherri snuggled up next to him. "I could talk to Peter. He's been around. I know he knows some people who may be able to make Bismarck disappear."

Kevin put his hands up. "Stop. I'm—*we're*—not going down that road. You and your friends aren't getting shit on them for my issues."

"Our friends."

Kevin smiled. "Our friends aren't getting into shit because of me."

"So, what are you going to do?"

"Maybe I'll just keep avoiding him. Maybe he'll do something stupid, and I won't have to do a damn thing."

Sherri lay her head on his shoulder and held his hands as they sat in silence.

"Whatever you decide I'll be with you," she finally said. "Just promise me it won't be something rash and stupid."

"My stupid days are behind me," Kevin said with as much sincerity as he could muster. "But it works both ways— promise me you won't ask anyone to take him out or make him disappear."

She crossed her heart. "I promise. But that doesn't mean if I see Bismarck walking down the street, I might just lose control of my car and run his ass over."

Kevin laughed. "And you're telling me not to do anything rash."

Sherri playfully pushed Kevin's thigh and he winced in real pain.

"Shit, Kevin, I'm sorry!" she waved her hands. "I forgot."

Kevin gave a pained smile. "Don't worry about it. It's been hit worse."

Sherri's eyes suddenly opened wide. "That's what happened the night at the fire show, isn't it? You hit the lesion on the chair."

"Uh huh. Our first-time meeting and I almost cried out like a little girl."

Sherri snorted, then reached down to her purse and pulled out a ticket. "Before I forget, I want to give you this. We're having a huge night-before Halloween show this year. Peter has got a great venue lined up. He lined up some big names from MTV to be there. This could be our shot of getting a network contract!"

"That's fantastic!" Kevin carefully folded up the ticket and put it in his pocket.

Sherri stretched her arms over her head then got off the couch. "I should get going," she said. "It's my week to open up the shop, so that means a very early morning."

"You sure I can't convince you to stay?" Kevin reached out and started to rub the inside of her thighs.

"Anyone ever tell you you're a very naughty man?" Sherri smiled and closed her eyes as Kevin's hand worked its way to her crotch.

He reached out and cupped her ass with his free hand. "I think you might have mentioned it once or twice." He started pulling her onto his lap when his cell phone, sitting on the kitchen table, began to ring again.

"Let it go," Sherry whispered.

Kevin stood up. "I won't answer it. I just need to know."

"So, was it Bismarck?" Sherri asked when the ringing finally stopped.

Kevin stood next to the kitchen table and shook his head. "No. It was Caesar."

"You can't live on-edge like this." Sherri walked over and held his arms. "You need to decide, one way or another, what you're going to do about this prick."

Kevin frowned at her. "Why are you calling Caesar a prick? You know he's a nice guy."

Sherri tapped him on his face. "One of these days that smart-ass mouth of yours is going to get you into trouble."

"Believe me, it already has." He leaned down and gently kissed her.

After a moment, Sherri pulled away. "I really have to go," she insisted. "If I stay, I have the feeling you're going to keep me up all night."

"It's only fair," Kevin said, pulling her back close. "You've got me up right now."

Sherri seductively smiled up at him. "Is that so?" She dropped to her knees and efficiency pulled his jeans and shorts down to his knees and bent in. "Then I guess I better take care of it."

Kevin looked down and watched her stroke and fondle him. He felt waves of pleasure wash from his groin into his body and tried to ignore the vision of Sherri, her lips almost touching the head of his cock, looking at the lesion on his thigh.

CHAPTER 15

"Look at that." Honsey pointed outside two days later at work. "Just like Christmas!"

Kevin saw the fat, wet snowflakes falling out of the dreary, cloud-choked sky and shook his head. "It's not even Halloween yet."

"So?" Honsey laughed. "This is Michigan. Hell, I can remember as a kid walking through half a foot of snow to go trick or treating."

"I'd rather have sunshine and seventy-degree weather."

Honsey snorted. "Ain't gonna get that here." He finished filling a rack of CDs and laughed again. "The snow won't last. It's just mother nature showing us what's in store come this winter."

Kevin finished locking up the cash register. "Need help with anything in back?"

"No, I think we've put in enough overtime this week." Honsey walked over to Kevin. "Everything all right with you?"

Besides having weird-ass lesions and a psychopath who wants me to help him rip you off? Kevin tiredly smiled. "Uh huh. Why?"

"Just checking," Honsey shrugged. "I know it can be hard getting back into civilian life. I've seen guys come out of the can with the best of intentions, and then fall back into the same shit that got 'em locked up in the first place."

Kevin kept his smile as his heart started to pound. *Does he know about me and Bismarck? How in the fuck could he know?*

"I hated Fairview," he said with total sincerity. "There's nothing—and I mean nothing—that could make me fuck up and be sent back there."

"That's good to hear. I really think the online store is going to make both of us some damn good money." Kevin nodded in agreement and then, before he even realized it, Honsey slapped him on the shoulder millimeters below the hair.

Kevin gasped and stepped back. Honsey's eyes opened wide with concern.

"You okay?"

"I'm fine," Kevin said through gritted teeth.

"I didn't think I hit you hard," Honsey mumbled. "My wife tells me that sometimes I don't remember my own strength, but—"

Kevin put his hands out. "It's okay. I got this nasty infected zit on my arm and it's tender . . ." Honsey kept starring at him and Kevin shrugged. "It doesn't seem fair does it? Thirty years old and still getting zits."

Honsey's face finally softened. "What's fair about life?" He walked in back and got both his and Kevin's jackets. "I'd offer you a ride home, but I'm picking up the wife tonight from work. Said she felt like she was coming down with the stomach flu."

Honsey opened the front door, and a gust of freezing wind blew in. Kevin quickly zipped up his tattered goose-down filled jacket and stepped outside. "No problem. The seven-P.M. bus is almost always on time. Let me know if you need to stay home with the misses tomorrow. I can get here early to open up."

Honsey joined Kevin outside and locked the door behind him. "She'll be fine—Hell, she has to be a tough woman to live with an ornery bastard like me!" He gave another hearty laugh. "At the rate we've been working we'll have our online gig up and running and bringing in the cash by November first. Then we all can sit back and smell the roses."

"Man, who shit their pants?"

Kevin glanced at the large black man in his mid-thirties, wearing a bright orange ski jacket sitting next to him on the Detroit Metro Bus.

The man scrunched his face and looked at Kevin. "Ain't that the nastiest shit you ever smelled?"

An invisible cloud of foulness finally hit Kevin's nostrils and he tiredly nodded.

"I wanna know who's shittin' their pants!" The man stood up—Kevin guessed him close to seven feet tall as he had to bend over to keep from hitting the roof—and looked around, then pointed a meaty finger at a rail-thin, middle-aged Hispanic man dressed in baggy brown corduroy pants and two hoodie sweatshirts sitting one row ahead on an aisle seat.

I have no issues with any other readers looking over the manuscript. However, I grew up and worked in downriver and midtown Detroit, and the above scene actually happened to a friend who was on a bus going to work one morning. Detroit is a rough, working class town, and there are some fantastic people living in it, as well as some truly nasty folks.

"He shit his fuckin' pants!" he hollered with a mixture of awe and disgust. "Look," he pointed at the Hispanic's foot, "you can see the shit runnin' out of his drawers!"

Kevin glanced over. A thin line of runny brown feces was dripping out of the guy's right pant leg onto his dirty white Nikes held together with electrical tape.

The bus slowed for a stop and the black man walked up to the driver. "You gonna let this guy shit all over your bus?"

"It ain't my bus," answered the driver, a young black woman with corn-rowed hair.

"So, you jus' gonna let him sit there and shit all over?"

The driver loudly sighed and glanced back. "Don't look like he's hurtin' anyone." She turned around and moved the bus back into traffic.

"This city's done gone straight to Hell," the black man muttered as he walked past Kevin to the back.

Kevin looked over at the Hispanic man. He was hunched over, arms tightly crossed over his cachectic chest, and he was talking to himself in a low, hushed voice. *If I start busting out with more hairs, people are going to be treating me just like they're treating you.*

Another wave of nauseating odor wafted Kevin's way. He moved over one seat and pressed against the window, thankful for the draft of cold air that smelled of diesel exhaust rather than steaming shit.

I sure hope Honsey's right about the online store taking off.

Kevin knew that Honsey was right about him being stressed to the max, and he was angry at himself for showing it. Even Caesar, who had come over the night before to share a six-pack and invite Kevin and Sherri over to dinner Saturday night, had commented on Kevin's hair-trigger emotions, telling him to 'just chill the fuck out'.

They had been sitting on the couch, chatting about Sherri, Kevin telling him about the October 30th MCFM show that Peter had scheduled at the Masonic Auditorium. As Kevin was saying how ecstatic she was about it, a sudden knock on the door caused him to visibly flinch.

"You gonna get that?" Caesar had asked after a moment filled with a dozen more knocks went by.

Kevin had pictured Bismarck standing on the rickety porch, dressed in freshly pressed dress pants and a lined leather jacket, a .38 special revolver tucked in his pocket to provide extra incentive for the planned robbery. "No. Probably got the wrong address."

After another dozen knocks Caesar stood up. "Fine. I'll get it."

"No!" Kevin's voice was louder than he intended. "It's probably just one of the crackheads looking for some money to score."

"Then I'll kick their ass off the porch." Before Kevin could say another word, Caesar had crossed the four steps from the couch to the front and opened the door. He sat paralyzed on the couch, wanting to turn away but unable to move a single muscle in his body.

It wasn't a crackhead or Bismarck. Instead there was a young man and woman, neither appearing older than twenty. The man had short cropped brown hair and a white shirt and tie slightly visible underneath a thick flannel overcoat, while the girl, thin and blond, with her hair pulled tight in a bun, wore a brown wool jacket covering a buttoned up white shirt and a knee- length black skirt.

"We should introduce ourselves," the man said. "I'm Jacob and my companion is Emma. We represent the Church of Jesus Christ of Latter-day Saints. May we come in to talk with you a bit?"

Caesar crossed his arms and stepped back. "Evening. What's up?"

Jacob handed Caesar a book. "We'd like to talk to you about how Jesus Christ walked on this Earth, on this very land we now call America—"

"I'm Catholic," Caesar bluntly told them. "I was raised Catholic and am a practicing Catholic and there's no way in Hell I'm interested being a Mormon." He glanced up and down the block. "You having any other luck around here?"

"Yours in the first house on this block that we've come to," Emma spoke. "There didn't seem to be anyone else home, although I just saw a car pull into the house down the block."

Caesar shook his head. "I wouldn't go there."

"Why is that?" Jacob asked.

"It's full of crackheads and meth addicts," Caesar warned them. "They'll steal the clothes off your back before you're done with your spiel."

The smile on the face of Jacob faded away. "We know it's not easy spreading the gospel of the Lord," he said, "but we know that our God will—"

"The Lord watches over those that use the brains that he gave them," Caesar said in a slow, even voice, "not those who act like idiots." He stepped toward them and pointed down the street. "Get in your car. Drive north on Woodward until you're past Eight Mile. Then pick any block and start practicing your preaching there. If, after six months you don't get shot or raped, then come back here and give this neighborhood a try."

Kevin smiled to himself as the bus slowed again. *Those two evangelists got a priceless lesson from Caesar. Hope they were smart enough to learn it.*

"West Willis Street next stop," the bus driver called out. Kevin zipped up his jacket and stepped out of the bus.

He was half-way to his house when he felt the vibration of his phone. He considered letting it ring but pulled it out of his pocket anyway and smiled when he saw the caller's number.

"Hi beautiful lady," he said to Sherri. "You going to make my night perfect and tell me you're coming over?"

"I wish," she answered, "although I do have some great news, unless you've already heard it."

"Can't say I've heard any news today," Kevin said. "Did they announce I've miraculously won the lottery without buying a ticket?"

"Almost as good. Bismarck's been arrested."

Kevin immediately stopped walking. "What? When?"

"I saw it on channel seven news just now. They didn't give many details, it was something like him breaking parole, but they showed him being put into a cop car in handcuffs. Kevin, with his priors he'll never see the outside of a prison again!"

A wave of immense relief washed over Kevin. "I can't believe it . . ." he uttered. "The bastard is finally gone."

"I know! And I have some more positive news. There's a party we're invited to at Dr. Rothstein's Saturday night. I know it's short notice—Peter is an airhead sometimes about shit like this—but it'll be really cool, I promise. Rothstein has got a great place in Creektown, and you'll, you know, be able to talk to him. About the lesions."

"Yeah." The smile faded from Kevin's face. "Did you say this Saturday?"

"Yes. Why?"

"We're supposed to be going over to Caesar and Maria's place Saturday night for dinner."

"Damn." She sighed. "Kevin, I'm really sorry."

"Listen, maybe we can make it over to Rothstein's house some other time." There was a long pause and Kevin pulled the phone away from his ear to see if he had lost the signal. He hadn't.

"Sherri, you still there?" he asked.

"I'm here." There was another pause before she continued. "This is important to me—to MCFM—and I really have to be there. Dr. Rothstein has done so much for us; the work he's done on Allen alone would have cost thousands more if he had gone to anyone else."

Kevin blew on his hand to try to warm it up. "This party at Rothstein's is that important to you?"

"It is. And like I said, you could talk to Dr. Rothstein about your problem."

Kevin thought for a few seconds, then spoke. "You're right. It is important. We'll go to Rothstein's Saturday night."

"Then I should call Caesar," Sherri said. "It's my fault we have to cancel."

"It's no one's fault." Kevin was aware of the tension in his voice and took a deep breath. "Look, it's fine. Caesar is cool. He'll understand."

"You sure?"

Kevin turned on his block and scanned the street: no cars or people around the crack house. "I'm sure," he nodded, quickly walking to his house. "I've got to dig my keys out of my pocket, so can I call you back in a couple minutes?"

"Sure." Another pause. "Kevin, I'm sorry about fucking up Saturday night."

"Don't worry about it. I'm sure you'll find some way to make it up to me. Talk to you in a couple." He hung up the phone, walked up the slippery stairs of his porch, and dug through his pockets.

He was just about to unlock the deadbolt when he thought he saw a movement—like a body quickly zooming in and out of a picture frame—from the corner of his eye. Kevin quickly turned around, slipped on the frozen wood of the porch, and fell hard on one knee.

"Shit!" His is keys tumbled out of his hands into the snow. He gingerly got up and looked around.

In the dim light of the lone streetlamp, thick white flakes of snow filled the air. There were no people, no cars, no dogs or other animals. Just snow and a bitterly cold wind that pushed the flakes through the air. *Maybe it was a ghost. It is getting close to Halloween.*

"There's no such things as ghosts," he remembered his father telling him when he was a child. "It's not the dead you need to worry about, my son,, it's the living"

"As always, Dad, you were right," Kevin said out loud while shaking off the snow from his keys. "And the living one named Bismarck is now behind bars—and if there's a God—will be there until he's a ghost."

CHAPTER 16

THEY SHOULD MAKE PEOPLE take their driving test in the snow," Sherri said, irritation in her voice as she and Kevin drove to Rothstein's party on Saturday night. "That way we wouldn't have to deal with so many assholes when the white shit starts falling early in the season."

Kevin nodded. Through the window he could see the huge sprawling GM Assembly Plant, a squat, concrete monolith covering block after city block.

"How far you think this traffic jam goes on?" he asked, looking at the long line of cars that crawled in stop and go traffic on Southbound I-75.

"There's probably an accident somewhere." Sherri hit the horn as a late-model Ford F-150 pickup tried to cut in front of them.

Kevin glanced over and the driver of the truck, a middle-aged white guy with close-cut gray hair mouthed 'fuck-you' and flipped him the bird. Kevin resisted the urge to respond in kind and instead put his hand on Sherri's thigh.

"We left in plenty of time," he comforted her. "I'm sure we'll make it there by eight."

Sherri glanced at her watch and sighed. "You're probably right." She dropped one hand to cover his. "So, Caesar wasn't pissed about the change in plans?"

Kevin shook his head. "Nah." He gave her leg a squeeze. "Caesar's an easy-going guy. We'll make it in a couple weeks or so."

Kevin sat back in the seat as they continued in the stop and go traffic. He felt guilty about lying to her about Caesar but had no stomach for turning an already unpleasant situation into something worse.

"C'mon, K, what am I supposed to tell Maria?" Caesar had said when Kevin had called him about the change of plans. "She went out and bought a shitload of food."

"I'm sorry," Kevin apologized over and over. "Just tell her something came up and—"

"I'm not lying to her."

"I'm not asking you to lie to her," Kevin said in a voice louder than he had intended. "I'm just saying that this party at Rothstein's house is important—*real* important—to Sherri."

"Forgive me for thinking it's important to get together with my best friend and his new girlfriend to come over once and break bread with me and my old lady."

"Man, you know it's not like that."

There had been a long pause before Caesar finally spoke. "Look, K, I don't mean to be going off on you. It's just that, you know, this dinner seemed pretty important to Maria for some reason, so—"

"I get it, Caesar. I promise I'll talk to Sherri about it and we'll get it rescheduled as soon as we can."

Sherri suddenly shook his arm and brought him out of his memory. "I told you it was a crash at the intersection."

The side of the freeway was lit up like Christmas. The blue and red flashing lights of cop cars illuminated a tangled mass of glass and steel, which bore the faint resemblance to a mini-van and sedan of unknown make.

"That couldn't have turned out well," Kevin mentioned as they passed the wreck.

"No argument from me." Sherri pushed on the gas and moved the car expertly into the left lane, passing a line of slower moving cars. "By the way, I wanted to tell you that I called the cops yesterday about Bismarck."

"What do you mean?"

"I called to see if I could get any more info about him and why he got tagged."

"I thought we had talked about this, Sherri." Kevin forced himself to keep his voice calm. "You said you were going to stay out of it."

"No, I said I wasn't going to have my friends beat the shit out of him. I never said anything about sitting back and watch a piece-of-shit thug like him fuck with my man."

Kevin took a deep breath. "I know you did it out of care and love, but really, I don't want you getting caught up in my shit, especially shit that came out of Fairview." He leaned over and kissed her cheek. "Your life is going great right now, and I would never want to be the one that fucks it up."

"Not gonna happen." She put her hand on top of his and held it tight. "I'm not going to let it."

Kevin smiled and forced himself to relax. "So, what did the cops say?"

"Typical bureaucratic bullshit: we can't comment on that, it's an ongoing investigation, blah blah blah . . ." She shook her head. "Pretty piss poor legal system when a scumbag like Bismarck gets anything less than a public hanging."

"You really need to do something about that mean streak of yours," Kevin teased her. "It's going to destroy your innocent girl image."

Sherri laughed for a short moment. "I lost that image a long time ago." She slowed the car and pulled off the freeway. "We should be there in a few minutes."

"Okay." Kevin looked out the window at the dimly lit buildings with tired fluorescent signs blinking everything from FREDDIES FRESH FISH to CASH CHECKS HERE!

Sherri turned the car south on St. Aubin Street and Kevin was instantly reminded of his neighborhood; deserted streets filled with garbage bags, torn sofas, ripped mattresses, the flotsam and jetsam of a dying city and its few remaining inhabitants.

"Don't tell me this doctor lives down here," Kevin said.

"No, he doesn't live anywhere near here. He's got a place off Jefferson."

"That's a relief. Hate to think what kind of doctor would have to live in the same kind of place as an ex-con."

"Once you and Honsey get the online store going, I'm sure you'll be able to get a place in a nicer neighborhood." Sherri turned north on Jefferson Avenue and the scene switched again to brightly lit restaurants and a steady stream of traffic.

"Maybe I'll get a place on the riverfront," Kevin suggested, looking out toward the dark blue Detroit River. As they passed over the MacArthur Bridge, he pointed out to the large island in the middle of the river. "You ever go to Belle Isle when you were a kid?"

"No. My dad said it was too dangerous."

"When Caesar and I were sixteen, we used to go there all the time. We'd get someone to buy us a twelve pack or a couple bottles of wine and drive out to the north end of the island." He looked out to the river and the island loomed dark and forlorn, like a long-forgotten piece of the Pleistocene Age dropped in the heart of the twenty-first century. "Did you know that herds of wild fallow deer roamed the island?"

"Can't say I did."

"They are weird-ass looking animals," Kevin continued. "Weigh maybe a hundred, hundred-twenty pounds but have these broad," he put his hands next to his head, thumbs touching his temples with his fingers spread wide, "shovel-shaped antlers that you swear are going to tip them over on their face." He laughed and shook his head. "We would sit out in the fields for hours, drinking our booze and watching the deer fight, fuck, whatever deer do."

Sherri reached over and rubbed his thigh—fortunately his left thigh, the one without the lesion—and smiled. "I wish I could have known you then."

"No, you don't. I was arrogant and stupid. You would have picked that up in a heartbeat and never given me a second glance."

"Maybe." She smiled again. "It's not a good thing to live in the past."

"You're right. It's not."

"Speaking of the past, I was talking to Roxanne last night—you remember her from the show?"

Kevin laughed. "Oh yeah. She's not easy to forget."

"Anyway, when she and I were talking, I told her about you being an ex-con."

Kevin shrugged. "It's no big deal. She and rest of the gang would find out sooner or later."

"I'm sure you're right. But knowing Roxanne as well as I do, she'll find a way to ask you about it. About why you got sent there." She gunned the car to get through a yellow light, then turned to look at him. "You told me the first night I came over that you got sent there for getting into a fight."

"That's right."

"But as I seem to remember, you somehow made me forget to ask you for the details."

Kevin raised his eyebrows. "Really?" He cowered against the window in mock fear when Sherri raised her fist. "Okay, maybe I did distract you that night." He paused for a moment. "You really want to hear about it? Not one of my more shining moments."

Sherri nodded but said nothing.

"It had been a bad day," Kevin began. "Around seven o'clock at night, I took a drive down to Monroe. Don't know why I went there, just kept on driving until I pulled off when I saw a bar that looked interesting. It was a typical dive—some pool tables, foosball machine, jukebox playing shitty 80's music."

He looked out the window at the stores passing by, their windows dark and covered with thick steel bars for protection. "Put a young guy full of anger, bitterness, and testosterone into a white-trash hillbilly heaven and you've just about got the perfect recipe for disaster. I started drinking and conning everyone I could into playing pool. By midnight I was stone drunk and had hustled a few hundred bucks."

"Did somebody try to rob you?"

"No. What happened was that I sat down to take a break and this group of four guys started doing an eight-ball shoot around. This little Hispanic guy—hell, he couldn't have been more than five-two—walked up to them and asked if he could join."

"And?"

Kevin put his hands behind his head and stretched his back. The vertebrae popping in his back sounded like sticks breaking in the confines of the car. "The biggest guy in the group—a couple inches taller than me with muscles like a body builder—looks at this little dude and spits a mouthful of beer in his face." He sighed. "To this day I don't know why it set me off. Maybe cause the Hispanic dude looked a little like Caesar, maybe because I just wanted to hit something. I stood up, walked over to the big dude, smiled, and hit him with a perfect right cross and broke his fucking jaw."

"Damn." Sherri stopped for another light and turned to Kevin. "Still, I've never heard of anyone getting sent to Fairview for six years for a simple A & B."

"My luck was running pretty much on shit those days,"

Kevin said. "That, and the fact that the big dude happened to be the son of the Chief of the Monroe County Sheriff's Department."

"Oh, Kevin . . ." Sherri pulled the car slowly away from the light then turned on the first road to the right. "I'll never complain about having bad luck again."

"But those days are over," Kevin stated. He looked out at a smattering of houses, a mix of small one bedrooms, two-story wood frames, and old style English Tudors, that lined the street, then back at Sherri. "Are we getting close?"

She slowed and pulled into the drive of a wood-sided, three story Tudor with a small, attached garage. "Better then close. We're here."

CHAPTER 17

KEVIN SQUINTED AS HIS eyes adjusted to the indoor light of Irwin Rothstein's house. A thirty- something woman with smooth, pale skin and eyebrows pierced with a half-dozen golden bars, took his and Sherri's jackets as well as their cellphones. While Kevin thought Sherri looked radiant in a long, red spaghetti-strap dress with a plunging back and neckline, exposing her multicolored tats, he felt underdressed in black khaki and a golden-hued sweater Caesar had given him as gift.

In a large room at the end of a brightly lit hallway, a number of other men and women milled about, some dressed in expensive-looking suits and dresses, others in jeans and torn t-shirts. Most of them were pierced, tattooed, or with some other type of body modification.

"Who are all these people?" Kevin whispered to Sherri.

"Some of Dr. Rothstein's patients, friends, leaders of the Midwest body-mod movement, even some politicians and other movers and shakers." She pointed at one couple— the man, tall and tanned, early thirties, with close-cropped blonde hair wearing black leather pants and vest, the woman in her late forties, short and busty and wearing a see-th-ru silver-mesh dress—having an animated conversation and smoking a cigar-sized blunt.

"Don't tell me she's the head of the Detroit City Council?" Kevin joked.

Sherri laughed. "Nope. She owns a web design and virtual advertising company that's running different content portals for high-end fashion designers. She also sets up video channels for small companies and groups. She'sworking on ours right now."

Kevin feigned a smile and felt very old. "Video channel? Like on YouTube?"

"It can be on YouTube, but there's a ton of other sites that we get our content out to the great unwashed masses."

A thought struck Kevin. "Content? Will there be filming tonight?"

Sherri laughed. "Here? No way. People that come to these events are very private. Why do you think they took our cellphones from us at the door?"

"To make some extra money?"

She laughed again and tugged on his arm. "C'mon, my smart-ass boyfriend. Let's go mingle with the beautiful people."

As they made their way down the hall, Kevin noticed the walls were covered in bookshelves and adorned with a variety of framed pictures, magazine covers, and newspaper clippings.

"Good to see another doctor not thinking he's God." He pointed to a faded cover of a DETROIT MONTHLY magazine. The face of a middle-aged man—short dark hair with strategically placed gray on the sides, light brown eyes, high cheekbones and prominent nose—was over a caption reading "Irwin Rothstein: Detroit's Doctor of the Year."

"Dr. Rothstein does have a big ego, but he's really a nice guy," Sherri said. She peered closer at one book on the shelves, then pulled it out.

Kevin looked over her shoulder; the title of the thick tome was *Germanic Neolithic Runes*.

"I think this is the book that I saw your tats and scarifications in," she explained, flipping through the pages. After a few seconds she handed the book to Kevin. "Here, knock yourself out."

He put the book back on the shelf. "I'm here to spend time with my girlfriend, not to look at dead German script." Kevin tilted his head and read off some titles of the numerous books. "Runic Magic in the Middle Ages. . . . The Sacred Stones of Externsteine. . . . Alchemy Throughout the Ages." He nudged Sherri. "Your Dr. Rothstein sure has an interesting library. I wonder if he's a witch."

"Warlock. That's what I think male witches are correctly called." Kevin looked at her and she started to laugh. "No, he's not a warlock or witch. At least I don't think so."

They continued their way down the hall and Kevin continued to scan the framed articles. He stopped midway down the hall.

"Wonder what this is about," he murmured, reading aloud the yellowed paper. "New York Times, September 13, 1937. A miracle cure for burns?" Kevin scanned the paper and read more. "David Solomon Rothstein, famed surgeon at the Berlin Medical Academy, announced yesterday a new procedure using human skin cells grown in the laboratory to replace skin destroyed by burns that previously would be a road to certain death. Dr. Rothstein states that . . . that . . ." he stopped speaking and turned to Sherri. "Think that this is Rothstein's grandfather?"

"Could be." Sherri pulled on his hand. "Let's go find him and you can ask."

The hallway emptied out into a large, circular ballroom and Kevin's first thought was that he had entered a Hollywood makeup studio. Off to the left, standing next to a roaring fireplace stood a tall, lean woman with long sharpened canines pushing out over full red lips, her deathly pale skin highlighted by a short black dress. To his right was a young man dressed in a green one-piece jumper with three divots across his forehead, looking as if someone had punched him repeatedly with a golf ball, leaving perfectly circular craters. The crater-headed man was standing next to the piano and talking to its player, an extremely muscular, deeply tanned man who was nude. Kevin couldn't help but notice the man's long, flaccid cock. The shaft was adorned with multiple rows of symmetrical, circular lumps from the base to the head, which was pierced with three rows of miniature barbells.

"I think I'm way under-dressed and too normal for this party," Kevin said.

"You look fine." She turned and kissed him. "I'm actually into guys with non-implanted cocks."

"That's good, since even for you there's no way in hell I'm getting my dick pierced or skewered."

Sherri laughed. "It's something though, isn't it? Dr. Rothstein did the penile lengthening as well as the bead implants."

"I'm sure Dianabol and a tanning booth took care of the rest of the look." Kevin continued to look around the room, trying not to be too conspicuous in his stares as more people, mods and non-mods, filled the room.

Sherri squeezed Kevin's hand. "He plays quite well, don't you think?"

Kevin drew his eyes away from the crowd. "Who?"

"The guy playing the piano." Sherri giggled. "I'm sorry—I forgot how overwhelming it can be the first time at one of Dr. Rothstein's gigs."

"It is surreal." He looked at the piano player and listened for a few seconds. "And you're right. He is good. Mozart, C major, if I remember correctly."

"I'm impressed."

"My mom made me take piano lessons for five years."

"You know, just when I think I'm beginning to know you, you bring up something that surprises me."

I'm sure there are some surprises you wouldn't want to hear.

"My dad always said to keep them guessing."

Sherri laughed, then she stood on her tiptoes and waved. "Hey, Peter! Delmond! Over here!"

Peter and Delmond, along with a middle-aged man, made their way through the crowd. It was only when they were closer that Kevin realized the man was Dr. Irwin Rothstein. He appeared short—Kevin guessed five foot six, with more white in his hair than in the Detroit Monthly picture—dressed in a gray suit, black shirt and red tie. Sherri's face lit up into a large smile when she saw him.

"Dr. Rothstein," she said before embracing him. "It's so good to see you again!"

"The pleasure is always mine." He stepped back and looking at Kevin. "I take it you're Sherri's new boyfriend?"

He extended his hand. "I am. Kevin Ciano." Rothstein's handshake was firm and confident.

"I hope you realize what a lucky man you are," Rothstein said, his gaze shifting back and forth from Kevin to Sherri.

Kevin nodded. "I do." He turned to Peter and Delmond. "Good to see you two again."

"Same here," Peter grinned. He turned to Rothstein. "Kevin met the gang at our last show at the Eastown Theatre."

"The one I unfortunately missed." Rothstein nodded, then spoke to Kevin. "I hope you'll be making the October 30th show? It could prove to be pivotal in the life of your girlfriend."

"A producer from HBO named David Steinman is in the east portrait room," Delmond explained. "We were just getting ready to go talk to him."

"That's great!" Sherri gushed. "Do you think we have a chance, Dr. Rothstein?"

"I absolutely do," he answered. "Since we're now all here, let's go have a chat with Mr. Steinman."

"Is Roxy coming?" asked Sherri.

Delmond looked at Peter and they shared a small laugh.

"Roxy's already met with David," he said, "so I think it'll be fine if we go chat with him without her."

"Where is she?" Sherri asked, looking around the room.

"The last time I saw her she was with the cat-woman over at the water-view bar." Delmond grabbed Peter around the waist and pulled him close.

"Cat-woman?" Kevin said.

"A patient of mine who feels she was a cat in an earlier life," Rothstein said. "I've been helping her with some changes."

"You need to see her," Peter said to both Sherri and Kevin. "The whiskers, ears, and tail are complete, and she now has a row of teats—" he motioned with his hands down his chest and abdomen—"that will blow your mind."

Rothstein immediately picked up on the puzzled look on Kevin's face. "The cat-woman is named Serval. She feels that she was at her happiest—as a cat—when she was pregnant, so we've added a few special modifications to help her on her journey." He looked at Sherri, then at Peter and Delmond. "Shall we go meet Mr. Steinman?"

Sherri turned to her boyfriend. "I know we've only been here a few minutes and it would be rude as hell for me to leave you alone, but—"

Kevin waved her off. "It's no problem. Go talk with Steinman. I've always wanted to have a rich and famous girlfriend."

"Thanks! Promise I won't be gone too long."

Kevin passively watched her meld into the crowd of people. *I should have asked her where I can get a drink.*

He looked around, saw nothing that looked like a bar, then made his way toward the piano player, who had taken a break from his music.

"How you doing?" Kevin asked him.

The man looked up at Kevin and smiled. "I'm doing well. What do you want to hear?"

Kevin shook his head. "I don't have a request. I just need to know where I can get a drink."

"Oh." The man's smile disappeared. "What's the matter? Don't like classical music?"

"No. I mean, yes, I like classical music. It's just that—"

The man gave a dismissive wave of his hand. "Don't worry about it. The only reason I'm here is that Rothstein has done cut-rate work for me and pays me top dollar to sit like a shaved monkey and play shit I detest."

Kevin took a step back, flustered. "Sorry to bother you."

"The bar is toward the back. First room on the right."

"Thanks." Kevin pushed through the ever-growing crowd of people to another cramped hallway, turned into the first room to his right, and was delighted to see a large, U-shaped bar in the corner. He ordered a double shot of vodka and downed it in one quick swallow, then ordered another double over ice.

"Having a tough night?" the bartender mused. He was a tall, slim black man, hair cut in a double-strip Mohawk with large, four-gauge barbells piercings through his eyebrows, nose, and lower lip.

Kevin took a sip of the iced vodka and smiled. "Just feeling a little out of my element . . ."

"Know what you mean," the bartender laughed. "I remember my first gig here. I figured that it would be a bunch of tight-ass white folks. Doctors and lawyers and shit, and that they'd look at me like a freak. Then I got here and realized that I was the one who was tight-assed!" He laughed again and looked at Kevin. "I know some really rad artists who could get you some nice piercings or tats if you like what you see tonight."

Kevin could already feel the vodka erasing away the sharp edges of tension and took another drink. "Piercings aren't my thing. However," he pulled up the sleeves of his sweater, "I got the tats covered."

The bartender peered down at Kevin's arms. "Damn." He moved closer and squinted. "Man, those are some rad tats and scars. Where did you get them?"

"Some guy up north," Kevin said, wondering why the hell he was showing them off.

"The colors are incredible," the man continued, still starring at Kevin's arms while moving his head from side to side like a dog listening to a complex command.

"Colors? There's no colors to them."

"No, look." The man grabbed Kevin's left arm in a surprisingly strong grip and twisted. "It's like they change from black to brown to deep red when you move your arm. 'Course, it could also be from the tiny hit of acid I took a couple hours ago!" He finally let go and looked up.

"What did they use to ink it?"

A memory blossomed in Kevin's mind—he was held down by Bismarck and two other assholes in Readona's cell, beaten into half-consciousness, while Jackson, a drooling, stinking lump of a man, held a homemade inking needle powered by an ancient sewing machine and slowly traced the designs on Kevin's arms. After that, Readona himself used a smuggled-in blowtorch to heat up the sharpened end of a coat-hanger to burn in the scarifications.

". . . okay?"

"What?" Kevin blinked and looked around.

"You looked like you were in never-never land and I asked if you were okay." The bartender chuckled deeply. "I think you're past your limit on the vodka."

Kevin took a deep breath and slowly exhaled. "I'm fine . . ." He grabbed his drink and quickly finished it. "In fact, I think I'd like another."

The bartender shrugged. "It's your liver."

Kevin watched the clear liquid pour into his glass and willed his pounding heart to slow. He looked down at his arms, the tats and scars the same black and white they had always been, the same haphazard—at least to Kevin—designs snaking up and down his forearms and onto his biceps.

I should've looked through the book Sherri showed me earlier; maybe there's something in there that can tell me what these fucking things mean, even though I can't believe Readona put any more thought into them than the other insane shit he did in the joint.

"So, you gonna tell me the secret ingredients of your tats?" the bartender said in a light tone, although Kevin could see a more primal curiosity reflected in the man's eyes.

"I don't really remember." Kevin pulled down his sleeves and forced a smile. "I was sort of out of it at the time they were done."

"That's too bad. Listen, maybe you could give me the name of the guy that—"

Kevin felt a tap on his left shoulder and turned. It was Roxanne. She was as tall as Kevin, courtesy of a stiletto high heels, her blond hair in cornrows, wearing a tight-fitting short black dress that did little to hid pierced nipples underneath.

"I was hoping you were going to show up," she said, leaning in and giving Kevin a quick kiss on the cheek. She looked past Kevin down the bar. "Where's Sherri?"

"She's off with Peter, Rothstein, and Delmond meeting with . . ." Kevin shook his head, ". . . with the producer whose name is escaping me."

"David Steinman." She laughed. "I did my time with the little weasel last night."

Kevin raised his eyebrows and Roxanne laughed again.

"He came down to Glamor Girls—the new strip club next to the downtown MGM Casino—to see me dance."

"How long you been working there?"

Roxanne shrugged. "Just a few months. It's easy money." She motioned to the bartender. "Large glass of ice water." She looked back to Kevin and winked. "I sent Steinman home a very happy customer last night. I'm sure Sherri and the rest of the gang will have no trouble convincing him to put all our pretty faces on TV."

She gulped down half her glass of water, took a deep breath, then finished the rest in another long swallow. She casually dropped it on the bar and motioned for a refill.

"Thirsty tonight?" Kevin asked.

Roxanne gave a mischievous smile. "Something like that."

Kevin looked more closely at her eyes. Her blue irises were almost completely devoured by dilated black pupils. "You're high."

Roxanne shrugged. "You got me." She jiggled her purse. "Scored some of the best E in town. I'm happy to share."

Kevin waved her off. "No thanks."

"Mr. Clean-and-Sober now, are we?"

Kevin held up his glass of vodka and took a drink. "Definitely not sober."

"Just my type," Roxy said, grabbing his free hand. "Tall, handsome, and drunk."

Kevin laughed but did nothing to pull his hand away. "Not drunk *(but pretty well on my way)*. Just pleasantly buzzed." He looked around at the menagerie of people in the room. "You know many of these people?"

"Some. Rothstein usually throws these things two-three times a year." She pulled his hand. "C'mon, let's go upstairs."

Kevin finished his drink in one swallow. "What's there?"

Roxanne looked at him and gave an evil laugh. "What? You think I'm going to try to jump your bones?"

Kevin cleared his throat. "Listen, Roxanne, I think that you're very attractive, but—"

"Yeah, I know, you and Sherri are head over heels in

love." She snickered as they made their way up a wide spiral staircase to the third floor. "Don't worry. I'm not going to get in the way of young love, even though I am surprised that you two are together."

Kevin frowned. "What do you mean by that?"

"You're not her type."

They reached the top of the stairs and for an instant, Kevin forgot their conversation. They were in a large circular ballroom, devoid of furniture except for couches and sitting chairs lining the walls, which were made up almost entirely of large picture windows.

A cool breeze embedded with odors of river water, diesel fumes and pot blew throughout the room where a dozen other people milled about, most gazing out of the windows and talking in hushed tones.

"Pretty impressive, isn't it?" Roxanne asked him, looking out over the Detroit River and at the twinkling lights of Windsor on the other side of the dark water. "Rothstein says this is his thinking room." She snorted and sat down on one of the couches, pulling Kevin down next to her. "My opinion is that it's where he brings his latest conquests to fuck."

"Why not both?"

She frowned. "What do you mean?"

"It can be both his thinking and fucking room."

"I suppose," she shrugged, "although I prefer not to think when I fuck."

Kevin finally disengaged his hand from Roxanne's and intertwined his fingers behind his head.

"What did you mean when you said that I wasn't Sherri's type?"

"I just meant her last couple boyfriends have been more of the artistic, effeminate types. The last guy she was with before you was this forty-five-year-old poetry writer." She pulled up her legs on the couch and Kevin moved away to keep from being speared by her heels.

"You're saying that I'm too much of a brutish thug for her to be with?"

Roxanne raised her eyebrows and shook her head. "Not at all." She stretched out her legs and moved closer to him. "Not that there's anything wrong with being a hot brutish thug." She suddenly stood up and pointed out the window. "Look!"

Kevin stood up and turned around. A large freighter was gliding silently on the river, rows of blinking lights two football fields long illuminating the dark water underneath.

"Wouldn't it be cool to be the captain of one of those ships?" Roxanne said, snuggling close to Kevin. "All that power, all the control at your beck and call—what a rush it would be."

Kevin took a half step away and crossed his arms. "I guess so, or at least until you crashed."

"Roxy?"

Kevin and Roxanne simultaneously turned to see a forty-something bronze-skinned woman of medium height saunter toward them. Her light-blue flowing dress had two slits up either side exposing her trim legs, while on her upper torso the dress had a wide-open V that closed at her navel. Above, her small breasts were exposed, while underneath them Kevin saw a row of four nipples on each side descending down her chest.

"Where did you go?" The woman asked Roxanne.

Kevin saw that the woman had a half-dozen, light colored five-inch-long whiskers protruding from the sides of her mouth and ears that came to a sharp point. *This must be Serval, the cat-woman Peter and Rothstein were talking about earlier.*

"You and Lamia seemed to be having quite the personal discussion," Roxanne answered. "I went off to find someone else to have fun with."

"Don't be jealous of Lamia," the woman told her. "She's

feeling overwhelmed by her recent mod, that's all." She finally turned to look at Kevin. "Are you the boy Roxy has decided to have fun with tonight?"

"Actually, Serval, this is Sherri's new boyfriend." Roxanne introduced him. "Don't you think he's much better than the last one?"

Serval gazed up and down at Kevin. "Much better. Maybe her taste in men is finally improving."

Kevin took a step back. "You know, speaking of Sherri, I probably should go see if she's done with her meeting with Steinman."

Roxanne shook her head. "She'll be fine. Sherri can take care of herself. And don't worry—while Serval can be very intimidating, she doesn't bite."

"She's lying," Serval smirked. "Sometimes I do bite."

Roxanne laughed. "You do, don't you?" She grabbed Kevin's left hand and thrust it at Serval's chest. "Here," she said, pushing his hand down on one row of teats, "tell me that these don't feel real."

Kevin felt the nubs; they were warm, rubbery, and grew firm under his touch. A soft purring coming out of the semi-closed mouth of Serval. Roxanne again leaned into him and this time he didn't resist. At least not until he heard the loud voice of a woman that he was sure was Sherri saying, "There you are!"

Kevin immediately pulled his hand off of Serval's chest, awkwardly stepped away from Roxanne, and wildly looked around. There was a small group of people on the other side of the room staring an attractive middle-aged woman wearing a flowing white dress with a crimson-colored velvet cape, sporting two devil horns emanating from the top of her forehead walking toward him.

There was no Sherri.

Roxanne broke out in raucous laughter. "Fuck, Kevin, you thought you were busted, didn't you?" She wrapped her arms around the woman with the devil horns in the white dress. "Lamia, you damn near gave Kevin here a heart attack!"

He forced a smile. His heart was pounding wildly in his chest and he felt sweat drop down his sides.

The woman named Lamia walked on unsteady legs toward the trio. When she reached them, Kevin could see her eyes were as massively dilated as Roxy's. *Is everyone at this party on drugs except me?*

Lamia put her hands on her small, bony hips and starred at Serval, totally ignoring Kevin. "What's going on? Why did you leave me?" Her voice was high and strained.

"You said you needed some alone time, honey," Serval replied in a cool, detached manner.

"But nobody is leaving you." She he spread out her arms wide, "Everyone here is family."

"No," Lamia replied, shaking her head as tears now fell from her eyes, "no one here knows what I'm going through right now. The transformation is just too much . . . just too much . . ."

"I know it's hard," Roxy said, stroking Lamia's face. "But I'm sure that Dr. Rothstein—"

"Irwin?" Lamia's eyes lit up and her crying stopped. "Where is he? I need to talk to him, to show him what miracle is happening." She grabbed Roxy's hand. "You'll help me find him, won't you?"

"Of course, "Roxy cooed, then turned to Kevin and rolled her eyes. "Let's go downstairs to the deck and see if there's there."

Serval clapped her hands. "That's a wonderful idea! I'm sure that Mr. Paul is down there giving samples from his latest bash of hash. It's so yummy that you'll get multiple O's from it!"

Roxanne pulled on Kevin's sweater. "C'mon, Kev, let's go see Mr. Paul and have multiple orgasms!"

Kevin disengaged her hand from his sweater. "Thanks for the offer, but I think I'll pass and wait here for Sherri."

Roxanne bent in and kissed him full on the lips. "Your loss," she said after she pulled away. "By the way, I just saw Sherri walk in."

Kevin turned around. Sherri was standing at the top of the stairs. As Roxanne and her friends passed by, Kevin saw Sherri say something to her. Roxanne stopped, waved her off, then continued on. Sherri starred at Kevin for a few seconds and then walked over to him.

"What the fuck did I just see?"

Kevin put his hands out in supplication. "Nothing. Roxanne's stoned on E."

"Oh, okay—that makes it fine for her to be kissing on you when I'm not around."

"No," Kevin replied, keeping his voice calm, "she wasn't kissing on me, she—"

Coldly, Sherri folded her arms. "You're telling me she didn't just kiss you? Are you really trying to sell that shit?"

Kevin waited a few seconds and tried to clear his vodka-addled head before answering. "I'm not saying that. Yeah, she kissed me. Because she's Roxy and she's stoned." He crossed his own arms, quickly uncrossed them, and moved closer to her. "Look, I'm sorry I let that happen. This is supposed to be your night and I know I just fucked it up for you. I'm sorry, okay, and I'll make sure I never let it happen again."

Sherri tried to smile and failed. "So, I guess that means I'll just have to believe you?"

"Sherri, it won't happen again. I promise." He moved closer to her and held her shoulders as she kept her arms crossed. "You're the best thing in my life right now and I'm very sorry I've hurt you. Forgive me?"

"I'm generally not the forgiving type," she answered quietly, "but I know Roxy very well, and realize she has no filter about anything." Sherri uncrossed her arms and sighed. "So yeah. This time I can forgive you. But don't ever put yourself in a situation where anything like that can happen with her again."

"I won't."

And you better be right because I definitely believe she's not fucking around.

Kevin kissed her on her forehead. "How'd it go with Steinman?"

Sherri's face loosened and she smiled. "It went good. Actually great! He wants to film our Devil's Night show and if that goes well, work to get us a series."

"That's great!" Kevin hugged her then stepped back. "M-C-F-M: The Series. Just promise that when you're rich and famous you won't forget the little people like me."

Sherri playfully pushed him away. "Not a chance. You're going to be with me every step of the way."

"Hey!" A large, rotund man dressed in 1960's hippy clothes yelled from the top of the stairs. "Dr. Rothstein want's everyone down in the ball room!"

"Know what this is about?" Kevin asked as he and Sherri made their way downstairs.

"Rothstein probably wants to tell everyone about our deal with Steinman."

Sherri stood on her tiptoes when they reached the edge of the crowded ballroom. Kevin was glad that he had used three layers of padding over the lesions on his shoulder and thigh as he was pressed tight against the fellow partygoers. The air around him was thick with odors of perfume, aftershave, sweat and alcohol, all mixing together in a redolent stew.

"Could I please have your attention?" Rothstein announced.

He towered over the crowd in the middle of the room; Kevin guessed he was standing on a stool.

"I want to thank you all for coming tonight," Rothstein

began. "It's always my pleasure and honor to have such a distinguished group of people from all walks of life join together to celebrate our diversity, our open-mindedness, our willingness to push beyond what is considered the norm to more fully embrace our true selves. Whoever or whatever they may be."

"We want to thank you for having us!" a loud baritone voice yelled out. The crowd erupted with applause.

Rothstein put both hands in the air, palms out. "It's truly not about me. Without all of you, I could never do what I have done or hope to do in the future."

Another round of applause filled the air.

"Now before I let you all of get back to enjoying yourselves," he continued, "I wanted to let you know that a very special group of people who go by the name of the Motor City Fire Masters have just been given an offer by David Steinman to have their show taped for an HBO special!" Rothstein began to clap, and the crowd again filled the air with noise. "It's been my great pleasure to work with these Fire Masters over the years to help them realize their dreams, and I hope that I can continue—"

"Irwin!" a high, nasal voice filled the air, and like the waters of the Red Sea, the crowd of people directly across from Kevin and perpendicular to Rothstein parted. Kevin finally saw the owner of the voice.

It was Lamia.

"Irwin!" she screeched again, taking two more deliberate steps into the ballroom, her skinny arms held off to the side like she was trying to fly.

"That woman is stoned out of her mind," Kevin whispered to Sherri. "You know what her story is?"

"She's one of Rothstein's old lovers. He's done a helluva lot of work on her."

Lamia now stood a few feet away from Rothstein and pointed a bony finger at him. "Why are you starting without me? We need to show them your masterpiece, we need to—"

"No, dear," Rothstein said. "It's not about your new work. It's about something else."

"Something else?" She moved closer to him. "There is nothing elseWhat you've given me is a miracle, a fucking miracle, and you should be telling the world about it!"

She took a step back and threw out her arms.

"Move away!" she yelled, still starring at Rothstein. "If he's afraid to show what his genius can do, then I'll have to do it for him!"

Lamia reached up and in one coordinated movement slide off her cape and dress. She was naked underneath. There was a collective gasp, a few muted applauses.

Rothstein stepped forward. "Lamia, please. You need to calm down and—"

"You're wrong, Irwin." She held out her arms again. "I was born for this."

"What the fuck is she talking about?" Kevin said to Sherri. "I—"

His voice stopped as Lamia turned in a slow circle and he was able to see what the crowd behind her had witnessed. Laying on her angular, pale back were two wings, like pictures of angels from an illustrated Old Testament, translucent and shimmering in the ballroom lights like gossamer rainbows.

Kevin gasped. *This can't be real.*

They werereal though, however fantastical and bizarre it appeared. People with implanted vampire fangs, cat teats, and now a demented, stoned woman with the wings of an angel.

"Lamia, this isn't making me happy," Rothstein spoke to her like a father talking to his petulant daughter. He picked up her dress and cape and held it out toward her. "You need to put these back on now, and then we'll—"

Lamia slapped the clothing away and then kicked out, catching Rothstein directly in the balls. He dropped to the floor, clutching his groin, while shouts of 'Holy shit!' and 'What the fuck!' erupted from the crowd.

"You don't tell me what to do anymore, Irwin!" Lamia shouted, her eyes open wide in a manic state of euphoria. "I've transcended flesh and blood, and now . . . now watch me fly!"

Her wings began to shake, to move, and then, like a gigantic flower exposed to sunlight, spread out wide. People fell over one another trying to step away from the fantastical appendages as they began to slowly move up and down. Lamia's face was contorted in concentration and the veins in her back, shoulders and neck bulged out like writhing worms.

Kevin grabbed Sherri and pulled her back.

"I can feel it!" Lamia screamed, the wings moving in jerking, frantic motions. "I can feel myself fly, I can feel—"

The next sounds were simultaneous: A shriek, a banshee wail from Lamia's mouth along with the wet noise of tearing of flesh, bone, and muscle as the left wing sheared itself off her back and fell into a crumpled, bloody mess on the floor.

CHAPTER 18

A PIERCING SCREAM TO THE left of Kevin. The guttural sounds of someone puking behind him. The pressure of Sherri's nails digging into his arm through his sweater. All these things assaulted Kevin's consciousness. Yet he felt disembodied, a specter to the events going on around him as the vision of Lamia, surrounded by an ever-widening pool of blood, took him back to Fairview.

To the time of the killing.

He had grabbed the guy—a seventeen-year-old kid busted for ten ounces of pot, who ended up at Fairview because of a disinterested court-appointed lawyer and a judge who was in a fight for re-election and didn't want to appear soft on drugs—from behind. The kid flailed wildly, but Kevin was stronger and easily pushed him up against the shower wall, slick with condensation.

Kevin slammed the kid's head into the concrete twice, the second time producing a wet, crunching sound that echoed in the deserted room. In that instant, Kevin used the razor-sharp knife given to him by Readona and brought it savagely across the kid's throat.

A high-pitched gurgling noise erupted from the spot where the kid's throat ended, and his slashed trachea began. Blood from severed carotid arteries sprayed against the wall like high pressure water from a ruptured hose, splattering back and bathing Kevin in a crimson sheen. He let go and the kids' body dropped to the floor like a puppet cut off from its master's strings.

Kevin had thought that the assault would cause immediate death. He was wrong. The kid feebly grabbed at his slashed throat, blood spurting out in ever-slowing pulsations like a dying fountain. His eyes, deep brown, dilated in fear, glossy with tears, stared up at Kevin in question and accusation.

"Just fucking die," Kevin hissed, wanting with all his might to leave, to run, yet knowing he had one more grisly task to perform before Readona and his monsters would finally leave him alone.

But the kid still didn't die. The blood that had been pushing forcefully through Kevin's fingers just a minute before was now coming out in weak dribbles, adding to the red pool slowly running down the drain the middle of the room. And just when Kevin thought he had to leave or lose what little was left of his sanity, the young man, his blood splattered face streaked with clear lines of tears, reached up with one bloody hand to Kevin and tried to speak.

The words were garbled, but loud enough to hear. Over and over again.

Help me.

"Kevin? Kevin!"

He blinked and was instantly back at Rothstein's, Sherri yelling in his face. "Kevin! You have to help!"

Kevin forced himself to focus. People were screaming and yelling, either standing catatonically still or shuffling aimlessly, as if their movement alone could bring back sense to the night. Rothstein was kneeling next to Lamia, using his hands to try to stop the bleeding.

"Someone call 9-1-1!" Rothstein shouted.

Sherri swore at her cell. "Fucking thing! Can't get a signal!" She looked up again at Kevin. "I'm gonna go outside and try. Please help Dr. Rothstein!"

Kevin took a deep breath. "Go. I'll do what I can in here."

Which is what? Watch Lamia bleed out just like you watched that kid at Fairview die?

"Lamia, can you hear me?" Rothstein was saying over and over, vainly attempting to stem the gush of blood with his hands. Lamia was corpse-white in color, her breath coming in shallow, fast gasps.

"We have to stop the bleeding," Kevin said, fully aware of how self-evident that statement was but not knowing what else to say.

Rothstein's hands were pressing down around the stump of what appeared to Kevin to be a broken piece of ceramic material, patches of its smooth dull whiteness visible underneath a covering of blood and blanched muscle, torn and frayed like chewed meat off a bone.

"We need some towels," Kevin said. . He urgently turned to the crowd and saw Delmond and Peter. "Get some towels!"

"And my emergency medical kit." Rothstein added. "It's in my second surgery suite downstairs."

"I can see the light, Irwin," Lamia murmured, her eyes fluttering like a tiny bird. "I'm ready to die."

"No one is dying tonight," Irwin replied through gritted teeth.

Kevin watched the blood continue to rhythmically pump out of Lamia's back through Rothstein's fingers. *You're either a great bullshitter, Doc, or know something I don't, because in my eyes this woman is dying right here and now.*

"Here!" It was Delmond holding white towels against his chest. "Peter should be here with your kit in a second."

"Is the ambulance here yet?" Rothstein replaced his hands with some towels and started pressing back down on the wound. Like magic, they began to turn crimson.

Kevin looked toward the front door. "I don't see any. Sherri was trying to call but was having trouble getting a signal."

"Here's your kit," Peter said, squatting down next to Rothstein.

"In it there's a white container," Rothstein explained. "Get it out, open it and then pour the entire contents on the wound after I remove the towels."

Kevin watched as Peter did pulled out a white jar, similar to the ones that contain peanut butter, and poured the contents—a dull, off-green colored powder—over the open wound. Rothstein immediately put both his closed hands, sans towels, back over the wounds and pressed down hard for another thirty seconds, then slowly pulled his hands away.

On Lamia's back, where there was just a moment before a gaping wound that was spurting blood, there was now a dark brown covering, like an ovoid-shaped pancake scab. The bleeding had stopped.

"What the hell is that stuff?" Kevin asked

"An emergency coagulant I developed," Rothstein said. "A mixture of hydrophilic polymers, potassium ferrate, and a few proprietary ingredients."

Kevin glanced at Peter, who shrugged.

"The ambulance is here!" Sherri called out from the hallway.

Rothstein looked up from Lamia. "Delmond, Peter-Clear the way for the EMT!"

"Irwin?" The voice was distant, hollow, and it took Kevin a few precious seconds to realize it was coming from Lamia. He eyes were barely open, and her mouth moved in jerky, birdlike movements. "Irwin, I'm sorry. . . ."

"An ambulance is here," Rothstein said. "I promise you'll

be fine."

"What do we have here?" a young, stocky black man wearing dark pants and a long sleeve shirt with DETROIT EMERGENCY SERVICES prominently stitched across the chest, asked before reaching Lamia. He was pulling a tattered looking gurney with an even younger Asian EMT accompanying him.

"Forty-nine-year-old female," Rothstein answered calmly. "She's suffered acute trauma to her left scapula and has lost a significant amount of blood."

"Son of a bitch," the man muttered as he finally got a full view of the scene. He quickly bent down and checked Lamia's pulse, all the while staying clear of the wing.

"She's stable," he said to his partner. "Let's get her on the gurney and then get an I.V. started."

"What is that thing?" the Asian EMT asked, nodding toward the wings.

"It doesn't matter," Rothstein sighed.. "The only thing that matters is getting this woman to the hospital now."

"Whatever you say," the black EMT said as he calmly inserted the I.V. needle into Lamia's pale, thin arm, "but that sure as hell ain't something you see every day."

CHAPTER 19

T HE EMTs MOVED QUICKLY and efficiently to load Lamia, sans her left wing, onto the gurney. Rothstein stayed
by her side until she was loaded into the ambulance.

"Where are they taking her?" Sherri asked Rothstein after he came back into the house.

"Detroit Receiving. I'm still friends with a few of the re-
constructive plastic surgeons there."

He ran his hands through disheveled hair.

"All that work . . ." he sighed and looked around. Many
people had already left and the few that remained were speaking in hushed tones as they made their way out.

Peter pointed to the already congealing pool of blood
that stretched out in a crimson stain over the ballroom floor.
"What can we use to clean this up?"

"There's a mop and bucket out in the riverside store-
room," Rothstein spoke, "along with some bleach and a box
of absorbent surgical towels."

Peter nodded. "I'll get Delmond, and we'll have this
cleaned up in no time."

Rothstein grimly smiled. "Thank you."

"Is Lamia going to be all right?" Kevin heard Roxanne say. He turned to his right to see her arm-in-arm with Serval.

"I think so," Rothstein answered. "The muscle and nerve damage were significant, but there weren't any major arteries severed, even though . . ." He waved at the blood now congealing on the floor, "it looks like a butcher shop in here."

"We were thinking of going to the hospital to be with her," Roxanne said to him, "unless you want us to stay here and help."

"I think that's a great idea to go," Sherri wrapped her arm around Kevin's. "We've got everything taken care of."

Roxanne shook her head. "Sherri, give it a rest."

Sherri pressed tight into Kevin. "Like I said—we've got everything taken care of around here."

Roxanne sighed. "Let's go, Serval. Sherri obviously isn't going to quit being in bitch mode anytime soon.'"

A minute after they left, Kevin heard loud footsteps and turned to see Peter and Delmond making their way into the ballroom. Peter carried a bucket and mop while Delmond's muscular arms were filled with two large boxes Kevin assumed held cleaning material.

"Let's get this cleaned up. But before the fun begins," Delmond retrieved a fifth of Maker's Mark bourbon out of one of the boxes, "I figured we could all use this." Delmond broke the red-wax seal off the bottle and took a long drink, then looked at Rothstein. "Hope you don't mind?"

"Not at all." He held out his hand and took a mouthful himself. "Probably the best idea anyone has had all night."

The five drank in silence for a few moments, passing around the bottle. On top of the earlier vodka he had pounded, Kevin felt the numbing effects of the bourbon and welcomed it. His thigh was still dully throbbing from a few minutes earlier. *Must have bumped it in all the bloody excitement.*

"Guess it's time to work," Peter finally said. He pulled out some latex gloves from the nearest box. Everyone except

Rothstein put on a pair.

"Shouldn't you be wearing these?" Sherri asked, looking at Rothstein while pointing at the gloves.

He shrugged. "Lamia and I knew each other very well," he said in a tired voice. "I have nothing to fear from her blood."

"What about the wing?" Kevin asked.

"Yes, what about the wing?" Rothstein echoed, looking at the crumpled object like a child looking at a broken favorite toy. He bent down and tenderly stroked the faux feathers. Both Peter and Delmond took a step back.

Kevin hesitated, then touched the wing. Even through the latex of his gloves it felt silky smooth. "What's it made out of?"

"An organic polymer base, fused with micro-acrylic fibers," Rothstein pondered aloud, "It's taken me twelve years to perfect it."

He finally looked away from the wing.

"I started work on it when I was in full-time practice, never dreaming that in twelve years . . ." his voice trailed off and he abruptly stood up. "Can you help me take it downstairs? I could do it myself—the material is very light—but I'd feel more comfortable if there was someone to help me. It's already been damaged enough."

Kevin glanced at Sherri, who was on her hands and knees, scrubbing the floor after Peter had soaked up the majority of the blood with a mop.

"I probably should stay up here and help clean," he proposed.

Sherri shook her head. "That's okay . . ."

Her eyes locked on Kevin's and he could almost see the thoughts forming over her head like in a comic strip: *Go with him and ask about the hairs!*

"Are you ready?" Rothstein had his hands wrapped around the bloody stump of tissue that an hour ago had been the base of Lamia's wing.

Kevin bent over and carefully picked up what he thought of as the corner of the wing, trying not to damage any of its spider web-fine material. When he straightened up the Maker's Mark seemed to rush to his brain, and he felt unsteady.

That would be great: fall down and break the wing.

"Are you all right?" Rothstein asked.

"I'm fine." Kevin took two deep breaths. "Which way are we going?"

"Back down the foyer and take a right at the last door on the left."

Side by side, they carried the wing to the door. The air was filled with the odor of formaldehyde, reminding Kevin of high-school biology class.

"You'll get used to the smell," Rothstein said as if reading Kevin's mind as they made their way to the basement. "Since the house is sitting on land next to the canal, the previous owners had an underground watertight wall built around the entire foundation."

He stopped and turned on the lights. Kevin squinted and a loud humming filled his ears.

"The noise will quiet down in a moment," Rothstein said. "The ventilation fans are programmed to run at maximum for two minutes to clean the air."

Kevin's eyes adjusted to the multiple rows of bright overhead florescent lights and the first thought he had was that he had stepped into a Hollywood rendition of a mad scientist's laboratory.

The entire area was twice the size of the ballroom. Three stainless steel operating tables—with human-shaped forms covered by opaque plastic sheeting—sat in the middle of the room underneath banks of large circular lights. One back wall was composed of two rooms with walls made of translucent Plexiglas. Everywhere else was medical and scientific equipment. Oxygen tanks, multiple refrigerators and LED monitors and oxygen tanks to rows of tables holding scalpels, tweezers, and all manner of surgical equipment, with everything neatly arranged on benches, tables, and pushcarts.

"Let's put the wing over here." Rothstein nodded toward a pool-table sized bench up against the nearest corner of the room. He moved a large microscope and a box of slides to the side and placed his end of the wing down.

"What do you think of my suite?" Rothstein asked while collecting a bottle of yellow-colored fluid, a large stainless-steel tray, and towel from an adjoining table.

"It's impressive." Kevin fixated on the area immediately above the table holding the wing.

On the wall were another dozen framed magazine and medical journal covers and articles like the ones that lined the upstairs foyer. He moved closer and realized that almost all of them were in German. One dated 1934 read Deutsches Arztelbatt with a picture of a stately young man with close-cropped blonde hair and piercing blue eyes below the title.

Rothstein placed the equipment down and put on a pair of gloves before pointing at the 1934 journal cover. "There's been only one physician on the cover of Arztelbatt." Pride laced his voice. "He was a brilliant man, my grandfather." He took a single-bladed saw from the metal tray and nonchalantly began sawing off the lump of skin, muscle and bone from the wing. Kevin stepped away from the table and grimaced.

"Sorry," Rothstein apologized. "I should have warned you." With one final push he cut through the bone, then wrapped up the mass in a towel before soaking it down.

Kevin watched him place the tray and its grisly contents into one of the coolers lining the wall. "You going to do some type of exam on that later on to see why it ripped?"

Rothstein snapped off the latex gloves and smiled. "That's right. Do you have medical training?"

"No. I enjoyed dissecting things in biology back in high school, but medicine . . ." Kevin shrugged. "Never saw myself doing all the work it took to get into medical school."

"It is a long, grueling road," Rothstein said. "My grandfather was my inspiration." He looked up at the faded cover of Deutsches Arzteblatt and smiled. "He was a genius. While physicians in Germany were still in the infancy of plastic surgery, he was perfecting techniques that weren't repeated for fifty years. He could have won a Nobel Prize, been recognized the world over, but then the German people put Hitler in power, and it all went to Hell."

"What happened to him?"

"He and my grandmother and my father—a ten-year-old boy—were sent to the Dachau prison camp in 1941. They would have all died there, and I never would have been born, except for my grandfather's courage." Rothstein picked up a towel from a nearby cart and began to carefully clean the frames along the wall. "He talked the camp physicians into letting him work with them. After he had gotten into their good graces, he managed to steal a gun from one of the guards. He used it to cause a diversion during the influx of new inmates so that a good number of prisoners, including my grandmother and father, could escape."

"But your grandfather didn't?"

"No." Rothstein finished cleaning the frame and neatly folded the towel and placed it next to the wing. "After the war was over and the U.S. Army liberated the camp, stories filtered out about my grandfather. How the German camp physicians, the ones that weren't executed for allowing him into their fold in the first place, used him as a test subject in their experiments on skin transplantation."

"What do you mean?"

"The Nazis thought it was apropos that the great Jewish plastic surgeon should die by having his own skin torn off, piece by piece, leaving him with no dermal layer. No skin at all, except for his face. Survivors of the camp said the German doctors kept him alive for five days. Five days of hearing his screams of pain and agony. Five days. . . ." Rothstein's voice trailed off and he wiped his eyes. "I'm sure it's hard for you to believe such monstrous evil ever existed, but it did. Unfortunately, I'm sure it still does."

Kevin thought of Bismarck and Readona but said nothing.

"Thank you for your help, Kevin," Rothstein murmured. He started toward the stairs, then turned around. "Do you mind helping out a bit more?"

"Not at all. What do you need?"

Rothstein smiled, his teeth looking an unreal shade of yellow in the florescent lights. "I need you to help me move some bodies."

CHAPTER 20

KEVIN TOOK A STEP back. "Bodies?"

Rothstein chuckled. "That does sound strange." He handed Kevin a clear, full-length plastic gown that covered his arms and legs. "Here. Put this on and I'll explain."

"The City of Detroit is financially moribund," Rothstein continued, putting on an identical gown. "Because of this, certain non-essential, or at least what the politicians consider non-essential, services have been greatly scaled back. One of them is the disposal of deceased indigents."

"I'm still not getting you," Kevin repeated, wishing he had stayed upstairs to clean up the blood.

"The poor, the destitute, the people that have no one to take care of them after they've died—hundreds of people a year—were literally being stacked like cordwood in the main city morgue because no one claimed them. Don't you remember the big scandal regarding it two years ago?"

Kevin shook his head. "I don't."

I was a little busy trying not to become a corpse myself at the time.

"No matter," Rothstein shrugged. He started to walk

toward the far wall of the basement to a large set of stain-less-steel double doors. Halfway there he turned around and motioned to Kevin. "Are you coming?"

Kevin suppressed a nervous laugh. *Of course I am. Who wouldn't want to walk into a locker that probably holds dead bodies?*

"So, the truncated story is that I made a deal with the city of Detroit to help them out with their problem," Rothstein explained. "I take a certain number of corpses every month that I use in perfecting my body morphing procedures."

He opened the doors and Kevin involuntarily shivered as a blast of cold air, tinged with the oily smell of formalde-hyde, enveloped him. It looked like a large meat locker with two rows of scaffolding on either side. All of them holding corpses.

Kevin tried to look straight ahead but still, out of the corners of his eyes, in the light filtering in from the basement he could see the bodies. Most were African American but there were a few Caucasians, their pasty white flesh hanging like limbed slabs of beef. Some were covered in clear plastic sheets that did nothing to dull the morbid nature of the scene.

Rothstein motioned to his right and Kevin glanced over at a large, African American man and an emaciated white woman. Both were wrapped in plastic. "These are the two we need to move."

"Move? Where?"

"To the elevator." Rothstein pointed to the back of the room and Kevin noticed a set of controls on the wall. "The previous owner of this house started out as a butcher and worked his way into becoming a master chef. He used this freezer both for his own use and later, for his catering business." He walked to the head of the large black man and grabbed his shoulders. "If you take the feet, we'll get him on the elevator and into the truck."

Kevin steadied himself and grabbed the man by both his feet.

"He's lighter than he looks," Rothstein said. "He's been completely eviscerated."

Rothstein was right. Besides being less heavy to carry then Kevin had thought, the man was also completely stiff, making the task akin to carrying a six-foot long box. Albeit a box made of flesh and bone.

With some maneuvering, they placed the body into the elevator and the creaky doors slowly shut. There was a jolt, and they began to move upwards.

"Once a week, a mover brings a truck with an insulated carrier in the side lot," Rothstein waited as the elevator climbed at a slow rate. "He takes the bodies down to a crematorium in River Rouge that disposes of them for a reasonable charge."

"Why doesn't Detroit just do the same thing?" Kevin asked.

"Some nonsensical union rules about transporting bodies outside of city limits with the use of non-union drivers."

The elevator lurched to a halt and Kevin almost dropped the body. After they had loaded it into the truck, they repeated the procedure a second time with the woman. Rothstein then closed the back door of the truck and walked to the elevator.

"You don't lock it?" Kevin asked.

Rothstein turned around. "What?"

"The truck. You don't lock it?"

Rothstein chuckled. "No. Who's going to steal dead bodies?"

"I guess you have a point."

They rode in silence back down to the basement. Even though the air was cooler, Kevin was sweating under the plastic gown and was happy to take it off. "Is there anything else you need help moving?" he asked, rolling up the sleeves of his sweater to try and cool off.

Rothstein said nothing as his eyes fixated on Kevin's arms.

"I got these tats and scars a while ago," he disclosed, trying to remain nonchalant. "I'm sure it's nothing you haven't seen in your line of work."

Rothstein walked closer and again looked at Kevin's exposed arms. "Those are very . . ." his voice went silent for a few seconds, ". . . unique designs. May I ask you who did them?"

"Someone I used to know." Kevin shifted uncomfortably on his feet and tried to think of a way to change the subject.

"Did he suggest the designs or were they something that you came up with?"

"His idea," Kevin said in complete honesty. "To tell you the truth, I was pretty out of it when they were done. *Which happens when you're repeatedly punched in the head,* he thought begrudgingly. "If I could go back in time, they're not something I would have picked."

Rothstein continued to stare as Kevin's arms but said nothing.

"Have you seen tattoo designs like this before?" Kevin asked.

"I can't say I've seen tats or scarifications like yours on anyone else before, but . . ." Rothstein finally looked up at Kevin. "Being in the business I am, one of my major interests is the history of body modification. Did you know that the ancient Sumerians had both tattooing and scarifications down to an exact science?"

"No. I didn't know that."

"We Americans like to think we're so *avant garde* about everything—culture, sex, body modification—yet the truth of the matter is that it's all been done before, and generally at a much higher and meaningful form."

"But my tats and scars . . . you've never seen them before on anyone?"

Rothstein rubbed his eyes with the back of his hands. "I think I perhaps have seen them in some of my travels, maybe some of my research books..." he shook his head. "I've drank too much tonight. Am I starting to ramble? When I drink too much I tend to do so." He patted Kevin on the shoulder—fortunately his left shoulder—and smiled.

"It's completely understandable about regretting your mods. We all have regrets in life." He spread his arms out wide and looked from shoulder to shoulder. "So . . .what do you think of all of this?"

"It's impressive. Can't say I've ever seen anything like it."

Rothstein laughed. "That is a very diplomatic answer. A lesser man might have said that he thinks I'm a 21st-Century Dr. Frankenstein."

"Dr. Frankenstein had his laboratory on a mountain, not in a basement next to a river."

Rothstein laughed again. "Very true. But like Dr. Frankenstein, I've been persecuted for my work." His mouth turned downward. "Seven years ago, I was chief of plastic surgery at Midwestern General Hospital and on the cover of Detroit Monthly Magazine. Then I was sued for twenty million dollars by a patient for a totally benign complication of a breast reduction surgery." His face became red, and he slammed his hand on a nearby table.

"The best part of it was that the lawyer taking the case was Samuel Rothstein, my first cousin. That lousy little prick just couldn't pass up the chance at getting back at me for being more successful than him."

"So, you lost the case?"

"No, but it was a pyrrhic victory." He pointed at the door to the stairs walked toward it. "The hospital's lawyer convinced me that it would be in my interest to settle out of court."

He turned to face Kevin.

"What they meant was that it was in the hospital's best

interest. Six months later I was kicked off staff not only at Midwestern, but at Edward J. Falcon, and every other hospital in town. I lost my mansion in Gross Point Farms, my car collection . . . everything." Rothstein took a deep breath and slowly exhaled. "That's not true. I didn't lose my heritage or my skills. I slowly began to do work on the side with people like Peter, like Lamia. People who are on the outer fringes of society but are willing to follow their inner voice to do what they need to do to be complete."

"Still, it must be hard," Kevin guessed, "to have once been on the inside and now just looking in."

"It was, at least for the first few years, but now . . ." he looked around the room. "Now I'm doing work that my grandfather would be proud of and will soon be doing surgeries unheard of in the mainstream world. All in all, I'm learning to be quite happy being different." He looked at Kevin again. "Can you understand that?"

Kevin suppressed a laugh. *I've got weird fucking growths on my body so yeah, I understand what it's like to be different.*

"I guess so."

Rothstein opened the door to the upstairs. "I suppose we should head back up. Your girlfriend might be worried that I've involved you in some bizarre medical experiments." Rothstein gave a hearty laugh.

Kevin did not. He was still thinking on the growths and how Sherri would bust his balls if he didn't ask Rothstein about them.

"Dr. Rothstein?"

"Yes?"

"I know this might sound weird, but I have this friend who's convinced that he has a skin condition called Morgellons." Kevin kicked at the floor. "I really hate to ask you about it, but when he heard I was going to a party hosted by a plastic surgeon, he practically begged me to ask you about them."

Rothstein shook his head. "I'm afraid I can't give you much information. In my younger days I would have said that Morgellons are nonsense, fodder for delusional conspiracy theorists. But as I've grown older and seen the incredible variations of the human condition . . ." he smiled at Kevin. "Morgellons have been described as everything from alien parasites to a clandestine government germ warfare project run amok. Since I'm not an expert in either area, I would suggest your friend find a dermatologist and start from there."

Sure. I'll just look up dermatologists that provide free care for folks with bizarre conditions and everything will be fine!

"Well, the problem there is that he doesn't have any insurance. You wouldn't happen to know any dermatologists that do free care, do you?"

Rothstein looked off in the distance for a few seconds, then shook his head. "Not off-hand, but if someone comes to mind, I'll be sure to let you know."

"I'd appreciate it," Kevin hoped his disappointment wasn't coming through in his voice. He followed Rothstein upstairs and into the ballroom. The floor was spotless with no evidence of the bloody carnage earlier that evening. Sherri and the rest were nowhere to be seen.

"Perhaps they're on the porch," Rothstein said, and he and Kevin walked to the back of the house. There, behind a row of picture windows stretching from wall to wall, he could see Sherri, Peter, and Delmond.

The thick smell of cannabis wafted in the air as Kevin stepped outside. The second-story porch reached out to the edge of a canal, its dark water reflecting the lights of the nearby homes.

Peter disengaged himself from Delmond's arms and walked over to Kevin and Rothstein. In the dim light emanating from gas lanterns hanging on all four sides of the porch, Delmond's cheeks were flushed, and his bloodshot eyes held dilated pupils.

"Did the doctor show you his playroom?" Peter asked Kevin. "Bet you've never seen anything like it, right?"

"No, I never have" Kevin took a miniature hookah from Peter and inhaled deeply.

Peter laughed, a light, easy sound. "Take it easy on that stuff. Delmond grows some very potent weed."

Kevin exhaled and quickly felt the effects of the pot tickling his brain. He looked over at Sherri, who was in deep discussion with Delmond.

"Don't worry about them," Peter said, waving his hand in the air. "When Delmond gets high he likes to wax philosophical. Sherri is matching him word for word."

"Have you ever been down to Creektown?" Rothstein said to Kevin, who was surprised to see the older man take a hit off the pipe.

"No." He looked up and down the canal. "I grew up in the Delray neighborhood and didn't even know this place existed."

"I think I'll go rescue your girlfriend from my boyfriend," Peter said. "His rants can get a bit much."

Rothstein took another hit from the pipe.. "Three miles of canals connecting to the river, all hidden by the decay surrounding it." He handed the pipe to Kevin. "Detroit has turned into two cities. A system of growing enclaves like Creektown, where people can live and have viable communities. Other parts of the city have turned into a zombie: dead without willing to lay down and die. While the enclaves live and grow, the rest of the town festers, decays, and regresses back to nature. Or to evil."

Rothstein handed the pipe to Kevin. "Where do you live?"

Kevin took a deep breath to try to clear his addled mind. "Off of Six Mile and Conners."

"A block of twenty to thirty houses, three or four with permanent residents and the rest unoccupied or used as dens for prostitution and drugs."

"That's the place," Kevin replied. "Do you know the area?"

"I know the city."

He went to pass the pipe back to Rothstein, but impulsively took another large hit. Kevin held the bitter smoke in his lungs for as long as he could stand before blowing it out in one long exhale, like a dragon emptying itself of its flame.

A horn from a large ore freighter on the river suddenly boomed into night and Kevin flinched. "Do those things do that very often?"

"I suppose all the time, although I really don't notice them. Like anything in life, you can train yourself to get used to anything, no matter how annoying."

"And here she is!" Kevin turned to see Peter walking with Sherri on his arm. "I told you I'd extricate her from the clutches of Delmond."

Kevin put out his hand and Sherri took it.

"So, did you and Delmond solve all the world's problems?" Rothstein asked cheekily.

Sherri smiled. "Not all of them. But we did get the ballroom cleaned up."

"I saw that," Rothstein commended her. "Very nice job."

"How 'bout you two?" Sherri asked. "Take care of what you needed to in the lab?"

"Kevin was a great help, in fact," Rothstein turned to Kevin, "I want to do some remodeling of my surgical suite in the next week or two and would most greatly appreciate your help."

"Sure," Kevin said, "but I don't have a car, so it might be spotty when I can get over."

"That's why there's Uber," Rothstein reminded him, patting Kevin on the shoulder. "Does thirty dollars an hour sound fair?"

"Very fair." Kevin squeezed Sherri's hand. "That will help

me get a car, so I don't have to employ my girlfriend to drive me all over."

Sherri smiled, but to him it seemed forced.

"It's not too bad of a job," she said," and it comes with some enjoyable benefits."

"Any of y'all feel like going to get some eats?" Delmond said, walking over to the group. "I've got a hankering for a dozen White Castles!"

Rothstein shook his head. "Not the healthiest diet."

Delmond rubbed his stomach. "No, but they're sure damn tasty!" He grabbed Peter's arm. "C'mon, boyfriend, let's go."

"We probably should head out too," Sherri said. "I need to catch up on my sleep—I've got four double shifts scheduled for next week so I can take time the week after to get ready for the show on the 30th."

"The show is going to be spectacular," Rothstein said. "It will be a night to truly remember."

CHAPTER 21

THE DRIVE BACK TO Kevin's house started in awkward silence. He was exhausted, his back throbbing so much that even under the blanket of pot and booze it pained him like a fresh toothache.

And here I thought I was still in good shape; one night of lifting some torn angel wings and dead bodies and I feel like a sixty-year-old man.

It was Sherri who broke the quiet. "What's wrong?"

"Nothing Why?"

"You're squirming around in the seat like a five-year-old."

Kevin looked out the window at the shimmering lights of the city and suddenly wished they could be going anywhere but back to his house in the middle of hell.

"Maybe I'm allergic to some of the chemicals that Rothstein had in his lab," he finally said.

Sherri glanced at him. "Did you ask him about the hairs?"

"Yeah. Sort of." Kevin ran his hands through his hair and looked back out the window.

"Sort of?"

"I asked him."

"And?"

Kevin turned toward her, arms crossed. "Damnit, Sherri, I asked him." Kevin's felt a dark ball of anger grow in his chest and took a deep breath to try and calm himself. "He said that he thought Morgellons were a crock of shit."

Sherri shook her head. "Rothstein may be weird, but he's not cruel. He wouldn't look you in the eye and tell you that you're crazy."

The ball grew in size. "Now I'm a liar again?"

Sherri gave an angry glance before exiting the freeway. Woodward Avenue was dark and ominous, a river of concrete surrounded by mountains of decay.

"If I didn't care about you, I wouldn't be on your ass about it." She turned to face him after stopping at a red light. "I'm not calling you a liar. It's wrong of you to accuse me of that."

Kevin's heart was beating so loud he was sure Sherri could hear it. In the deep recesses of his mind, he knew she was right, knew that she was saying the things she was saying out of love. However, that part of him had been smothered by six years of life in Fairview, and it was easy—far too easy—to revert back to a primitive survival instinct that had kept him alive.

He looked into her eyes and said in a very even tone, "Maybe you should call up Delmond and see what he has to say about it."

Sherri's face tightened. "What's that supposed to mean?"

Kevin turned away and looked out the window. "The light's turned green."

"I know the fucking light is green! What do you mean I should call Delmond?"

"I mean you were having a deep conversation with him. It was about me, right?"

Sherri stared at him, jaw open, until she finally turned and began to drive when the light turned green a second time.

"We need to put this on hold right now," she said in a voice that held the sharpness of a razor blade.

"I just want to know why you were getting advice about me from a gay guy."

"Number one, you don't know what you're talking about. Number two, what the fuck does Delmond being gay have to do with anything?"

"I don't give a shit how people get their nut off. It's just that he dates men, not women. Asking him about me is like asking me what it feels like to suck a guy's cock."

Sherri sat stone faced, hands tightly gripping the wheel. For a few fleeting seconds, Kevin thought she was going to come back with a retort about his time in Fairview. How perhaps he did know what it was like to be throat-fucked, and if she spoke those words, he would open the car door and get out, moving or not.

Instead, she finally said, "I wasn't talking to him about you, Kevin. He and Roxanne are close, okay? I was talking to him about Roxanne."

A small light of recognition went off in Kevin's mind. "This is all about Roxanne trying to kiss me."

"She wasn't just trying, and you sure as hell weren't putting up a fight."

Kevin started to speak and she put up a hand. "I don't need someone fucking around on me. I've been in that situation before, and I won't put up with it again."

"I'm not a middle-aged poet," Kevin said, and in one corner of his mind he instantly regretted it.

Sherri laughed, a tired sound. "Roxanne . . . she is something, isn't she?"

She pulled onto Kevin's street and he swore he could feel a suffocating cloud of despair wash over him.

Rothstein was right. This place is evil. He laid his head back on the seat and was instantly asleep.

"Kevin? We're at your house."

He opened his eyes and looked around. The dim light of the streetlamp washed over his house, giving it an ethereal yellow sheen "Okay." He took a deep breath to try to clear his head before turning toward her. "Look Sherri, I'm sorry if I've been an asshole. With all the shit that went down to-night . . . the blood (*but not as much blood as when you murdered that kid in Fairview*), helping Rothstein in his freaky-ass basement lab, the booze and weed . . ." Kevin touched her arm. "It brought out the asshole in me and I'm sorry for how I've been to you. You, of all people, don't deserve it."

He thought he could detect a softening of her face. "Apology accepted."

He took her hand and kissed it. "You want to come in?"

Her brow furrowed and she jerked her hand away. "You told me you were sorry because you just want to fuck?"

"No!" Kevin shook his head. "Look, we're both tired and high, okay? I meant it when I said I was sorry. That shit with Roxy was just that—stupid shit. It won't happen again."

"I hope not." Sherri leaned over and kissed him, then sat back. "But I'm not staying."

The ball of anger inside Kevin bloomed again with fero-cious intensity. "We have one argument and you're leaving?"

"Kevin, I'm tired, I'm still pissed at you, and I'm working three double shifts next week. I'm going home to get some sleep. That's it."

Kevin tried hard to extinguish the anger, and if he was honest with himself, the fear, that churned in his gut. He wanted to say, to scream, 'I don't want to be alone! I was alone for six years in that shithole called Fairview and after watching all the craziness tonight and being freaked out by Rothstein, the last thing in the world I want right now is to be alone!'

Instead, he got out, slammed the door, and walked into the silence of his house.

The headlights from Sherri's car traced twin lines of bright light on the walls before they faded away and left Kevin standing alone in the darkness.

You should call her, a tiny voice in the back of his head said. *Call her, tell her you're sorry again, and she'll come back.*

"She won't come back," Kevin said out loud.

Then call Roxanne. The thought bloomed in his head like an artistic inspiration. *She'll come over. You know she will. She'll make you forget about Sherri, make all the pain go far away.*

"I must be more stoned than I thought," Kevin muttered, finally turning on the kitchen light. A roach the size of a small mouse scattered off the countertop onto the floor before disappearing behind the refrigerator. "To think about even calling Roxanne . . ."

He rubbed his eyes with the back of his knuckles and made his way to his bedroom. In the deep recesses of his mind the thought of Roxanne regressed, rolled itself up like a microscopic pill bug, and slept.

Kevin checked for rats and bugs before sitting down on his bed. He pulled off his sweater and looked at the hair on his shoulder. It lay flat against his skin like a skinny black worm, an alien presence that offended him to his core.

"You need to come out," he said to the hair. It was as clear to Kevin as a perfect spring morning—his life had begun to spiral out of the control the morning the lesion holding the hair appeared, a physical manifestation of the bad karma that had descended upon him.

He dried his suddenly damp fingers on crumpled bedsheets. Memories of the pain the first time he had tried to pull the hair out almost stopped him, but he was ready now. He was high enough, drunk enough, determined enough to accept whatever pain came with the action.

The hair moved.

It was like the tail of an angry snake, a short, snapping

motion. Kevin screamed and scrambled backward on the bed. The hair twitched once more, then lay still on his shoulder.

"Fuck. FUCK!" Kevin yelled as loud as he could.

He continued staring with wide eyes at the hair, the *thing* on his shoulder all the while sitting as still as he could on the bed.

"It didn't fucking move," he said after a minute of silence, his eyes never leaving his shoulder and the hair that lay on it. "I must have twitched, or it's just the pot and booze and stress . . ."

He sat totally still for another five minutes, then slowly, carefully got up and walked into the kitchen where he found the last bottle of whiskey. Picking it up with his left hand (*don't want to disturb the sleeping little hair-thing on my shoulder again because if I see it move one more time, I'm apt to just cut off my entire fucking arm with a rusty saw*) he went back to his bed and methodically drained the quarter bottle until the darkness of sleep finally, mercifully, washed over him.

PART II

There is no coming to consciousness without pain.

—*Carl Jung*

CHAPTER 22

⌐T⌐HE DREAM ENDED IN an explosion of blood.
⌐⌐ Kevin awoke in a state of panic, his heart pounding
wildly, sheets soaked with sweat, hands gripping the side of
the bed like a man adrift in the ocean holding onto a lifeboat.
Weak rays of sunlight snaked through the blinds casting crazy quilt patterns on the walls, while the low droning of the
furnace gave Kevin little comfort that he was truly awake.

He concentrated on slowing his breathing. The brutal
memory of the dream still seeped into his consciousness like
pus oozing from an open wound.

"It was just a fucking dream," he said to himself, forcing
his hands to unclench. "A crazy alcohol and drug-induced
dream . . ."

And while the dream was unsettling, moribund, and
strange to the extreme, what was unsettling to Kevin was that
he was a man who never remembered his dreams.

His fiancé, Lisa, was just the opposite. She would always
tell him her dreams, vivid, technicolor spectacles. Kevin once
told her that dreaming was too exhausting and that was one
of the reasons she needed at least ten hours of sleep to feel

rested, while he could get by on five or six.

Like many other times in their relationship, she was not amused.

Except on that very morning, he remembered. Kevin could still see the afterimages of the dream flickering in his periphery, like ghosts. He had been in a huge courtyard, large as a dozen empty football fields. The sky above appeared alive, rolling with thick clouds colored in shades of red, brown and black. Around the courtyard stood massively high guard towers like at Fairview, but shaped like crude imitations of sculptured phalluses.

Kevin walked toward the closest tower. The ground beneath his feet was soft and spongy, each step causing a putrid rotting-meat odor to permeate the air.

For some reason he stopped, and the ground began to undulate and pulsate, like the belly of a pregnant woman holding a kicking fetus.

"It's quite disconcerting, don't you think?" Kevin heard behind him in a soft, taunting voice. He turned and screamed.

It was Readona. In the real world, the man who inhabited Kevin's waking nightmare at Fairview was nondescript, almost mousey, yet in Kevin's dream he was a ten-foot tall Adonis adorned in flowing golden robes.

"What is this?" Kevin asked, his voice halting and dry.

"This?" Readona spread out his arms and pirouetted on feet that were covered in iridescent green scales. "This is my—*our*—home."

"No," Kevin said. "This isn't real. My home is in Detroit. You're still in Fairview, and—"

"I'm sorry, Kevin," Readona said, like a third grade schoolteacher talking to a recalcitrant student, "this is our home now."

He pointed to the horizon and Kevin saw mountains, ethereal shimmering conical shapes that almost touched the clouds.

"Can you hear them?" Readona cocked his massive head toward the summits. "I believe they're calling our names. Shall we give them our regards?"

"I'm not going anywhere with you. This isn't real."

Readona shrugged his thick shoulders. "It's as real as anything else in your shitty excuse for a life." He began to walk, giant legs propelling him insanely fast across the open plain. In what seemed like mere seconds, the giant dream-Readona was a tiny speck on the dull horizon, yet when he began to speak, it sounded to Kevin as if he was standing next to him.

"You really need to come over here," Readona said in a sing-song voice. "The view is incredible. I think I can even see the son!"

"No!" Kevin began to run, his legs numb and leaden, but he pushed on for what seemed like hours until he was next to Readona, who was standing at the base of one of the mountains.

"My son," Kevin said, his voice now a hoarse whisper. "Where is my son?"

"He's fine," Readona said. He pointed to the crook of his insanely muscled left arm and there, swaddled in white cloth, was a baby.

A living, breathing baby boy.

"Give him to me," Kevin demanded. A low moaning sound began to reverberate in the air.

Readona smiled, a too-large mouth filled up with razor-sharp teeth like that of a hungry shark. "I don't think so," he said, pulling the baby closer to his chest.

"Give me my son, you fucking monster!" Kevin snarled with all the force he could muster.

"I'll tell you what," Readona offered, "let's ask his mother. If she says yes, then I'll consider it."

"His mother?" Kevin said, taken aback by the statement. "Lisa's not here."

Readona pointed at the mountain and again smiled his

huge shark smile. "Everyone is here."

Kevin turned and stared. There was something wrong about the boulders at the base of the range. They kept going in and out of focus, like they were . . . moving.

That was it, Kevin realized with horror. The mountain, not just the base but the whole fucking peak was moving, and suddenly the entire scene came into crystal clear focus: it was made up of bodies.

Millions upon millions of writhing, contorting bodies, covered in the hair-like things on Kevin's shoulder.

"What's the matter?" Readona mocked, his voice nearly drowned out by the moans and screams of the people-mountain. "You're not happy to see your ex?"

Kevin tried to back away but he couldn't. His feet had sunk ankle deep into the earth. He wanted to close his eyes, to clasp his hands over his ears to drown out the overpowering sound of the people but he couldn't move, his arms useless war clubs hanging by his side, his eyelids frozen open as if held by invisible strings. He could see Lisa, her once-beautiful face nearly unrecognizable from the thick mass of hairs covering it; packed next to her, he thought he could recognize Caesar and Maria, but they were quickly pulled into the guts of the mountain, only to be replaced by other screaming bodies.

"This is ours, Kevin!" he heard Readona shout. "This is ours! Welcome to—"

The cacophony increased in volume by ten, drowning out Readona's voice. Kevin had no voice left, just a pitiful desert-dry whisper of horror as the last shreds of sanity unraveled in his mind, finally snapping when Readona smiled one last time, then like twisting the cap off a bottle of beer, pulled off the baby's head just as the dream-world erupted in an orgy of blood.

Kevin rubbed his face and looked over at the picture of himself, his mother and Lisa, still sitting crookedly on the nightstand where he had placed it before falling asleep.

That dream should teach me teach me to not get all sentimental about memories that should stay buried. Kevin pushed himself up on one elbow and reached out from under the covers to put the picture back into the nightstand. A fine cloud of dead skin wafted into the air with the motion, and Kevin finally noticed misshapen streaks of blood on the linens.

"Not again," Kevin said hoarsely, staring at his right arm as it remained dark and swollen, like he had been in a bruising fight. He slowly reached up, turned on the light, and immediately forgot about the dream.

Running in perfect parallel lines next to his tats and scarifications were six raised areas of skin, and out of three of those were more hairs, smaller but identical to the one on his shoulder. Underneath the other three lesions he could make out more hairs, like dark, terrible butterflies in their translucent cocoon getting ready to hatch.

Kevin forced down the panic building in his gut and walked to the bathroom where he found two new fully formed hairs sprouting from his left upper thigh and a perfectly lined row of three grape-sized lesions running up his breastbone to just beneath his Adam's apple.

He stood on the cold linoleum floor for another twenty minutes, scanning and feeling every part of his body that he could reach for more evidence of the hairs, like a junkie looking for one more vein to shoot.

Kevin tallied the findings up in his mind: six long hairs, three sprouted, three waiting to pop on his right arm. Two newly sprouted hairs on his left leg. The row of lesions on his chest, two lesions on his back and of course, the original hair on his right shoulder.

He sat down on the cracked floor, body wet with sweat, hands shaking with adrenaline and fear. As he tried to think of what he was going to do next, Kevin gazed down at his genitals. There, hiding in the tangle of public hair at the base of his penis, was a dime-sized lesion.

He pawed at the skin like a chimpanzee grooming its mate. *It has to be just an area of irritated skin. I haven't shaved my pubes in while maybe it's just an ingrown hair and—*

It's not just a hair, a deeper, malicious voice in his mind countered. *It's something special like all the rest, hairs that have a mind of their own, hairs that your little girlfriend certainly won't be happy to see*!

"Fuck!" His voice was loud and frantic. Kevin stood up and drew a fist back to punch the bathroom door or wall. Do anything, something to release the rage and terror that swelled in his chest.

Instead, he looked in the mirror. Looked at his face contorted with anger and fear, at his clenched left fist. Slowly, Kevin relaxed his arm and let it drop to his side.

"No." He used the sound of his voice to steady himself. "You're not going to lose it. You're *not* going to lose it."

Kevin walked into the bedroom and grabbed his cellphone. He went to hit Sherri's number and noticed with irritation that the battery icon was on low, even though he had just charged the phone. *Please answer baby. Please.*

Kevin called her three times, and each time heard the same words "Sorry I'm not answering, but hey, if you took the time the call why not take the time to leave a message!"

He left no message.

Kevin stared at the phone then punched in another number. *I hate to put this on you, Caesar, but I don't know what else to do.*

Caesar answered on the second ring.

"Hi Kev. Listen, we're just getting ready to go to church, but—"

"I have more of the hairs, Caesar."

There was quiet, then the muted sounds of hushed voices before Caesar spoke again. "Are you ready for me to take you to a doctor?"

Kevin looked at his right arm, at the fine, coal-black hairs laying docile across his pale skin. "Yeah, Caesar. I'm ready."

CHAPTER 23

CAESAR SHOWED UP TWENTY minutes later. Kevin used the time to find the loosest clothing he owned, consisting of gray sweatpants and an extra-large DETROIT LIONS sweatshirt his grandmother had gotten him for Christmas ten years previous.

Except for perfunctory hellos, both men were silent for the few couple minutes they drove down Woodward Avenue.

"Where are we going?" Kevin finally asked. The early Sunday morning street was totally deserted, making it feel like they were the only inhabitants of a great abandoned city.

Caesar cleared his throat. "Edward J. Falcon hospital."

"The Bird House? Why go all the way downriver? Receiving is closer. Hell, Mercy is closer."

"I called both their ERs on the way over. There's a three hour wait at each. A nurse at the Bird House said there's only a twenty- or thirty-minute wait there."

Kevin nodded. "I really appreciate this, C. When I woke up this morning and saw more of the hairs . . . I didn't know who else to call."

Caesar continued to stare straight ahead as he turned the

car onto Fort Street. "I'm surprised you didn't call Sherri to take you."

"I tried. We had a fight last night and she didn't answer this morning." Kevin reached over and gently put his arm on Caesar's shoulder. "I'm sorry the way I dissed you and Maria about dinner. It was a lame way to treat my brother."

Caesar smiled "Fine. You're forgiven. How was the party that you dissed your brother for?"

"Except for the blood, dead bodies, and me being an ass-hole and kissing another woman, it was great."

Caesar raised his eyebrows. "You're shitting me about the bloody dead bodies, right?"

"Blood *and* dead bodies. And no, I'm not shitting you."

"What the hell were they doing there? Making a snuff vid?"

Kevin shook his head. "No. Just Class-A weirdness."

Caesar remained quiet for a moment. "Sounds like a story best told over a few beers," he finally said.

"That it is." Kevin looked out the window again. "You don't know if the Bird House offers free ER care, do you?"

"Don't start that shit again about not being able to afford getting checked out," Caesar said. "We'll be there in ten minutes and I'll be damned if I'm driving all the way downriver to have you pussy out on me."

"I'm not going to pussy out on you."

"That's my boy." Caesar cleared his throat again. "Wanna hear some good news?"

"I'd love to hear some good news."

"Maria's pregnant."

"That's great. Though I didn't know you guys were trying to get pregnant."

Caesar shrugged. "We didn't tell anybody, but have been trying for over a year. We figured that maybe it just wasn't meant to be."

"I'm happy for you. For both of you. How far along is

she?"

"Twelve weeks. She wanted to start telling everyone last month, but I wanted to hold off in case . . ." he stopped speaking and grimaced. "Sorry, K, I know how much, well, how much it hurt you when Lisa miscarried."

"It's okay. I've come to peace with that period of my life."

Except for having horrible nightmares about monsters tearing the heads off infants, I'm just fine about that time when my life went completely to Hell.

"Glad to hear that." Caesar tapped on the steering wheel with both hands and looked at Kevin. "To tell you the truth, I'm scared shitless."

"Why? Isn't Maria doing well?"

"It's nothing like that" Caesar slowed the car as it went over the Fort Street-Rouge River Bridge. "It's being a father. What the hell do I know about being a dad? It's not like my old man was a role model for anything except drinking and beating his wife and son."

"You're nothing like your dad," Kevin said. "You're a good man, Caesar. A good friend, a damn good husband. I have no doubt you'll be a great father."

"You really think so?

"I know so."

"Thanks." Caesar slowed the car as he drove up to a tiny guard house on the periphery of a seven-story hospital parking lot.

"There's no one in there," Kevin said. "Just park."

"Chill, K." Caesar parked the car four rows away from the Emergency Room entrance. "You ready?"

Kevin rubbed his eyes with the palm of his hands. "I need some coffee."

"I'm sure they have coffee inside," Caesar said. "Let's go."

"You don't have to come in," Kevin told him. "You should go see your mom. She lives just down the road."

"I know where my mom lives." Caesar opened his door

and got out. Kevin followed his lead.

"That is one ugly building," Kevin said, staring up at the Bird House. Seven stories at its tallest point, it looked to him as if a giant had dropped three different-sized concrete rectangles in no discernible pattern.

"It's a place filled with sick and dying people. It's supposed to be ugly." Caesar took a half-dozen steps toward the entrance, then stopped and turned around. "Kev, let's go."

Kevin sighed. "Fine. But I'm not letting them do anything crazy to me in there, you hear?"

"They're not going to do anything crazy to you." Caesar put his hands on his hips. "Now let's get this taken care of."

Kevin followed his best friend into the ER waiting room. Inside the basketball arena-sized area painted bright blue and green were a dozen rows of mostly empty seats. A woman and three small, sniffling children sat at one end of the room. Another twenty-something woman, her bleached-blonde hair pulled up in a tight bun and wearing a tattered jean jacket and camouflage sweatpants sat middle row, softly humming to herself.

"I'll get us a seat," Caesar said. He pointed to a window with a small opening on the other side of the room. "Why don't you go check in."

Kevin walked across the room, which smelled faintly of urine, sweat, and cigarettes, to the check-in window.

"Hi," he said to the bored looking receptionist—a middle-aged black woman wearing bright blue hospital scrubs and diligently doing a crossword puzzle in a haphazardly folded newspaper. "Is this where I check in?"

The woman looked up over the edge of her reading glasses. "Uh huh. I need your driver's license and insurance card."

"I'm sorry," Kevin said, "I don't have either one." He pulled out his State of Michigan I.D. card and placed it in the stainless-steel holder below the Plexiglas window. The woman picked it up, looked at it a few seconds, then looked at Kevin.

"You got an insurance card?"

"No."

The woman sighed before handing Kevin back his I.D. along with a clipboard with a dozen sheets of paper attached to it. "Fill out these papers—front and back—then hand them to the nurse when you're called."

"Do you have any idea how long the wait will be?"

The woman sat partway up on her seat and looked in the waiting room. "There's only a few people ahead of you. Shouldn't be too long."

"Okay. Thanks."

"What'd they say?" Caesar asked after Kevin made his way back to his seat.

"Said they have a magic cure for weird-hair-disease and it only costs a buck ninety-nine."

"Glad you still have your sense of humor."

"You know me," Kevin said as he began to fill out the first line of the first page, "always looking on the bright side of life."

CHAPTER 24

Fifteen minutes later, Caesar nudged Kevin with a sharp elbow to the ribs. "They're calling for you."

He stood up and walked to the far end of the waiting room, where a short Hispanic orderly stood in front of a set of swinging doors.

"I'll need your clipboard," the man requested before leading Kevin into the hallway filled with eight exam cubicles partitioned with off-white curtains.

He motioned Kevin inside the last exam room to the left. "A nurse will be in to take your vital signs shortly," he said before leaving.

I should have brought in a magazine. Kevin looked at the clock on the wall. Its large black hands read 11:32 a.m. He had been in the exam room for less than five minutes and was already feeling like it had been a hundred years.

He heard voices in the hallway and a few seconds later a man with short, unkempt brown hair and a sharp, angular face wearing a white lab coat pushed open the drapes and walked in.

"Hello, Mr . . ." the man looked quizzically at a screen of

a notebook- sized computer tablet, "Maldenado?"

"You got the wrong guy," Kevin said. "My name is Kevin Ciano."

"Shit." The man tapped on the screen several times, then finally smiled. "There we go. Kevin Ciano." He finally looked up. "So what can we do for you today?"

"It's kind of hard to explain."

"Don't be shy," the man—whose name tag read Sherman Ickes, M.D.—said, sitting down on a small stool in the corner of the cramped room. "Believe me, there's isn't anything I haven't heard or seen here in the Bird House ER."

"I have these growths. They started popping up a few weeks ago and—"

"Don't worry about it." Ickes looked back and forth from Kevin to his computer screen. His voice was pressured, like he'd drank one-to-many cappuccinos. "I've seen a number of herpes cases this past month. Now the good news is that there's medication that can . . ." He stopped speaking and stared at the computer screen again. "Where the hell are your vital signs?"

"No one has been in here to take them," Kevin said. "The orderly said something about a nurse coming in but—"

Ickes waved him off. "Nurses are on strike. Only a few part-timers and non-union ones are here, and they're spread way too thin." He reached out for Kevin's right arm. "I need to get your blood pressure."

Kevin offered his left arm. "I'd rather you do this one."

Ickes shrugged, took Kevin's arm and pulled up the sleeve. He gazed at the tats and scars a few seconds before placing on the blood pressure cuff and pumping it up.

"Interesting ink and scarifications," Ickes said a minute later while taking off the cuff. "You get them around here?"

"No. Chicago."

"Nice town," Ickes said off-handedly as he worked intently on the tablet. "Too bad I never have any time to go there."

He finally looked up at Kevin. "Okay, Mr. Ciano, I'm going to have my associate come in to give you a look and then we'll get you fixed up with some medication for your herpes."

"I don't have herpes," Kevin said.

Ickes frowned. "You don't? Where did you get tested?"

"I haven't gotten tested." Kevin forced himself to remain calm, even though his heart was starting to pound. "I think it's some type of weird skin disease. I went to the library a couple weeks ago and did some internet searching and I think it might be a condition called Morgellons."

Ickes gave a condescending smile. "The internet is a great thing, but there's also a lot of crap out there. Nonetheless—" he tapped the screen of the tablet once more for another minute, "I'm sure one of my colleagues, Dr. Crockett, will be able to help." Ickes turned and was out of the cubicle before Kevin could respond.

He slowly watched as the hands on the clock turned. Fifteen minutes. Twenty. Twenty-five. *If someone doesn't come in the next five minutes I'm out of here. Caesar can bitch at me all he wants but I'll be damned if I'm waiting here for someone else to blow me off.*

Five minutes later Kevin was getting ready to leave when a young man with short blonde hair and wire-rimmed glasses walked into the room. He was dressed in a sharp dark blue shirt, black slacks and an expensive-appearing black and blue tie. He also had a stethoscope around his neck and a computer tablet in his hands.

"I'm Dr. Crockett," he said, "a third-year resident working with Dr. Ickes. He's told me you think you have herpes that might need some medication."

"I don't have herpes." This time Kevin didn't try to keep the frustration out of his voice.

"Oh." Crockett looked at the tablet, tapped the screen a few times with his index finger, then looked at Kevin. "So, what then can we help you with, Mr. Ciano?"

"I have these hair-like things. They started showing up three weeks ago. First on my shoulder, then on my leg and arm."

Crockett nodded. "Hair-like things . . . have you given any thought of what they might be?"

"I did some searching on-line. There's this condition called Morgellons that seem to fit some of my symptoms."

"I'm familiar with that." He sat down next to Kevin on the exam table and smiled. "So, is anything else going on?"

"What do you mean?"

"Any other problems you might be having," Crockett said. "Any other skin problems you're worried about, hearing or seeing things that maybe are frightening to you, having—"

Kevin got up from the exam table. "What are you talking about?" He looked at the man's name tag, which was clipped to his belt. "What kind of doctor are you?"

"I'm a third-year psychiatry resident," Crockett replied. "And there's no reason to get angry. We're just here to help."

"Really?" Kevin reached down and in one motion took off his sweatshirt. "Tell me how you can help this."

Crockett's eyes went wide. He pointed at the hairs on Kevin's arm and shoulder. "Are those things real?"

"No. They're hallucinations."

Crockett stepped away from the exam table. "Are there any more of those . . . growths on your body?"

"I have some on my back and leg." Kevin pointed to his chest. "I think this row of bumps here are more of them growing. Have you ever seen anything like this?"

The young doctor shook his head. "Never." He took a deep breath then put on a pair of latex gloves.

Kevin's breath quickened. "What are you doing?"

"We need to do a biopsy of one of those protrusions," Crockett said. Kevin heard a trace of uncertainly in the man's voice. "That way we can find out for sure what they are."

"A biopsy," Kevin said. "You mean cut it out?"

"That's right," Crockett said as he looked through some cabinets for equipment.

"I don't know," Kevin said, suddenly feeling chilled without his sweatshirt on. "I tried to pull one out, and . . ."

"And what?"

"It hurt."

Crockett finally turned around, having assembled a collection of sterile dressing, suture material, forceps, a scalpel, and a syringe.

"I'll inject some medicine called Lidocaine—" he paused. "You're not allergic to lidocaine, are you?"

"I don't think so."

"Good. I'll inject the medicine right around one of the protrusions and that will completely numb up the area."

"You sure?"

Crockett smiled. "I'm sure." He looked at the counter-top where he had assembled his instruments. "Did the nurse put the consent form over here?"

"I haven't seen a nurse since I've been here."

"We can't do the procedure without a consent form," Crockett said, as much to himself as to Kevin. "Administration would have my ass."

He began flipping through a filing cabinet filled with papers.

"So how many skin lesion biopsies have you done?" Kevin asked.

Crockett glanced over his shoulder, then continued on with his consent form quest. "Don't worry. I've done my share."

"How many?"

Crockett finally stopped his search and turned to look at Kevin.

"Kevin, it's not a complicated procedure, okay? I observed biopsies all the time when I was an intern, and—"

"You've never done any, have you? I'm just going to be

a damn guinea pig for you to get your quota or training or something like that, right?"

Crockett sighed. "Look, this is a teaching hospital—that means that patients who come in here have to realize—"

"Code Yellow in the ER waiting area!" the overhead speakers suddenly blared.

"Wait here," Crockett said, then dashed out of the cubicle.

This is fucking crazy. Kevin could hear some muted voices out in the lobby of the ER but nothing definitive. *What the hell is Code Yellow? Somebody take a big piss?*

He looked back down and his eyes wandered to the instruments that Crockett was collecting; forceps, sterile gauze, surgical tape, scalpel . . .

He stared at the scalpel, the stainless-steel blade shining in the glare of the overhead fluorescent lights like a newly cut diamond. The cacophony of voices beyond the thin veils of the cubicle continued in their garbled chatter as Kevin walked over to the instrument tray.

That doctor is crazy if he thinks I'm going to let him practice his cutting skills on me. Kevin reached down with his right hand and picked up the scalpel (it was heavier than he had imagined) and examined the razor-sharp blade. *This would do the job though, wouldn't it? Definitely faster than those cheap-ass scissors I tried to cut it with and much more efficient than just trying to pull it out.*

An involuntary shiver ran up his spine as he remembered the night before. Kevin turned his head and looked at his shoulder, at the thick, ink-black hair-like thing resting silently on his skin.

"You didn't move," he said in a hushed voice. "You couldn't have moved."

It was the hash, the bourbon, the exhaustion of one terrible fucking night playing with my mind.

You're just a hair. A thick, ugly, weird hair.

Before he could think any more about it, Kevin grabbed the scalpel and in one quick motion, placed it at the base of the hair on his shoulder and started to cut.

The hair whipped away like a hooked worm; a jolt of pain surged from his shoulder to his arm and fingers. Kevin screamed and dropped the scalpel. Blood quickly formed around the base of the hair and ran down his arm onto the floor.

"Fuck. Fuck. *Fuck*," Kevin awkwardly grabbed some sterile gauze.

He pressed it down on the hair and surrounding skin and another wave of pain erupted. Through gritted teeth he kept keep pressing and was just finishing taping it down when Dr. Crockett walked back into the cubicle.

"What's going on?" he said, first looking at Kevin, then at the scalpel and blood on the floor, then back at Kevin. "What are you doing?"

"Nothing." Kevin backed up to the exam table and quickly put on his sweatshirt.

"What did you do?" Crockett's voice was calm, yet his wide eyes betrayed his confusion.

"Nothing that concerns you." Kevin took a step toward the hallway and Crockett blocked his escape.

"Listen, Kevin," Crockett began, "you obviously have some type of condition that's bothering you. I can see how concerned you are about it, and I want you to know that I'm concerned. If you'll just sit back down on the exam table, we can get a biopsy of that hair and make sure it's not something we need to be concerned with."

"Is this a fucking prison?"

"No, but—"

"I'm leaving." Kevin brushed his way past Crockett, down the hallway and back into the waiting room, which was now three quarters filled. The ache in his shoulder and arm still hurt like a just pulled tooth and he checked twice to see if blood was running down his shirt sleeve to his hand.

Caesar was intently reading a tattered copy of the *Detroit Metro Times* before looking up when Kevin tapped him on the shoulder.

"Hey," Caesar said. "You get everything taken care of?"

"Yeah." Kevin looked over his shoulder. Crockett and a nurse were looking at him. "Let's go."

"Sure." Caesar stood up and arched his back. "So, what'd they do to the hairs?"

"I'll tell you in the car." Kevin took Caesar's arm and pushed him toward the exit.

"What's the big hurry?"

"I just want to leave." Kevin forced himself to keep moving forward and not look back. He tried changing the subject, "What was the problem out here earlier? I heard a lot of commotion."

"You remember that blonde chick in here earlier, the one wearing the camo sweats?"

"Not really, but I'll take your word for it."

"Ten to fifteen minutes after you went into the back, she started talking to herself really loud and rocking back and forth. A nurse or orderly came out and tried quieting her down."

"I take it she didn't listen."

"You got that right." They reached Caesar's car in the parking lot and he unlocked the doors.

"Before anybody could do anything, she started pulling out her hair—and I mean pulling it out by the fuckin' roots. I saw her grab a whole handful; one second there was hair on her head and the next second there was just a fist-sized area of bloody scalp."

"That's pleasant," Kevin said in a sarcastic tone, "especially to a man with his own special hair problem."

"Shit, K, I didn't mean anything like that." Caesar kept apologizing all the way out of the parking lot until Kevin cut him off.

"I know you didn't mean anything by it. Let's just move onto something else."

"Sure." They drove in silence for another five minutes until Caesar pulled onto the freeway. "One more thing about that chick—she kept saying something about this dude, kept saying 'I want Nehemiah! Nehemiah can heal me!'"

"So what?" Kevin asked, his head starting to throb with a deep headache. "Probably her dad, or boyfriend."

"Yeah, but . . ." Caesar shook his head. "That name, Nehemiah, I seem to remember it from somewhere." He glanced at Kevin. "It ring any bell with you?"

"No."

Caesar shrugged. "No big deal. So, what did the doctors say about your hair problem?"

"Not a lot." Kevin closed his eyes and laid his head back on the seat, being careful to not put any pressure on his shoulder.

"They take one off? Send it to some lab or something like that?"

"No."

"So, what did they do?"

There was silence in the car until Caesar slammed his hand on the steering wheel. "You didn't let them do anything, did you?"

Kevin finally opened his eyes and looked out the window, watched the gray, overcast sky pass by at seventy miles per hour.

"The doctor was going to cut one off. I was going to let him do it, but they called that code yellow and he took off out of the room."

"And that was it?"

Kevin finally looked over at Caesar. "No. when Crockett left, I decided to cut off the one, the original hair, on my shoulder. Just when I started it . . . it moved."

"The hair on your shoulder moved?"

"Yes." Kevin glanced at his shoulder and then quickly turned away, as if the mere act of looking would cause the hair to come back to life. "I took a scalpel that Crockett was going to use and went to cut off the hair and it—" a sudden chill ran throughout his entire body—" moved. Like a tail of a rat caught in a trap. It fucking *moved.*"

Caesar stared straight ahead. He finally cleared his throat. "Kevin, it's not that I don't believe you, but . . ." his voice trailed off and he finally looked at his friend. "You're under a ton of stress, and stress can do bad things to people, can play with their minds."

"I'm not crazy!" Kevin took a deep breath and slowly exhaled. "If I was sitting where you're at, I'd probably be thinking the same things that you are. But you saw it. You looked at it up close. It's not a hair, it's not a growth, it's something else. And whatever it is, it moved."

They drove in silence the rest of the way to Kevin's house. Caesar pulled into the driveway and turned off the car before turning to face Kevin.

"I need to get home," Caesar said. "Maria wasn't feeling good, and I promised I'd head straight back after taking you to the hospital."

"You told her what was going on with me?"

Caesar shook his head. "No. I said you had a bad case of the flu and needed to get it taken care of, so you didn't miss any work."

"So, you lied to your wife for me," Kevin said. "What kind of friend does that make me?"

"A friend who got me out of more jams than I care to remember," Caesar mused. "Listen, K, what I said before about . . . about the hair moving and you, I just want you to know that—"

Kevin put up his hands. "It's okay. Sometimes I still think I'm imagining it. I wish I was imagining it. But I'm not, Caesar. I'm *not*."

"I'll ask around at work tomorrow, see if the guys know of any dermatologists who work for free, or at least on a sliding scale." He put the car in reverse but kept his foot on the brake. "You gonna be okay? I mean, I could call Maria and tell her that you're really sick and I need to stay with you a while."

"Go home to your wife," Kevin said. "I'll be fine."

"You sure?"

"I'm sure."

"Okay, but listen—call the health department tomorrow—maybe they can hook you up with a doc who can take those damn things out without charging you big bucks."

"I'll do that."

"I mean it, K."

Kevin went to leave, then stopped. "Caesar—you got any pain meds with you, any Tylenol or Motrin or aspirin?"

"Shoulder still hurting?"

Kevin nodded. "It's not bad now, but when I think about trying to get to sleep . . ." his voice trailed off and he said nothing more.

Caesar put the car in park, reached across the seat and opened the glove compartment. "I have these," he said, handing Kevin a pill bottle. "Got 'em a few months ago from my doc after jacking my back at work."

Kevin read the label: Acetometaphen/hydrocodone. Generic for Norco 325/10.

"Maria doesn't like me taking them," Caesar continued. "Says it makes me too goofy. I was going to just throw them away, but now I'm glad I didn't."

"Me too." Kevin quickly pocketed the bottle. "Thanks man. Now go home, say hi to Maria for me and tell her congratulations about the baby."

He watched Caesar drive away then went into the house. He grabbed the last beer in his refrigerator and sat down on the couch and used it to down one of the Norco's. The cool, carbonated liquid felt like heaven in his parched mouth, and he drank it greedily, only stopping when his cell phone started ringing. Before he looked at the number, he thought it was Sherri or Caesar.

It was neither.

CHAPTER 25

*I*T CAN'T BE HIM. *It can't be*!

Kevin finally answered the call on the fifth ring. "What the fuck do you want?"

"How come it took you so long to answer?" Bismarck's voice was smooth as a barber's straight-edge razor.

"None of your damn business."" Kevin cleared his throat. "I heard you were in jail."

"Oh, that," Bismarck said, as if dismissing a minor inconvenience. "It was a misunderstanding."

"I'm sure that's what the kid said after you or some of your friends threatened him. Am I right?"

Bismarck laughed. "Kevin, what are we going to do with you?"

"How about leaving me the hell alone?"

"No, Kevin, I don't think so. The fact is that we're going to take care of business tomorrow night."

"What do you mean?"

"The shitty little record store you work at, remember? We're going to fucking rob it."

"I can't." Kevin tried to force himself to hang up, to destroy the phone, to completely sever his connection with Bismarck.

"Sure you can. You need to—"

Kevin pulled the phone away from his ear and Bismarck's voice faded away into disembodied chatter. He starred at the phone and wondered just how far he would have to go to escape the Hell his life had turned into.

"Where are you?" Bismarck's voice called out from the phone.

Kevin suddenly had the image of a miniature Bismarck standing on the floor, screaming up to him like a tiny cartoon figure.

Kevin brought the phone back up to his ear. "The signal must have dropped." He suppressed a manic laugh that was forming in his gut, his mind still imagining the cartoon Bismarck on the floor, jumping up and down and throwing a fit. "What did you say?"

"You need to pay attention, Ciano," Bismarck said, voice laced with irritation.

"Sure." Kevin swallowed down the laughter which was still building inside. "I'm all ears."

"Are you high?"

"No (*at least not until the Norco kicks in*)." Laughter now at the top of his chest, pushing against his larynx.

"Good. I need you clear tomorrow night for this job." Kevin raised his foot over the imaginary Bismarck on the floor and the tiny man's face lit up in terror. "I'll pick you up at your house at midnight." He brought his foot down and the cartoon Bismarck flattened into a paper-thin figure beneath his shoe.

"I can't wait," Kevin said before the ball of laughter burst out of his mouth.

"What the fuck are you laughing at?" he heard Bismarck say over the sound of his own manic howls.

Kevin pushed the 'end' button, dropped the phone on

the couch and collapsed on the floor, his sides aching, tears falling from his eyes as he struggled to breathe.

Finally, after what felt like forever, the laughter ceased.

It took longer for the tears.

Bismarck called back ten minutes later. He reiterated that he would be coming over to Kevin's at midnight the next evening—Monday—to pick him up to rob Honsey's store.

"Why do you need me to help?" Kevin had asked.

"Because you know how to turn off the security system and cameras, as well as the combination of the store safe," Bismarck answered as if they were the most obvious reasons in the world.

"There is no store safe."

"Sure, there is. Every little worthless store like Honsey's has a safe, and by now he's told you the combination so you can open and close on your own."

"What if I just don't answer my door when you come over tomorrow night?"

"Then I'd have to kick it in and pull your punk-ass out," Bismarck replied in a jovial tone before hanging up.

Kevin spent the rest of the afternoon moping around the house. He cleaned the bathroom twice. Mopped the kitchen floor; vacuumed the flakes of dead skin that littered his bedroom floor like dried autumn leaves.

He knew that Bismarck would be at his house the following evening as sure as the sun rose in the east. And just as sure, Kevin knew that robbing the store wouldn't make Bismarck slink away and never bother him again. The robbery would just be one more thing Bismarck (*and Readona, don't forget about the deranged puppet-master*) could and would use to blackmail him.

There was only one way to end this madness.

He had to kill Bismarck.

☉   ☉   ☉

A blustery north wind cut through Kevin's tattered winter jacket as he made his way outside to the bus stop the next morning. The dying maple tree in front of his house was nearly devoid of leaves, its gnarled limbs reaching out in silent supplication.

Kevin took a deep breath and welcomed the cold burn in his lungs. He hoped it would clear his addled brain. While the Norco had helped to dull the pain in his shoulder, his sleep was still restless and filled with thoughts of killing Bismarck.

He went over his plan again after he got on the bus, making sure to sit in the back by himself to lessen the chances of someone bumping into him and hitting the hairs. When Bismarck came over, he would invite him in. Then, in an unguarded moment, Kevin would knock him out, or at least stun him enough so that he could pull out a knife that he would hide in the couch to cut the man's throat. Then, he'd wrap him up in some old bed linens and hide the body in one of the abandoned houses down the block and hope that the stray dogs and coyotes that roamed the neighborhood wouldn't dig him out.

Yeah, it's a great plan, except for the thousand and one ways it would go wrong. Kevin tried to put the thoughts of Bismarck and the coming night out of his mind as he got off the bus and opened Honsey's store. *I need to see the light in this brutal darkness, that on Wednesday night I get to go see my beautiful girlfriend work to achieve her dream.*

Sherri had called him not fifteen minutes after his conversation with Bismarck, telling him about a MCFM rehearsal at the Masonic for the big devil's night show. Kevin had promised her he'd be there. *Sure—that's plenty of time to get over there after slitting Bismarck's throat, cleaning my house and getting rid of the body.*

He had just finished turning on the lights and turning off the security system when the store's phone underneath the front counter rang. He had ribbed Honsey a time or two about still having a landline.

"I'm old-fashioned," Honsey had said. "And besides, this phone never runs out of batteries."

Kevin reached for the phone then hesitated. *What if it's Bismarck? What if he wants to come over now? What if . . .*

The phone continued ringing and Kevin finally picked it up.

"Hello?"

"Kevin?" the voice was ragged, muffled, but he was sure—pretty sure—it wasn't Bismarck.

"Yeah?"

"It's me."

"Who?"

"Honsey!" He loudly coughed multiple times and Kevin momentarily pulled the phone away from his ear. "Where have you been?"

Kevin looked at the clock on the opposite corner wall. It read 7:04. "I got in at seven."

Honsey sighed. "You were supposed to be there at six to work on the website, remember?"

No, I didn't remember. I had a few other things on my mind last night.

"I'm sorry," Kevin said. "I must have forgotten."

Another sigh, this one even louder. "Fine. You do remember about working on the website this morning, right?"

"Yes, I remember now. Sorry I didn't get in. I'll stay late tonight to make sure everything gets done."

Hell, maybe I'll just stay until Bismarck gets here and I can help rob the place and then lock up in one easy step!

"Good. By the way, I'm gonna be late getting in today. Think you can handle things?"

"Sure." Kevin waited a few seconds, then, "are you okay?"

"My wife has breast cancer." Honsey said it matter-of-factly, like talking about a coming snowstorm or the latest loss by the Lions. "Had to take her to the hospital last night. She wasn't breathing well and had been throwing up all weekend."

"Damn., I'm sorry to hear that. Is there anything I can do to help?"

"Not unless you're on a first name basis with God." Honsey gave a deep sigh. "It's so fucked up. I just switched our medical insurance six months ago to some cheap-ass HMO, figured I could get us on a better plan once the online store took off early next year. But now that means none of the big hospitals with fancy oncology departments will even look at her case. If I had just kept us on our regular insurance, then maybe—"

"Maybe's aren't worth shit in this world," Kevin said. "You've told me that multiple times."

"I know," Honsey said in a quieter voice, "but knowing sure ain't helping my wife." He cleared his throat. "I'm gonna be leaning on you a lot in the next few weeks, Kevin. You up for that?"

"I'm up for it," Kevin said, hoping Honsey couldn't detect the lie in his voice.

"Thanks." Another pause. "Listen, you think you could run things yourself today?"

"Of course. I'll call if I have any questions."

"All right. I'll try to come in this afternoon."

"It's fine. I'll take care of everything."

"Kevin, I really appreciate this. I'll make it up to you, I promise."

"Don't worry about it. Just help your wife." Kevin hung up the phone before Honsey could say any more.

The day at the store went by uneventfully except for when, while replacing some unstable CD holders in the back of the store, Kevin slipped and hit his right arm directly on the newly erupted hairs. Like before, the pain was sharp and instantaneous, shooting down into his hand and up into his biceps. He took another Norco after that, rationalizing that he couldn't be in pain all day and run the store but making sure he took no more the rest of the day so as to be sharp for his encounter with Bismarck.

Otherwise, it was the usual: customers came, customers went, a few even spent some money. In between, Kevin worked on the website, and by 8 P.M., when he put up the closed sign and locked the front door, he had managed to forget a time or two his coming task at hand.

It all came back in full force when he went to turn on the security system. Kevin's fingers lingered over the numbers, stained and faded from the thousands of times Honsey had methodically tapped the code.

I'm sorry, Honsey. But I'm backed against a very hard wall and don't have anywhere to turn.

I hope you haven't decided to save some pennies on some cut-rate insurance policy like you did with your health insurance in order to try to make things better in the end, because sometimes things don't turn out better even when you try. Sometimes things just go straight to hell no matter what you do.

"Or don't do," Kevin said out loud. He turned away without turning on the security system, shut off the lights, and quickly walked out the door.

The north wind had brought a storm filled with rain and sleet, turning Kevin's porch into a slick, slushy obstacle course by the time he reached home. He fumbled with his keys and cursed himself for not bringing gloves.

Maybe Bismarck will decide the weather is too bad, then immediately chided himself. *Bismarck would be coming even if Jesus and the Four Horsemen of the Apocalypse came riding out of the clouds.*

Kevin sat on the couch and pulled out his phone. The white glowing numbers read 9:30.

Two and a half hours. One hundred and fifty minutes to—

The phone began ringing and Kevin dropped it like it was a piece of radioactive waste. It bounced silently off the cushion of the couch onto the floor and continued its song.

Kevin quickly picked it up and looked at the number. It wasn't one he was familiar with. Caesar, Sherri, or even Bismarck.

Maybe it's Honsey—no, that's not his number—maybe it's—

The phone went quiet. Kevin stared at the number until a new chirping tone let him know that the caller had left a voice message.

Kevin waited a moment, then hit the voice mail button on the phone and turned the volume to max.

"Hello. This message is for Kevin. This is Dr. Rothstein. I hope you remember me. I wanted to get in touch with you regarding some work I'd like to get done on my house in the next week. I believe we talked about this the night you were over with your lovely girlfriend. I hope you'll give me a call as soon as possible so we can get this arranged." He cleared his throat then continued. "Also, I have some . . . interesting information about the body art—your tattoos and scarifications—adorning your arms. You had said you knew nothing about their origins or meanings, so I took it upon myself to do some research. Anyway, we can talk about it more at our next encounter. Have a good evening."

Kevin had completely forgotten about Rothstein's offer of work. *I need to get back in touch with him since I certainly could use the money.*

And the information about the scars and tats; what was that about?

Maybe it's something from those books Sherri and I were looking at. The memory of that night came flooding back to him. *I was going to go back to look at them, but then that mess with the winged woman happened ...*

Kevin carefully pulled up the sleeves of his sweatshirt, the motion causing a dull but very real pain spreading throughout his right arm. He looked at the scars, at the tattoos, at the 3 hair-things that lay quiescent on his skin and the other three that were still covered by a thin layer of skin.

Maybe there is a connection between the hairs and the 'work' Readona did on me, but how or what? He rubbed his eyes with the palms of his hands and sat down. *Maybe that sick fuck put something in me, like those Morgellon things I read about. But what would he gain by that? Readona was nuts but there was always a reason, no matter how fucked up, for things he did. What could he gain by doing something like this to me? And if it is some type of disease, some parasite, what the hell do the figures and shapes of the tats matter, why would Rothstein say that—*

Kevin's thoughts were interrupted when headlights flashed into the living room then quickly disappeared.

Kevin looked at the wall clock. 9:57.

It must have been someone turning around in the driveway. There's no way it could be Bismarck, he said midnight, not ten.

The knock on the door was solid, loud and inpatient. Not the friendly rhythmic knock of Caesar. Not the soft, inviting knock of Sherri.

Kevin knew it was Bismarck.

CHAPTER 26

"WHO IS IT?" KEVIN said loudly.

"Open the door, Ciano," came the muffled reply from Bismarck. "It's freezing out here."

"Just a second." Kevin stood frozen in the living-room, his head jerking back and forth from the front door to the kitchen. After a few seconds, he ran into the kitchen, got a large carving knife, and after jamming it between the cushions of the couch, answered the door.

Bismarck's dark hair was white with snow and he shook it off like a wet dog. "What the fuck took you so long?"

"I was taking a shit."

"Uh huh." Bismarck glanced around the house and Kevin prayed he had pushed the knife deep enough into the couch.

"Why the fuck do we live in such a nasty-ass state like Michigan?" Bismarck continued, brushing snow off his leather overcoat onto the floor. "One of these days I'm going to move to Florida."

"Why don't you leave right now? Get a jump on morning rush hour traffic."

Bismarck winked at Kevin. "Glad to see you still have

your sense of humor. You ready to hit it, sport?"

"I never said yes to your proposal." Kevin said the words before he had time to think of their potential ramifications.

"There was no proposal. It was a statement of fact." He took off his jacket, then carefully placed it on the back of the couch before sitting down.

Kevin forced himself not to stare at the couch, to where the knife was buried between the padding. He could visualize the handle, could see in his mind's eye the sharp blade just centimeters from Bismarck.

He could also see, quite plainly, the shining, nickel-plated semi-automatic handgun nestled in a shoulder holster over Bismarck's left chest.

"You like the piece?" Bismarck unsnapped the holster and casually pulled the weapon out. "Desert Eagle .357. Those Jews are quite good at making guns." He pointed it at Kevin and smiled. "At this distance, the hole going in would be small, but going out would be the size of a baseball."

"You're a tough man holding a piece. How 'bout you put it away and we'll see how tough you are?"

"Now, now, Kevin, that's no way to talk to your partner in crime." Bismarck casually slid the gun back into its holster. "Get a jacket on and let's take care of business."

Kevin took a step back and crossed his arms. "I thought you said that you were coming at midnight."

"Did I?" Bismarck leaned back into the couch and smiled. "Guess I just couldn't wait to have fun with my old pal."

"Why are you doing this?"

"I told you: I need some money."

"Bullshit. There's a lot of other ways you can get cash. Ways that don't involve me."

"This rip-off of your boss is really bothering you." Bismarck laughed, a high-pitched, grating sound, and it was all Kevin could do to not fling himself onto the couch and jam the knife into the larger man's guts.

"Everything about you bothers me." Kevin's heart was pounding, sweat ran down his sides, and the hair on his shoulder and arms began to throb.

"You're breaking my heart," Bismarck said. In one smooth motion he pulled out the gun again and motioned the barrel at Kevin. "Sit down in that ratty looking chair of yours."

"Why?"

"Because I have a .357 pointed at your chest and I'll kill you if you don't."

Kevin tried to swallow and found his mouth dry. "Fuck you," he finally said. "This is my house, shitty as it may be, and I'll be damned if I'm taking orders from you."

Bismarck gave a low chuckle then put the gun down in his lap. "You are something. Too stupid for my tastes, but..." he shook his head again. "Fine. You don't want to rip off the store, then how about we change the plans."

Kevin frowned. "What do you mean?"

"I mean I have another proposition in lieu of our night-time thievery."

A chill ran down Kevin's spine and the hairs—his real hairs—on his arms stood on end.

"Like what?"

Bismarck laced his fingers together and cracked them. The sounds echoed like tiny firecrackers in the confines of the living-room. "You know, for all your bravado and ma-chismo, you are very naive. At Fairview for six years and you still have no clue. You learned nothing."

"I learned what evil, sick fucks you assholes are."

Bismarck smiled again, but this smile was predatory, like a lion getting ready to devour a helpless gazelle. "No, Kevin, you didn't learn." He casually put his hand on the gun. "But you will. Get naked."

Kevin took a step back. "What?"

Bismarck wagged the barrel of the gun at Kevin. "Get

naked. Take your clothes off. Show me what you got."

"You're fucking crazy," Kevin scoffed, a thick sense of revulsion slowly building in his chest.

"C'mon, Kev, don't be a prude. What's so hard about doing a little strip tease for me?"

"I'm not taking my clothes off."

*He's going to have to shoot me before I play sick games again
like what happened at Fairview.*

"I know you know that I used to watch you in the shower
at Fairview." Bismarck balanced the butt of the gun on his
right thigh and began to rub his crotch with his left. "I'd get
so hot seeing you in there, soaping up that tight ass of yours,
that I'd cum in a minute while beating off."

"I don't care if you shoot a load in your pants right now.
I'm not stripping for you."

Bismarck pointed the gun at Kevin's head. "I'm not giving you a choice. Just like I'm not going to give that little
nigger that I scoped out this morning a choice."

Kevin kept his eyes on Bismarck and didn't allow himself
to focus on the gun. "What are you talking about?"

"I'm talking about some hot piece of kiddie chocolate ass
I saw walking home by himself this morning," Bismarck said,
still rubbing his crotch. "Tomorrow I'm going to offer that
little cotton-picker a ride, take him back to my crib, and have
me some fun!"

Kevin could see it in his mind: Bismarck, all cordial and
proper, maybe offering the kid a ride, or some money, or
both. And the kid, either already too jaded and cynical to
care or one of the rare ones that still held childhood dear to
their hearts and would never believe a grownup could be the
devil in disguise.

"So, what do you say, Kevin? Need to hear more to be
convinced?"

"No. I've heard enough." Kevin was at his tipping point,
a razor thin precipice that on one side held all the doubts, all

the fears that had carried him along since that fateful night in Monroe. On the other side was an empty canyon of darkness. He choose the latter.

Bismarck's cold-blue eyes grew wide in amazement as Kevin grabbed the barrel of the gun with his left hand and pulled while simultaneously throwing a hard, straight punch with his right fist. His knuckled collided with Bismarck's upper lip and Kevin felt the satisfying crack of teeth breaking.

In one quick, brutal motion Kevin wrenched the gun from Bismarck's hand and stepped back.

"Tell me why you're really here," Kevin said, pointing the gun at Bismarck's chest.

Bismarck spit a large wad of blood onto the floor. "Fuck you, Ciano."

Kevin's right fist shot out and tagged Bismarck on the mouth again. "I'll be happy to stand here and slowly beat you to death. Your choice."

"You have no fucking idea what's going on here, do you?" Blood and spittle dripped out of Bismarck's busted mouth. "You think this is all about robbing some half-ass record store or me fucking some stupid little nigger?"

Kevin hit Bismarck in the mouth for the third time and felt another tooth crack. "I do," he said, "and since I'm the one beating the shit out of you and holding the gun, then—"

Bismarck moved faster than Kevin thought possible. His right foot shot out and buried itself into Kevin's scrotum. He crumpled to the floor while Bismarck grabbed his wrist and gave a vicious twist. Kevin felt and heard a snap—ligament or bone? —and dropped the gun, the pain in his balls and wrist fighting for supremacy.

Kevin forced opened his eyes and looked up from the floor. Bismarck was standing over him, the Desert Eagle .357 pointed at Kevin's head. His eyes were dilated in anger and he wiped away a long string of crimson sputum with the back of his hand and flung it off with an angry snap of his wrist.

He finally smiled, his Hollywood white, straight teeth coated with blood and pulled back the hammer of the gun.

Kevin stared at the barrel, and the only thought that went through his mind was that he would never get to tell Sherri again how much he truly loved her.

But he was wrong.

Bismarck did the first of three things that amazed and stupefied Kevin: He took a deep breath and slowly let it out, but instead of pulling the trigger, he uncocked the gun and put it back in its holster. He then knelt next to Kevin and hit him with a quick, vicious punch to the jaw. Kevin's head popped back, and he felt his world condense into a small point of black.

"Now we're going to see," Kevin heard a voice say, seemingly far away, as he struggled to pull himself together.

"This could have been so fucking easy," Bismarck continued, talking to himself as much as to Kevin. "But no! You had to play the tough guy, had to show me you were still the bad-ass punk from Fairview."

Kevin concentrated with everything he had and willed himself to open his eyes, to become aware again even as he was slowly slipping into the abyss of unconsciousness.

Only to see Bismarck still on his knees, holding his sweatshirt that he had torn off of him, looking down with eyes wide with excitement.

"It worked . . . it fucking worked!" Bismarck said, his voice laced with awe and wonder. "If only Charles could see . . ."

CHAPTER 27

KEVIN REGAINED CONSCIOUSNESS THIRTY minutes later. Bismarck was gone. For the rest of the night, he laid on the couch, ice wrapped in a dirty towel over his aching, swollen wrist.

He was able to doze on and off throughout the early morning hours, courtesy of two Norco's, trying to piece together the meaning of the insanity that was his meeting with Bismarck. Questions glowed in Kevin's mind like microscopic fireflies.—*What the fuck was Bismarck looking at after he had torn my shirt off? Was it the hair-things? And what was that shit about Readona?*

"If only Charles could see," Kevin whispered, repeating what Bismarck had said, or at least what he remembered him saying.

Maybe I imagined it all. Maybe it was just a bad dream.

Except an over-active subconscious wouldn't explain the blood splatter on the floor and his wrist aching like a rotten tooth.

Kevin finally got off the couch at 6 a.m. the next morning and made his way to the shower. The warm water caused his wrist to hurt more, and as he was drying off, he opened the bottle of Norco.

Half a dozen left. He starred at the pills and wondered what he would do when they were gone.

"Fuck it," he said out loud before popping one in his mouth and dry swallowing it.

He toweled off quickly, not bothering to do the detailed body scan he had ritualistically performed since the new hair-things appeared.

I'd feel if there were new ones. I'd know.

But what if they're different? A tiny, snickering voice in his mind whispered. *What if there's a*

new crop of tiny hairs covering your back and your balls? Wouldn't that be a surprise to Sherri?

"There's no fucking new hairs!" Kevin's voice echoed in the small confines of the bathroom.

He angrily rubbed the steam off the mirror and looked at his face. His lower lip where Bismarck had hit him was swollen like a marble-sized dark red balloon.

"Bet Bismarck looks worse," he said to the reflection, which didn't reply.

His cell rang and he jumped.

This better not be Bismarck.

It wasn't.

"Hello Honsey. I'm sorry I'm not at the store yet. I didn't think that—"

"Did you watch the news this morning?"

"What?"

"The news. On television. Channel Two to be precise."

What the hell is he talking about? "I don't have a television."

More silence.

"What's going on, Adam?" Kevin continued. "Is your wife worse?"

"No," Honsey said, irritation lacing his voice. "This has

to do with the store. It was broken into last night."

But we didn't break into the store! "Really? Did they steal anything?"

"No. Nothing was stolen. Though that's only because some Good Samaritan anonymously called the break-in to the cops when the prick was still in my store."

"That's good," Kevin said, glad Honsey couldn't see his shaking hands or hear his pounding heart.

"It's great because you left the security system off, meaning that if Mr. Anonymous hadn't called it in, the perp would have cleaned me out."

"I'm sorry," Kevin said, hoping that Honsey couldn't hear the lie in his voice. "Listen, I want you to take out as much money in my next paycheck to—"

"The cops called me around one this morning to come down to the store," Honsey continued. "You know, see what was stolen, broken, etcetera. I get down there and the cops still had the perp in their car. I got a good look at him." He cleared his throat. "I remembered the asshole from the day he came into the store. There was something going on between you and him."

Bismarck? He broke into the store himself last night? "What are you saying?"

"I'm saying that you knew about the break-in!" Honsey replied, his voice loud and angry. "You left the fucking security system off so your buddy could rip me off!"

"Listen, you got it all wrong. It's—"

"I thought you were different," Honsey said, his voice more subdued. "I really thought you had your act together."

"I can explain. Just give me one more chance."

"I gave you one more chance when I hired you straight out of the pen. You're fired. I won't tell anyone at the DOC about this, but if I ever see you around my store, your ass will be back in Fairview in a heartbeat. And you can be sure that I'll be changing the locks and security code."

The phone went silent. Kevin resisted the urge to throw it against the wall and instead placed it very carefully down on the end table next to the couch.

He closed his eyes and took several deep, slow breaths, willing his heart to slow its frantic pounding. "What am I supposed to do now?" he asked aloud, looking around his barren house. "No car, no job . . . hell, I'm living the American fucking dream."

His phone rang again and Kevin thought, hoped, for one crazy second that it was Honsey calling to recant on his recent outburst and give Kevin another chance.

He looked at the number. It was Sherri.

"Hey," he answered, hoping she couldn't hear the disappointment he felt, immediately replaced by the guilt that he was feeling disappointed.

"Hey yourself."

"How come you're not getting ready for work?" Kevin said.

"I was getting ready," she said. "Just wanted to call to see if you're okay."

Okay? Well, besides having crazy hair-things sprouting out of my body, getting beat up last night, and being fired this morning, then yeah, I'm doing great!

"I'm okay," Kevin lied. "Why?"

"Bismarck. I saw him on the news again this morning. He broke into your record store."

"I know."

Fuck! Why did I say that?

"You know? How?" Kevin could imagine her brow furrowed, eyes squinted in confusion.

"Honsey called a few minutes ago," Kevin said, not able to think up a lie that would sound at all true. "He thinks I had something to do with it."

"Did you?"

The question caught Kevin so much off guard that pulled

the phone away from his ear and looked at it as if it were a rotten apple he had bit into.

"Kevin?" he heard her tiny voice say.

He placed the phone back to his ear. "Yeah. I'm here."

"Did you have anything to do with it?"

A dark part of him became instantly angry, wanted to say, to shout, *how dare you ask me a question like that, the man who you've been sleeping with, the man who you say you love.*

The more rational part answered, "I don't know. Bismarck came over last night. He wanted my help to rob the store. I told him no. We had a fight. He left."

"Are you hurt?"

"My wrist is fucked up," Kevin said, feeling a hundred years old. "I don't think it's broke."

"Are you going into work?"

Kevin suppressed a hollow laugh. "No. Honsey fired me."

"Oh, Kevin," Sherri said, and now he could picture her face, eyes wide with grief and sympathy, and he wondered how he ever got so lucky to have her in his life. "I'll take some sick time from work and come over in a couple hours."

"Don't. I don't want you to jeopardize your job. They're not that easy to come by around here."

"Fuck that. I've never used one minute of sick time. They can do without me today."

"If you're sure . . ."

"I'm sure."

"Then it would be great to see you." Kevin sat back on the couch and closed his eyes. "Do me a favor and bring something to wrap my wrist along with a bottle of booze, okay?"

Kevin had finally put away the knife from the couch after giving in to the sedating effects of three Norco's in less than twelve hours when he saw Sherri's car pull up in his driveway.

"Hey handsome. What the hell is going on at the crack-house?" Sherri said as she walked in. "There's got to be at least a half-dozen cars there."

"I think they're having a big end of the month sale. Out with the old merchandise and in with the new."

"This looks painful," Sherri said, lightly touching the dark bruise on Kevin's face.

"I've had worse." Kevin pulled her closer for a long, deep kiss, ignoring the throbbing of his lip. "I missed you . . ."

"Me too." Sherri pulled out a wrist splint and two fifths of whiskey from a paper-bag she was carrying. "Here's your orders." She filled two glasses with whiskey and water and handed one to Kevin.

"How come you're keeping it so dark in here?" Sherri asked, opening the shades on the front window. "You need to let some light in—it's actually nice and sunny out today."

Kevin sat down on the couch in the shadows and shrugged. "Guess I'm feeling like a vampire."

Sherri peered at him. "Are you high?"

Kevin took a long drink of the whiskey. A lie immediately formed in his mind, but he pushed it away.

"Caesar had a few spare Norco's he gave to me. I took one this morning (*and two last night but those don't count, right?*). Between my face, my wrist and my shoulder . . ." he shrugged again and said nothing more.

Sherri sipped her whiskey and sat next to him. "Norco's and booze aren't a good mix."

Kevin grinned. "Actually, they're a great mix." When Sherri didn't laugh at his joke, he put the glass down on the floor. "You're right. I'll be a good boy and not mix my sedatives."

"I'm not your mom," Sherri said, her face tightening." You can do whatever you like."

Kevin put his hands up, palms out. "You're right. Thanks for calling me on it. I won't do it again."

Sherri relaxed and patted him on the knee. "Thanks."

"Was your boss pissed about you taking off early?"

"She'll get over it. I told her I was getting bad period cramps." She looked at Kevin's left hand and wrist. "Looks painful."

"It is." He pointed to the wrist splint. "You want to put that on for me?"

"Sure. We can play doctor and nurse."

"Why not?" Kevin said as Sherri carefully placed the black wrist splint on Kevin. "We can pretend you're a horny patient who wants a pelvic exam."

Sherri laughed and finished putting on the splint. "I think you're the one who's horny."

"Only with you."

"Let's keep it that way."

"I will." Kevin looked down at the splint. "Thanks for getting this. Feels better already."

"I'm glad." Sherri looked at his right hand and pointed to his knuckles. "I can see why Bismarck's face looked like hamburger."

"He deserved it. Actually, he deserved a lot more."

"Is there something here you're not telling me?" Sherri said in a quiet voice. "I remember the story about Bismarck in prison, but . . ." she looked into his eyes ". . . it just seems like it's more than old allegiances gone bad."

"Look, I told you before that I did some bad shit in prison. Bad. And now it's coming back to haunt me."

"How bad are we talking here? What the hell besides killing someone could they hang over your head to make you do their bidding on the outside?"

Kevin looked down at her, saw her shift on the couch, watched her hands shake ever so slightly as she lit a cigarette and knew that if he told her about killing the kid (*he wasn't a kid, he was seventeen years old and how the hell was I supposed to know how old he was?*) she would leave that instant and never come back.

"I hurt people for them. I was their enforcer. If I didn't

help him, Bismarck said he and Readona would go to the release board and tell them and that I'd end up back at Fairview." He sat back down next to Sherri on the couch. "I can't go back there. I don't know how I made it out of there alive the first time. If I had to go back . . ."

His voice trailed off and he shook his head.

"I remember my brother telling me that words couldn't convey the rotten nature of that place." Sherri turned to look for an ashtray on the coffee table and, not finding one, went into the kitchen and tapped the cigarette ashes into the sink. "I'm gone for what—three days—and you throw out the ashtray already?" shesaid, , weakly smiling as she did so.

"Sorry. I think it broke last night during my discussion with Bismarck."

"I can imagine." She took one last drag on the cigarette and the embers glowed like a devil eye in the dimness of the kitchen. "Once our show is over, I'll have to make sure that I'm over here on a more regular basis so that—"

Her sentence was cut short by a loud bang outside the house. Kevin turned and walked to the front window.

"Get down," he said in a tone that left no room for discussion.

"What?"

"Get down," Kevin repeated. "I think that was a gunshot."

"I'm not getting down," Sherri said, walking over to stand next to him. "You're not the only one who grew up in Detroit."

Kevin looked at her, opened his mouth to say something, then carefully pushed open the drapes.

A rusted late 1990s Toyota Celica, smoke billowing from a battered tailpipe that dragged on the road, sat in front of the crack-house. There were three people—two girls and an older man—clamoring around the driver, who was in animated conversation with one of the girls. The car suddenly backfired again, a loud, throaty bang, and Sherri twitched.

"Thought you were a tough Detroit chick," Kevin said.

Sherri elbowed him in the ribs. "I am. Don't forget it." She peered around Kevin's shoulder. "How old you think those girls are?"

"Fifteen?"

Sherri shook her head. "Uh-uh. Maybe thirteen. Tops." She took a long drink of whiskey and Kevin fought down a strong urge to drink his.

"I couldn't give a damn if adults want to put poison in their bodies," she said after wiping her mouth with the back of her hand, "but to sell that shit to kids . . ." Sherri shook her head again and walked away from the window. "There's a lot of evil, sick bastards in the world."

Kevin had an image of Bismarck and involuntarily shuddered. *You have no idea just how evil people can be.*

"It's hard to see people bringing kids into this world with all the shit going on."

"Yeah. I know." Kevin turned to face her. "You ever think of having kids?"

Sherri shook her head. "Not really. I used to, but now . . ." she shrugged. "I started getting the depo shot three years ago to keep from getting pregnant and the older I get, the less I think I want kids." She put her arm around his waist. "How 'bout you? Think you want to be a dad someday?"

"I don't know. I haven't thought about it since . . ."

"Since when?"

He took her hand and in silence, lead Sherri to his bedroom. "Remember when we drove over to Rothsteins, and I told you about the incident in Monroe?" he asked after they had both sat down on his bed.

"Yeah. So?"

"I told you it had been a bad day." He sighed and motioned to her. "You got any more smokes?"

Sherri dug into her jeans and pulled out a crumpled pack

of American Spirits. She took two from the pack, lit them both, then handed one to Kevin.

He took it with a trembling hand and inhaled deeply. The acrid smoke burned his throat and lungs, and Kevin suppressed a cough. "There's something I want to show you," he said. Opening the top drawer of his nightstand, he pulled out a 5-by-7-inch photo in a simple wooden frame.

Sherri took hold of the frame and looked at the picture of the young man with long hair tied in a ponytail that hung lazily over his bare left shoulder standing in-between two women. The woman to his right appeared to be in her late forties to early fifties, with short cut light brown hair, dressed in jean cut-offs and a Detroit Tigers t-shirt. The woman to the man's left was younger—twenty-one or twenty-two at the most—with thick dark hair that flowed radiantly onto her chest. She was wearing a light-pink bikini that did nothing to hide an obvious early pregnancy. The young man, who had his arm draped languidly over her shoulder, had a tight grin, like he was holding something in, while the young woman was beaming a joyous smile that could not be faked.

Sherri finally handed the picture back to Kevin. She took a drag from her cigarette, looked over at him, and raised one eyebrow. She took another drag and slowly blew the smoke out. "So you were . . . are, a dad. Did you just figure to surprise me with it one day or keep a little secret?"

"I don't why I didn't show it to you before." Kevin took another puff off his cigarette, then dropped it on the floor and crushed it out with his foot. "It's not that I didn't want you to know, but . . ." his voice trailed off and he put his hand on her leg.

She sighed, then put her hand over Kevin's. "How old were you?"

"Twenty-two."

She glanced at the photo again. "You look younger than that."

"Everybody looks younger before they spend time in the joint." Kevin looked at the picture and a tired smile formed on his face. "That's my mom and Lisa, my fiancée. She was ninteen."

"How far along was she?"

"Fourteen weeks." Kevin carefully put the picture down on his bed. "We were up at Sleeping Bear Dunes National Park in the picture. My mom went because Lisa had been having some cramping and spotting the week before. Even though she got a full checkup and normal ultrasound at her doctor's, my mom was still worried."

"Why are you telling me this?" Sherri pulled her hand away and stood up. "To let me know that you have some ex-wife or fiancée somewhere who has your kid?"

"A week after that picture was taken, we were back home. It was a Friday night. Lisa and I were at my place, a little one-bedroom apartment in Hamtramck, and she started having cramps again."

He stopped speaking and rubbed his eyes with his palms.

"The cramps were worse," Kevin continued. "I wanted to call 9-1-1, but Lisa said she was fine. That we couldn't afford a trip to the ER." He gave a sour laugh. "She said it was from the spaghetti dinner I cooked for us that night."

Kevin stood up and the full impact of the whiskey hit him in a thick rush. He reached out to keep from falling and Sherri caught his arm.

"It wasn't the food, was it?" She said in a quiet voice, holding him steady.

"Lisa went into the bathroom. I wanted to go with her, but she wouldn't let me. I stood outside the door and listened to her, heard her start crying, then heard her start screaming."

Kevin folded his arms tightly across his chest.

"I kicked the door in. She was laying on the floor, her jeans and panties around her ankles, soaked with blood. I thought she was dead."

"... but she wasn't."

"No. I reached down to touch her, and she pushed away. Her mouth was open, but nothing came out, like someone had cut off her tongue. I didn't know what had happened, what to do until . . ." he took a huge gulp of air and let it out in a loud sigh, ". . . for some reason I turned around and looked in the toilet."

"Kevin, you don't have to—"

"My son was floating in the fucking toilet. My son . . ." his voice cracked and he took another deep breath, "I didn't think a fourteen-week old fetus would be big, but he . . ." Kevin again stopped speaking and held his middle finger and thumb far apart, ". . . was about this long. He had a little penis floating in the water between his perfectly formed legs and his fingers were so tiny and his eyes . . ." He turned to look at Sherri and she could see tears dripping down his cheeks, ". . . were open. How in the fuck could it have open eyes?"

Kevin sat back down on the bed.

"I flushed my son down the fucking toilet," he said, "then cleaned up Lisa and got very, very drunk."

Sherri put her arm around his shoulder. "I am so sorry."

"That was the day I gave up," he said. "Gave up on everything—on Lisa, on my health, on my life. I felt like I had died. I think of that day as T-D-O-D—The Day of Death. I never understood—never knew—what people meant when their soul died. But on that day, I learned.

"I was fired a few months after that for not showing up for work or showing up drunk and stoned. Lisa and I went bad fast. I was so much into my own self-pity I wasn't there for her. A week after being fired she left me. It was that night when I went to a little bar in Monroe and found out how truly bad life could get."

They sat in silence for a few moments before Sherri broke the spell. "What happened to Lisa?"

"No idea. I think she headed to California. She always

said she hated Michigan." Kevin shook his head. "I don't blame her for an instant. Hell, I never even thought about what the miscarriage, that rotten fucking night, did to her." He stood up, wobbling slightly. "Want another drink?"

She shook her head. "I have rehearsal tomorrow night. There's a ton of shit I need to get done before then."

"Oh. Yeah."

Sherri got up and looked down at Kevin. "Why did you tell me that story?"

Kevin sighed. "I don't know. Maybe to let you know I'm not the same self-centered asshole I was. At least I don't think I am. (*I bet that kid who you butchered at Fairview to save you own skin might beg to differ on that!*) To let you know that me being an ignorant asshole the other night with Roxy was just that: me being stupid and ignorant, no more, no less."

Kevin grabbed her hand. "I love you, Sherri, and I'm going to do everything I can to be the best man I can be for you. I need you to believe me when I say that."

She pulled his hand to her mouth and kissed it. "I believe you. And while I could say I know how bad that night was, the fact of the matter is I don't. I've never been pregnant, never had a miscarriage, never had to deal with that kind of Hell." She stood up, took a long drink, then crossed her arms. "And so, I don't want you to take what I'm going to say wrong, to think that I'm some callous, unfeeling bitch."

"I know you're not."

"You might in a moment."

"Why?"

"Kevin, I believe actions speak louder than words. You can't be wallowing in your own self-pity and drowning it away with booze and drugs."

"I don't think I'm doing that."

"Well, I think you are, and this is not a path you want to go down, because if you do . . ." she turned to look at him and he saw she still had tears in her eyes, ". . . then I won't go down there with you."

"What are you talking about?"

"What happened to you, with Lisa, with your unborn son, all the shit at Fairview—it's done." She lit another cigarette. "I've had bad shit happen to me too. Maybe not as bad as what happened to you, but to me at the time, it was. I also tried to drown myself with drugs, with booze, with random hook-ups with men and women just as screwed up as I was. But I learned that you can't let that bad shit define you or shape you, because if you do, that time in your life has won. You have to let it go."

The face of the man-child he butchered at Fairview flashed in Kevin's mind. The dark brown eyes, wide with terror, mouth gaping open and shut like a fish out of water, blood spurting out onto the cold, grimy shower tiles.

"I-I don't know how to do that," Kevin said in a near whisper. "I don't know how to let it all go."

Sherri held his hands. "I know it's shitty. I *know*. But you have to decide that you're going to get through it and let it go. If you don't," she put her hand under his chin, "I can't be with you. I can't go into that dark hole of self-destructive pain again . . ."

He pulled her tight and they kissed, tongues entwined, and Kevin reached around and unsnapped her bra. Her nipples became hard under his fingers and soft moans escaped her throat.

"I have to go," Sherri reluctantly said after finally pulling away. "But before I leave-" she slid off the couch to her knees and smiled up at Kevin as she expertly unsnapped his jeans and pulled them along with his underwear down to his hips. Kevin closed his eyes and felt himself grow hard as he waited for her touch.

"Kevin . . ." Sherri's voice went silent, and he looked down. She was staring at his cock.

No, not there—she's looking at the damn gauze you put on

that bump at the base of your dick!

"What's wrong?" Kevin asked.

She looked up at him, a frown on her face. "Why do you have gauze wrapped around the base of your cock?"

He suddenly felt stupid with his jeans around his hips and his dick quickly going limp. "There's a bump down there. It's probably just an ingrown hair, but . . ."

"Bumps? You mean more of those hair things?"

"I don't know!" Kevin said, louder than he intended. "I thought I saw one (*and don't bother to tell her about the new tricks the hair on your shoulder can do or the new ones on your arms or chest because that would just add fuel to the fire*). I'm probably just being paranoid."

Sherri pushed herself away and up. "Damnit, Kevin, you have to get those things taken care of! If you're getting more of them, it could be something serious." She bent down, quickly kissed Kevin, then walked to the door. "Promise me you'll get those hairs and bumps looked at tomorrow."

"I'll get a taxi and take me over to the DMC Urgent Care," he said, knowing full well it was a lie.

"Promise?"

Kevin pulled his pants up and forced a smile. "Sure. Anything for you, my love."

"Good." She opened the door, then turned back around. "You're going to come to the rehearsal tomorrow night, right?"

"Of course. I wouldn't miss it for anything in the world."

"You're going to be amazed! I love you."

"I love you too," Kevin said. He didn't to get up to watch her leave.

Kevin sat on the couch for another five minutes, staring listlessly at the wall, before finally getting up to grab the half-empty bottle of whiskey in the kitchen. He carefully made his way to his room where he methodically finished the rest of the alcohol in even, measured drinks.

CHAPTER 28

I T WAS THE WORST hangover of Kevin's life. He had awoken at seven the next morning, head throbbing in perfect timing to his racing heart, mouth dry and cottony, his entire body feeling like he had been beat and thrown down two flights of stairs. His skin from head to toe felt raw and itchy and he forced himself into the shower to try and bring some relief to his misery, even forgoing the bottle of Norco that sat next to his bed.

The sensation of the warm water hitting his skin was at first soothing, but quickly turned into a feeling of rough sandpaper being dragged over his body. The itching in his arms, chest and groin grew from annoying to unbearable, and as Kevin scratched, his skin came off.

It was like the after-effects of a bad sunburn; long strips of skin peeled off like a shedding snake. Underneath the skin, descending down his chest in a perfect line, were a row of coal-black hairs sticking out like short hypodermic needles. Both his arms now held even longer hairs intertwined between his scars and tats, looking like some crazed organic framing. And in his groin was a thick, short hair protruding out of the skin at the base of his dick like a miniature coal-black unicorn horn. He reached down, nails caked with bloody skin brushed his finger across it. It was hard, stiff like bristles on a brush of steel wool, and a sharp, burning sensation shot up his cock and into his balls.

Kevin caught his breath, held down a bolus of vomit forming in his gut, and stepped out of the shower.

"This can't be real," he said aloud, wishing with all his will that he was just having a twisted dream, a nightmare that he would soon awake from.

This is no nightmare, a tiny, dark voice in his head whispered. *This is real, your own fucked up reality, and won't Sherri be surprised when she finds out her boyfriend is turning into the wolf-man!*

"I gotta go to back to that the fucking doctor," Kevin said, standing up on shaking legs. "I'll go see that psychiatrist, tell him to cut off these fucking things no matter how painful it is."

No, you won't, the dark voice in his head responded. *You remember how much it hurt, how sick you felt when you tried to pull one out. How the hell are you going to handle having a whole fucking bunch of them cut out?*

His mind raced for an answer to that question as he eyes fell upon the hair on his right shoulder. It was now at least three inches long and as thick as a pencil. It lay like a sleeping alien life-form, and Kevin had the maddening urge to grab it and pull, pain and agony be damned. Pull until its deep, dark roots were free of his body.

"I should have done it when you first came out," Kevin said to the hair. "I should have pulled you out the first chance I had."

But you didn't, the same dark voice chided him. *You didn't have the guts, didn't have what it takes to face something head on and—*

"Fuck it," Kevin said and without further thought,

grabbed the hair.

He tried to brace himself for the pain, tried to ready himself for the agony he knew would follow his desperate actions, but it was different. Instead of the piercing, burning pain he had felt just a few minutes before when he touched the hair on his groin, this time the ache—while not as severe—was deeper, spreading like a rapidly expanding wave throughout his whole chest. Kevin braced himself against the sink, holding tight onto the hair, when it happened.

The only thing he could compare it to was when he was ten years old and tried to catch night crawlers, big, fat worms that came out at night in the empty, over-grown lot next to his parents' house. The worms, when grabbed with eager little hands, would secrete a slime that made them almost impossible to hold onto and pull out of their earthen lairs.

It was the same with the hair. One second Kevin had a tight grip on it, and the next second it was wet, slippery, coated with a thick sheen that glistened like gasoline on water.

Kevin let go of the hair and looked at his fingers. They were coated with an oily mucous that even at arm's length held a repugnant odor, like rotting meat left in the heat of the summer sun.

He stared at his fingers, then at the hair on his shoulder. Kevin could feel his mind shutting down, involuting from all the insanity that had invaded his tiny corner of the world, and part of him welcomed the looming bottomless pit of madness that he could at last find refuge in. And as that part grew stronger and stripped away the last vestiges of hope in his world, his eyes fell upon a coffee mug sitting on the edge of the bathroom sink. A nondescript mug made from yellowing porcelain with a faded old English D on the side. A mug that held two toothbrushes.

His and Sherrie's.

Kevin forced himself to focus on those two, small inconsequential items, things that he looked at every time he went into the bathroom but only noticed when he used it. He made those things the center of his universe, the things that he could hold onto, things that allowed him to crawl away from the edge of the abyss, if only for a few minutes more.

After what felt like hours, Kevin left the bathroom, put on a loose-fitting shirt and a pair of boxers, and made his way out into the living-room. Weak rays of sunlight filtered through the thick shades of the living-room window and Kevin looked for his cellphone.

I have to go see Rothstein. I can go over, help him do whatever he wants me to do, and tell him his payment can be telling me what these fucking things on my body are.

And what if he doesn't know? That dark voice whispered. *What if he's just as repulsed as you know Sherri will be?*

"Fuck you," Kevin answered the voice. "He'll know." *He has to know. He has to.*

Kevin found the phone wedged in-between the cushions of his couch. Just as he picked it up it started to ring, and for a second he crazily thought that his mind had dialed Rothstein's number.

But a glance at the tiny screen showed he hadn't achieved the power of telekinesis. It was Caesar.

"Hey," Kevin said.

"Hey Kev. What's up?"

Now that's the million-dollar question of the day, isn't it?

"That's sort of tough to answer," Kevin said.

"Why? You having some type of trouble?"

No, my friend, no trouble here—just me and my weird hair-growths hanging out. "No, just, you know . . . the usual stuff."

Oh. Okay. Listen K, I just wanted to blow you up and apologize for not calling sooner," Caesar said. "Been super-busy with Maria and baby things you know, and stuff at work, but then I saw Bismarck on TV and figured I'd better see what's going on."

"Yeah. Bismarck certainly figures into what's going on."
Kevin cleared his throat. "You want to come over tonight?"

"I was calling about that too. Thought that if I can clear
it with Maria, I could come over after work and take you to
the rehearsal for the show."

Damn. That's right. Sherri's rehearsal is tonight. Kevin
thought about the new hairs, about having to deal with people touching him, bumping into him. "I don't know, brother.
I'm feeling shitty. I don't know if I can make it."

A sigh from Caesar, then, "Okay. I'll just spend a few
minutes at the rehearsal then drop by your place afterwards.
How's that?"

"That would be great. See you then." Kevin hung up
without another word.

He desperately wanted to tell Caesar about Honsey,
about work, about the new hairs, but was still too wired. *You
can tell him tonight. What's the worst that can happen? Except
for sprouting a thousand new hairs between now and then and
looking like a b- movie monster reject.*

Kevin punched in Rothstein's phone number and took a
deep breath as the connection was made. *He'll be able to help,
he'll be able to—*

"Hello, this is Dr. Rothstein."

"Hi, Dr. Rothstein. This is Kevin Ciano. We met last
week at your party."

"Of course. Kevin. It's so good to hear from you."

"Thanks. Listen, you had said something about needing some work done at your house and asked me to call you
this week, so . . ." Kevin waited for a response and when one
wasn't immediately forthcoming, he was afraid the connection had been lost.

"That's right," Rothstein finally spoke. "I'm sorry. I completely forgot. I've just gotten invited to go over to Hungary
in three days to speak to a European conference on advanced
body modification techniques. It's a significant opportunity

for me and I've spent every waking minute on polishing my presentation."

That's really nice, doc. Doesn't do shit for me, though.

"That's great," Kevin said, trying to hide any disappointment in his voice. "How long are you going to be over there?"

"Four weeks." He laughed and Kevin could almost see his perfect white teeth framed by his tanned face. "Of course, if I get an offer to teach and do research over there, I might not ever come back to this narrow-minded country."

"I'm glad for you," Kevin said, desperately trying to think of some way to quickly end the conversation.

"Are you going to see the rehearsal tonight?" Rothstein asked, then just as quickly added, "But of course you are. I'm sure Sherri tells you about it daily. What time are you going to be there? We can talk about what I need done at the house then."

Kevin felt a surge of crazy hope blossom instantly in his chest. "Yeah, sure, that would be great. I planned on being there before the show started."

"Of course," Rothstein said. "I plan to be there around nine, so I'll see you there then?"

"Yes, that sound's great," Kevin forced a smile onto his own face, "I'll see you tonight."

CHAPTER 29

KEVIN TOOK THE LAST of the Norco's a half hour before he and Caesar left for the rehearsal. He had measured his intake throughout the day so that the narcotic kept both the pain away—pain which was increasingly become constant, whether or not the hairs were disturbed—and helped addle his brain over obsessing. Leaving his house, Kevin had nearly fallen down the porch stairs. Caesar said nothing until they began to drive.

" I'm glad you decided to come see the rehearsal," Caesar said. "I'm sure Sherri would have been really disappointed if you weren't there."

Kevin nodded but said nothing.

"So, what's really up?" Caesar asked. "Haven't seen you this stoned since our senior year in high school."

Kevin looked over at his friend. "It's that obvious?"

"Yeah Kev. It is."

"Thing are fucked up, Caesar."

"Then talk to me, Bro."

"There's a lot to say." Kevin took a deep breath and slowly exhaled. "And none of it good."

Caesar tapped his hand on the steering wheel and craned his neck to the far edge of the front window. "Wonder how far this damn traffic jam goes?"

They had been sitting in a long line of cars moving at a snail's pace for the last twenty minutes on southbound I-75. During that time Kevin had told Caesar about Bismarck, about Honsey and being fired.

And about the hairs.

Caesar had remained mostly silent during Kevin's outpouring, only offering a word of encouragement here and there. It was only after he told him about the new hairs that Caesar remarked, forcefully, that Kevin needed to get them looked at and expressed relief that he planned to see Rothstein after the rehearsal.

Kevin pointed at the exit sign ahead which read Ramsey 1/4 mile. "You could exit there. That puts us pretty close to the Masonic if I remember correctly."

"I think you're right." Caesar gunned the engine and cut into the exit lane in front of a metallic blue BMW 535ci. The driver of the car laid on the horn and flashed his brights several times.

"I think the guy behind you has anger management issues."

Caesar smiled and put his middle finger up to the rearview mirror. "Definitely. Good for him I don't."

The BMW followed Caesar to the intersection, then turned left as Caesar turned right.

"Man, this area hasn't changed," Caesar said as he drove slowly through street after street of abandoned houses and buildings.

"It was a rough place even back when we were growing up."

"This ain't rough, K. This is dead."

They drove three more blocks in silence, the one unbroken streetlight in the area casting a feeble yellow light into the quiet darkness.

Caesar loudly sighed as they stopped at the next intersection. "You have any idea where we are?"

"Yeah. Fucking lost."

"We're not lost. I'm ninety-nine percent sure that Ramsey intersects with Freemont, and from there the Masonic is just a few blocks away on the corner of Temple."

"Turn left."

"You think this is Freemont?"

Kevin shrugged. "No idea, seeing as how all the street signs have long been torn down. Turn anyway."

The destruction around them grew even worse. Kevin was reminded of a 20th-century history class and pictures of Dresden, Germany after being firebombed by the allies in World War II.

"If we don't figure out where we are in the next two blocks I'm turning around," Caesar said while blowing through the next stop sign after quickly looking from side to side. "Maria will have my ass if something happens and—"

"There!" Kevin pointed down the block at a large terra-cotta bowl with flames and black smoke billowing from its core. "Either that's the place or the crackheads are getting creative in their fire skills."

After turning onto Temple, the neo-gothic architecture of the Masonic auditorium came into view, with a half-dozen more of the flaming pots illuminating the limestone walls of the massive building.

"Guess it's just more than a night of practice." Caesar pulled into the large parking lot that held at fifty cars across the street from the building.

He parked and looked at Kevin. "I'm sorry. I wasn't thinking. You want me to just let you off in front while I park?"

"Why? Now I'm a fucking cripple that can't even walk?"

"I just thought that, with, you know, the new hairs and all that . . ."

Kevinshook his head. "No, it's on me. I'm the one that needs to apologize for all the shit I've laid on you." He shook his head then laid it back on the seat and closed his eyes. "I feel like I'm ready to lose it."

Caesar pulled the car into the lot and turned off the engine. After a moment of silence, he cleared his throat.

"I know things are looking—no, not looking—*are* shitty for you right now. But you're the toughest bastard I've ever known, and I know you'll make it through this."

"The shit I went through after Lisa miscarried, then going to Fairview . . . I didn't think there could be any worse things than that." He opened his eyes and turned toward Caesar. "This," he motioned with both hands at his body, "this insanity is something too crazy to be real, but it is. And I have no fucking idea why it's happening . . ."

"I don't know either. But you need to know that there's people that care about you, that love you, that'll help you get through this."

"I appreciate it. I truly do." Kevin slowly smiled. "Damn, we're sure getting mushy in our old age, aren't we?"

. "Nah. We're just growing up." He pulled a small bag of pot out from underneath the seat. "Told Maria this is the last bag I'm smoking."

He rolled up a fat joint and lit it up and inhaled deeply, then handed it to Kevin, who did the same. The car began to fill with smoke and Kevin rolled his window down, the damp, cold night air giving him chills.

"I've been so damn busy crying on your shoulder I haven't let you get a word in edgewise," Kevin said after exhaling a large cloud of smoke.

Caesar shrugged. "Not much to say. It's just me—Caesar Ramirez—a married, working class guy leading a thoroughly working-class life."

Kevin laughed. "No, seriously, man, get me caught up. How's Maria and the baby? How's work? They finally pull their head out of their ass and promote you?"

"Maria's doing great. Had an ultrasound the other day and the baby is looking just fine."

"You know if it's a boy or girl?"

"Boy." Caesar shook his head again. "Still can't believe that I'm gonna be a dad."

"Like I said before, you're going to do great."

"I told Maria I wanted you to be the boy's godfather," Caesar said between puffs.

"You're kidding, right?"

"No. I mean it. The kid needs someone to look up to, someone tough, someone that can—"

"It takes more than just knowing how to use your fists to be tough," Kevin said after taking another deep hit off the joint and slowly exhaling. "Like being a good husband, having a steady job, busting your ass day in and day out to give your family more than you had." He patted Caesar on the shoulder. "You're a tough man."

Kevin took another hit and laughed as he exhaled.

"And besides, you have to believe in God to be a godfather, right?" He looked out the window into the overcast sky. "If there's a God, he either forgot about me a long time ago or has decided I'm the second coming of Job. Either way, I'm not cut out to be your child's godfather."

Caesar took one last hit off the joint then stubbed it out and dropped the joint in the ashtray. "I'm not giving up on you just yet."

Kevin rubbed his eyes and took a deep breath. "Man, that was some killer weed."

Caesar nodded. "Yeah, it is. Between me and you, I'm gonna miss the ganja. If giving it up keeps Maria happy though, then so be it."

"So, what about the job?" Kevin asked. "They promote

you yet or am I gonna have to go down there and kick some sense into them?"

"They're giving me a promotion to district manager."

"That's great! When does it start?"

"January the First. Coming up fast."

"They throwing enough cash your way?"

"Yeah, it's a nice raise. But . . ." Caesar turned to Kevin. "I have to take a transfer for the position. To Indianapolis."

"As in Indiana?"

"Yeah."

"Starting in January? That's only two months from now."

"Uh huh." Caesar tried to smile. "I was gonna tell you. It's just that it's been so damn busy at work, then trying to get our shit together at home . . ." his voice trailed off and an air of heavy silence hung in the car.

"Where are you guys going to live?" Kevin finally said, as much to break the lull in the conversation as to gain the information.

"They're going to rent us a house. And said they'd help rent out our place up here."

"Damn. That's some big changes." Kevin took a deep breath and slowly exhaled. "I'm glad for you, C. You deserve it. You gotta do what's right for yourself and your family."

"Indy isn't that far from here."

Kevin weakly smiled. "It is without a car." He opened the door and got out. A cold blast of air hit him, and he swore he could feel the hair on his shoulder shiver in protest. "C'mon, let's go see the show."

CHAPTER 30

A SHORT, BALD HEADED WOMAN with pendulous breasts, wearing a black leather loin-skin, greeted Kevin and Caesar after they walked through the massive Oak front doors of the Auditorium. They were in a long, rectangular shaped entrance area with another thirty or so men and women milling about. Some were young, others middle aged, but almost all had some type of costume or body piercing or visible tattoo.

"I need to see your tickets, honey," the large-breasted woman said to Kevin in a high, little-girl voice.

He looked to Caesar, who shrugged.

"We don't have any tickets," Kevin said, resisting the urge to rub the woman's shiny head. "My girlfriend is part of the show."

"No tickets, no entrance," she told them in that same sweet little voice.

"Since when do you need tickets for a rehearsal?" Caesar asked.

"Since it's what I was told."

"Look, we really do know the people in MCFM," Caesar said. "Just go and ask—"

"Is there a problem here?" Kevin turned to his right. A gigantic black man—he guessed seven-foot-tall—dressed in full Viking regalia and carrying what appeared to be a very authentic broad-headed axe, eyed them suspiciously.

Kevin shook his head. "No problem. Just a misunderstanding."

Caesar tugged on Kevin's coat. "Let's step out a minute. I'll call Peter and—"

"We can settle this right now," he said, his eyes still locked on the Faux-Viking. The large man took another step forward.

Kevin didn't move. "My girlfriend, Sherri invited me to come over to—"

"You Kevin Ciano?" the man asked.

Kevin began to feel light-headed and realized he was holding his breath. "Yeah."

The Viking's face softened. "They're okay," he said to the bald-headed woman.

"If Sven says you're okay, then you're okay," the woman said to Kevin and Caesar. She pointed to another set of doors. "Go on in. I'm pretty sure you missed the rehearsal show but I think there's another one later tonight."

"Thanks," Kevin said, following Caesar into the next room.

It was decorated area the size of two basketball courts, half-filled with more garishly-dressed men and women and reeking of cannabis. The large open area had a marble floor polished to brilliance, and the ceiling was opulent with intricate wood carvings.

Caesar looked around, then shook his head, laughing. "A bald goth chick with saggy tits and a giant black guy with an axe named Sven. Never a boring moment with MCFM."

Kevin had to silently agree on that.

"Speaking of Sven," Caesar pulled a fat joint out of his jacket pocket and lit it up, "what was the deal in there, Kev?

You looked like you were ready to tear that guy's throat out."

"Guess I'm just not mellowed out enough yet." He took a deep hit off the joint and tried not to cough.

"Hey Boys!" they both turned to see Roxanne waving at them from the far-left corner of the room. She made her way over to them wearing nothing but a thigh-length white MCFM t-shirt which only partially hid her black thong.

"Hi, Caesar," she hugged him, then turned to Kevin and immediately kissed him on the lips before he had time to react.

"You're in a good mood," Caesar said, barely suppressing laughter.

Roxanne put her hands on her hips—hiking up the t-shirt—and pouted. "What are you talking about? I'm always in a good mood!"

"You are," Caesar pointed out, "but you just seem especially happy tonight."

She laughed with a flair of cheer in her voice. "It's a great night—rehearsal was kickin', we're almost sold out for the show, and now you two," she turned toward Kevin and winked, "are here. What more could a girl ask for?"

"Speaking of the rehearsal," Kevin was reminded, "I thought it wasn't going to start until ten."

Roxanne shrugged. "Our show's producer, Steven, said he wanted it early." She moved closer to Kevin and he took a small step back.

"Why?" Caesar asked.

Roxanne frowned. "Why what?"

"Why did Steven want the rehearsal moved up?" Kevin asked again. He was struck by how constricted her pupils were and wondered just what Roxanne had taken to be so high.

"I don't know. Something about all the big-wigs that are putting money up for the show were here early and why not let them see it first—sort of like a premiere of a premiere!"

She laughed again and did a pirouette.

"If you already did the show, then why are they still selling tickets?" Caesar asked.

Roxanne looked at Kevin, then at Caesar. "What the fuck is up with you two and your questions?"

"Just curious guys," Kevin answered.

"I know what guys like you are curious about," Roxanne said. She slid up next to Kevin and grabbed his hand before placing it on her crotch. He felt her heat and dampness before pulling his hand away.

"C'mon, Roxanne," Kevin said, trying to maintain his composure, "you're going to get me into trouble with Sherri."

She took a step back. "Sherri is not some little innocent maiden. Believe me, she's done some very freaky shit in her time."

"I got no problem with that," Kevin nodded. "I'm a live and let live type of guy. Speaking of Sherri, where is she?"

Roxanne crossed her arms and frowned again. "You're hurting my feelings. She'll be okay sharing you with me for a while."

Kevin let his eyes drift down to Roxanne's thong. He took a hit off the joint and offered it to her. "How about if we share this with you and call it even?"

Roxanne took two hits off the joint. She pursed her lips and slowly blew the smoke out in tight, perfect rings. "I guess we can play later," she finally said, then took Kevin's hand again and led him through the crowd.

"Now you'll see why MCFM are going to be the next big thing," she proclaimed, standing next to an inconspicuous set of plain wooden double doors. Roxanne opened them with a flourish, and they stepped inside.

It was a theatre, with row after row of high-backed seats covered in red velvet. A cathedral ceiling soared high above them and massive crystal chandeliers hung down and glittered like diamonds. On each side of the theatre were rows of opera balconies. Kevin could see some people lounging in them. A bouquet of odors mingled in the warm air—the oily smell of kerosene, the sweetness of cannabis, with an underlying medley of cigarette smoke, electrically-generated ozone and sweat.

"This is quite the place," Kevin said. , "How'd you guys manage to swing it?"

"More fucking questions," Roxanne groaned, absently scratching her arm. "It was Stevie Levine, our new producer, who got it. Don't know who he owed or blowed but I don't care. This place is gonna put us in the spotlight where we belong!"

"Holy shit," Caesar exclaimed, pointing to one of the opera balconies towards the back. "You see that?"

Kevin looked up. A woman—thin, naked, with short blonde hair—was bent over, holding onto the side of the balcony while behind her, a thickly muscled man in a Panama hat and unbuttoned white dress shirt was rhythmically thrusting back and forth

"They're fucking!" Caesar said.

"Yes, they are," Roxanne said matter-of-factly. She moved closer to Kevin and pointed with one finger toward the couple. "That can't be . . ." she paused for a dramatic second, "That can't be who I think it is, can it?"

Kevin rubbed his eyes and peered up again. The woman was sideways, and it was hard to see her face, but if he squinted hard enough to focus, he thought he could make out enough features.

Enough to think it might be Sherri.

"Do you think that's Sherri?" Kevin said in a near whisper.

Roxanne shrugged. "It does look like her, doesn't it?"

Kevin squinted and tried to focus. *What the fuck? I'm high but damned if that doesn't look like her*! He grabbed Roxy's arm. "How do I get up there?"

"What are you talking about?" Caesar said. "Let 'em screw in peace."

Kevin turned to him. "I think that's Sherri!"

"It's not Sherri," Caesar countered. "Hell, it doesn't even look like her, Kev."

"Calm down," Roxanne tried reassuring him. "It's not your little girlfriend up there."

Kevin let go of Roxanne's arm. "I thought you just said—"

She clapped her hands together. "I was just fucking with you. That's Steven. He was hitting on me before he found that little wench he's boning." Roxanne crossed her arms and gave a wicked laugh. "She was so fucked up on coke and speedballs she couldn't even say her name. Probably doesn't even realize she's getting screwed."

Kevin's heart was still beating wildly as Roxanne put hand on the small of his back and led him toward the stage.

"C'mon, tiger," she spoke in a flirtatious manner. "I'll show you that your little Sherri is safe and sound in back and not up in the balcony getting a dick up her ass."

Kevin took deep breathes and tried to regain his composure. Instead of mellowing him out, he felt the pot had made him anxious, edgy, and he needed something to dull the razor's edge. "You got something to drink backstage?" he asked.

Roxanne laughed again. "Something to drink? Honey, we got the works!"

They walked onto the stage toward the heavy curtain. draping down like a giant crimson cloak. Kevin was struck with a feeling of deja-vu; it was exactly like the first time when he met the group at the Fillmore, all of them in back, engaged in animated conversation, surrounded by equipment, totally comfortable with their places in life. And he, the outsider, coming into their culture of tats and scarifications and piercings and anarchy and being welcomed with open arms.

But there were differences. Instead of everyone sitting around, mellow and joking, Kevin could feel the tension, hanging thick and palpable like a cloud of dense smoke. All coalesced around dozens of people halfway in the back, most of them looking up at Peter, who was six feet in the air, suspended by at least twenty-five hooks piercing him all over his nude body.

Roxanne bounced over to the group. "Hey—I thought we were doing this scene later!"

Sherri, who was standing to one side and monitoring the ropes attached to a large rigging apparatus that held a number of pulleys and cables, glanced over. "It is later," she replied in a pissed-off voice. "Where have you been? We could have used another Bio here."

"Excuse me," Roxanne said, pursing her lips and shaking her head. "And you're welcome for me finding your stud." She stiffly marched over, grabbed a pair of latex gloves, and stood next to Delmond, who was looking back and forth between Peter and an iPad he held out at arm's length.

Kevin moved next to Sherri. "Hi baby."

"Hi." She gave him a quick kiss then looked back at the ropes. "Sorry, kinda busy right now."

"No problem. Do your job." Kevin looked back up at Peter; the hooks ran from his back and chest down to his knees and arms, keeping him suspended in a concave, reclining shape. His left arm was held straight, and he was stretching out his hand, as if attempting to touch an unseen entity with his fingers.

"He's doing Adam from Michelangelo's painting on the Sistine Chapel," Kevin surmised at seeing the familiar pose. "Right?"

Sherri smiled. "Sexy and smart, just how I like my man." She motioned with her head toward Delmond. "It's okay to get closer if you want."

Kevin turned to Caesar, who shook his head. "Not me. I like watching the show, not seeing how the magic is done."

Delmond wore a pair of hospital scrubs with the DMC logo printed in block letters across the left back pocket, and a MCFM t-shirt. Even in the cool air he was perspiring, beads of sweat cascading down his dark face. He looked at his iPad—Kevin spotted the famous painting on it, Adam leisurely stretching out his left hand, his index finger almost touching God—then at Peter.

"Your left arm needs to be just touching your kneecap," Delmond instructed him.

Peter looked over, his face calm and serene, as if he were reclining on a sofa watching a favorite movie. "Okay, puppet-master, make it happen."

Delmond motioned to a thin young man with a scraggly goatee and wearing a faded "Mao for President!" t-shirt featuring a grinning skull sandwiched between the lettering. He held four lines of ropes that were connected to a series of dull black pulleys which snaked down to four hooks impaled in Peter's upper arm, forearm, and wrist.

"Chaz, let the two distal arm lines down so that his mid-forearm is lightly touching his kneecap," Delmond said to the goatee-man.

"Ah . . ." Chaz stammered. "The distal ones are—"

Delmond shook his head. "The last one on his forearm and the wrist!" He glanced at Kevin then back at Chaz. "I thought you were supposed to get a decent rigger and puller. You mean to tell me you don't know the terms distal and proximal?"

Peter loudly cleared his throat. "Delmond, chill out." He looked at Chaz. "My boyfriend is a perfectionist. Don't take anything he says personally."

"Damn right I'm a perfectionist when my man is hanging in the air with twenty-five fucking hooks in him," Delmond said. He looked back at Chaz. "Now you gonna do what I just told you or not?"

"Okay." Chaz fumbled with the ropes for a few seconds before pulling lightly on the two in his left hand, causing Peter's right shoulder and upper forearm to move up.

"C'mon, man!" Delmond protested. "If you can't get this right then get the fuck out."

"I got it," Chaz l said, then tugged on the ropes in his right hand before letting them go limp. Peter's arm jerked up and Kevin heard a distinct sound of tearing.

"Oh fuck!" Chaz said, his voice high with emotion, looking back and forth from Peter to Delmond. "I'm so sorry I'm so sorry I'm—"

Peter took a deep breath and slowly exhaled. "It's fine, Chaz. Shit sometimes . . . happens."

Kevin took two steps closer to Chaz and saw that the hook in the middle of Peter's forearm was pulled sideways rather than in a U-shape like all the rest. From the jagged hole that was now in Peter's arm dripped a steady stream of blood.

The crimson drops fell on the scuffed-up hardwood floor and Kevin had to back out of the way to avoid from being hit. They splattered into strange shapes, patterns of dark red that caught Kevin's gaze. He blinked and stared at the floor, the patterns eerily reminding him of the Rorschach that crazy shrink in Fairview tormented him with. *That pattern, looking like an upside-down octopus in the middle of a burnt down forest, is just like the one that—*

Two things happened simultaneously: the hair on his shoulder seemed to move, to stretch out like a dog lounging in the sun, and someone's hand touched Kevin's other shoulder. He heard a frightened, throaty yell, and realized it was coming from him.

"Hey, handsome. Chill out." It was Roxanne. She stood next to him, hand still on his shoulder, her other hand holding a bucket filled with rags soaking in a greenish solution that gave off a sickly-sweet odor. "I just need to clean this little mess up, so if you could step back, I'd appreciate it."

Kevin squeezed his hands into fists, feeling nails bite into his palm, tried to focus on that sensation rather than the hair on his shoulder. "Yeah. Sure."

"Never took you for the squeamish type." Roxanne cleaned the floor while Peter was being lowered. "Wasn't it hard to be a fighter if you couldn't stand the sight of blood?"

"Maybe that's why I'm not a fighter anymore." He looked around. "Where's Sherri?"

"I think the fire queen went to get a couple more piercers to help unhook Peter."

"Is he going to be okay?" Kevin looked at Peter, who was surrounded by six people, Delmond angrily talking to all of them.

"He'll be fine." Roxanne finished cleaning up and threw the rags, streaking with red, into the bucket. "It was just a small tear." She stood up and arched her back and Kevin's eyes wandered to her chest.

Roxanne caught his gaze and winked. "Better not let Sherri see you copping a look."

She picked up the bucket and headed to the back just as Sherri was coming out with two other women, one tall with ebony skin and a large afro, the other pale and middle-aged.

"The glamor of performing," Sherri drawled as she walked by Kevin, "is never as glamourous as it seems."

Kevin followed her over to Peter, who was sitting, legs outstretched, arms at his side, on a white sheet. There were some blood stains on his arm and leg, but Kevin didn't notice any more active bleeding.

"This is why we need more rigging," Delmond was saying to Peter, who shook his head.

"It was an accident, plain and simple. If we have more ropes it'll make the illusion that much harder to pull off." He looked over and caught sight of Kevin. "Hey, Kevin! Good to see you again!"

"Likewise." He looked closer at Peter's left arm. There was an ugly-looking jagged tear through the skin.

"Where the hell is Roxy?" Delmond asked, who was squatted down next to Peter.

"She went backstage," Kevin recalled.

"She needs to get her ass out front and center." Delmond looked at Sherri and her companions. "Guess you can unhook him."

Sherri and the two women, all wearing skin-colored latex gloves, began expertly removing the hooks from Peter.

Delmond looked over his shoulder at the rest of the people watching. "Y'all can go. Thanks for your help."

"I don't see Chaz," Peter said as he watched the crew leave.

Delmond cleared his throat. "He left."

"You mean you told him to leave," Peter countered.

Delmond shrugged. "Same difference."

"It wasn't his fault," Peter said. "I think that hook was through an old scar, so it wasn't as strong as the others."

"It wasn't through scar tissue," Delmond said with a note of certainty. "I was the one who rigged you up, remember?"

Sherri and the other women stood up, the hooks and rigging laid out in two neat lines on the sheet. They had finished in less than two minutes.

"You want the hooks sterilized right now?" Sherri asked Delmond.

"I don't know," he replied. "Still want to give some thought about re-doing this whole scene, maybe more hooks, added rigging—"

"And I say no," Peter cut in. "It's my ass up in the air, remember?"

"And I'm lead rigger and piercer," Delmond countered, "meaning it's my job and responsibility."

Peter shook his head. "Let's run this by an impartial observer like . . ." he turned to Kevin. "So, young man, don't you think it would be an incredible scene to see this lovely lady here," he pointed at Sherri, "naked as the day she was born, standing on top of a soon-to-be-incinerated wooden pyre, touching fingers, ala Adam and God on the Sistine Chapel, with a lean, handsome man like myself who appears floating in midair? I'll have on special paint that will glow under UV light so the ropes and pulleys will almost be invisible. It'll look like I'm levitating out of a cloud of dark smoke."

"Sounds cool, but seeing you get torn up with a bunch of hooks isn't my thing."

"We'll talk about this later," Delmond insisted, the tone of his voice leaving no room for argument.

Peter casually shrugged. "We can talk all you want, but there will be no more ropes."

"Are you two boys fighting again?" Roxanne returned carrying a black leather doctor's bag. She winked once again at Kevin. "Isn't young love just so cute?"

"Cut that smart-ass mouth and get him sewed up," Delmond snapped before walking to the back with Sherri following.

Roxanne sat down cross-legged next to Peter. She removed a pair of gloves, a stainless-steel needle holder and some suture material from the bag.

"Ready for this?" she asked Peter.

He nodded once. "Make me pretty again."

"You're already pretty." Roxanne began weaving the nylon sutures in and out of the jagged tear and bringing the frayed edges of skin together perfectly.

"Nice job," Kevin commented.

"Thanks," Roxanne said, still suturing. "I'm good at a lot of things. Just ask Sherri."

Kevin watched, Roxanne pushing the U-shaped suture needle through Peter's tattooed skin and wondered how come there was no bleeding.

Peter looked at Kevin and smiled. "I can see from the questioning looking on your face that you're probably thinking 'how in the hell can she be doing that without him bleeding?' Am I right?"

Kevin nodded.

Peter tapped his head with his free hand. "It's all in the mind. There are Yoga masters who can slow their heart rate down to two beats a minute. O stay immersed in ice water for days with no ill effects. Medically proven and validated, even though modern science says it can't be done."

"There," Roxanne said, cutting away the suture material. "All done."

"Thanks." Peter got up and stretched his back, multiple pops filling the air.

"Is that how you deal with the pain of being suspended?" Kevin asked, trying to push down a sudden deep spike of ache radiating from the hair on his shoulder.

"Exactly!" Peter moved closer to Kevin, as did Roxanne.

"It's the shit we hold up here—" Peter again tapped his skull, "the physic—YES pain, not as in reading minds, but our negative thoughts and emotions, as well as what we hold in our heart . . ." he thumped his chest twice with a closed fist, "the spiritual pain, that will kill us. Physical pain can be controlled, subdued, and even embraced. It's the last thing to kill you." He reached over and patted Kevin on the shoulder, millimeters away from the hair, which Kevin swore he could feel move. "You control the mind, and you can control anything."

"Is that so, Jedi Master?" Roxanne teased him. "Then how come you don't just levitate?"

Peter smiled. "Won't you be surprised the day I do."

"Anybody here ready for a drink?"

Kevin turned to see Delmond carrying a box in one muscular arm and a cooler in the other. He put both down on stage.

Delmond pulled out a bottle of vodka from the box. "The MCFM bar is now officially open. If y'all want something to drink, get off your lazy asses, and get some!"

"There you go, stud," Roxanne said to Kevin before pinching him on the ass. "Time to get liquored up!"

"Where's Sherri?" Kevin asked Delmond.

"She was talking to some guy in the back," Delmond answered. "She'll be out any second."

"You sure she didn't take a stroll up to the balcony?" Roxanne asked innocently.

Caesar gave her a hard nudge with his elbow. "Knock it off. It ain't funny."

Roxanne frowned and flipped Caesar off. "I think it's damn funny."

"Think I'll go back and get her," Kevin said.

Roxanne grabbed his hand. "Sherri is a big girl. Stay here and have a drink with me." She took a long swallow of vodka.

Kevin shook his head. "No thanks. I'm more of a bourbon guy." He quickly found a bottle of Maker's Mark, peeled the red wax covering off the top, and took a swallow. The golden liquid burned hot in his esophagus; he found that the small voice in his head telling him he was walking the razors edge by combining the Norco with pot and now booze was easy to ignore.

"Slow down there, tiger," Roxanne said. "I don't want Sherri, at least when she gets back from who knows where, to think I was getting her BF drunk so I could take advantage of him.'"

"I'm fine," Kevin told her. "I've done this a time or two before." He looked around. Still no Sherri.

That's because she's still up in the opera balcony taking it up the ass! a darker voice in the recesses of his mind urgently whispered. He tried very hard to shut that voice up.

"Hey guys, you starting the party without me?" It was Sherri, now wearing a short blue dress and black high heels.

She walked up to Kevin and kissed him. "Hi handsome. Want a date?"

Kevin smiled. "Sure." He took her hand, his other still holding the bottle of bourbon, and walked to the corner of the stage.

"What's going on?" Kevin said, looking at Sherri.

"What do you mean?"

He looked her up and down. "I mean what's with the little blue dress and FMPs?"

Sherri jerked her hand away and stepped back. "What the fuck, Kevin? I thought it might be nice to dress up for you. I thought maybe you'd appreciate it. I thought my boyfriend would be happy to see me instead of acting like an asshole."

"Look, it's just that . . . when we were coming in, we saw this girl up in the balcony with . . . and then I come back here to see you and you disappear in back and—"

"You're making no fucking sense!" She put her hands on her hips. "If there's anyone who should be pissed it's me. You're way late, miss the rehearsal, then come strolling in back with Roxanne. And now you're-you're implicating that I've been fucking around on you?"

Kevin took another hit off the bottle. "I'm sorry."

Sherri shook her head. "You know, Kevin, you've been saying that a lot lately." She took a step closer and peered in his eyes. "You're high as hell, aren't you?"

"I took another Norco to help ease the pain. What's the fucking problem?"

She crossed her arms, looked over at the group then back at Kevin. "A few years ago, I watched someone I was close to kill themselves with Vicodin and whiskey. I don't feel like reliving that time in my life."

"Did that someone have a bunch of painful, ugly-ass hair things sprouting out of them?" Kevin sharply said, then took another drink, even though his head was swirling and felt his words becoming fat and lazy.

"No, Kevin, they didn't." She took a deep breath and slowly exhaled, then uncrossed her arms. "Are there more of them? The hairs?"

"Yeah. There's more."

She touched his hand. "I'm sorry. What did the doctors say?"

Kevin shook his head and regretted it an instant later as a wave of vertigo washed over him. "What doctors?"

"You said you were going to go in today to see a doctor, remember? You promised me you'd go in today."

"I did go see someone!" he angrily said. "I went to the fucking Bird House, okay? Me and Caesar. You can go ask him if you think I'm lying."

Sherri glanced over at Caesar. "Fine. I believe you. What did they say?"

"They said they didn't know what the hairs were," Kevin answered, his head still spinning. "They wanted to cut one off."

"I'm sure they did. To see what it was. And—"

Kevin ran his hands through his hair. His brain felt slow and all he wanted was to crawl into the bottle of bourbon and not come out. "And nothing. Something came up, and there was this emergency that the doctor had to go to, and . . ."

"You didn't get anything done?" Sherri interrupted. "You didn't get one of the hairs cut off and examined so they could see what it is?"

It's a fucking living, moving nightmare that's slowly eating away what's left of my sanity! "That's right," Kevin said, not caring anymore if his words were slurred or unintelligible. "And to tell you the truth, I'm fine with that because I've tried to take them off and it hurts. Hurts like fucking hell."

"It hurts." She stared at him. "Kevin, I hate to break it to you, but sometimes shit that you need to do *does* hurt!" She paced around, not caring that half the group was now looking over their way. "You told me you used to fight! You of all people should be able to deal with pain!"

"Everybody seems to be reminding me of that part of my life tonight, and you know what? Maybe I've had my fucking fill of pain and blood! You ever think of that?"

Kevin heard someone clear their throat behind him. It was Caesar.

"I was voted by the group to come over to see if you lovers wanted to join us," he said. "And to see if everything is okay."

Kevin took a deep breath and looked at Sherri. "Everything is as good as it can be right now, Caesar."

"Tell the group we'll be over in a second," Sherri said. After Caesar walked away, she moved closer to Kevin.

"Kevin, I'm on your side, okay? I'm not going to say I know exactly how you feel, because I don't. But I do know you're a good man, a strong man, and if you let me, I'll help you get through this."

Kevin went to talk, paused, then finally spoke. "I appreciate it, Sherri. I do. It's just that . . ." he shook his head and took her hand. "C'mon, let's go try and have some fun."

"Everything okay with you two lovebirds?" Roxanne asked when they got back and sat down on folding chairs next to the others.

"We're fine," Sherri tersely replied. She sat down next to Peter. He handed her a fat joint and she inhaled deeply.

Roxanne motioned her to pass the joint. "So, what do you think about your girlfriend being a star?" she asked Kevin.

"What do you mean?"

Roxanne looked at Sherri. "You didn't tell him yet?"

Sherri turned to Kevin. "Our first show is totally sold out, and they're already working on booking us in November for three more nights!"

Kevin grinned. "That's great! Once those royalty checks

start coming in, I can sit around and become your full-time fuck toy." He took a small sip of Maker's.

"I like this man!" Delmond said heartily. He turned to Peter. "How 'bout it, boyfriend? Can I quit MCFM and be your lazy fuck-toy?"

Peter laughed, then took his boyfriend's face in his hands and gave him a kiss. "No damn way," he said after pulling away. He turned to Sherri and pointed to the back. "Did you talk to Tyler about the funeral pyre fire-pots?"

"I did. He thought there might have been an issue with the ignition timer," she said. "Nothing to worry about."

Peter shook his head. "I beg to differ. If you wouldn't have been suspended so high—"

"What are you talking about?" Kevin asked. "Problems with things blowing up seem like an issue to me, especially when it involves the woman I love."

"Aww, that's so sweet," Roxanne chimed in. "What happened was that the fire pots—the half-dozen, very large fire pots—went off a bit too soon and almost torched your lover during her grand finale."

Kevin turned to Sherri. "You okay?"

Sherri waved him off. "I'm fine." She lit a cigarette then glared at Roxanne. "Roxanne is, as usual, exaggerating things."

Roxanne laughed. "Bullshit. You know you were almost a Shish Kebab up ther."

"It won't happen again," Sherri reassured him. She motioned with her hand at Roxanne. "You gonna walk around all nearly naked? I seem to remember you had some pants on when you got here tonight."

Roxanne took one last draw on the joint, now a tiny roach, then spit on her fingers before crushing it out. "Honey, I hate to tell you this, but you're showing the entire world your tits, ass, and pussy at every show. Or did you forget that?"

"It's a *show*, Roxanne."

"I don't think anyone minds what I show them," Roxanne giggled. "Besides, this isn't nearly naked" She pulled off her t-shirt and threw it at Sherri, "*This* is nearly naked!"

Peter and Delmond both clapped as Roxanne danced seductively around the group. Sherri shook her head but said nothing.

"Nice of you guys to have some high-end stuff," Kevin said to Peter, tipping the bottle of Maker's toward him before taking another drink. His brain already felt thick and foggy, but he welcomed the chemical veil that also put a thick veil over his anxiety and pain.

Peter smiled. "Courtesy of our producers. If they want to buy it, then we'll certainly drink it."

"You can stop your little dance now," Sherri said to Roxanne, who was still gyrating around the group, "or take it out to the reception area."

She stopped and pouted at Sherri. "Maybe I will. Our sponsors are very hands on, and I certainly have what they want to touch."

"Hey there, girl," Delmond said, "not all of them." He stood up, pulled down his sweatpants and wagged his large penis back and forth. "Some prefer to touch this!"

Roxanne broke out in manic laughter. "You are such a whore!"

Peter lit up another joint and offered it to Kevin. "See? This is what happens when you get a bunch of freaks together."

Kevin tersely smiled. *You have no idea about being a freak.* He suddenly had the urge to strip naked, to tear off his clothes and scream, *you want to see a real freak—well here it is folks! This is the freakiest shit you will ever see!*

Instead, he took another quick draw off the bottle and hoped no one saw his shaking hands.

"What's on tap for the rest of the night?" Caesar asked

Peter.

"Not much. Check all the equipment, especially the firepots, then head home, get a few hours sleep and do it all again tomorrow. Sans the crowd, of course."

"But the crowd will be back Saturday night," Sherri said, moving her chair closer to Kevin's. "It's going to be incredible!"

"I can't wait to see it," Kevin said, but his mind was wandering and there was something irritating his brain, a sluggish ethereal caterpillar that slowly crawled through his cortex that was just out of reach. It distracted him from the conversation and twice he could sense Sherri becoming perplexed at his behavior, but it was an itch that just had to be scratched and then it happened—the caterpillar metamorphosised into a fully formed thought.

"Dr. Rothstein." The words escaped Kevin's lips before he was consciously aware he had spoken.

Sherri frowned at him. "What?"

He looked around. Caesar, Peter, and Delmond were in animated conversation and Roxanne was sitting back, headphones from her iPad pumping music into her drug-soaked brain. "Have any of you seen Dr. Rothstein?"

Peter nodded. "Yeah. He was here earlier for the show."

Kevin's heart began to pound. "Did he leave?"

"I don't know. Said he was going to hang out with some friends for a while." Peter nudged Roxanne, who, still sitting back with her eyes closed and a half-lit joint in her mouth, put up her middle finger. He cocked his index finger and snapped her sharply on the thigh.

Her eyes popped open. "What the fuck?" She glared at Peter and threw the joint at his face.

"Chill out, girl," Delmond said. He picked up the joint and shook it at her. "No need to be wasting good dope."

"There's no need to be fucking with me either," Roxanne shot back.

"Just trying to help out Kevin here," Peter said. "He's wondering if anybody knows where Dr. Rothstein is."

"Oh." Her demeanor changed instantly, reminding Kevin of chameleons that change color when evading predators or hunting prey. "He said he was going to get with some friends." She squirmed around in the chair and looked from side to side. "Anybody seen my purse?"

"I have it," Sherri said. "Don't you remember asking me to hold onto it for you?"

"Of course, I do," Roxanne snatched the purse from her. "What do you think I am, high?" She broke out in a high-pitched giggle.

Kevin stood up and he felt a rush of blood drain from his drug-infused brain. Vertigo washed over him, and he grabbed the back of the chair for support.

"You okay?" Sherri asked.

"He's fine," Roxanne said, still pawing through her purse. "He just can't hold his liquor."

"That's right," Kevin said weakly, trying to concentrate to stop the spinning room. "I'm turning into a lightweight in my old age." He looked down at Sherri. "I'm going to go find Rothstein to, you know, ask him about my bum shoulder."

"That's a good idea." She pushed away from her chair. "I'll go with you."

"No, you won't." Both Kevin and Sherri looked over at Peter, who was standing with a short, dour-looking middle-aged man wearing a pair of dark blue overalls.

"Excuse me?" Sherri said, hands on hips.

"I want me, you and Tyler to go check out the firepots," Peter said, putting his arm on the shorter man who visibly flinched at the touch but said nothing.

"You can do it without me," Sherri said.

"No, we can't," Peter countered. "You know this equipment inside and out. We need to get this fixed. Now."

"Stay and get this fixed," Kevin said. "I'll find Rothstein."

"You have no idea where to look," Sherri countered. "He could be anywhere."

"Then I better get going," he said, kissing her once then stepping back. "Come look for me if I'm not back by daybreak."

As he turned to leave, Kevin saw Roxanne get up.

"Where are you going?" Sherri asked her.

Roxanne threw her purse over her shoulder. "I'm going to take a piss. Want to come and watch?" She sauntered off, swaying her hips in an exaggerated motion.

"It shouldn't take me too long to take care of this," Sherri said to Kevin after Roxanne had walked past the curtain. "Stick around for a few minutes then I can go with you."

He pulled her close. "Listen, if what happened at the rehearsal is even half as significant as Roxy said, then you need to stay here and take care of this, no matter how long it takes."

"All right. I'll be waiting here for you." She kissed him passionately. "I love you, Kevin."

"I love you too."

"You going somewhere?" Kevin heard Caesar ask. He turned and his friend was sitting cross-legged on the floor, sharing a thick blunt with Delmond.

"I need to talk to Rothstein."

"Oh." Caesar took a short toke on the joint, then his bloodshot eyes opened wide. "Oh, yeah. That makes sense. Know how long you're going to be?"

Kevin shook his head. "No idea. What time you need to leave?"

Caesar looked at his watch. "It's 10:30, so pretty soon."

"I'll take Kevin home," Sherri said. "As long as he can afford to pay the fare."

"I think I can cover that," Kevin commented. As if to rebuke him, the hairs on his thigh sent a jolt of pain down his leg. He let himself grimace once he had left the stage and desperately wished for another Norco.

He left the theatre and went back into the double-bas-
ketball court-sized room and looked around. The crowd was
thinning. There was no sign of Rothstein.

How in the hell am I gonna find him? Kevin looked
around again and felt a small, tight ball of panic coalesce in
his gut. *I'm high as shit and this place is fucking huge. Even
if we're on the same floor he could be in the room next to me
and—*

Kevin yelled when someone pinched him on the ass.

"Shit, Kevin, chill the fuck out!" It was Roxanne.

"I thought you said you were going to take a piss." Kevin's heart was beating so loud and fast he was sure the entire
room could hear it.

"That was just for your girlfriend. She would have lost
her jealous mind if I said I was going with you."

"You don't need to come with me. I'll be fine."

"Oh, sure. You're more fucked up than me and totally
look like you know where you're going." She reached down
and grabbed both her breasts. "Besides, I need to see the
good doctor myself. I think the girls need to bulk up."

"Look, Roxanne, I appreciate it," Kevin said, wishing he
could think of something to say to make her leave. "But really, I'm okay, and besides, if Sherri—"

"Is there a problem between you too?" she interrupted,
her voice changing to subdued and concerned. "You know
you can talk to me about it, right? I mean, me and Sherri go
back a long way."

"It's nothing like that. I have some stuff, some old boxing
injuries, going on in my ribs and shoulder. It just hurts like
hell when someone touches me in the wrong way."

"Why didn't you say so?" Roxanne dug into her purse
and a few seconds later came up with two dark blue, oblong
tablets. "Oxy. These are my travel pills. I keep my main stash
at home." She popped one in her mouth and swallowed, then
handed him the other one. "Here, take this and in twenty

minutes it will be all better."

Kevin looked at the pills. Before he could properly think, he threw it into his mouth and swallowed.

Roxanne gave a wicked laugh. "Just like a pro." She grabbed his hand and pulled him through the room. "C'mon, pretty boy, let's go see the wizard!"

CHAPTER 31

Roxy was wrong. It only took fifteen minutes for Kevin to feel the narcotic French kiss of the OxyContin.

They were in a small dark room on the sixth floor after walking up the stairway past a trio of very drunk drag queens when a thick curtain of artificial serenity descended over his consciousness. He thought it would be the same as the Norco, but it was different; whereas the former was more of a coating over his pain, both mental and physical. With the Oxy, Kevin felt more stoned yet more aware of life, as if the sharp edges of his existence had been smoothed out and all the bad pushed into one corner and locked away. He took a deep breath and leaned against the wall, inadvertently bumping his right shoulder.

Even the pain in his shoulder was different. He felt it, but it wasn't sharp and deep. It was shallow, superficial, like the sting of a small bee. Not pleasant, but nothing that would bring him to his knees.

"Hey, lover, you okay?" Kevin heard Roxy say, her voice melodic and soothing.

"Yeah. Kevin licked his lips, which felt like Jell-O. "I'm

fine."

Roxy moved closer. "The Oxy kicked in for you, didn't it?" She traced an index finger over his face and Kevin didn't stop her.

"You think you feel good now, just wait until you fuck on this shit," she whispered in his ear. "Makes sex without it a damn bore." Roxanne ran the tip of her tongue around the inside of his ear and to Kevin it felt as if tiny flicks of electricity were teasing his skin. "We could fuck right here. No one would know."

"Unless someone happened to come in." Kevin laughed at the thought.

"I'd make 'em pay to watch the show," Roxanne said while her hands expertly unbuckled his pants.

Kevin leaned back onto the wall and closed his eyes, giving himself into the pleasure as Roxanne grabbed the head of his cock and greedily began to tease and caress it. He almost let himself go completely, would have fucked her in that very room, if the last vestiges of his rational mind hadn't latched onto the thought of finding Rothstein and telling Sherri he loved her.

"Stop," he said.

"I don't think so."

Kevin grabbed her wrists and pushed them away. "I need to see Rothstein," his words felt thick on his tongue. He pushed his cock back into his underwear and awkwardly pulled up his pants.

"Find Rothstein?" Roxy backed away, frowning. "I hate to break it to you, but the Masonic is a big fucking place and there's about zero chance of you finding the good doctor tonight."

"He's got to be here somewhere," Kevin said, a dulled panic fighting through his new buzz. "If we just keep looking we can—"

"I'm about done with this hide and seek little game,"

Roxanne groaned. "I came here tonight to practice and party."

Kevin took a deep breath and tried to steady himself, but it was no use. The world twisted and turned like a hazy kaleidoscope.

You fucked up. The Norco, the pot, then the booze and now the oxy. How in the hell are you supposed to find Rothstein when you're so damn high?

"Where the hell are we?" Kevin finally looked around at the room he and Roxanne were standing in.

It was small, the size of a normal sized home living room, with tiled inlaid floors colored black and white in the shape of a large X. The only furniture in the room was a large, high-backed chair, completely covered in red velvet with a misshapen set of Ram's horns hanging on the wall above it.

Roxanne shrugged. " Probably one of their Satanic ritual rooms."

"What?"

"The Mason's. They're into some very nefarious shit. Didn't you know that?"

"No. I didn't."

"Well, it's true. Just because I'm a hot blonde with a fine ass and big tits doesn't mean I don't know things."

"Look, I didn't mean anything by it," Kevin said, wishing that he never let her come with him. "I just want to find Rothstein."

Roxanne sighed and put her hands on her hips. "And just how do you expect us to do that, Kevin? Want me to wave my magic wand and make him appear?" She pawed her breasts and crotch looking for an imaginary wand, then looked at Kevin and shrugged. "Sorry honey. No magic wand tonight."

"We have to think of something!" Kevin said, ignoring Roxy's theatrics.

"I don't wanna think. Makes my brain hurt."

Kevin rubbed his temples, trying to unsuccessfully will

away the chemical fog that held his brain in a tight, stupefying grasp. As he leaned up against the wall, he felt something in his back pocket jab into his lower back . . .

"My phone," he said, pulling his cell out, feeling like he had made the discovery of the ages. "We can call Rothstein."

"Well, duh," Roxy said, pulling a phone out of her purse. "I can do that too!"

They walked out of the room into a dimly lit, cramped hallway and tried to call. Neither phone had a signal.

"See honey?" Roxy said, "the universe doesn't want you to do anything more than fuck me senseless."

"Fuck the universe," Kevin mumbled. "I gotta find him."

"Fine. You go on your search. I'm going back downstairs to see if there's any kind of party left." She held out her hand. "Want to join me?"

"I need to find Rothstein," Kevin muttered again, trying desperately to hold onto to the thought before it was lost in the oxy-alcohol haze. "We've already been downstairs and I don't think that—"

"I bet he's down there," Roxane said, as if stating the most obvious fact in the world. "I bet he's probably down there looking for you right now!"

"Roxanne," Kevin threw up his arms, which felt like helium balloons, "why do you think that?"

"Why not?" she said, grabbing his hand and pulling him toward the stairs. "Most people are down there, so it just makes sense that's where he'd be."

"I guess that makes sense."

"If I see the good doctor, I'll let him know you're looking for him," Roxy kissed him on the cheek and disappeared down the stairwell.

Kevin stood, the quiet of the hallway a sudden juxtaposition to Roxy's chatter just a moment before.

Maybe she's right. Maybe Rothstein is back downstairs and here I am, standing on God-knows-what floor, high as shit and waiting for him to magically show up like a genie from a bottle.

A single, sharp cry suddenly cut through the air. Kevin jerked his head from side to side and saw nothing. He was still looking when there was another cry, then a long moment of silence before . . .

"You got any spare rope?"

The voice came from behind Kevin. He turned around and a wave of vertigo blossomed, and he had to throw both hands out to the walls to keep himself from falling.

"Hey, man, take it easy." Kevin squinted and saw a head, almost black, protruding out of the wall ten feet down the hallway.

The head began to elongate, like being pulled out of the polished woodwork with invisible hands. Kevin's screamed. *What the fuck is this place maybe Roxy is right and there's some supernatural Satanic shit going on and . . .*

Kevin finally stopped screaming as the head became a chest which became an entire body.

It's just a guy dressed in black. Kevin took two deep breathes to try and still his wildly beating heart. *There must be a door there that I didn't see and that's where he came from.*

The large man wasclad full in black: hood, leather face mask, skin-tight leather shirt and pants, and army-style boots. He sauntered down the hall and starred at Kevin.

"You look stoned as hell!" the man said before breaking out in laughter. His eyes appeared wide as owls underneath the mask. He leaned close to Kevin. "What are you on? Got any more?"

Kevin backed away, his head still spinning. "I'm not feeling well," he moaned. "I'm having a bad night."

"Bad night? The bitch we're stringing up in our little dungeon down the hall is the one in for a bad night," the man snickered, following Kevin step for step. "You're welcome to come in and partake of the festivities. Believe me, that kinky little slut is all about the more the merrier. That is, of course, if you're willing to share your goodies."

"I don't have any goodies," Kevin told him, the surge of adrenaline momentarily clearing his brain.

He wondered how far he was from the stairwell but too paranoid to look away, afraid that the black leather-clad man would take him to the dungeon and string him up like a flesh and blood piñata.

"Sure, you do," the man said, his voice deep, silky smooth. "Now be a good boy and share and—"

Kevin turned and bolted. By blind luck or memory, he found the stairwell and stumbled down, sure at any moment that a large, leather-clad hand would grab him and pull him back up into a dungeon filled with S&M deviants. He would be trapped there forever like in the old black and white re-runs of *Twilight Zone* he and Caesar would watch as kids, a private hell where he would be roped up like a rodeo steer and tortured while the hairs-things continued to grow out of him like perverted organic monsters feasting on his flesh and blood.

Kevin finally stopped running in the middle of a stair-well, out of breath, and looked behind.

There was nothing. No leather-clad monster, no bloat-ed, bipedal hair-things torn free of his body. Nothing except hissing florescent lights and the sound of his own labored breathing.

You gotta pull it together, man. Get your shit together. Rothstein is out there. Focus on that.

Kevin heard footsteps coming toward him and he backed against the wall, fists instinctively up in a fighting position.

It was a young couple, no older then eighteen. The girl, short and skinny wearing a skin-tight red dress with close-cropped snow-white hair, let out a squeak and grabbed her boyfriend. He was a boy only an inch taller than her, wearing ragged jeans and a new MCFM t-shirt.

The boy smiled. "Chill out, man," he said in a surprisingly

deep voice. "We're not looking for trouble."

"Me neither."

"You come from the private gig up here?" the boy asked, a thin arm still wrapped protectively around the girl. "We're looking for it."

"No," Kevin said, a picture of the leather-clad man flashing in his mind, "I'm heading downstairs."

"See?" the boy said to the girl. "The man here say's there's nothing up there. Let's head back down and—"

"I wanna check it out myself," the girl said, pulling away from the boy in an act of bravado. "Amber said it's gonna be awesome, and you promised you'd at least try."

The boy looked at Kevin. "You sure there was nothing going on up there?"

"I don't know." Kevin could feel the adrenaline surge wear off and the witch's brew of narcotic-alcohol-pot take over his brain. "There's a lot of crazy stuff going on in this place tonight."

The girl's eyes widened, and she tugged on the boy's hand. "Let's go! I bet things are just starting!"

Kevin starred at her young, unlined face and wondered if she was even eighteen. *You have no idea what things are just starting.*

"I really don't think there's anything up here," Kevin said. "You should just go back downstairs."

The girl frowned. "You just said there's a lot of things going on up here."

"No, no, I didn't say that," Kevin stuttered, his words feeling fat and unformed in his mouth. "

"He's fucking high," the girl said to the boy, pushing out her chest and showing hard nipples pressing against tight fabric. She then told Kevin with open contempt, "We're not stupid fuckin' kids. We know there's some kickin' shit going on up here!"

The boy looked at Kevin with eyes that said, *help me con-*

vince her to leave because she's a junkie for kicks but I'm afraid that the shit we're going to find is going to be bad!

Kevin shrugged and said nothing.

"C'mon," the girl said, pulling the boy past him. "We don't need to be hanging out in the stairwell with some buzz-kill old man."

Kevin watched them disappear into the darkness. Even if he heard them scream, he couldn't turn around. He had to, had to . . .

"What was I doing?" Kevin said out loud. "I was looking for someone but now . . ."

He almost let himself slump down on the steps, to lay down like a full-grown fetus and pass out, to sleep when he slapped himself—hard—twice on the face, the second-time drawing blood from his lower lip.

Rothstein. The name came slow and laboriously, but it came. *I was going see Dr. Rothstein.*

"You need to pull it together," he said aloud, his voice sounding strange and foreign. "You can do this. You *have* to do this."

He took three long deep breaths then continued down the stairs. *I'll stop at each floor and see if he's there. That's the only thing I can do. Stop, look, then go on.*

He opened the first door off the stairs and was amazed to find himself in the Masonic blue room again. There were a number of people in it. Kevin guessed thirty or so and he began scanning the room for Rothstein.

I don't see him. *Damnit, what if I've missed him. Now he'll be going out of the country for God-knows how long and—*

Kevin thought he heard the stairwell door slam shut two seconds before a hand fell on his shoulder and he once again screamed.

CHAPTER 32

HE WAS SURE IT was the black-clad dungeon master, or the boy holding the bloody, mangled remains of his girlfriend.

Kevin was wrong on both counts.

"My Lord, Kevin, what's wrong?"

It was Dr. Rothstein, impeccably dressed in a dark charcoal Armani suit and a silver silk tie.

"I'm sorry," Kevin said, his voice cracking. "It's just that . . . I thought you were . . . I've had a rough night."

"I'm sorry to hear that." Rothstein said. "I ran into Roxanne fifteen minutes ago and she said you had something to talk to me about." He pointed to a corner of the room that was unoccupied. "That looks like a good place to chat."

"Sure.." Kevin followed Rothstein and tried to hold down his nervousness.

"Kevin, I have to ask you," Rothstein began, "are you using drugs?" Before Kevin could say anything, Rothstein put one hand up. "I ask not because I'm a prude or crazed anti-drug crusader, but you appear somewhat paranoid, and your pupils are quite constricted in this dim light."

"I took an OxyContin (*along with some Norco's and booze and pot, but hey, who's counting?*)" Kevin said, "because of this pain I have in my right shoulder—an old injury from my boxing days."

Rothstein looked at Kevin for a few seconds, then nodded his head. "You don't do drugs on a regular basis?"

"No!" Kevin said it with more force than he intended. He took a deep breath and tried to smile. "I was just in a lot of pain.."

Rothstein smiled, but Kevin could tell it was forced. "I see. Should I be worried that this shoulder problem is going to stop you from doing work for me while I'm in Europe as we spoke about before?"

Work? What work? Son-of-a-bitch, why did I let myself get so fucking high?

"No. No problem. I'll be fine."

That's good." Rothstein pulled out his wallet. "Here's two hundred dollars to get you started," he said, handing Kevin four fifty-dollar bills. "I could tell you everything that needs to be done, but I'm sure I'd forget something. I've left a list on the main dining room table. If you have any questions, I've also left some numbers that you can try to reach me at, although I've heard the phone service in Hungary leaves something to be desired." He handed Kevin a set of keys. "The larger key is for the front door deadbolt. The smaller key is to the freezer downstairs."

"The freezer to move the bodies to?" Even in his mentally obtunded state, Kevin was unable to forget moving the corpses Rothstein used to practice on.

"That's right. I'll be working on a new procedure right before I leave, and there's a chance I'll need some of the specimens moved to the freezer to be cremated." He looked closely at Kevin. "You won't have a problem with that, will you?"

"Of course not." (*At least not if I can find some more drugs to take.*)

"Excellent." Rothstein looked at his watch. "I'd love to stay and talk more, but I'm due to meet a very lovely lady at the Windsor Casino, so do you have any more questions?"

He's going to think you're a crazed freak if you show him the hairs! Just walk away and—

"Can I show you something?" Kevin blurted out in one quick string of words.

Rothstein stepped back and folded his arms. "Show me what?"

Kevin looked around the room. "Ah . . . can we just find a more private spot?"

Rothstein narrowed his eyes. For a few seconds Kevin thought that he was going to say no, was going to ask for his money back, but then the doctor's eyes softened, and he nodded.

"Of course. I know how difficult sensitive things like this can be." He walked out of the room into the empty hallway and Kevin followed him into the men's room halfway down the hall.

"It looks like we have the place to ourselves," he said.. "Now, if you just drop your pants, then—"

"What?" Kevin took a step back. "Why the fuck would I do that?"

"So, I can look at your genitals," Rothstein said as if it were the most obvious fact in the world. "I can't tell you what type of sexually transmitted infection you have, without first having a look."

"No," Kevin said, emphatically shaking his head. "It's not anything like that!"

"Oh. I'm sorry. Knowing both Roxanne's and Sherri's proclivity for sex, I just thought that you three had picked something up."

Kevin took a deep breath and without further thought, pulled off his sweater and then the gauze wrapped around his arms. When he was done, he held them out. "This is my problem."

Rothstein peered at the tats, the brandings, and the hair-things that snaked their way from and around the designs. His eyes finally moved up Kevin's right shoulder.

When Rothstein reached out to touch the largest of the hairs, Kevin visibly flinched. "They hurt if you touch them," he said, feeling weak for saying it.

"How long have you been beset by these?"

"The ones on my arm are recent. The one on my shoulder came out a month or so ago."

"Are they anywhere else?"

"A few on my back and legs." (*And one at the base of my dick but I really don't think you need to know that.*)

"Do you have tattoos and branding there also?"

"No. Why?"

Rothstein looked around the restroom again, then checked all the stalls, before speaking.

"I've seen designs like yours before." Rothstein moved closer. "See this?" He traced his finger in the air over one of the scars, a long line with a triangle attached to the middle. "It's a German rune, a thyth. An ancient letter if you will." He pointed at another scar and adjoining tattoo. "See here? This N-like figure next to this sharp S? They're symbols for uraz, standing for manifestation and power, and sugil, which has many meanings, but the most common being a cosmic energy or life-giving force. I know a few more, but the rest . . ." he shook his head. "I have no idea."

"Okay," Kevin said slowly. "So Readona, the guy who did these, had a thing for old German letters. So what?"

"After you came to my party, and after your help with the resulting chaos of that evening, I spent some time researching the figures and designs. I realized I've seen some of those designs, these very same markings, at *Blizingsleben* and *Externsteine*, two areas in Germany connected to the occult."

"The occult? Readona was fucked up, but I never got the

sense he was into witchcraft or other shit like that. And even if he was, why put them on me?"

"I don't know." Rothstein took another step back. "Like my grandfather, I'm a man of medicine and science, but I've seen things in Europe and read translations of ancient texts that have made me question if we truly should discount the ancient myths and beliefs of our Stone Age ancestors."

"What are you talking about?" Kevin suddenly felt chilled and put his shirt back on. "Do you think that these brands, these tats are somehow connected to the hair-things? I mean, how could that be?"

"I don't know. I'm just saying that I've never seen anything like those hairs, and it appears that the person who did your scars and tattoos had an intimate knowledge of German runic magic. Sometimes in life Kevin, the things that we discount out of hand are the very things that are the truth."

"So, what the fuck am I supposed to do? Find a fucking German witch-doctor to cure me of this curse?" Kevin hit one of the lavatory doors with his fist. "This has to be a big joke, right? I mean, you're a fucking physician!"

Rothstein took a long deep breath. "I wish this was an elaborate joke, but it's not." He pulled out his wallet and handed Kevin a business card. "Here's the contact number for a colleague, one of the few I still am congenial with in town, who's an excellent dermatologist. If I were you, I would get in to see him as soon as possible to have these hairs, as well as the branding and tattoos, removed at once."

"I don't have insurance," Kevin said in a dejected tone. "Does he do charity cases?"

"I don't know." Rothstein sighed. "I believe he's currently at a conference in Palm Springs. I'll call him when I get back from Europe to see if I can help get you in."

"So, I'm just supposed to do what? Live with these fucking things as they get bigger and bigger?" Kevin carefully leaned against the wall, exhaustion blooming in him like a summertime storm. "Look, Doc, I'm sorry if I sound like I'm going off on you . . . I just hoped that you'd have an answer for me, something normal, something not so fucking crazy."

There was a moment of quiet, then Rothstein touched Kevin lightly on the hand. "Have you given any consideration about talking to the man who did these markings?"

"Talk to Readona?" Kevin shook his head. "I'd rather be dead then have *any* contact with that motherfucker ever again."

"I've never been to prison, Kevin, and I never want to. I can only imagine what kind of evil festers in such a place, but if this Readona put these markings on you, perhaps he did it for a reason."

"No!" Kevin emphatically repeated himself. "I can't go back there. I promised myself when I walked out through those gates, I'd never set foot in that fucking place again."

"I know it sounds like a horrible choice, but sometimes we have to break promises to ourselves in order to find the answers we need." Rothstein finally moved toward the door. "I'm sorry, but I have to go. I hope you find the strength to find the answers you need. I'll call you when I get back in the states."

Kevin stood in the bathroom another five minutes, wishing he had more Oxy to put himself into a thoughtless stupor. Suddenly, three twenty-something men, all dressed in black leather chaps and billowing white robes, stumbled in and began groping and kissing each other.

"Have fun," Kevin said to the trio, who paid him no heed as he walked out, still deep in thought regarding Rothstein's words.

He's fucking crazy. That has to be it. Spent too much time around cadavers dipped in formaldehyde and it's cooked his brain.

"But what if he's right?" Kevin wasn't aware he was

speaking out loud until a tall, lean woman wearing a Masonic Auditorium security badge lightly tapped him on the arm. "Excuse me, sir. Did you say something? Are you okay?" Kevin looked up. "Sure."

Actually, I'm fantastic! Got these weird-ass growths sprouting from me that this doctor has told me might be caused by an ancient German curse. How the fuck could I be better?

"We're going to be closing, soon," she said, "so you'll have to be leaving."

"Sure." He started to pull out his phone to call Sherri when he heard a woman shout his voice. He looked up and saw Roxanne walking over to him.

"Hey, sexy," she greeted. "Did you and the good doctor get together? I told him you were lost in the upper regions of this place trying to find him."

"I did. Thanks for letting him know I was looking for him."

"Anything for you." She moved in and kissed him full on the lips while placing something in his palm. "Call me if you ever want to have some real fun."

Kevin looked down at his hand. She had a placed a Glamor Girls card in it with her cell phone number written in neat numbers on the top.

"Thanks," he said, then realized the woman standing two arm's length away and glaring at him was Sherri.

"You shit!" she said, and for a second Kevin wasn't sure if she was talking to him or Roxy, who quickly walked away. "I've spent an hour looking for you and here you are, having a grand time with the slut of MCFM!"

Kevin took a deep breath and slowly exhaled. "I don't know how long you've been there, Sheri, but Roxy kissed me. She's stoned out of her mind and acting like she always acts."

Sheri walked unsteadily up to him. "You expect to pull that 'I'm so innocent' crap again?"

"You're obviously drunk, I've had a rotten fucking night,

so how 'bout we cancel this drama-fest right now and go home."

"Go home?" Sherri's voice was high and loud. "Fuck you, Kevin!"

"What the hell's wrong with you?"

"You think I'm blind? You think I don't know that you were fucking her when you were supposed to be looking for Rothstein?"

"I didn't fuck her!" *Maybe I wanted to, but I didn't and don't I get any credit for that*?

"I can't believe you," she said. "The biggest night of my career is coming up and you're messing with my head just for some crazy bitch like Roxy!"

"Your fucking career?" Kevin stepped closer and pinned Sherri against the wall. "I've got God-knows-what growing on me, *in* me, and you're worried about is your fucking career?"

Sherri shoved him hard and he had to throw his arms out to keep his balance to not fall flat on his ass.

"And what are you doing about your 'problem', Kevin? What have you done to try and take care of it?"

"I've gone to a doctor. It wasn't my fault he was a fucking quack!"

"Then go to another one!" Sherri crossed her arms tightly over her chest. "I can't do this. Not now." She dug in her purse and threw two twenty-dollar bills at him. "Here. Call a cab. Call Roxy. I don't fucking care. Just don't call me."

"I don't need your damn money!" Kevin balled up the bills and threw them at her as she walked away.

"I'm going to have to ask you to keep your voice down," he heard someone say behind him. Kevin turned to see the same security guard from before.

"Sorry," Kevin said. "My girlfriend and I were having a little disagreement."

The woman nodded. "Yes. I know. Everyone heard the

little disagreement."

Kevin walked outside into the cold. There were few cars, no cabs, and no Sherri. Thick, wet snowflakes tumbled haphazardly out of the dark sky and chilled him to the bone. He reached into his pocket to get his phone and try and call a cab when his hand brushed Roxy's card.

Kevin pulled it out and stared at the phone number scrawled on top. *If you call her, you know you're going to fuck her and that definitely will put an end to the Sherri and Kevin experiment.* Yet even with that absolute certainty, he kept the card out when a pair of hands reached from behind and covered his eyes.

"Guess who?"

It was Roxy.

"I thought you left." Kevin turned around to face her.

"And I thought you were going home with Sherri," Roxy said, smiling mischievously.

"We had an argument."

"I'm sorry." She giggled and pulled her coat tighter, "but Sherri can be a high maintenance gal. You should've asked me out before you started fucking her."

"We'll work it out," Kevin said, suddenly wishing he had taken the time to call a cab. "I was just getting ready to call a cab."

"I already called one," Roxy said. "You can come over to my place and chill awhile. I promise to give you all the juicy stories about Sherri-baby!" She laughed, then dug into her purse and pulled out another ovoid blue pill.

An Oxy.

"It's your lucky day," she continued. "I found two more of these buried at the bottom of my purse. You look like you can use this one."

Kevin looked at her, looked at the pill, then opened up his mouth. Roxy put it on his tongue and he swallowed it just as the cab pulled up to the curb.

CHAPTER 33

THE INTERIOR OF THE cab smelled of moldy upholstery and cheap aftershave. Roxy snuggled up to Kevin and lay her head on his shoulder. The one sans the hair.

"Sherri pissed off?"

Kevin sighed. "Yeah. Sherri pissed off."

Roxy sat up and laughed. "She'll get over it soon enough. Sherri gets mad fast, but she gets over things fast too."

"She said I didn't give a shit about the show," Kevin drawled, "or something to that effect." He looked at Roxy. "How the fuck could she think something like that?"

"The show's the show. It'll happen and then it'll be over, and people will move on." Roxy lit up a cigarette and blew smoke at the prominent NO SMOKING sign on the back of the seat. The cab driver, a thin, middle aged man with pale skin and a pock-marked face, looked back in the mirror but said nothing.

"You're not jazzed about it?" Kevin asked. "I thought it was going to get you a TV gig and all that rich and famous shit."

"The only thing that's going to get us a TV gig are my

blowjob skills." Roxanne shook her head and looked out the window. "Nothing lasts forever. That's why you have to live for the moment. Sooner or later, bad shit is going to fuck you over."

You mean bad shit like weird-ass hair things growing out of your body? "That's one way to look at things."

"It's the only way." Roxy smiled and leaned in to kiss him before her phone began ringing in her purse. She pulled it out and looked at the number. "I have to get this."

Kevin sat back in the seat, his face feeling numb yet at the same time sparkling with heat. *You shouldn't have taken another oxy. Just like you shouldn't have gotten into this cab with Roxy. Which goes along with every other fucking shouldn't have in your damn life.*

"I'm on my way home," he heard Roxy say, her face etched in a tight smile. "I'm tired, honey. It was a long day."

Kevin saw her listening intently before slowly nodding. "Okay, honey, five minutes. Just wait outside the door."

Roxy turned off her phone. "Sorry, baby," she said to Kevin, "have to make a quick pit stop." She leaned forward and said an address to the driver.

"What's going on?" Kevin asked.

"Have to stop at G-Girls and see a client," Roxy answered, as if discussing a clinical case at a doctor's office. "It'll only take me a couple minutes."

"G-Girls?"

"Glamor Girls. Where I dance for extra cash."

"That's right . . . I remember." Kevin looked out the window. The few streetlights that were working bathed the sidewalks and barred windows of small shops in muted shades of black and gray.

They drove in silence until the cab pulled over to the curb next to nondescript one story brick building and a large sign which blared out **Glamor Girls!** in eye-numbing florescent orange.

"Stay in the car," Roxy said to Kevin as she climbed out. "I don't want you dumping me for any little hard-body that's dancing tonight."

Kevin blinked and tried to focus but it was no use. The second Oxy was already performing narcotic magic and he felt it coat his brain with a syrupy sheen.

The cab driver turned around and gave Kevin a yellow-toothed gargoyle grin.

"You're a lucky man to have a woman like that," he said. "Maybe I'll have to come down and see her dance one night."

"You should do that," Kevin sighed. "She puts on a helluva show."

"Really?" The guy's bloodshot green eyes lit up. "She give any extras?"

"Extras?" Kevin leaned forward, a scowl on his face. "What do you mean by that?"

"I don't mean anything!" He quickly turned and grabbed the wheel.

Kevin sat back and closed his eyes. *Why the hell are you fucking with this guy?* a tiny voice in his head asked, and just as quickly, another voice, sounding the same but somehow different, answered, *because you can. Because it's fun to fuck with weak people,* "Especially when you're higher than hell."

"What's that?" the driver said. "What did you say?"

Kevin opened his eyes. "I didn't say anything."

"Yes, you did. You said something about being high." He turned around again to face Kevin. "I don't mind stopping at a strip club, the meter's still running you know, but if she's here to pick up drugs—"

"She's not here to pick up drugs," Kevin said slowly, making sure to correctly enunciate every word. "Just saying hi to an old friend." He had to work to keep himself form laughing after saying the word 'hi.' The laughter stayed trapped in his chest, but a large grin still broke out on his face.

The driver smiled back, taking Kevin's drug-induced mania as a sign of friendliness. "I believe you. It's just that in my line of business—"

He stopped speaking when the back door jerked open.

"Is this the motherfucker you're dumpin' me for?" a large, white guy (his face dark from too many sessions in the tanning booth) said, his body halfway in the cab. His breath smelled of expensive scotch and it wafted into the cab like a yellow cloud.

Kevin guessed the guy to be in his late forties or early fifties, with slicked back dyed black hair. He had the build of a professional athlete gone to seed from too much booze and too many high calorie dinners, a large, gelatinous belly overhanging an expensive leather belt and freshly pressed slacks.

"Eric, don't be a dick!" Roxy grabbed the man by both shoulders and tried to pull him out of the cab.

"Don't call me a dick!" Eric turned around and pointed a sausage-sized finger in Roxy's face.

With a quick motion, Roxy grabbed his finger with one hand and his wrist with the other. She stepped to the side and bent his finger at what seemed to Kevin to be an impossible angle while twisting his wrist. The result was that Eric, who easily outweighed Roxy by a hundred and fifty pounds, dropped to his knees.

"You're breaking my finger!" he yelled in a high-pitched voice.

"Are you gonna stop being a dick?" Roxy asked, still holding tight.

"Yes!" Eric answered, thick tears dropping down his flushed cheeks.

She finally let go before helping Eric to his feet. She brushed away his tears and shooed away a few onlookers that had come out of the club to watch the spectacle.

"I'm sorry, honey," she said to Eric, "but you remember what I told you last time when you started some shit when you saw me with another guy?"

Eric nodded like a chastised six-year-old. "I didn't think you meant it."

"Now you know I mean what I say." Roxy took Eric's face in her hands and kissed him gently on the cheek, then whispered something in his ear that brought a smile to the man's face.

"You promise?" he said, beaming.

"Of course." Roxy reached around and pinched him on his ample ass. "I'll see you next week." She got in the cab and motioned the driver to continue.

"What was that about?" Kevin asked after they pulled away from the club.

Roxy ran her fingers through her hair. "That was Eric. Played football for the Lions back in the day before he blew out his knee. A nice guy who likes to throw his money around as well as his weight."

"I take it he's a regular at the club?"

"Uh huh." She winked at him, then laughed. "Regularly passes me twenties for dry humping him during two and half minute songs. He gets blue balls and I get his cash!"

The cab started moving again. "That move you did," Kevin said, wagging his index finger. "That was slick."

Roxy shrugged. "I dated a guy who did some martial arts. I showed him some of my moves and he showed me some of his." She snuggled up next to Kevin. The pressure of her body on the hairs was dulled by the oxy but he could still feel it, a deep ache that seemed to permeate his whole being.

"Eric has a mean bark but he's harmless as hell." Roxy opened up her purse and pointed at a small plastic bag filled with something that Kevin couldn't make out. "He scored some sweet coke," she said in a conspiratorial whisper. "Best Columbian money can buy."

Kevin smiled and it felt like his grin would split his face in two. "That's great," he whispered back. "I was just thinking that I needed some more drugs to make this a perfect night."

Roxy pinched his mouth with two fingers. "You are such a smart-ass at times, you know that?"

"I've been told that a time or two," Kevin said, his words feeling heavy on his tongue.

Three minutes later the cab pulled down a side street and up to a small set of condominiums.

"Thanks, sweetheart," Roxy said to the cabdriver. She handed him a twenty. "Keep the change."

Kevin looked at the meter. It read $19.20.

Roxanne got out the cab and turned around. "Earth to Kevin? You getting out?"

A tiny voice, distant, muted by the oxy and booze, struggled to be heard. *Stay in the cab. Tell the driver your address. You have enough cash at home to pay him. If you get out now then—*

"Kevin?" He opened his eyes to see a hand, long, thin, with nails painted bright red, reaching out. Roxy laughed and he felt her grab his arm—somehow missing the hairs—and he was outside, the air cold and bitter, burning his lungs with each shallow breath.

"You ever ask yourself why in the fuck we live in Michigan?" Roxy said as she fumbled getting her key in the lock. "It's so damn cold my nipples are as hard as diamonds!"

She finally got the lock open, and they entered a foyer leading directly into a living-room filled with a large, L-shaped black leather couch, two small coffee tables, a desk holding a computer and printer. In between the two arms of the couch was a small desk with framed pictures of MCFM. A small thin-screen TV hung on the far wall.

"Welcome to my little abode." Roxy threw her purse on the couch before turning on one standing light in the corner of the room. "Make yourself comfortable—I'm gonna go freshen up. If you have to use the bathroom there's one around the corner next to the basement stairs."

Kevin lazily threw his jacket on one far end of the couch

next to her purse and watched Roxy walk upstairs. *Look at that beautiful ass. In just a few minutes it's going to be bobbing up and down on your cock as she fucks you silly*!

"Why are you here?" he said to himself in a quiet, slurred voice. The Oxy was wrapped around his brain like a thick spider web, making the world move in sedated confusion.

He walked in the bathroom to take a piss, and afterwards, while washing his hands, he looked in the mirror.

"You, sir, are quite fucked up," he said to his reflection. His hair was tousled and wet from the snow, his skin was flushed, and his pupils were large circles of black. He tapped once, twice on the mirror.

It's a medicine cabinet, dipshit. I bet she's got some good stuff in there!

Kevin opened it. There lay a three-quarters squeezed tube of toothpaste, a small travel bottle of mouthwash, and three prescription bottles. He pulled those down and looked at the labels.

Xanax. Nope, don't need any more downers. Viagra— hmmm, must keep them here for guys like Eric.

The third bottle was the charm. 'Oxycodone 10 mg' it read, and it was almost full. Kevin dumped a dozen pills in his hand and put them in his pocket.

He was back sitting on the couch, contemplating whether or not to take another Oxy, when Roxanne came downstairs, carrying what looked like a large white pen in her hand. She was wearing a short black silk robe, opened enough in the front so that Kevin could see most of her ample breasts.

She stood next to the couch and bent over. "Ready to have some fun?"

Kevin looked up. "I was born for fun."

"That's the spirit!" she knelt down, and Kevin finally saw that he thought was pen was actually a fire starter, the kind used for gas grills. When she flicked it on, the blue flame illu-minated a basketball sized pot in the shadows on the end of the couch. Roxy placed the tip of the lighter to the pot and it silently erupted an eight-inch-high wall of flame.

"Isn't that kind of dangerous?" Kevin asked. "Having a fire pot in the house?"

Roxy shrugged. "Life is dangerous. Besides, I got a thing for fire. It gets me hot and wet."

She sat next to him and untied her robe. She was naked underneath.

"I already did my line upstairs." She pulled out the bag of coke and expertly tapped a line on top of one breast. "Your turn."

Without hesitation Kevin put his face down and inhaled in one quick sweep. He sat back and squeezed his eyes shut and forced himself not to sneeze.

"Oh my God, you should see your face!" Roxy laughed, a high hysterical sound that hurt Kevin's ears. "Your eyes are all scrunched up, your mouth is in a tight pucker. It looks like you just smelled a piece of shit!"

"Glad I'm providing you with some amusement," Kevin said, wiping his eyes.

"You turning into a sensitive pussy?" She wiped his upper lip with one index finger then put it in her mouth and sucked seductively. "Don't want to be wasting any of that good coke."

"Certainly not," Kevin said, already feeling the coke fight with the Oxy to speed up his brain.

"How's that shoulder?" Roxy asked, snuggling up next to Kevin. She grabbed one of his hands and put it between her legs and he could feel her heat, her slippery wetness.

"It hurts."

"Then this is your lucky night. I give great massages."

Bet you've never given a massage to someone with weird-ass hair things growing all over their body. "That's a helluva offer, but I don't think I'm up for one of those tonight."

Roxy pouted, then laughed. "That's okay. I think I know

what muscle you really want massaged." She expertly unbuckled his belt and zipped down his pants. Kevin closed his
eyes and laid his head back and was hard in seconds as Roxy
worked his shaft with one, then both hands. He pushed all
thoughts of everything else away, of Sherri, of—

Shit. The hair by my dick!

"What's this?"

Kevin opened his eyes. Roxy was squatted between his
knees, his underwear pulled down so that his cock and balls,
and one short, black hair-thing, were visible.

"It's just a weird pube," Kevin said with as much false sincerity he could muster.

Roxy looked up with a frown. "You need to shave, baby.
The full bush look went out of style in the 90s."

"Guess I'm just old fashioned."

"I know what!" Roxy clapped her hands together. "I
could shave you right now!"

Kevin quickly shook his head. "How 'bout later?" He
reached down and put her hands on his semi-tumescent penis. "Finish me up first, okay?"

"Promise you'll let me shave you?"

"I promise."

Roxy winked at him. "Okay. Now just lay back and be a
good boy while Roxy gives you the best blow-job you've ever
had."

"How could I refuse that?" Kevin closed his eyes again as
Roxy began to assault him with her hands and mouth.

Even with the mental numbing of the drugs, in just a few
minutes he felt himself worked to the edge. As the pressure
built up in his balls, he opened his eyes to see Roxy—who
had pulled a pair of tweezers from her purse—-grabbing and
pulling out the black hair.

The pain, although dulled by the oxy, was still immediate
and deep. Without thought he jerked away from Roxy, who
held the hair up high like a hunter with his trophy kill, her

face etched with revulsion.

The hair-thing was moving, wiggling like a stuck worm on a hook. Roxy screamed and gave a sharp snap to her wrist which sent the hair flying off the tweezers and toward the fire pot. It landed on the edge, and the madness of the situation escalated to pure insanity as Kevin saw the hairs roots—double the length of the hair—acting like miniature spindly legs, balancing the coal-black thing from falling in the pot, holding on with tiny toe-like projections.

"What the fuck!" Roxanne screamed over and over while Kevin sat dumbly, incredulous at the sight of the hair thing flailing like a demonic armless drunken man before finally falling into the fire.

There was a quick hiss, like bacon frying in a pan. A needle thin line of smoke, black and oily, snaked its way up into the air. A few seconds later came the smell, an impossibly foul odor of putrefied meat and steaming shit.

"What the fuck?" Roxy said again, her voice loud, filled with confusion and anger. "What the *fuck* was that?"

"It was just a hair…" Kevin kept staring at the pot, half-expecting the hair-thing to come crawling back out of the fire like a monster from a B-horror movie that just wouldn't die.

"Just a hair?" Roxanne's voice increased in intensity and pitch with every word. "It was, was, standing on the side of the pot! What the fuck kind of hair does—" her voice suddenly stopped, and Kevin finally looked over. Her eyes were open wide, and she pointed at him with a shaking finger. "Shit! Kevin, you're bleeding like a stuck pig!"

Kevin looked down at his groin. There was a growing pool of blood dripping between his thighs and covering his now-limp dick. *How in the hell can one little hair cause so much bleeding? Maybe I'll die of blood loss. What a helluva caption on the evening news: Man Dies After Bloody Blowjob!*

Roxy ran into the kitchen and grabbed a dirty towel off a chair and threw it at him. "Push that up against it." When he was slow to, move Roxy pointed at him. "C'mon, Kevin, you're bleeding all over my couch!"

"I'm sorry." The room began to spin as the pain worked through the Oxy and made Kevin sick to his stomach.

"You look terrible."

"I'll be fine . . ." Kevin closed his eyes and tried to pull it together. "Just give me a minute here."

"You need to leave." Roxy's voice was cold and hard.

"What"? Kevin looked at her. She stood in the hallway, arms tightly crossed.

"You need to leave. This is just too fucking crazy. I don't know what the fuck that thing was I pulled off your groin but it sure as hell wasn't just a pube!" She shook her head vigorously, like trying to shake water out of her ears. "It was fucking moving! It stood on the edge of the pot. It was fucking alive!"

"It wasn't alive. We're high, Roxy. Both of us. I didn't see anything like that. It was just a . . . a hair."

"I know what I saw!" She took a step back. "I told you I'm smart. I read a lot of shit. Maybe that hair-thing was something that the government infected you with in prison, some type of new disease that they're testing out for germ warfare or to depopulate the planet!"

"It was just a fucking hair!" Kevin's voice was louder than he intended and he quickly put up one hand, the one that wasn't pressing a towel to his bleeding crotch. "Listen, I didn't mean to yell, okay? It's just that . . . hairs aren't alive, Roxy. I mean, it's dark in here and the fire pot makes all sorts of weird shadows and—"

Roxanne opened the hallway door she was standing next to and pulled out a short-barreled twelve-gauge pump shotgun. She pointed it at Kevin.

"What the hell?" he pulled up his pants, keeping the towel on his groin. "Roxanne, put that damn gun away!"

"You need to leave. Now." Her voice was quiet and cold.

"Things are finally going good for me. I make sweet money at Glamor Girls. MCFM is finally taking off. Crazy shit like this . . ." she wagged the gun back and forth and Kevin's eyes never left the barrel, which seemed impossibly huge. "This crazy shit is something I don't need in my life."

"Okay, Roxy. I'm moving. See, I'm moving." Kevin kept eye contact with her and as he slowly backed toward the front door.

"I'm sorry, Kevin," Roxy said, still pointing the gun at him. "I just wanted to have some fun, but this is just too fucking crazy."

"Yeah. It is," Kevin said before closing the door behind him and stepping out into the cold night air.

CHAPTER 34

K EVIN WAS LYING ON the floor of his house next to the couch when the sound of his cell phone woke him. He sat up, illuminated by the weak rays of sunlight coming in from the front window, totally disoriented to where he was or how he got there. It was only after the phone went silent that he realized he was home.

What the fuck happened last night? Where are my fucking clothes? Kevin looked around and found them in a pile next to the couch. Feeling chilled, he went to put on his sweater when he noticed it was covered in vomit. Disgusted, he balled it up and threw in in a corner.

"I feel like shit . . ."

The words came out cracked, heavy, and his mouth felt and tasted like it had been stuffed with cotton balls soaked with piss. When Kevin put his hands to his face and slowly rubbed his forehead and temples, his skin felt odd, like touching a mannequin in the department store, and there was a smell . . .

He put his fingers up his nose and inhaled. Underneath the odors of cigarettes, booze and pot there was a subtler, almost sublime yet very real smell of rot, of decaying meat—

And then he remembered sitting at Roxy's, hearing her screams, watching as the hair-thing she tore from the base of his dick meet its untimely end in a pot of fire and giving off a stench that would forever be seared into Kevin's consciousness.

With shaking hands, Kevin slowly unwrapped the blood-soaked towel around his groin. *If there's more hairs down there I'll lose it. I'll crawl into a bottle of whiskey and never come out.*

Kevin looked down at his groin, dried blood streaking his thighs, cock, and balls. There were no more hair-things, just a crimson crusted, jagged pea-sized hole where the hair that Roxy had pulled out had been. He gazed at his arms, at his thighs, at his shoulder, at the black projections sprouting out of his skin, and a powerful shudder raked his body.

What if Rothstein was right? What if, somehow, Readona has put something, something evil into me and now it's pushing its way out? Kevin tried to think it through, but the effort was like climbing Everest. His brain was beyond frayed, it was fried, burnt out from too much alcohol, too many drugs, too little sleep and too much horror that couldn't be real but was.

His eyes fell upon the cell phone wedged into the far cushion of the couch, and even crawling over to it was a feat, his body drained of energy and every muscle and joint aching with a deep, gnawing pain. The screen indicated one new voicemail from Caesar. He almost dialed back out of habit then realized he had no desire to speak to anyone and doubted he could put a coherent sentence together.

I need a smoke. Kevin reached into his pocket and grabbed a crumpled pack of cigarettes. He put one in his mouth. *Need a light to get this cancer stick lit, dumbass.* He reached back into both pockets. only to find no lighter, but there were a handful of pills. He pulled one out and stared at it, much like a monkey might gaze in dumb wonder at a brightly lit neon downtown billboard.

More memories of the previous night finally trickled into his mind—an Oxy.

I stole drugs from Roxy, right after we went to her house after the Masonic . . .

"Sherri." The word escaped his mouth on its own volition.

Can't you just imagine the look on her pretty little face when Roxy tells her about the wild and crazy antics of last night?

Kevin picked up his phone and almost dialed her before he dropped it on the floor. *You can't call her. What are you going to say? Hi Sherri, just wanna say sorry about last night and by the way, don't believe any shit Roxy tells you even though it's probably all true.*

"You pushed her away," Kevin said out loud, "just like you pushed away Lisa, like you've pushed away everyone in your life who gave a damn about you."

Kevin felt his heart began to race as a sluggish ball of panic built up in his chest. *What did that asshole shrink at Fairview say? That I had a subconscious hatred of myself and that I felt that I didn't deserve to be happy or have anyone in my life that made me happy?*

"And I told him he was full of shit." *But he wasn't full of shit, was he Kevin? You're the one full of shit. You should have listened to him.*

Why in the fuck was that asshole so interested in me? Why the fuck was I any different?

"And why do I have these fucking insane hairs?" Kevin screamed the question. The room remained silent.

He looked down at his arms again, at the thick hair-thing laying comfortably on his shoulder. *Rothstein said it: the hairs are more than just that, they're connected to the scars and tats that Readona forced on me. That demented fuck must know what they are. And if he knows, he'll know how to get rid of them.*

"But you know how he works," Kevin reminded himself. "He only does things face to face."

He took a deep breath and popped the oxy that he was still holding like a gold doubloon into his mouth.

He had no choice. He would have to go back.

To the Fairview State Penitentiary.

To Hell.

CHAPTER 35

KEVIN STAYED IN AN Oxy and alcohol-induced haze for the rest of the day after he had called the bus company regarding their schedule to Fairview. He moved in and out of consciousness laying on the couch, time both compressing and elongating. He felt like shit, his body alternating between heavy sweats and bone-wracking chills, the hairs an ever-present reminder that nightmares could become real.

The last bus of the day left at 5 P.M. and got up to Fairview at 10 P.M. so that loved ones and family could spend an entire next day with their husbands/fathers/lovers locked up behind cold steel bars. Kevin reserved a seat, called the one Fairview Motel (**Harry's Happy Hillside Family Motel and Lodge**) where he was able to get the last room available. Between the ticket and the motel and the taxi ride home from Roxy's, he had burned through most of his remaining cash. Not really anything left for rent, for food, for anything. He was in to going to Fairview.

All in.

He finally forced himself to get ready, grabbing a dust-laden camo knapsack—it had been his father's in Vietnam—out of his tiny closet and threw in some clothes. Jeans, sweat-shirts, the only clean pair of socks and underwear he could find.

4:20 P.M. the clock on his nightstand read. He had hoped Caesar could take him to the bus stop, but the message on his phone shot down that idea. Caesar and Maria were headed down to Indiana for a week to look at houses, leaving Kevin at the mercy of public transportation.

I should get going to the bus stop. He picked up the knapsack, which felt far heavier to him than he knew it was, then went into the kitchen and threw in his last two bottles of whiskey, along with the rest of the Oxys he had wrapped in paper towel.

Kevin walked outside and a strong northerly wind blew a fine mist of freezing rain in his face. He turned to lock the door and heard a car pull up in the driveway.

It was Sherrie.

Kevin stood halfway down the steps. It took every ounce of his fading strength to not run inside and lock himself in.

Sherrie got out and opened up an orange umbrella emblazoned with the Detroit Tiger's old English D.

"You going somewhere?" She pointed at the knapsack.

Kevin tried to swallow but his mouth was dry. "Yeah."

They stood in silence, the only sound in Kevin's ears the pounding of his heart.

Sherrie walked closer. "God, Kevin, you stink. What's that smell?"

Kevin took a step back. Could she smell the hairs, the subliminal stinking rot?

"Did you come over here just to comment on my personal hygiene?" Kevin regretted the words instantly as they left his lips but unable to bring them back.

Sherrie flinched as if he had slapped her. "Yeah, that's me. A nagging, nasty bitch."

"No, that's not you." He so wished he had left five minutes earlier. "It's just that, it's been a shitty twenty-four hours."

"Really? Her voice was high with emotion. "Well, let me clue you in that it hasn't been great for me either." She tried to cross her arms, but the umbrella made it awkward. "You want to know why that is?"

Kevin said nothing and she continued.

"It's because my boyfriend, the man I thought I was in love with, was with another woman last night." She glared at him and Kevin wished for all the world he could undo what he had done. "Did you really go home with her?"

Kevin had no energy left to lie. "Yeah."

"Did you fuck her?"

He thought of Roxy on the couch, his dick in her hand and mouth before it all went bad. "No. I didn't fuck her."

Sherrie's eyes narrowed, then she slapped him. Hard enough to draw blood. Kevin felt a thick drop form on his lip and let it travel down his chin, not caring.

"I loved you!"

He finally wiped the blood away with the back of his hand and looked at it, half expecting to see tiny, black hair things wiggling in the crimson like obscene sperm. "Loved . . . that sounds past tense."

Her shoulders slumped. "Sometimes you can be the coldest man I ever met. You say shit that—" her voice cracked, and Kevin could tell she was fighting back tears, "—cuts right to my heart."

"One of the few talents I have. Pushing away those I love."

Sherri blinked once, twice, like awakening from a bad dream. "You're right. You do that very well." She turned and began to walk back to her car.

"I'm going to Fairview." He didn't know why he said it. Maybe just to tell someone, that the words would somehow justify it, sanctify the unholy madness that pushed him back to a place he swore on his mother's grave he would never return to again.

She turned around. "You're going where?"

"To Fairview State Penitentiary. The prison."

"Why?"

"To see Readona."

Sherrie frowned. "The guy that tatted you? That scarred you? The guy you called a fucking monster?"

"Yeah. That guy." He pulled up his sleeves, the cold air and rain like acid on his skin. "I need to know why he gave me these, how they're connected with those fucking hair-things that are growing out of me."

Sherri slowly walked over to him, each step measured, but still moved closer. With each step, Kevin allowed himself the crazy hope that there was a still chance between them.

"Kevin, let's go see a doctor." She held out her hand. "I'll take you to the ER right now."

Kevin shook his head. "They can't do anything there!" His voice became louder with each word, but he couldn't hold back. "It's something else, maybe something I did, karma coming back around to balance it out."

Sherri continued to beckon him. "Kevin, I can see you're stoned, but listen to yourself: what the hell could you have possibly done that—"

"I killed someone!" he screamed and even before the words left his lips, he knew that he had just destroyed the last link between himself and the woman that he loved.

Sherrie gasped, stepped back. "You killed someone? When?"

He rubbed his eyes with the back of his hands. "At Fairview. He was a kid. Seventeen. I didn't know him. Never met him. I just fucking killed him . . ." (*and cut out his heart, why not go all the way and tell her that too?*)

Her eyes opened wide, and he knew she would always see him as nothing more than a murderer from that second on.

"You killed a boy? Why would you do that? Did this Readona tell you to murder someone and you . . . you just did it?"

"You don't know what it was like," Kevin sobbed, his voice filled with self-pity and pain and the words began to fall out on their own, a verbal orgasm that he couldn't cease even if he wanted to. "It was him or me. *Him-or-me*! Don't fucking judge me, don't think I'm a monster unless you've been in that god-forsaken hell and—"

"What if it would have been my brother?" Sherrie's words were soft, quiet, and they carried the weight of the world. "Would you have killed him?" Her arms fell to her sides and she dropped the umbrella. "You would have, wouldn't you?"

Kevin stepped closer and put out his arms. "Sherrie, please just try to understand, I—"

She hit him again in the face, but this time with a closed fist and Kevin felt a tooth loosen. She pulled back to hit him again and this time he caught her hand mid-way thru the punch.

She screamed, "Who the fuck are you? You're not the man I fell in love with, you can't be, because if you are than that makes me . . ." her words ceased, and she backed away.

"Readona made me do it. They were going to kill me. I didn't have a choice. I swear, I didn't have a choice."

"You always have a choice. Everything we do in this fucking world. You always have a choice. And you . . . you chose to murder."

She finally picked up her umbrella and flicked out the water from it.

"Go," she said. "Go back to Fairview. To that fucking evil place. You belong there.".

Kevin stood in the rain another five minutes after she had left, the water soaking him to his skin. He thought he could feel the hair on his shoulder twitch with indignation.

CHAPTER 36

"MOMMY, WHEN IS THE bus coming to take us to go see Daddy?"

Kevin glanced from the corner of the Harry's Happy Motel lobby in Fairview at the small freckled -faced boy, seven or eight years old, with close-cropped red hair and a cherubic face.

The boy's mother, a dour-looking, pencil-thin twenty-something woman wearing a bright orange goose down jacket, frowned. "I told you before, the damn shuttle will get here when it gets here." She shook her head and stormed outside and lit up a cigarette.

He glanced to see give kid give him a 'don't worry about her, she's just scared' shrug. Kevin nodded then pressed himself back into the corner.

He had been awake since four a.m. in the hard double bed of Harry's Happy Motel, staring at the ceiling while listening to callers on an early-morning radio talk show. The major topics were alien abductions, MK-ULTRA mind control, and chemtrails being used to either poison the planet, stop global warming, or kill the aliens that were enslaving people with MK-ULTRA mind control.

Kevin had mulled the idea of calling—*I wonder if the conspiracy folks would have any ideas about my hairs?*—but since his phone battery was almost dead, he decided against it.

I wonder how many times Caesar or my mom stayed here when they came up to see me. Kevin Ciano, Prisoner Number 552476. We never really know what we're doing to our families by being in that hell hole called Fairview. All the time we're so worried about ourselves—trying to survive, trying to get by day to day, that we forgot all the pain and suffering we caused to those we said we loved.

Like what you're still doing to Sherrie, a tiny malignant voice in the Kevin's skull taunted him.

"What's that?" the hotel clerk, a pale-skinned short man with receding gray hair and a gravelly voice standing behind the counter, said to Kevin.

"I didn't say anything," Kevin said.

"Yes, you did! You said F-you, but you used the F-word instead of just saying the letter."

A crazed grin began to pull at the corners of Kevin's mouth, fueled by the absurdity of the man's statement. "I'm sorry if I said anything. I was just thinking of someone that I had an argument with."

The man pointed a shoulder at the freckled-faced boy. "There's kids in here, mister, so watch it."

"I'll do that." Kevin glanced at the clock on the wall behind the counter. "Do you know when the shuttle is getting here?" A murmur of agreements with the question came from the other dozen or so people in the lobby.

The man glanced at the clock. "It's eight-twenty-two. They shoulda been here twelve minutes ago."

And I should have kept to my own business back in Monroe so I wouldn't be standing here waiting for a fucking shuttle to take me to Hell!

"Yeah, I know that," Kevin said, trying to keep his voice even and calm. "I thought maybe you heard about the bus having a problem, or running late, or—"

"Don't know nothin' else about the bus and that's that." The man turned and walked into the back room.

Maybe the shuttle broke down, the tiny voice deep in Kevin's head chided. He shook his head in rebuttal and rolled the solitary Oxy tablet he had in his pocket around and around with his left thumb and forefinger. *Take it, you know you want to take it,* the voice urged him, *that's why you put it in your pocket. Hell, you're already anxious enough about going back and now you're going to let yourself Jones about one fucking pill?*

Kevin couldn't argue with that; he was feeling sweaty and anxious—on top of the ever-present deep, dull ache permeating his entire body, and knew at least part of the agony was his body crying out for more oxy.

"Look, mommy, there's a bus!" A young black girl, nine or ten, pointed outside. Kevin looked and saw the shuttle, painted yellow and green (*the same colors of the showers at Fairview, isn't that a nice touch?*).

The small crowd pushed forward, and someone bumped Kevin on his right shoulder, hitting the hair and causing a sharp needle of pain shooting down his arm. *C'mon, Kevin, take the oxy! It'll make everything all right!*

Kevin knew it certainly would not make everything all right, even as he dry-swallowed the pill before getting on the shuttle.

"Name?"

Kevin looked blankly at the Fairview guard, a burly, middle-aged Hispanic man with a brush cut and weary eyes. For a brief second his mind went totally blank before his mouth formed the words 'Kevin Ciano'.

"Please spell the last name."

Kevin enunciated the letters, hoping that he wasn't slurring his words. He had almost had a panic attack on the ride over, convinced that he would be piss-tested and they would detect the Oxy in his system and never let him leave.

Nobody was tested for anything though. After entering through the outer gates of the prison, they got off at the unloading station, where all the guests went through a metal detector and a pat down. The dour-looking woman with the freckled-faced boy set the detector screaming and was promptly escorted away, her boy walking silently by her side.

The guard had typed in Kevin's name and after thirty seconds, looked up. "Most cons who leave here aren't in a big hurry to visit."

"Can't imagine why that is. I mean, Fairview being the hidden gem of Northern Michigan." All the posturing, the false bravado, that had kept him alive for six years at Fairview came back in an instant, even over his pain and narcotic high.

The guard grunted and a small smile formed on his face as he gazed back at the computer screen at his desk and continued typing. Kevin looked around at the holding area, a large room with cheap plastic seats and a large-screen TV on the far wall. And at the end of the room, behind the guard, was a —thick door, the small glass window in it laced with wire, behind which was the first true entrance to Fairview.

The guard looked up from the computer screen again. "Any cigarettes?"

"What?"

"Smokes. Cigarettes." The guard pointed to a sign to Kevin's right fixed high on the wall.

NO SMOKING IN ANY PRISONER AREA! it proclaimed in both English and Spanish.

Kevin chuckled. "No smoking. All the other shit that goes down in this hellhole and you guys are now worried about smoking?" He dug his fingernails in his palms to stop his laughter, because if he started laughing, really let it out, he'd only stop when he was strapped in a strait jacket and loaded with Haldol.

The guard shrugged his meaty shoulders. "Between me and you, I agree. Still, rules are rules . . ."

Kevin reached into his pants pocket and pulled out a half full pack of smokes. "Here you go. Don't smoke 'em all at once. Bad for your health."

The guard threw the pack into a large oil-drum shaped container that held at least a hundred other packs. "Name of the prisoner you're coming to see?"

"Readona. Charles Readona."

The guard typed some more and looked up. "Says here that Charles Readona is doing detail in the library today so he's unavailable to meet."

"That's not acceptable."

The guard frowned. "What did you say?"

"You heard me. Let Readona know that Kevin Ciano is here to see him. I'm sure he'll find a way to make it happen."

The guard glanced from side to side. "I'm a good judge of character, which is why I've been able to do this job for twenty-one years and not get killed or hang myself, and I sense you're a decent guy. If you know anything about Readona, then you know you should just walk away. Now."

"I need to talk to him." Kevin appreciated the guards caring but found it very misplaced. "If Charles finds out I was here and wasn't allowed to talk to him, I would imagine your health and longevity on the job might come to a sudden end."

The guard pushed himself away from the desk and stood up. "Your choice."

He turned around, typed in a code on the entrance door, then unlocked a huge deadbolt with a key that hung around his neck. There was an audible click, the door opened, and Kevin followed the guard into Hell.

He had blocked it out. The sights, the smells of Clorox disinfectant, of sweat, of cum, all mingled together into one churning cloud of dark, savage defeat, but it all flooded back to him. Kevin felt surreal, like an out-of-body experience, following the guards past row after row of caged cells, some empty, some holding men wearing gray and brown prison garb, men that looked far past beaten and resigned.

"Bipedal monkeys," was what Readona called the mass of prisoners, "all hooting and calling for food and sex and someone to lead them."

And you're going to talk to this crazy motherfucker. Maybe you're the one who's crazy.

They entered a hallway that instead of holding cells, had a dozen rooms on either side, each closed off with thick steel doors. The guard led Kevin to the last room on the left and ran a card through a key reader.

"I'll let Mr. Readona know that you're here."

Kevin nodded in acknowledgement before the guard left and shut the door behind him. At the click of the lock, he involuntary flinched and had the illusion that the room suddenly collapsed inward.

I should have taken more Oxy. Kevin looked around the room.

It was cramped, the size of a small bedroom, with a rectangular wooden table with two more of the cheap green plastic seats that littered the waiting room on each side. In the corner, high on the ceiling, was a security camera, a bright red LED blinking on and off below the wide-open lens. Kevin suppressed a sudden urge to start mugging at the camera, to start making obscene gestures, to drop his pants and shake his pale ass at whoever was doing their shift of monitoring the system.

Instead, he sat down on the chair facing the door and propped his feet up on the table. Kevin closed his eyes and in thirty seconds was in the world of Oxy twilight sleep, random thoughts and sights flashing through his head. *Maybe they'll forget about me here. Maybe I'll stay locked in this room,*

*growing old and gray, becoming part of the furniture, and some
enterprising guard will make a YouTube clip of the famous
chair-shaped-like-a-man of Fairview Penitentiary and he'll become an overnight star . . .*

"Kevin! How good to see you!"

Kevin opened his eyes. There was a nondescript man in
his mid-sixties with thinning brown hair and soft green eyes
standing across from him, a man that could pass in the outside world as a banker or doctor or real estate agent.

It was Charles Readona.

CHAPTER 37

READONA SAT DOWN IN the chair on the opposite side of the table from Kevin. He crossed his arms and leaned back in the chair. balancing perfectly on two legs. "How was the ride up? Strike up any meaningful conversations with any of the unwashed masses of the outside world?"

Kevin stared at Readona and let the anger and rage that began to boil in his guts burn away his underlying fear. "Being outside is a lot better than being behind bars like a fucking animal. Like you are."

Readona let the chair drop back with a metallic clunk and uncrossed his arms. "That's not the way to talk to someone you obviously felt the need to see, now is it?"

Does he know why I'm here? How the fuck can that be?

Readona chuckled, a mild, innocuous sound, exposing his small, white teeth. "You and all the rest are so limited in your worldview. Has it ever occurred to you that I might want to be here at Fairview? You see it as punishment and torture—I see it as liberation. It's you and all the rest that are behind bars, Kevin. In here I'm freer than I've ever been."

"You keep telling yourself that," Kevin said, "and maybe

in twenty years you'll actually start to believe that self-ag-
grandizing bullshit. Of course, you'll still be here because
your sentence is what, one hundred and fifty years behind
bars?" He pushed away from the table and the chair made a
high-pitched screeching sound. "Me, I'm quite happy to be
away from this shit-hole, away from all the murderers and
psychopaths like you."

Readona placed his elbows on the table and folded his
hands together, resting his chin on his outstretched thumbs.
"Like me?"

"Especially like you."

"And yet . . ." Readona let his voice trail off for a moment
and stared at Kevin, "you came back."

Kevin took a deep breath. *Never should have taken that
Oxy. I need to be clear headed; I need to . . .*

"Can I tell you a secret?" Readona asked, and before
Kevin could answer, the older man continued. "I will be out
of here soon. Do you know why I'm certain of that?"

"Because you're a delusional asshole?"

Readona chucked again, although this time more quietly. "No, Kevin. Because of you."

"What's that mean?"

"Come, Kevin. While I do enjoy our little banter, let's cut
to the chase."

*Fuck. What am I doing here? He's playing me, just like he
always played me!*

"Okay, let's cuts to the chase," Kevin finally said. "What
are they?"

Readona frowned. "They? You'll have to be a bit more,
specific."

Kevin stood up and slammed his fists on the table. "You
know damn well what I'm talking about."

Readona shook his head. "I'm sorry, but you're far too
emotional—and high, yes, I can tell by your dilated pupils
and slurring speech that you're quite stoned." He pushed

away from the table. "I think our time here is ended."

No!" Kevin stood over Readona, who looked up at the monitors for a brief second before resuming eye contact with Kevin.

"You touch me, and guards will be in here in an instant," Readona spoke in a calm voice.

"Maybe. Maybe not. Are you willing to bet your life on that?"

"Still full of that self-inflated bravado." He looked Kevin up and down. "Let me see them and I'll tell you what you want to know."

Kevin began unbuttoning his shirt before looking up again at the monitor. "I'm really not into giving the world a free show."

"Of course." Readona gave a quick wave of his hand and the red light on the camera went dead. "There. It's just you and me now."

"It is."" Kevin looked down at Readona and knew he could kill him, could break his neck, beat him into a bloody mess, and nothing could stop him.

"You're thinking that you could kill me right now, aren't you?" Readona said in a serene voice. "And you could. You're younger, stronger, and much more savage than I am. There's nothing I could do to stop you. But if you do that, if you give in to that animalistic urge, then you'll never know . . ." He interlaced his fingers in his lap and sat back in the chair.

Kevin's hands began to shake. The room became hot and airless and suffocating odors of the place flooded his olfactory senses and brought on instant nausea. Kevin forced himself to finish taking off his shirt and wrappings that covered the hairs, willed himself not to puke as Readona sat and said nothing.

Just watched.

Waited.

And then smiled and took a deep, sharp, breath, like a

man on the edge of an orgasm.

"They're beautiful," Readona said in a near whisper. "Bismarck was right."

Kevin stepped back. "Bismarck? What's he got to do with anything?"

Readona licked his lips with a small, cat-like tongue. "When he came to see you. It was a means to an end, just as everything else in the universe ultimately is." His brows furrowed for a few seconds, then smiled. "Oh my. You really thought that Bismarck came to see you for some other reason? And then so quickly let himself be caught so he could come back here?"

Kevin grabbed his clothes and quickly put them back on. "Show's over," he snarled impatiently. "Now it's your turn. What the fuck are these things and how do I get them off me?"

Readona stared at Kevin for what seemed like hours. Finally, he cleared his throat. "They're the accumulation of over forty years of study. Of work, of multiple failures on my part. They are the life from the seeds that will usher in a new world. They are, in one possible word, perfection."

"That's great. And again, how do I get these fucking little hair-things of perfection off me?"

Readona laughed. Not a chuckle, but a straight from the gut laugh. "You can't get them off you. They're part of you, as much as your heart, your head, your cock. Haven't you realized that yet?"

"What I'm realizing," Kevin said, his voice shaking, unable to mask his fear and hate, "is that you're a complete piece of shit. An impotent old fuck who talks big words when actually you're just a trailer-trash high school dropout from northern Michigan who ended up behind bars for raping and butchering a little girl when the world was a very different place. You're fucking insane, and I'm just as crazy coming here thinking you'll give some answers on what these things are."

"Are you done with your profane-laden tirade? If not, carry on. I have all the time in the world. The question is, do you?"

Kevin stepped back and ran his hands through his hair, feeling like a fat balloon that had been pierced with a sharp knife. He didn't know how, but he felt in his gut, through his fear, the oxy, all rational thought, that Readona did know what was going on. And there was not a fucking thing he could do but listen. "Fine. Explain this gift to me and maybe I'll decide not to kill you today."

Readona pushed his chair back so that he was again balancing on two legs. "It's a very long story. I've always had an interest—no, actually a *calling*—to the study of things that are thought of by most as esoteric, as foolish, as long dead superstitions. Wwhat I came to realize early in life is that all of this," he spread his arms out wide, "all of what we call rational civilization is just a thin veneer over forces that control our lives and destinies."

Kevin snorted. "That explains everything. Thanks for clearing it up for me."

"That's better!" Readona said. "That's the Kevin Ciano I knew: arrogant but unsure, cocky but frightened. The perfect vessel for my seeds."

"That's the second time you've mentioned 'seeds,'" Kevin said. "You telling me you actually put some type of fucking seeds in me?"

"You really are going to make me explain it all, aren't you?" Readona crossed him arms then continued.

"I won't bore you with my early years and work, since you wouldn't appreciate it even if I told you. Suffice to say, in 1971 as a young man of nineteen I was stationed in Detmond, Germany. During that time, I took advantage of my military status and traveled extensively. One area that piqued my interest was a very unique rock formation called—"

"Externsteine." It took Kevin a few seconds for his drug-addled brain to realize that the word came out of his mouth.

Readona slowly nodded. "Yes." His eyes narrowed as he gazed at Kevin. "How did you know that?"

"I read a lot." *It's exactly what Rothstein told me. Could he have been right about the tats and scars?*

"Of course, you do. You're Kevin Ciano, scholar and gentlemen." Readona clapped his hands together and Kevin nearly jumped. "Let's continue the lesson then, shall we?"

Kevin glared and said nothing.

"As you know then, Externsteine has been used since pre-historic times by man as a religious and venerated site. The Nazis even proposed turning it into a sacred grove in com-memoration of their Aryan ancestors. Today it attracts all the usual New Age idiots who travel to watch the sun rise during the solstices."

"What the fuck does it have to do with the hairs?"

"Oh, Kevin, they are so much more then hairs! But I suppose there's no reason not to call them hairs, since there's really no word in our language to adequately describe them."

"Try."

"There are things, *truths*, that most people wouldn't believe, but truths none-the-less. At Externsteine, there are marking, pictographs, in underground tunnels that are closed to the public. The people who have seen them call them scribblings, ancient nonsensical paintings by savages, but what people today fail to remember is that in those times, man had nothing else but his own ancient technology, his magic, if you will, to take control of his environment, lest he be consumed by it."

Keep him talking. Maybe he'll say something that actually makes sense and tell me something that will help get these damn things off me! "So, you found these magical spells written on rocks in Germany that the Nazis thought were dope. How come they didn't use them to win World War II?"

"They tried, except the Nazis were akin to children playing with grenades. They thought they knew what to do but stopped far short of what was needed."

Magical writing in German caves that the Nazis tried to use. It's like a fucking bad Hollywood script on acid. "But you, Charles Readona, have figured out how to use these magical pictures to do what?"

"Pictographs." Readona pointed at Kevin's arms. "Your marks, the tattoos, the scars I gave you, are more powerful than you can imagine. I've tried with others, but you were the perfect vessel. When Dr. Denison—"

"Who?" Kevin began to sweat. The name sounded familiar, but the damn oxy addled his memories to dull, washed-out pictures he was unable to see clearly.

"Denison," Readona repeated. "Our esteemed Fairview psychiatrist. Or to be more precise, our late psychiatrist. He had an unfortunate accident and was killed. Regardless, he assured me after your sessions with him that you were the perfect vessel. The work, the magic, I was attempting isn't easy. It requires fertile ground on which to develop and grow."

Keep him talking. "I'm the ground?"

Readona smiled. "Yes, exactly! You're the fertilizing soil: rich, strong, able to withstand the power from the markings which are, to continue the analogy, the seeds."

Kevin's mouth was dry, his breathing fast and shallow. "What you did to me, what you put on me, they're just tats, just scars."

"No, Kevin," Readona mused, "they're very special. The scars are copied exactly from the pictographs at Externsteine and the tattoos are unique in all the world, colored with sweat, semen and ash made from men's bones and entrails, infused with the flesh and blood of a dead boys heart."

Kevin starred insanely at his arms, suddenly wishing he had an axe to cut them off. A memory bloomed into life like an exploding supernova of being at Roxy's, his pants and shorts down to his hips, blood pooling in his groin while a nightmare come alive, a hair-thing pulled from his body, tettered-balanced!-on the edge of a firepot and *Oh-my-Lord that damn thing was really alive and no matter how fucking crazy Readona is he's telling me the truth*!

"The hairs . . . the things growing on me . . . when will they stop?"

"I honestly don't know." Readona rubbed his chin with one hand. "From how they looked, it might be a while yet."

"A while?" Kevin's voice was loud, shrill. "How long is a *while*? A week? A month? A fucking year?"

Readona put his hands up, palms out. "Settle down. It does no good to get upset. You've done well so far. There's no reason to think you won't be able to carry on until they're ready."

Kevin wanted to get up, to go the door and pound on it until he was let out and run away until his lungs burst, or his heart gave out. Instead, he asked in a nearwhisper, "Ready for what?"

"For them to fall off and continue to grow."

"Fall off and grow," Kevin repeated, and suddenly he remembered a dream he had long ago, a dream of endless gray skies and earth with blood-soaked soil, of impossibly huge, phallic-shaped, monstrous things reaching to the heavens with millions of bodies covering their horrific sides. "And when that happens, what?"

Readona spread his arms wide, like an old-time preacher reaching the conclusion of his hellfire and brimstone sermon. "When they finish growing, when they are ready to start life on their own, then it will be a new age, a *Gotterdammerung*: a disastrous, perfect conclusion of events."

"What are you?" Kevin said, wishing he had another oxy, a hundred Oxys to swallow and drown out the insanity that was choking out what was left of his world.

"A man. Just like you."

"No," Kevin said, shaking his head. "You can't be just a man."

"Just a man?" Readona frowned. "Kevin, man is everything! Creators, destroyers, saints—"

"Monsters." The word fell from Kevin's mouth without conscious thought.

"Yes. That too. But even monsters can create things of infinite, terrible beauty."

"I'll kill myself. You said I'm the soil, the nourishment for these things, so if I kill myself, they'll die."

"You won't kill yourself. It takes a very special person to end their own life, to go against that hard wiring inside us that makes us do everything or anything to live. Like murdering a seventeen-year-old boy."

"But you're saying these hairs, these things, are feeding off me, right?" Kevin said, trying to block out the truth of Readona's words. "So, I either die from that or from my own hand. Either way, dead is dead."

"They won't necessarily kill you. If you're strong enough, then there's a chance that you'll survive."

"I'll have them taken out," Kevin said, his mind still racing, "I'll find a doctor and have them cut out or—"

"I told you earlier: you can't take them out of you. Maybe one or two, but all of them? It would be like trying to tear your own guts out."

Kevin slumped, felt like he had been gut-punched. "You've had all this planned out . . . everything from me talking with that damn crazy shrink to murdering that poor boy . . ."

Readona nodded. "You're finally coming to an understanding. You see, this ancient technology, this *magic*, is very hard, and very specific. Truthfully, I wasn't sure that the heart you supplied would work." He gazed off in the distance and interlaced his hands across his chest, as if contemplating some bucolic scene. "When I was a young man, I thought that I could accomplish this task myself, but due to a number of unseen circumstances, along with my own hubris, I was wrong, and ended up here at Fairview."

"When you butchered that little girl decadesago," Kevin said. "That's why you killed her? For her heart? To grow these," he looked at his arms, "*things* on someone else?"

Readona's face tightened, and for an instant Kevin could see s split in the man's armor, a glimpse into his rage and anger. Just as quickly though, he sighed and smiled. "Only the dead live in the past, Kevin, and I am very much alive, just as you are, and will continue to be, if—"

Kevin's anger and adrenaline overrode the stupefying effects of the Oxy and he took Readona by the throat, lifted him out of his chair and slammed him against the wall.

"How about if I take your heart like you took that little girls, or how you made me take that boys?" Kevin said, his voice angry and loud while Readona's eyes bugged out and he squirmed like a coyote in a trap. "How 'bout if I tear that rotted piece of meat out of your scrawny chest and shove it down your throat and watch you choke on it? Would that work for your fucking magic? Would it?"

Readona feebly pulled at Kevin's wrists to no avail.

I could kill him right now, Kevin thought, and the idea was so powerful, so intoxicating, so liberating that he almost did it, almost committed his second murder at Fairview, before finally letting Readona go.

"Killing you isn't worth coming back to this hell hole," Kevin realized, "no matter how good it would make me feel. I'll find a way to get rid of this, this shit you've put in me. I *will.*"

He walked to the door, the adrenaline surge of the moment already wearing off. He was exhausted, aching, and wanted nothing more than to leave and never look back.

But when Readona began to speak, he still turned

around.

"Your anger was always your best and worst trait," Readona said, his voice raw. "Anger at the world, at yourself, at all the self-imposed injustices you rail against. All have kept you from embracing your potential."

"And what is my fucking potential?" Kevin asked. "To be the dirt for your *things*?"

"You look at it all wrong. You should be happy, proud, to be carrying these harbingers of a new future. As much as I choose you, they choose you also."

Kevin felt dizzy and nauseated. He slumped against the door to keep from falling as Readona continued on.

"You are special, Kevin. More than you know, more then *I* first knew." Readona tapped his head. "Here is where true power lies. Thought. Concentration. Intention. My thoughts and intentions gave you your gifts, and now you can make it your own."

"And then what?" Kevin demanded, "That they won't kill me?"

Readona smiled. "Everyone dies, but not everyone can live again in the new age that you can help bring about."

Again, a flash of the nightmare. "An age of death and monsters."

"Look around you, at the world we live in. We already live in an age of death and monsters."

For that, Kevin had no reply.

"I can teach you how to live, how to rule in the new age," Readona continued, his voice holding a manic edge. "All you need to do is ask. Of course, there will be a price." He smiled and licked his lips like a lion slurping away blood after a messy kill. "More blood would have to be found, more life would have to be sacrificed, but life always has a price. And you've shown me already you're very capable of paying that price."

"Never again." Kevin shook his head vigorously and instantly regretted it, the nausea doubling and vertigo causing the room to spin like an out-of-control circus carousel.

"We'll see." Readona stood up and walked over to Kevin, then tapped lightly but methodically on the door. In ten seconds, two guards were there.

"You know where to find me, Kevin. But I wouldn't wait too long. Our mutual friends . . . they look very hungry to me."

CHAPTER 38

K EVIN GLANCED OUT THE smudged bus window, watching the scattered lights of Detroit pass by in slow motion. They had traveled a mile during the last twenty minutes and the rest of the passengers were becoming more vocal about their displeasure.

"Are we ever gonna get off this mutherfuckin' bus?" A large black man with a smoothly shaved head and scowling face yelled to the front. "Why the fuck you goin' so fuckin' slow?"

The driver of the bus, an anorexic-appearing, middle-aged white woman with stringy red hair and large, peace-sign earrings, stared straight ahead and said nothing. Which was exactly the way she had been ever since picking up the passengers at Fairview five hours earlier. Despite an increasing barrage of insults, accusations, and profanity, the woman sat silent and stoic.

Kevin glanced at her. Just the kind to snap. *One more insult and she'll slam on the brakes, stop the bus in the middle of the road, pull out an AR-15 and spray us all until we look like bloody hamburger.*

"I bet it's potholes," a portly young woman in a tattered, brightly-colored ski jacket (and reeking of pot) sitting next to Kevin said. "I bet it's a bunch of them potholes that can eat cars and buses and shit."

"If them pot-hoes be good at eatin' pussy then I can't wait 'till we get there!" another young woman sitting with twin young boys said from the front of the bus. The woman next to Kevin broke out in spastic laughter.

I should never have gone back to Fairview. Kevin closed his eyes and rested his head back on the hard seat as the bus began continued to move in fits and starts. *I forgot just how crazy Readona is. What he said about the hairs, about some fucked-up ancient magic and how I'm the ground for the seeds to grow . . . how can shit like that be true?*

But it is true, another voice in his head said, this one dark, malevolent. *You know he's right. Somehow, he's tapped into something dark and evil and you're on the short end of that fucked stick.*

A sudden jarring of the bus brought Kevin out of his thoughts. The ski jacket-wearing woman next to him turned and punched him on the right shoulder.

"That bitch up front was right!" she said gleefully. "Them was some big fuckin' potholes!"

The blow on Kevin's shoulder wasn't on the hair but close, causing a sharp pain to cascade down his arm and up into his neck. He grimaced and glared at the woman.

"What?" she said, frowning. "Did I hit you too hard, pretty boy?"

She shook her head and moved away from him.

Kevin took a deep breath and closed his eyes again as the bus speed up, trying to focus away from the pain which still throbbed in his arm and shoulder. He hadn't taken another Oxy and he was already feeling a global pain settle into his joints and muscles.

That's nothing compared to how you're going to feel when

the hairs get bigger, a dark voice in his head said.

Readona's a liar, Kevin mentally countered. *A bug-fuck crazy liar.*

Deep down you know he's not, the dark voice countered, *and since he's not, what are you going to do?*

There's nothing I can do. I'll be fucked.

No, you won't! the voice shouted. *Not if you listen to him, if you walk with him down his path to a destination only someone like him can guide you to.*

"Six mile and Schafer stop coming up," the bus driver called out.

Kevin raised his hand. "That's mine." He clumsily picked up the knapsack with both hands and walked to the front of the bus as it crawled to a stop.

"It's starting already," the driver said with a voice that sounded coarse and rough from decades of cigarettes.

Kevin looked at her. "What's starting?"

The woman pointed out the large front window of the bus. In the distance, down one darkened city block, Kevin could see the remains of a dilapidated house burning in the night.

"It's October 30th," the driver explained. "The night that all of Detroit's young devils attempt to burn down the city." She shook her head again and coughed. "Good luck to 'em, I say. Let it burn. Let it all burn."

Kevin stepped off the bus. Snow and freezing rain propelled by a blustery north wind stung his face and hands as he quickly made his way down the block. The only lights illuminating the gloom of the early evening were coming from the crack house.

Must have got a new shipment of product in. The penetrating sound of rap music filtered out through the closed windows and heavily fortified doors of the house. *At least one industry in this town is still going strong.*

His own house was cold and dark. Kevin could see his

breath when he turned a light. *I bet the furnace pilot light blew out.*

He was right.

After re-lighting the pilot, Kevin sat on the couch. He could feel the pressure of his clothing on the hairs, a dull, enveloping ache that mixed with a deeper, nauseating pain that came in waves. And there was the smell again, an undercurrent of rot and decay that emanated from his pores like smoke from a burnt steak.

It's going to be like this the rest of my life. Those fucking things growing, getting deeper, before they fall off and do only God and Readona knows what.

You know what they'll do, the dark voice in his head chirped. *You've seen it. They'll grow and grow and bring about Readona's new world, and all you have to do is embrace it and you can be part of that world.*

"Embrace Readona," Kevin said out loud. "How in the fuck can I even be saying those words?"

But it's the only way, the voice continued. *Can't you see you've been going about this situation all wrong? All you've done is fight it, rail against it, and where has it gotten you? Sitting cold and alone at home, basking in your own sour stench, when you could be a part of something new, something wondrous, something that is coming whether or not you embrace it.*

"Fuck!" Kevin's anguished scream echoed in the tight confines of the house.

He yelled again, and again before pawing through his knapsack and finding the rest of the Oxys. With shaking hands, he placed them on the coffee table in a line.

Six left. He picked one up, uncapped his last bottle of whiskey, and took a long draw after swallowing the pill. *What will I do when they're gone? Hell, maybe I'll just waltz on over to Roxy's and see if she'll loan me a few more, or maybe ask Sherri. . . .*

His eyes moved to the window, and he swore he could

see flickering tongues of fire dancing in the night through the shades. Devil's Night, the night of fire in Detroit, the night of MCFM's big show at the Masonic.

"All of them will be embracing their strangeness," Kevin said, getting up from the couch to pace. "Delmond, Peter, Roxy, Sherri." The thought of her choked him up and he clenched his fists tight, feeling his dirty nails bite into the flesh of his palms to keep him from crying. "They aren't ashamed, aren't afraid of what they know in their hearts they are . . ."

And you need to be like them! the dark voice cried out. *Embrace what you are—a fighter, a warrior, a—*

"Murderer." Kevin spun around the room, looking for the source of the raspy voice before his addled brain realized it was his.

There was a loud knock on the door. Another knock. And another.

It's Sherri! She's come over before the show! Kevin ran to the door, still holding onto the bottle of whiskey.

It wasn't Sherri. Instead, there stood a young man and woman, neither older than twenty. The man had short cropped brown hair and a white shirt and tie slightly visible underneath a thick flannel overcoat, while the girl, thin, blond, with her hair pulled tight in a bun, wore a brightly colored ski jacket over a buttoned up white shirt and a knee-length black skirt. They both looked vaguely familiar, but Kevin couldn't recall from where or when.

The girl offered her right hand in greeting. She smelled of soap and shampoo, odors of a world he no longer belonged in.

"We should introduce, or I should say reintroduce our-selves," the man said. "I'm Jacob and my companion is Emma. We represent the Church of Jesus Christ of Latter-day Saints. We were here a few weeks ago and weren't able to talk with you. Is now a better time?"

That's right—Caesar gave them shit.

"No," Kevin said, "it's not." Kevin was suddenly aware of the bottle in his hand.

"We understand it can be hard to talk," Emma said. "It's just that we think that it's very important that you hear—"

"About how God loves me?" Kevin interrupted, anger erupting inside him. "Let me tell you why God doesn't love me. Or you. Or anyone. He can't. Because he, she, or it doesn't fucking exist."

"I have to disagree," Emma rebuked him. "God is real. He is ever lasting. And preaching the word of the Lord is never a waste of time."

"Really?" Kevin looked up and down the block. "Do you know where you're at?" Before they could answer, he sourly laughed. "You're in Hell. And in Hell, I doubt the word of the Lord is taken seriously."

"It's people in areas like this that need to hear about the love of God the most," Jacob said, even as he took a step back. "That's why Emma and I specifically asked to come back to this area of Detroit to do our mission work."

"Is that so?" Kevin crossed his arms to try to retain some body heat. "How did you two get here?"

"We walked," Jacob said. "Our area to cover is—"

"I know you fucking walked!" Kevin said, his voice hard. "I mean how did you get to this wonderful little neighborhood of mine?"

"We had a driver drop us off," Emma said, totally nonplused by Kevin's demeanor. "Yours is the first block. We have five more to cover."

Kevin snorted. "You really have no fucking idea, do you?" He pointed down the block at the crack house. "Remember that place there? While you might think I'm not the friendliest guy in the world, the animals that live there make me a saint, or whatever the hell you guys have in your church."

"The Lord will protect us from any evil," Jacob said in a

voice that wasn't convincing.

Kevin's eyes narrowed. "You think so? Let's see how well he protects you when you knock on that door. First off, they'll let you in." He looked at the Jacob, then Emma. "Then they'll beat you senseless before running a train on both of you, then they'll get to the really nasty shit."

Emma pulled her coat tight. "I'm sorry you're so bitter about life."

"You need this," Jacob said, handing him the Book of Mormon.

Kevin slapped it out of his hand. The book flew over the railing and onto the wet grass. "And you—both of you— need to wake the fuck up." He shook his head. "Get out of here. Call your ride and get out of here. There's nothing you can do for me or anyone else in this shithole."

"Give yourself to God," Jacob said. "He can do anything."

"God." Kevin said the word as if it were bitter poison. "There's no God. There's nothing in this world except pain and evil."

The girl's eyes narrowed. "You're wrong". Her voice was surprisingly hard. "There is a God. I've seen how he can work miracles."

"Really?" Kevin said. "Did he get you into your favorite college? Give your mommy and daddy the money to buy you a new car you wanted?"

"My father raped me when I was eleven." Emma said this matter-of-factly, her voice low and stoic. "Right after I had my first period. He kept doing it until I ran away at fifteen. He made me get three abortions."

Jacob stared at her with wide eyes but said nothing.

"I know evil," Emma continued. "I looked it in the eye for four long years." She reached out and touched Kevin on the arm. "You can't let it win."

"Don't go to that house." It was all Kevin could say.

Emma continued to look at him for a few seconds more,

then nodded. "We won't." When Jacob began to protest, she gave him a look thatsilenced him. .

"I don't know what's going on with you that's caused you to be so angry and bitter," Emma said to Kevin, "but you need to face it. With God, without God, you need to face it." She walked off the porch and picked up the Book of Mormon and placed it in her purse before looking up one more time at Kevin. "There's some houses you can't avoid."

Kevin stood in the doorway until Jacob and Emma's driver came and picked them up. He stood there for another moment, the cold north wind working its way into his bones. He welcomed it, welcomed the numbness that came with it, helping to keep at bay the ever-present ache that held his body. It was only when his teeth began chattering that he went back inside.

How can someone have faith in an all-loving God without being blind to all the shit in the world? Kevin took a drink from the bottle and welcomed the burn in his esophagus. *If there's any God, it's a crazed, demented child-king getting off watching us torture, maim, and kill each other.*

"Maybe I should give my old priest a call," he said to the empty room, "see if he can do an exorcism on me. I can just imagine the conversation—'Father Daniels, I have these evil hair-things on me that some crazy fucking convict sorcerer at Fairview Penitentiary put into me. How 'bout spouting some scripture and dousing me with holy water for old times' sake?'"

The room was silent. Kevin felt a ball of panic and despair rising in his chest. He washed it down with another mouthful of whiskey.

No, all that would get me is an admission to the psych ward. Maybe I really do need an exorcist.

Or a healer. Fuck, there was talk of a healer when I first met the gang . . .

Kevin sat down on the couch and tried to remember

when he first met Sherrie at the Eastown Theatre, back when it all hard started.

"What was that guy's name?" Kevin rubbed the sides of his temples and tried to force his brain to work. "I can see us all sitting there, with Sherrie and Roxanne arguing about some guy that had been cured of AIDs by this healer . . . Fuck!"

He got up and began to pace in the living-room while trying desperately to remember the healer's name. The Oxy and booze slowed his thoughts down to rambling, almost incoherent words that he could almost see floating in the cold air.

"Nehemiah. . . . That was his name. Nehemiah." A grim smile formed on his face. "They said he walked the streets off . . . off Woodward, in downtown."

Are you sure it was Woodward? Maybe it was Livernois, or Schafer. How can you be sure when you're so fucking high? And that area covers what, two, maybe three-square miles? You really think you can find some inner-city preacher-healer on Devil's Night?

"I have to," Kevin spoke. "I don't have a choice."

Sure, there is. Just take another Oxy to wipe away the pain and doubt, get some sleep, and call Readona. It's the only way you can save yourself, the only way you can—

"Shut the fuck up!" Kevin slammed his palm on the side of his head, knocking himself to his knees. "I have to find Nehemiah," he muttered, head bowed, nausea and vertigo causing the room to feel like it was in the middle of an ocean storm. "I have to find him, I have to . . ."

And if you don't? the voice taunted him.

For that question, Kevin had no answer.

CHAPTER 39

KEVIN HAD THE CAB driver drop him off at Woodward and Three Mile. From there, he began wandering the back roads and alleyways in a wild hope of finding Nehemiah and his mysterious church. Each step was an exercise in pain, aching in his legs and gut extending up into his chest and arms. His clothes felt like raw wool and the pressure of his coat made his sweatshirt act like sandpaper grating on raw skin. He rolled the remaining Oxys around in his pocket like tiny ball bearings and wondered what it would feel like to take every last one of them.

There were few people on the darkened streets, and those that were gave Kevin a wide berth, as if able to sense he was a 21st-century leper, one not worth the time or effort to accost. Snow was falling in fits as Kevin finally took a break under one of the few streetlamps that were working. He lit a cigarette and looked up at the street sign. The original had been torn down and in its place was a crude wooden plaque with the words **Wellcum Too Paradice!** painted in bright red letters. A skeleton-thin rat stood on one end of the plaque, looking down with black eyes.

Kevin took a long drag on the cigarette. *Maybe this is paradise. Maybe everything is getting to be so fucked up that this is as good as it gets.*

"You lost?"

Kevin dropped his smoke. Turning around, he came face to face with a tall, thin black man, his head covered in a torn cap, his eyes magnified behind thick glasses. Hard lines of time cut across his ebony face like the work of a mad surgeon, and his lips were cracked and colored with frozen blood.

"No," Kevin said, "but I really don't know where I'm going."

"Then you're lost." The man said it as a known fact.

Kevin slowly nodded. "Yeah. Maybe I am."

"We find a lot of them that are lost." The man spoke in a voice that was quiet but powerful.

"Are you Nehemiah?" Kevin asked, carefully enunciating his words. He felt stupid for saying it, knowing it was a million to one shot that happened to be who the man was.

The man looked at Kevin for a few seconds, then turned and began to walk down the darkened street.

It's gotta be him! It has to be! Kevin kept telling himself this over and over as he followed the man through streets lined with abandoned, burned-out houses and alleyways filled with trash that smelled of rot and death. Snow continued to fall, blowing about in biting gusts. The hairs-things ached in protest.

They finally turned on a street that had one working streetlamp. Between two boarded-up storefronts there was a decrepit appearing two-story brick building with a sign above it reading **Parkland Ave. Spiritual Clinic**. Above the sign were yellow Neon lights flashing **Je_us _aves**.

The man stopped in front of a small group of people and pointed to the sign. "This is what you need."

"Nehemiah?" Kevin said. "Is this your church?"

"He ain't Nehemiah." he turned to see an anorexic thin,

forty-something woman, her skin pale and blotchy, wearing a two-sizes-too-big hunter-orange goose down jacket. "He's just some old crackhead."

"Isn't this Nehemiah's church?" Kevin asked.

"The one and only!" The woman looked up at the blinking Neon sign and crossed herself. "It's a very special place."

"I've heard that." Kevin looked around more closely at the group of a dozen or so people, men and women alike, in front of the building.

Most of the people were dressed in decent clothing, and there were none that were ranting and raving. Yet they all gave off the aura of helplessness, of needing something just out of reach.

"So what'chew got?" the woman asked Kevin. "I gots me hep C and a shot liver."

Kevin shrugged. *Oh, it's just a little case of evil hair things that are eating me alive.* "Hard to explain."

"It's okay, honey." The woman touched him lightly on the shoulder and Kevin forced himself not to flinch. "We all got something, right? Otherwise, why would be standing out here waitin' for Nehemiah?"

I don't know about you, but I'm here 'cause I got nowhere else to go. "Like I said, it's hard to explain." He moved away from the woman and toward the fringes of the crowd. He could smell the sweet odor of pot rising in the cold air and looked around, finally spying a woman who looked to be his own age holding a blunt the size of a large cigar.

"Excuse me," Kevin said to a woman. She had a head full of thick red hair bundled haphazardly under a too-small wool camp and wore a heavy navy-blue overcoat. "Do you know if Nehemiah is going to be here soon?"

She looked him up and down with light green eyes, then shrugged. "Hard to say. Could be here soon, could be here later." She shrugged again and took a hit off the joint, then handed it to Kevin. He took it and inhaled deeply; the tip of the blunt glowed a brilliant red, a solitary evil eye seeing nothing.

The smoke was acrid and bitter. Kevin was only able to hold it in his lungs a few seconds before exhaling in a spasm of coughs.

The woman laughed and hit the joint. "What's the matter?" she said in a mocking tone, "this your first time smoking high-grade weed?"

"I'm fine," Kevin said, taking the joint again from her. This time he forced himself to hold the smoke in as long as he could.

"Sorry, man, but I really think you're a virgin," the woman said before suddenly looking concerned. "Unless . . . you don't have lung cancer, do you? I mean, if you do and I've been doggin' you, then I'm sorry."

Kevin waved her off. "I don't have lung cancer." To prove it to her he took another hit, and this time, he didn't cough. "See," he displayed, handing back the joint, "all better now."

The woman gave him a sly smile. "Good." She looked around the crowd. "You ever meet Nehemiah?"

"No. You?"

The woman laughed. "Nah, I'm just here to offer moral support to a friend of mine." She pointed to a large black man with flowing dreadlocks pacing anxiously in front of the building. "I think he's a hypochondriac, but he thinks he has Ebola or some crazy shit like that."

"Well, if he does, that would be—" Kevin suddenly felt a wave of vertigo wash over him like a tsunami and reached out and grabbed the woman to keep from falling.

"Hey, man, you okay?" she asked.

Kevin took several deep breaths to try to clear his head. "I don't know, I just feel real . . . off . . ."

"What's goin' on here?" he heard a man's deep voice say as he realized he had his eyes closed. He opened them to see the woman's friend standing by her side.

"Don't know," the woman said. "This dude just started lookin' real off."

Kevin let go of her shoulder and tried to regain his equilibrium. He looked up at the **Je_us _aves** Neon lights and to his amazement, the e and the s were bleeding bright yellow blood. It fell in slow-motion luminescent drops, splattering in the snow and on the people standing underneath it.

"You been spicin' up them blunts again with K?" the large black man with dreadlocks asked the woman.

She smiled and gave a crazed giggle. "Just a little," she said, holding her hands and inch or two apart before spreading them out as far as she could, "or maybe a lot!"

"Just go with it," the man said to Kevin. "It'll be gone in a few hours."

"I need to see Nehemiah." Kevin's voice sounding muted and distant to himself. He looked around and long trails of liquid light colored red and green snaked from the bodies of the people around him. "Do you know when he's going to be here?"

"Nobody knows," dreadlock man said.

"What do you mean?"

"No one knows if he's coming back at all," the red-haired woman said.

Kevin took off his jacket, sweat forming on his body in wet sticky patches. "I don't understand. Has he left?"

"He left a long time ago," the woman said. She turned to her friend. "How long has it been? Months? Years?"

The man scowled and waved her off. "It's been awhile. He said he'd be back. He tol' everyone he'd be back."

"No way," Kevin said, shaking his head despite his dizziness. "He's the last fucking hope I've got."

"You can't swear!" It was the woman in the orange jacket, suddenly appearing and getting in Kevin's face. "This is a holy place!"

Kevin laughed, a sick, guttural sound. "Is it?" He stepped

back and took off his jacket, twirling it clumsily around like a stripper with her G-string, then took off his sweatshirt with trembling hands. "How's this, honey? Think this place is holy enough to heal this shit?"

The orange-jacket woman scrambled backward like a crab being chased by a hungry gull. "What the hell?" she kept saying over and over, pointing at Kevin like a kid seeing Santa Claus for the very first time.

"What the hell are those things?" the black man with the dreadlocks asked, staring at Kevin but not moving any closer. "Are they real?"

"I think they're moving!" his red-haired friend said. "The big thick one on his shoulder, I think it moved!"

"Yeah . . . they move," Kevin said, looking down at his arms, then at his shoulder. He suddenly felt deflated, like a balloon stuck with a sharp pin. "They move, and they grow," then another burst of manic energy, sending his mind racing and his heart pounding, "and they'll grow and grow and when they're ready," he threw his arms high in the air, "they'll grow a thousand feet tall and eat all of you!"

"This dude is seriously crazy," dreadlock man said, grabbing his friend's arm and pulling her away. "He definitely can't handle K. You shoulda never gave him any."

The woman angrily pulled away. "What? Now it's my fault this pretty boy is a pussy?" She turned in a huff and walked across the street, dreadlock man following.

"You are fucked, man," the woman in the orange goosedown vest said to Kevin. "You got some bad mojo goin' on and you *real* fucked."

"I know that," Kevin said. "I just don't know what to do about it."

There was a tap on his shoulder and Kevin turned, fully expecting to see either God or the devil standing behind him. Instead, it was the thin black man who had first lead him there. He was holding Kevin's shirt and jacket in outstretched hands.

"You best put these back on," the man suggested, "least you freeze to death out here."

"It feels good without them," Kevin replied, then

Reluctantly, put his sweatshirt then jacket back on, the weight of the garments causing tiny slivers of dull pain to course throughout his body. He dug in his pants pocket for another Oxy.

"You don't need that," the old man said as Kevin went to take the Oxy.

"You're wrong," Kevin said, then swallowed the pill. "What I need is a lot more of 'em. Know where I can get 'em?"

The old man pointed to the left and right. "Everywhere. Anywhere. Half this town is on drugs and the other half wants to be."

"You're gonna want to be too when these things growing on me start falling off and . . ."

"And what?"

Kevin starred at the old man. The lines on his face now appeared thicker, deeper, allowing Kevin to see facial muscle, tendons, facial bones, shiny white like the new fallen snow.

"Don't those hurt?" Kevin asked, pointing at the old man's face. "How come they don't bleed?"

The old man finally smiled, a mouthful of crooked, blackened teeth. He ran an arthritic index finger over his face. "These are my lifelines. They show all the battles I've won and lost . . ." He pointed at Kevin's arms. "Those things you got on you, they're marks of your battle, too."

"No. They're not mine, they were put there by someone, somebody evil."

"They're yours," the old man said with a note of finality. "You need to come to grips with that. Yours and no one else's."

Kevin looked around. The orange-jacketed woman, all

the rest of the people waiting for Nehemiah, waiting for salvation standing underneath the hissing fluorescent lights proclaiming **Je_us _aves**, were gone.

"Where did they go?" Kevin said, turning around in a slow circle. "Maybe they weren't really here." He squinted at the old man. "Are you real? Is any of this real?"

"As real as it gets."

"I'm so fucked . . ." Kevin sat clumsily on the concrete, the cold dampness immediately soaking through his jeans. He ran his fingers in the translucent globs of light that fell haphazardly from the fluorescent lights, the sensation of steel wool pricking his fingers.

"I know this yellow shit from the lights ain't real," Kevin slurred, drawing smiley faces in the imaginary liquid, "but the things on my arms are, and they're killin' me."

He looked up at the old man, who said nothing.

"I killed a boy," Kevin said without thought or care. "I murdered a boy, in prison. I slit his throat then cut out his heart and some evil monster—" he looked his arms and thought he could see inside his skin, could visualize the roots of the hairs, spreading like the web of some malicious, hell-spawned spider, "—used it to make the ink that made the tats on my arms." The horror of it bloomed like an atomic bomb in Kevin's mind. "I'm just as much a monster as Readona is. Just as much . . . a monster . . ."

Kevin looked around. The old man was gone. He was alone, sitting underneath the hissing yellow florescent sign of the Parkland Ave. Spiritual Clinic, his ass soaked, his body racked with pain, with few drugs and no hope.

Another shiver racked his body, and he stuffed his hands in his pockets, feeling on one side his cell phone, the other tablets of oxy. He pulled out of the phone and looked at it, willing someone, anyone, to call him.

The phone remained silent.

I wonder what Caesar is doing now? Sherri's probably at

the Masonic already, getting ready for the show. Maybe I should call Readona and—

"Fuck." *How can I even think that?*

Because he holds the key, a voice in his addled brain replied. *Call him, go back to him, embrace the gift he's given you and you'll be free of all the pain and doubt!*

"No! He's a fucking liar, he can't be trusted!"

He told you'd he protect you at Fairview and he did, the voice countered. *He didn't lie to you, he saved your worthless, pathetic life!*

But what I had to do . . . what I did . . . and then, like a movie come to life in his brain, he saw it all again, standing naked in the corner of the shower, the boy—Waylon, that was his name, Waylon—cutting his throat in one savage stroke, watching him bleed out and then turning him on his back and plunging the knife in the skinny kid's chest, the knife getting stuck for a moment in one of his ribs and Kevin, bathed in blood like some prison-bound vampire, laughing hysterically, tugging with all his strength to get the knife free. Then, hacking and sawing through muscle, sinew, bone until he saw the heart and he tried to pull it out but it was encased in the boy like an oyster unwilling to give up its pearl so Kevin had to chop and cut some more until he had the quivering, slippery organ in his shaking hands, then wrapping it up like a butcher with a pork chop and delivering it, still warm, to Readona, who held the heart like a priceless diamond. The look on his face appeared like a lover in the throes of orgasmic ecstasy.

"I'd rather die than be with you . . . be like you." Kevin looked up at the dark, overcast sky in an OxyContin and ketamine-induced haze and spied the unlit remains of the twenty-five-story tall Hendricks Office Tower, a few blocks away.

"You were wrong, old man . . ." Kevin said in a raspy voice, gazing at the steel and concrete monolith. "I do have the guts to kill myself. I *do*."

CHAPTER 40

KEVIN ROLLED THE REMAINING Oxys in his pocket with one shaking hand as he unsteadily made his way toward the Hendricks Tower. The pills were smooth, cool against his skin. He derived a moribund calmness from their sensual feel.

He turned off Grand River Avenue onto a side-street and was surprised to find a number of cars traveling down the unnamed pothole-scarred road. Kevin was even more surprised two blocks down to see that the Hendricks Tower, instead of being the dilapidated, abandoned building that he remembered, was brightly lit in its first three floors, a steady stream of well-dressed people entering and leaving.

A tall, muscular black man in his mid-twenties, wearing a light tan overcoat covering a freshly pressed tuxedo stood in front of two large oak doors that served as the entrance to the building. Kevin took a deep breath, tried to will away the shimmering drug-induced golden aura around the man, and walked up.

"Can I help you?" the man asked in a no-nonsense voice.

Kevin gave the best fake-sober smile he could muster.

"I'm here to meet a friend. We used to hang out at this place when it was a trashed empty building. Glad to see it come back alive."

"Uh huh." The man put out one meaty hand. "You got a ticket?"

Kevin reached into his pocket, then shrugged. His shoulders felt like lead bricks. "Guess I must have forgotten it. But if you just let me in, I'm sure my friend will—"

The man took a half-step closer. Faint odors of expensive aftershave followed, leaving a trail of tiny sparkling lights in their wake.

"Why don't you continue on your way," the man said in a quiet voice that held a steel edge. "We don't need your type around here."

"What type is that?"

The man smiled. One front tooth was capped in gold, the same color of his aura. "The alcoholic meth-smoking type shit that gives this city a bad name."

A couple, the man in his late-forties dressed in a charcoal gray Armani suit with a younger woman, wearing a low-cut blood-red dress, pushed by Kevin, laughing and smiling, appearing as if they had the entire world in their well-manicured hands. The doorman gave them a brief glance and let them through.

"So, they can get in and I can't?" Kevin said. "Isn't that discrimination?"

The man reached out in one fast motion, his large hand landing on Kevin's arm. He squeezed and Kevin forced himself not to cry out in pain.

"Turn around and walk away," the man said, putting more force into his grip, "or I'm going to fuck you up real bad." He finally released his grip and Kevin stepped away.

"You're too late." Kevin took a deep breath to try to clear his head as his shoulder screamed in dull agony. "I'm already fucked up real bad."

Kevin pushed his way through another half dozen revilers, each touch sending Oxy-dulled slivers of pain shooting throughout his body and made his way back onto the sidestreets. Three blocks in and he was already in a different world of darkened avenues, burned out homes and piles of rubbish.

So, you just going to wander around all night and freeze to death or are you going to do what you need to do?

Kevin tried to force his stoned mind to function. *What other fucking trashed buildings are around here that I can do the deed at?*

"C'mon, think," he said with gritted teeth. "You and Caesar used to come down here all the time, there's plenty of other dead buildings to ... to ..."

It suddenly came to him in a vivid, ketamine-colored memory: sitting with Caesar on Devil's Night on top of the Lee Plaza, a once opulent residential hotel rising off West Grand Boulevard. They had enlarged a hole in the razor-wired topped fencing barricading the once art-deco architectural masterpiece and made their way merrily through the ransacked, abandoned building. Caesar had made Kevin stop in the buildings formerly stately ballroom and play some off-key tunes on a broken piano, sitting in a dusty heap on the cracked and littered floor. After the musical interlude, fueled with two large blunts and a pint of cheap rum, they climbed the narrow stairwell to the top and watched the city burn, isolated fires scattered for miles across the otherwise darkened streets.

The large hair-thing on his shoulder twitched like the tail on a hungry rat. *Maybe I should name you. How about Little Readona? You like that?*

The hair said nothing.

Lee Plaza would be the perfect place to end it—maybe not as high as the Highland Tower, but at fifteen stories, plenty high to get the job done right. Kevin looked around and tried to get his bearings—he walked half a block to his left when he decided it was the wrong way.

Fuck. It all looked the same. He was on a block with half a dozen boarded-up row houses, their wood and vinyl sidings torn away like skin flayed from a tortured prisoner. The rest of the land gone wild, filled with thick tangles of brambles, stunted trees and piles of rubble from houses long torn down. *I need to go back to the Tower—I remember me and Caesar could see it from Lee Plaza.*

Kevin turned around when a cherry red Chevy Tahoe pulled onto the street and screeched to a stop in front of one of the abandoned houses. Five white guys in their late teens, dressed in matching black leather trench-coats,got out of the car.

"This is it, man!" the shortest of the men said loudly while pointing at the house. "This looks like a great place to get the party started."

"Urban renewal at its finest, motherfucker!" another of the men, taller with a scraggly goat-tee that appeared to be formed from dozens of six-inch long writhing black worms said when he spied Kevin. "Hey! Who the fuck are you?"

Kevin put up his hands.. "Just passin' by."

"Remember that dog we toasted last month?" the short man said to the worm-goatee man, who had grabbed a bottle with a rag stuffed in top from the Tahoe. "That was some crazy shit, seein' that fuckin' thing run around on fire." He lit the rag with a lighter and orange flames lit up his acne-scarred face. "Wonder what it would be like to see a man on fire."

"Bet it would be da bomb," another of the men, this one weighing at least three-hundred pounds and wearing thick round glasses, said in a surprisingly high voice. He pulled out a pistol from underneath his trench-coat. "You a nigger-lover, boy?"

"I don't want any problems," Kevin said.

He tried to back away, but his feet felt glued to the pavement. *Run, asshole, run!*

"Looks like a Dee-troit nigger-lover to me," worm-goatee man said, still holding the flaming Molotov cocktail. "Looks like a nigger-lover that needs to be toasted." When he cocked his arm back to throw the bottle, Kevin finally forced his feet and legs to move and ran down the street.

There was one gunshot, then two more.

With each ear-numbing blast, Kevin expected to feel the sharp bite of a bullet tearing through his flesh, yet each time there was only the crazed laughter of the men and the thought that ran through his head of 'why are you running, you want to die, why not let them do it for you' but he couldn't stop, couldn't let himself be put down like some poor dog. He cut through the backyard of an abandoned house, tripped and fell amidst the rotting garbage and remains of burnt furniture and broken toys and thought for a second of just lying there, becoming part of the forsaken flotsam and jetsam of the urban wasteland before another gunshot sent thunder into the night and Kevin returned to running for his life.

He finally slowed, his breath coming in short, painful gasps, his legs heavy with fatigue. Snow had started falling again in wet, thick flakes. An early 20th-century Georgian-style house, its roof collapsed, and windows broken out, loomed silently to his right; to his left was a one-story U-shaped brick building that Kevin guessed had perhaps been an elementary school. That was back when there were people in the neighborhoods, when children ran in the streets laughing with joy while they played stickball or street hockey. Now there was nothing—no families, no children, no life.

Kevin looked around and realized he could have been in Pripyat, Ukraine, in any other urban wasteland lost, left for dead, abandoned to the inexorable maw of entropy. He strained to hear any signs of life but the only sounds he could hear over the pounding of his heart were distant echoes—cars, sirens, mechanical rumblings all churned together to make one hazy cloud of a still-living world just outside his reach.

An enormous flood of loneliness enveloped him, a deep, visceral sensation. He was alone. Truly alone.

Except for the hairs, can't forget them because they certainly haven't forgotten you, and if Readona is right, maybe they're almost ready to pop and hatch out of your skin like some demented magic trick and then you all can sit down and hash out your issues like the reasonable, rational monsters you are.

A heaving sob erupted from this throat and thick tears blossomed in his eyes. *Fuck you, don't you start crying like some weak little bitch. You need to man up and finish this now!*

Kevin brushed his face with the sleeve of his jacket that stank with the foul odors of cigarettes, whiskey, and old sweat. He looked at the school and began to make his way toward it when some dim memory came alight in his drug-addled mind. It had been on the same night he and Caesar had broken into Lee Plaza; they had walked in around in the nearby neighborhoods, even then becoming broken and decrepit, and spent time on the basketball court of a small elementary school shooting hoops with rocks and anything else they could find to throw. If this was the school, then Lee Plaza was just a few blocks ahead.

Kevin finally saw the basketball court, one of the stands bent at the base like a rusting miniature leaning tower of Pisa, the netting long rotted away. On the court he realized he was walking on a sea of broken plastic and glass. The court was awash in cell phones, all of them crushed beyond repair.

A drug dealer's cell phone graveyard. Kevin absently pushed one busted phone around with his shoe and amazingly, it began ringing.

What the fuck? All of the phones began singing, a thousand different ring tones, getting louder and louder. Kevin put his hands to his ears but still the sounds came through. *It's not real, it's the drugs, I've turned into a damned pathetic junky just like the assholes I used to detest in high school and in the joint!*

"You're not ringing!" He couldn't hear his screaming voice over the cacophony of sounds but continued to scream until just as abruptly as it all started, all was quiet.

He held his hands to his ears for a few more seconds then slowly pulled them away. *You gotta pull it together, you gotta—*

Another ringing, this one muted but familiar, coming from his cell phone inside his pants pocket. Kevin frantically grabbed the phone and cocked his arm back to throw it as far as he could when another thought exploded in his mind: *What if it's real?*

He held the phone out at arm's length and forced his eyes to focus on the small plastic screen: The caller ID read *Sherri.*

"Hello?" he said, and nearly cried out in joy when he heard Sherri's voice in return.

"Kevin? What's going on? I didn't think you were going to answer."

"I . . . I'm having a bad night." *This has to be real, it has to be her and not some fucked up trick of my mind!* "I didn't know if it was really you."

"What are you talking about? What's wrong? Where are you?"

"Somewhere in Detroit . . ." He looked around. "I don't know where . . ." He took a deep breath and tried to focus. "How are you? Did the show go okay?"

"The show starts in ten minutes. I thought maybe . . . maybe you would be here to see it."

He could imagine her standing on stage and remembered the first time they had met—she was so beautiful, confident, strong. His heart broke even more. *How could I have fucked things up so damn bad?*

"I'd give anything to be there . . ." His voice began to crack with emotion. "I'm so fucking sorry, Sherri, for everything I did, for the shit I said, the shit I did with Roxy, for the horrible shit I did in prison . . . everything has just spiraled out of control, and I just . . . just fucked it all up . . ."

There was no response. Kevin pulled the phone from his ear. The screen was dark.

"Sherri?" Kevin looked at the screen. It was completely dark. No battery light, no imaginary phosphorus glow. Just dark and dead like all the other phones in the graveyard.

"Fuck." Kevin dropped the phone and smashed it with his foot. "Fuck! Fuck! *Fuck!*" His screams cut through the air and a dog howled in the distance, as in answer to Kevin's anguish.

He screamed until his voice was a rough whisper and his throat raw. There was nothing more to say, no more good-byes to make.

Kevin walked through three more blocks of burned out and abandoned houses before coming upon Lee Plaza. It was unchanged since the last time he had been there with Caesar: same faded out orange-glazed brick, windows on every story busted out, surrounded by razor-wire topped fencing that had enough holes cut through it so that a platoon of men could pass through.

He slowly made his way down the first-floor hallway, his cigarette lighter casting a sickly yellowish glow to the few remaining plaster rosettes on the ceiling, an early Art Deco masterpiece that had long since been broken and vandalized by thieves and urban explorers.

Kevin tripped over a large pile of rubbish and almost went sprawling onto the floor. *Should have brought a flashlight. Amazing the things you forget when you're going to kill yourself.*

He continued down the hall, trying to remember where the stairwell was, when, looking around, he saw the stateroom and the piano he had played a thousand lifetimes ago. Kevin held the lighter up high and walked into the room; a thick stench of urine and mold caused his eyes to water. He gazed upon the remains of the piano which had been smashed into a hundred pieces, yellowing ivory keys scattered about the floor like the broken teeth of a fallen giant. The keys began to move, undulating slowly like porcelain worms come to life, and before they began playing songs from Kevin's long-lost youth, he moved on.

Where in the fuck is that stairwell? I know me and Caesar went to the top from this floor. Kevin was at the end of the hallway which was filled from floor to ceiling with debris. *If I have to dig my way through all that shit . . .*

He slowly turned around in a circle, eyes squinted in concentration, and suddenly, there in the weak shadows cast by his lighter, he saw the stairwell entrance.

Kevin entered the narrow walkway and was hit with a cold wave of air blowing from somewhere above. He walked up the stairs, his legs already starting to scream by the time he reached the third floor. By the sixth floor he was gasping for air and the muscles in his thighs were spasming.

He stopped for a moment, his chest heaving, sweat rolling down his sides. Nine more floors and the thought seemed impossible.

"No," Kevin said through gritted teeth as he forced himself to start walking again. "No fucking way am I quitting now. Not now."

He dug deep into his memories, of when he was an amateur boxer, of sitting on his stool between rounds, hands and wrists aching with pain, blood running down his face, legs feeling like useless slabs of clay. Still, when the bell rang, he was able to pull the strength from deep inside and fight on.

"One more round," he kept repeating as he climbed to the seventh floor, eighth floor . . . until the stairs ended at a closed door on floor fifteen. *If this fucking thing's locked I swear to whatever god is still listening to me that I'll rip my wrists open with my own fucking teeth and bleed out here in this stairwell.*

Kevin tentatively reached out and touched the door handle. It opened with barely a push.

He walked onto the roof. Northernly winds battered him in bone-chilling cold and odors of burning wood and incinerated garbage from the fires that dotted the landscape of Detroit.

He pulled the six remaining Oxys out of his pocket and put them in his mouth, then swallowed them with a mouthful of whiskey. Fifteen stories below, the traffic on Grand Avenue looked like toy cars, their tiny headlights weakly illuminating the gloom that held the city like a malevolent force.

His eyes drifted north, where it seemed a million years ago, he had attended a party at Dr. Rothstein's and helped save the life of a fallen angel. In that part of Detroit, fires were absent. The only lights were from houses lining the canals breaking through the darkness of the night.

On his right shoulder, he felt the largest hair move.

"What's the matter, afraid I'm down to my last few minutes?" Kevin could visualize the hair—thick, pulsating, growing tiny arms and legs. He laughed maniacally at the thought. "Worried that your easy meal is going to turn into a useless pile of shattered bones and guts?"

Maybe they are scared. Maybe they're scared they're going to die with me—but then, another thought—*What if they don't die? What if they crawl out of me like sentient, evil worms, burrow in the ground and either wait for another poor slob to attach themselves to, or . . .*

He suddenly had a vision of a dream—of the hairs morphed into monstrous, phallic shaped things rising up from across the Earth into a blood red sky pregnant with misshaped, coal black clouds writhing like an angry ocean. *Where did that come from? I think it was a dream, or maybe something Readona put in my head . . . why can't I remember?*

Kevin squeezed his head with the palms of his hands, trying to force out the memories, to make his mind focus but it was so damn hard over the booze, over the drugs, over the doubt and fear . . .

What if it's true? If those fucking things don't die, I just won't be killing myself, I'll be killing Sherri and Caesar and everyone!

"Fuck!" His scream sounded like the howling of a wounded animal and he screamed it again and again. *Every damn decision I've made in my entire life has been fucked up. Why would this one be any different?*

"Who's there?"

Kevin stepped away from the edge and turned around. There was no one he could see, but again heard the voice. He squinted at the pitted concrete room surrounding the main elevator shaft and mechanics in the middle of the roof, and there, behind it, he detected a flickering of light and wisps of smoke.

Behind the elevator room was a fifty-five-gallon steel drum, flames of yellow and red leaping from its interior, sending sparkling hallucinogenic crystals of unbelievably bright white light into the coal-dark air. Around the drum sat two emaciated middle-aged men, both wearing tattered wool overcoats; the one closest to the drum had sickly yellow, acne-scarred skin and wore a bright orange hunters cap while other, a darker skinned man, had a too-small black cowboy hat covering a mass of greasy gray hair.

"Who are you?" Kevin asked aloud. "Are you real?"

The man with the orange cap gave a raspy laugh. "Hell yes, Chief, we're real. You high?"

"Yeah," Kevin answered, still mesmerized by the star-shaped sparks rising from the steel drum.

The orange-cap man perked up. "You got any more stuff?"

"No. Took 'em all."

The orange cap man frowned, then shrugged. "That's okay. Me and Juan should be all set for the night, right, Juan?"

"Uh huh," the cowboy-hat wearing man named Juan grunted in reply.

Kevin moved closer to the men and the raging fire in the drum. The warmth from the flames felt like a lover's soft caress on his frozen skin.

"My name's Jimmy-D," the man with the orange cap said, then pointed to the cowboy-hat wearing man. "I already told you Juan's name, right?"

"Yeah." Kevin was feeling the full effects of the six Oxys working into his brain, their muscular drug-fingers soothing his frayed neurons. They were relaxing them, turning them off one by one.

"What you guys doin' up here?" he asked, still not convinced the men were anything but drug-induced ghosts.

"Keepin' safe from all the crazy shit that's goin' down on the streets tonight," Jimmy-D explained. "And doing some prospecting."

"Some what?"

"Finding shit to sell. This city is a gold mine. Just need to know where to look and I know, see? I used to own a salvage company, was doin' alright, and then ..." Jimmy-D's eyes drifted off for a moment and he shook his head, "but then, well then ..." he suddenly slapped himself on the side of his face, and the blow gave off a hollow, wet sound, "... then shit just happened but I still know how to find stuff to sell, right, Juan?"

"Uh huh," Juan answered.

"What are you doin' up here, Chief?" Jimmy-D asked.

Kevin finally tore his stare away from the sparks and tried to think. *What the fuck was he doing up here?*

"Chief? You still with us?"

Kevin looked at Jimmy-D, then out at the outline of the city. "I came up here to ... to kill myself."

"No shit?" Jimmy-D raised an eyebrow. "Really? That's pretty heavy shit ..."

Juan slowly looked at Kevin. "How you gunna do it?" he asked in a baritone voice.

"I was gonna jump."

Juan nodded. "That'll do it."

"Why you wanna kill yourself, Chief?" Jimmy-D asked.

"I got some . . . some bad shit goin' on, and . . . and I couldn't think of anything else to do, but now . . ." Kevin awkwardly sat down next to the men. "You think that killin' myself's a stupid thing to do?"

"It's your choice, Chief," Jimmy-D shrugged. "We all got to die sometime." He motioned to Juan.

"Lemme have the junk, man. I'm startin' to get itchy."

Juan dug into a pocket of his ratty coat and pulled out a small, rectangular piece of aluminum foil that he handed it to Jimmy-D, who emptied the contents of the aluminum foil onto a tablespoon.

"We'd share with you, but we both got the AIDS," Jimmy-D said matter-of-factly to Kevin while pouring some water from a bottle over the heroin on the spoon before firing up a lighter underneath it. "Me and Juan just get high with each other now."

"That's okay," Kevin said, "I'm good." His eyelids felt like they were miniature wet burlap bags, so damn heavy, and it would be so nice to close his eyes and . . .

"Fuck." Kevin opened his eyes, looked around: He was still sitting cross-legged, the fire in the drum crackling, Jimmy-D passing Juan a used-looking syringe who injected what was left into a spidery vein on his hand.

"What's wrong, Chief?" Jimmy-D asked, his words slow and slurred.

"How long have I been out?" Kevin asked, his heart pounding.

Jimmy-D shrugged. "A couple minutes maybe?"

Kevin stood up. His heart continued to pound, and he was hot, so damn hot from sitting by the fire that he tore off his jacket and sweater and embraced the bitter cold air that blew in tight swirls on the roof.

"What the fuck are those things?" Juan asked, pointing at Kevin with a shaking, arthritic finger.

"I don't know," Kevin said.. "Somebody told me that they were some type of curse, of bad magic, shit put in me to grow." He shook his head and instantly regretted it as his world tipped sideways, causing Kevin to nearly fall onto the drum.

"Holy shit!" Jimmy-D pointed excitedly at Kevin's shoulder. "Did that hair-shit on your shoulder move? Did you see that, man? That thing moved!"

Juan slowly nodded. "Uh huh. Moved like a fuckin' mouse in a trap."

"Yeah, they move. They're fuckin' alive," Kevin droned, looking at the shoulder hair, which had become still. "They're alive and killing me and I don't know how to stop them . . ."

"Why don't you pull 'em out?" Jimmy-D offered.

Kevin frowned. "I can't, I mean, I tried before and it didn't work."

"Nah, just fuckin' pull 'em out!" Jimmy-D opened his mouth and pointed to his lower jaw. "See down here? My teeth were fuckin' rotten, so I took pliers and yanked 'em out." He tapped his forehead hard with a dirty index finger and it sounded like a woodpecker on a hollow tree. "They was rotten and woulda killed me, infection going straight into my head." He grinned, a slow heroin smile and pulled from his pants a pair of rusted pliers, waving them around in slow motion like a mad conductor in front of an invisible orchestra. "But I pulled 'em out and now everything is fine!"

"That hadda hurt like hell," Kevin said.

"Yeah, it hurt," Jimmy-D agreed, "but they was doin' me no good and hurtin' like hell anyway, so I figured if I could just get through one big hurt, then all the hurt would go away. Besides, the pain is all in here anyway—" he tapped himself hard on the head, "—and pain never kilt anyone. 'Least that's what my old man used to tell me before beatin' me with a baseball bat, that dirty rotten motherfucker!"

"A friend told me that me that too," Kevin vaguely remembered asking Peter how he could handle the pain of being suspended. "And he wasn't even high."

"What's that, Chief?" Jimmy-D said, and it took Kevin a moment to realize the question was directed at him.

"My friend . . . used to do this wild shit with ropes and cables and hooks and . . . I didn't know how he handled the pain."

"Fuck, the one on your chest moved!" Jimmy-D. "Did you see it that time, Juan?"

"Maybe. I don't know. We're all high." Juan chuckled a hoarse sound, his eyes closed.

Realization dawned on Kevin, "It's the fire . . ."

The thought blasted through his addled mind, and a memory as clear and bright as the noon-day sun appeared before his eyes, the memory of being at Roxy's, of her pulling out the hair in his groin and flinging it into the firepot, the black nightmarish thing writhing on the edge like an unsteady tightrope walker before falling and being consumed by the flames.

"It's the fire. That's how they can die!" Kevin looked at the largest hair on his shoulder. "Naughty Little Readona, wanting me to jump off this building so you could grow into the sky and kill everyone! But I know your secret: you don't like fire but I'm going to feed you and all your evil, rotten brothers to it!"

Jimmy-D frowned. "You gonna kill yourself by settin' yourself on fire? That'll make it smell real bad up here."

"No," Kevin said, "I'm gonna burn the hairs in the fire."

"How you gonna do that without burnin' yourself?" Juan asked in his slow, low voice.

"He'll use my pliers to pull 'em off!" Jimmy-D said, looking at Kevin. "Right? Did I guess right?"

"Yeah, you guessed right." Kevin could feel more of the hairs moving, as if awakening to their grim fate. "I'm gonna need both of you to help me, though. Can you do that?"

"Sure Chief," Jimmy-D said, "we'll help you." He looked at the pliers sitting beside him. "Those are my special pliers, you know. I don't let just anyone use them." He carefully handed them to Kevin. "Don't break 'em, okay?"

Kevin took them and smiled. He couldn't remember the last time he smiled. "I won't." He carefully threw an armful of wood next to the drum into the fire, then placed a thin, rectangular foot-and-a-half-long piece of metal bumper from a junked car on top of the trash can.

"If I start bleeding too much, one of you is going to have to cauterize the wounds with this." Kevin pointed at the piece of bumper, whose end began to glow blue and gold with the heat. "You understand?"

"I can do that," Jimmy-E said. "Blood don't bother me at all." He looked at the hairs all across Kevin's body. "You gonna have some nasty scars when it's done . . ."

Kevin thought of the scars on the back of Peter and smiled again. "My friends have scars too. They won't mind." He took a deep breath and looked at both the men. "If I pass out, one of you has to promise me you'll finish the job. Every one of these fucking hairs has to be pulled out and put into the fire. Understand?" He bent down and waved the pliers at them. "They have to go into the fire, understand? Don't let them fall on the ground, over the edge, or touch either of you! Into-the-fucking-fire!"

"Yeah, yeah, we got it," Jimmy-D, irritation in his voice, told him. "Don't need to yell at us. We ain't stupid, you know."

"So, who's first?" Kevin said, looking down at his body, over his legs and arms, until his blurry vision fell upon the long, solitary hair on his right shoulder.

It started to twitch and move, as if it knew what he was planning.

Taking a deep breath, Kevin grabbed the hair with the pliers and pulled.

The End

Acknowledgements

MY THANKS TO THOSE that helped bring this work to completion and print, including friends and colleagues of the Taos Toolbox class of 2011, Walter Jon Williams and Nancy Kress, members of the MSU writing workshop, and my editor, Cedric G! Bacon.